UNDOING

CRAZY

A novel

COLETTE WINLOCK

Oaktown Press, May 2013
Oakland, California

Copyright (c) 2013 by Colette Winlock

Library of Congress Cataloging-in-Publication data
Winlock, Colette, 1955--.
Library of Congress Control Number: 2013939538
CreateSpace Independent Publishing Platform North Charleston, SC

Undoing Crazy / by Colette Winlock.—Oaktown Press.
ISBN: 0615807925
ISBN-13: 9780615807928

1. African American—mental health—Fiction
2. Women—Black—social life and customs—Fiction.
3. Mental health—women—United States.

Cover art by Jeanette Madden
Author Photo by Lenn Keller
Cover Design by Kim Mason

For information regarding special discounts for bulk purchases
contact owc@email.com

Printed in the United States of America
10 9 8 7 6 5 4 3 2 1

Dedicated to all friends and families in search of better.

UNDOING

CRAZY

A novel

CHAPTER ONE

Mmph . . . can't they applaud like regular people—and just clap their hands?

Dana, my best friend, dragged me to this house of poetry, and truth is, all this finger-snapping and foot-stomping echoing in the high ceilings makes me think clapping is not part of the expected behavior here. The MC jumps onto the stage and embraces the solidly built young man who's caused all this commotion. He gives him one of those brother-hugs with a tight fist to his chest. As he leans into the performer's body, his other arm waves in the air, drawing the people in, encouraging an already pumped up audience to prolong their admiration.

"Was that powerful or what ya'll? Give it up for One Mo' Time. Show your love people."

One Mo' folds his hands in front of his chest and takes his bow, exiting the stage with a stride and shoulder-dip that reeks of confidence—he knows he did good.

"Our next performer is no stranger to the Black Dot Café, so let's hear it for the Queen."

A woman, far younger than Dana or I, with shapely hips and wearing a purple-and-white headdress steps up to the stage. Her bust line is not small at all, so I know she's had more than her share of attention. The Queen stares out, waits for the crowd to settle down, then she untangles the black mike off its silvery stand, pulling on the long cord to move as close to the audience as the stage will allow. The Queen looks across the room to make sure everyone is paying attention, throws the wrap around her neck, takes a prolonged and noticeable deep breath, and begins. "I call this . . . Now What, Mama?"

"Black people don't commit suicide
No . . . we look like greens cooking way too long
Minds limp, soaked in despair
Hearts simmered out
Needing
Wanting
Waiting
For something
To feed our soul
Mama says drink the pot liquor—
We do as told
Fat back and salt disguise bad as good
Stomachs and emotions stay twisted all day
We lie down to a fitful rest
Sun comes up but we're still under
It's all the same . . . and we wonder
What now, Mama?
The pot liquor's gone."

The Queen ends her performance to a silent room. When I look around, I notice something I haven't seen or heard all night. Until now, every artist has been lavished with snapping fingers, sometimes even moans of approval, but now, not a yes, foot-stomp, or pop fills the air. And honestly, I'm not sure what to think about that last recital, either. The café is small, chairs and tables are packed all the way back to the door with rows of young people standing along the walls—and still not a peep from anyone. I imagine that, like me, they're not sure what to think.

How did she get to be so bold she's calling out mamas? Who is this small woman who now makes me think the stage is larger than when she first stepped onto it? Maybe she grew up fast without a mama to help her know how to live, to keep her straight about things. The long purple skirt she wears hangs so low it touches the stage and looks like a drape.

Dana, who often in the name of doing her research will literally pull on my arm to take me somewhere isn't leaning into my shoulder, or jabbing my side with an elbow. And, to my surprise, like the rest of the room, her fingers aren't snapping, either.

For a while, the Queen has a stare-off with the audience, and when she points out into the room, crossing her arm over the stage to pause at each corner, it's just long enough to let you know that she meant to stop. Wait a minute, she's not pointing at me, is she? My weight shifts and my hips squirm in the small wooden seat—her eyes have indeed landed on me. I look at Dana, but she's fixated on the Queen, who now has her fingers stretched out towards me with her palm open. Seated in front of us are two young women wearing naturals like back in the sixties. They lean away from each other opening a clear path to where I'm seated; our chairs are so close to the stage that there's no mistaking exactly who the Queen is pointing at.

"So, tell us . . . how will you feed our twisted souls?"

The room's hushed with the kind of quiet sound that everyone can hear. I'm not going to turn around to verify it, but really, I feel 50 pairs of eyes looking in my direction. A single spotlight from the ceiling shines onto the Queen's thin hands. She's grabbing an amber necklace with a fist so tight her knuckles stand high and *damn it* she's still pointing at me with her other hand. She lowers her eyes and then repeats the question, again right to me. I know she's not expecting me to say anything, to have an answer—I'm not part of this. The way she's nodding her head reminds me of someone who's delivered their message and now they want to make sure you received it. All this attention brings a warm wave across my face and before I look away, I see her smile in satisfaction.

Outside the spotlight, the drummer ends an impromptu solo with a loud thump and the two performers exchange nods of appreciation. When the Queen turns back to face the audience, she flips her purple skirt and bows her bust line down to her hips. Then, slowly, like popcorn, an audience that'd been silent with private after-thoughts decides to show its approval. Snaps become louder, whispered *aaahs* and *mmms* jump from one person to the next. It's as if people know exactly when it's their turn. The sound reminds me of the cicada I heard when I was sent away to Texas, all day the large insects filled the air with rolling clicks and pops.

Now Dana is waving her hand in the air. She's snapping her thumb and middle finger in time with everyone else's delayed reaction. I guess the Queen is pleased with the growing response because she's dropped her head even deeper and longer than her previous bow.

Oh God, I don't know what to make of all this.

I think this underground club is meant for people much younger and definitely hipper than us, but Dana's carrying on like she's one of them. I think we stand out like a sore thumb; maybe that's why the Queen called me out. I have on the brown-and-orange pantsuit I sometimes wear to church. Dana's still dressed in a matching black jacket and skirt with high-heeled pumps of the same color, in what she calls her "power uniform" for working at the university. It doesn't take a sharp eye to see that we're much older than this congregation of spoken word admirers.

The MC doesn't jump up so fast this time. Instead, he saunters onto the stage nodding his head and grinning, and extends a bent arm for the Queen to grab on to as he escorts her off the stage. Dana leans towards me. I pull back some, but she's determined to whisper in my ear.

"So, what do you think?"

10

"Her stare gave me the creeps," I confess. "That girl was messing with me."

"She was using you for a dramatic ending." Dana smiles.

Clearly, we didn't have the same experience. I cross my arms and look away, staring at the now empty stage.

"Well, she could have picked somebody else. If, and that's *if*, I ever come again I'm sitting as far away from that stage as I can get."

"Mama says drink the pot liquor—we do as told."

As Dana repeats the line of poetry to no one in particular, I'm trying to decide if I should go to the bathroom now or during the next act when the line will have gone down.

"Don't you love the symbolism of the greens?" Dana says to me.

"Somehow, I don't see her making too many pots."

To me, the Queen looks barely in her twenties. My need to pee is getting stronger than my need to just sit and pretend that people aren't looking at me, like the retro-naturals in front of us who keep turning around and whispering.

"Things get passed on. There's code in her brain that says, 'drink the pot liquor.' Dana throws her head back like a mad scientist and laughs. "She's definitely going in my research. She's an example how memories are passed on from one generation to the next."

"Oh please, to you everything is a research study."

I know I sounded snide. I am so through with Dana and her night out in the field. "She's just talking about cooking greens, Ms. Researcher."

"Is that all you got from her poem? What about the opening line? 'Black people don't commit suicide.'"

"What's so surprising—haven't you heard of anyone doing that before?"

My voice is so blasé that Dana gives me a weird look.

"I know black people consider suicide, but I know a lot more stewing like the Queen says about those greens." Dana's eyes cast down in my direction when she says this but I ignore her look.

11

"Greens are not stew and pot liquor is only the minerals cooked out from the greens—everyone knows that."

Okay Carla . . . why are you feeling so defensive about cooking greens?

"Actually, our suicide rates are going up," Dana tells me in her researcher tone of voice.

Here goes Professor Dana. I try not to roll my eyes when she starts her lecture.

"It's still less than other groups, but a good many do just what that child's performance was about."

At least we agree that girl looks awfully young.

"Profound, Dr. Washington. I'm going to the bathroom."

I leave my seat, not bothering to look back at my friend, who is so caught up in the motif she doesn't see that I'm not as excited about being in this atmosphere as she is.

"Should I come with you?" Dana calls after me.

I shake my head at the singsong sound in her voice.

"Thank you, but I think I can handle this on my own."

The restroom is all of maybe fifteen steps from our seats. I need a moment to regroup from my unexpected participation in that last performance.

The Black Dot Café, though nicely decorated, isn't any bigger than an average living room; it reminds me of the model apartments I looked at when I went to an open house in the new Uptown district. There are so many people here that even though it's a short trip, I have to keep saying, 'excuse me,' to join a line of men and women standing in front of the same door.

As I wait my turn for the bathroom, I see the Queen is making her way through the crowd. Her skirt is still dragging on the floor, and she's saying a flirtatious "Hi" to each person she passes. I'm sure I see her winking at everyone with that look of satisfaction still on her face. When she arrives where I'm standing, her small-framed body layered in cloth brushes by me without the hello she's given to everyone else.

A familiar freeze creeps into my stomach and the best I can do is start counting black and white tiles on the floor. I think she's still messing with me. If she used me for a dramatic ending as Dana says, it looks like she wants to continue playing it out, but there's no way she could know my stomach feels so twisted, my soul so emptied, that sometimes all I do is lay in bed and ask myself if there is anything else to expect from life.

I don't remember ever seeing her before she got on the stage; how could she know? Why didn't she pick Dana or the women in front of us? Maybe just that quick, she saw enough of me to decide her final question was fitting.

"How you doing?"

A deep voice that sounds like Barry White interrupts me counting the floor tiles. The words belong to the young man in front of me who has now turned around. He's wearing a camouflage field jacket, his facial hair is nubby and he's got thick locks that touch his shoulders. He looks to be about thirty—and he's smiling—at me.

"First time here?" he asks, stuffing his hands in his pockets.

"Yes."

My gaze changes from the floor to the flyers tacked on the wall and I pretend to be interested in the announcements for upcoming events. Although he's not doing anything but grinning, I'm uncomfortable with his attention.

"So, how you doing? How's this vibe for you?"

"It's alright."

Careful, I tell myself. Maybe he'll turn back around if I don't sound too interested. His voice is distinctive, not at all what I'd expect from such a young-looking man. He may be attractive, but he's too close to my nephew's age to think about entertaining his advances. When it's his turn for the unisex bathroom, I let out a sigh of relief that he and his smile have disappeared behind the closed door.

After I return to my seat, Dana whispers, "One more."

13

There are four more acts to go, but maybe she's finally decoded what my crossed arms mean. Dana's enjoyed herself—her finger snaps have been louder and longer than anyone else's. All night, she's acted as if the couple seated next to us are long-lost friends. I had other things to do—I'm the one who needed to stay home tonight. This is the last weekend before school starts and there's still Mama and my hair to do.

I guess the last performance was underwhelming because the crowd's finger snaps are light.

Dana looks over at me and says, "Let's go."

Finally, we can leave the café to walk the few blocks back to her car, and go home. On the way out, Dana is still playing "I'm one of you" and speaks to almost everyone we pass as we leave.

Oh no.

The young man with the locks is standing at the edge of the sidewalk right outside the door to the café. That smile is still on his face and he's rocking on his heels with his hands still stuffed in his pockets.

"May I escort you two beautiful women to your ride?"

I shake my head, no.

"Yes," Dana says. "We would love that. Thank you."

I remain silent for our walk down an unlit street, counting cars parked halfway on the sidewalk and the number of broken warehouse windows in a neighborhood that looks like it's still trying to decide if it's coming up or going down.

Dana's chatting her head off with our new companion, as if we are strolling through a park. When we arrive at her pale yellow Volkswagon bug, he escorts her to the driver's side. She unlocks the door, he opens it, and before she gets in Dana gives him a hug. He approaches my side of the car with a look that says he's expecting a repeated hug, but after Dana pulls up the lock, I slip into the seat and say, "Thank you."

My handshake is quick and I shut the car door. Dana waves goodbye and as we drive away, she turns on the radio. I look over at my friend of fifteen years and think that she's oblivious to how I'm feeling.

Dana and I met hitchhiking down Carlos Bee Boulevard in Hayward. It was the seventies then, and we were both taking classes at Cal State. We ran into each other all the time, especially at the bus stop. I'd be waiting for an always-late bus at the corner, and I'd see Dana walk a little further down the hill to put her thumb out. I soon learned that almost no one waited for the bus and that hitchhiking was the popular way to get down the hill. One day, while I stood by myself waiting, Dana with her voice trailing as she walked past me, asked if I wanted to join her for the ride down. She was tall, wearing the same pair of silver-studded jeans and a matching jacket that she always wore, and her huge Angela Davis red natural was blowing in the wind. I remember thinking then she looked way too hip to be hanging out with me. I still don't know how we've stayed friends for so long.

"Inspiring wasn't it?" Dana says.

I'd been wondering who would be the first to break the silence between us.

"Didn't you see me shake my head 'no' to that young man?" I say.

"No, I didn't. But even if I did, I still would have said, 'Yes.'"

"I guess I don't matter then."

"Oh stop, Carla. There's no harm in letting youngsters show their version of gallant. Besides, he was cute in that natural kind of way."

"I'm sure David would have something to say about that."

"Now you know my darling, precious husband is not the least bit jealous. He says it gives young black men practice when older women let them display chivalry. It helps them know how to treat women their own age."

"Oh he does? Your wonder boy is special then."

I think of Dana's husband and how at first, I wasn't sure if David was the man for her. Maybe for dates and good times, but marry him? He was a brooder. I didn't understand what she saw in such a tall, lanky, and quiet man. He was good looking, and he still is. His pure chocolate skin, thick eyebrows, and matching moustache make him appear confident—which is why I didn't understand his sullen moods. I didn't know if he could feed the free spirit I knew my friend to possess. Before they married, I asked her if she was sure about him and without questioning herself, she assured me that he was the one she needed.

"Doesn't school start this week?" Dana asks, ignoring that I called her husband the 'wonder boy.'

"Tuesday." I sigh and stare out the car window watching the ripples on Lake Merritt move in uniform waves.

"Are you ready?"

"Ready as I'll get. Tomorrow I get my hair done. Then on to Mama's for her school-starts-tomorrow ritual."

"Mmmm, is it that time already? The summer went by fast." Dana removes one hand from the steering wheel to pat my shoulder in sympathy. "I think I'll take the long way to your place and go around the lake for a lap or two."

"Make it as many as you want," I say, "I'm not in a hurry anymore."

Dana plays with the radio buttons and stops on 91.1. It's KCSM, our favorite jazz station and we both settle into the bucket seats of her convertible for a spontaneous cruise around Lake Merritt.

"You want the top down?" Dana asks.

"No. I'm a little cold."

We've been doing this since college. Sometimes, like tonight, I've needed more time before going home, and other days it's been Dana who wasn't ready to go directly home and needed a few lake laps to talk about something on her mind. Tonight, though, I don't feel like talking.

The moon is full and bright, its image reflects on the water like a spotlight. As Dana drives, I notice my slump is a little lower than hers. I find myself preoccupied with the string of lights that circle Lake Merritt. As I count the tiny bulbs, I imagine that the dark space between each one represents lost meaning for things that used to matter.

Yes, Mama. The pot liquor is gone. *What do I do now?*

CHAPTER TWO

When your hair isn't right, you don't feel right. I'm lying awake in bed before sunrise. It's awfully early to think about what to do or what not to do. No amount of trying to keep my eyes closed is putting me back to sleep or giving me answers. Maybe my sleeplessness would make sense if it were a friend's wedding day or the morning before a big night out, or even like that time when I worried all night that my graduation pictures weren't going to come out right.

Still, for me, an African American woman, every day can seem like a big hair day, and even more so when my twice-a-month appointment at Charlene's Beauty Shop rears its ugly head on the calendar. On those days, what to do with my hair takes on enormous meaning. I find myself wondering, who will it make sense for?

My mother once said this about my hair:

"Carla, if you want a good job, you can't keep wearing your hair raw, looking unkempt like you did in college."

I had just graduated and, like thousands of newly degreed people, I was job-hunting for a teaching position. Mama and I were sitting in the kitchen in our home on Chester Street. She had been asking me about my plans and wanted to know if I was going to move back home, and what kind of school I wanted to work at. She was proud I'd become a teacher. It was the mid-seventies, and all across the nation it seemed like everyone was trying to regroup from black unrest. To have Eve Sinclair's daughter, with all my wooly hair, mistaken for one of those young people who face trouble bigger than themselves, (meaning, the Black Panther movement that grew out of our West Oakland neighborhood), well, that would never do.

I remember that day looking at my reflection in the toaster that sat on the counter, my big bushy natural was pulled back with an orange headband and tight curls rimmed my face. I remember thinking *I like my hair this way.*

"You gon' have to change it Sister, that's all there is to it," Mama said. "This is your fourth interview. If you don't do something 'bout them nappy edges and that thick bush you call a hairstyle, people gon' think you trying to be an instigator or something. They not gon' hire you."

"Mama, it's not that serious. It's just hair."

"You need to tighten it up. But don't get a perm," she cautioned. "The lye will burn your scalp. But a hot comb—now that'll tame it real good."

I went through a series of interviews for a teaching position at a middle school in Oakland, each one with people who didn't look like they had any thoughts about taming their own hair. However, mine had been tamed, and I got the job. My success at getting hired seemed to forever cement in Mama's mind that she was right, and it forever cemented in my mind that domesticated hair with a hot comb was the only way I would be acceptable. It's 1996, and even though I'm forty-six and definitely a grown woman, today, Mama's words still ring in my ears.

I make myself get out of bed and head off to my Saturday appointment to sit in air thick with the smell of blue grease on a hot comb and hope in vain that I won't spend most of my day getting my hair done. As soon as I hit the door, Charlene points me towards the wash area so I won't leave if she gets backed up. After some considerable time sitting with my head wrapped in a towel, she waves for me to sit in her chair.

Charlene's beauty shop is in a shotgun storefront with wall-to-wall mirrors. Three women sit behind me with their heads still wrapped, turning magazine pages quickly, but not reading. I can see they're keeping their eyes on me. I think they're probably hoping to be the next one waved over to sit in this chair.

Every two weeks I'm supposed to return. I try to stretch it to three, more if I can, but I see Mama on a regular basis and without fail she will let me know when my hair is "going back" and that I need to go see Charlene.

When I sit down in the oversized salon chair and place my shoes on the metal bar meant for your feet, Charlene looks straight at me through the mirror, frowning and shaking her head as if I've done something wrong.

"You took a little longer than usual to get in," she says. "And, oh my goodness look at this nappy kitchen. But don't worry, I'll take care of it."

It's the same thing Mama told me last week. I watch as Charlene runs the steaming hot comb through my hair with all the expertise and care of a master baker frosting a cake. It's gotten so I know which hot comb out of the dozen on the counter she will decide to use, I know when it's time for the three-inch hair clips, and when she'll say, "Hold your ear."

Even though I haven't liked doing this for a long time, I have to admit: Charlene knows how to straighten hair. All the years I've come to her, I have only been burned twice.

"There. Look at you now." Charlene steps back to admire her work.

She's done—it's tamed. When I look in the mirror, I know this flat bob that hangs to my shoulders and the straight cut bangs across my forehead no longer work for me, but I still do it. Truth is, I'm not ready for the look on Mama's face. Who knows what she'll say if I keep my nappy hair twisted in tight curls like it wants to be?

I work hard, and I can't remember when weekends stopped being a time to create a life that involved anything besides school and Mama. It's been months since I've headed over to San Francisco for enjoyment, where I could mindlessly walk around the skyscraper buildings, have lunch on Fisherman's Wharf, or visit the museums. For many years, I'd pay the toll for admission to the amusement park called, "The City," believing I could do anything I wanted; even blend in with the tourists.

Often, I pretended I was from a different country. I would say to an unsuspecting tourist who wanted to strike up conversation that I was from Ghana, Kenya, or sometimes Zimbabwe. My cocoa-brown skin that doesn't show a trace of my light-skinned father, made it easy to say I was from an African country, that I was a successful businesswoman on vacation. I'd get lost in my longing to be someone else and my stories became quite elaborate. Somewhere, a German couple believes they met the daughter of a prince.

When I went to the Fillmore District, it felt like I was sneaking out to visit the clubs like my brother Clarence did when he was younger. I remember watching him slip out the back door to go to the clubs that were close to our neighborhood on Seventh Street. I know Mama doesn't like me going to The City; she didn't like Clarence going out, either. A long time ago, I stopped telling her about me going over there because whenever I did, she would just frown about what she called my "wandering ways." Most of the time, I'd go by myself. Sometimes, Dana came with me, but I liked going alone so I could imagine having a different life.

But it's already Sunday. I lost a lot of time going out with Dana on Friday and yesterday Charlene took the whole afternoon to muzzle my hair. Then I was at Mama's half the night for dinner and our—or her "school is starting" ritual. By the time I got home, I was whupped.

Mama loved my hair and told me so, saying, "You look real nice, baby. Maybe when you get some time, you can take me to the shop. I sure miss Charlene." I played my part in the ritual. I let Mama inspect my hair, remind me how I couldn't find work until I got it straightened, and tell me all the things she misses about where we used to live, when everything was different. I reminded her, again, school started on Tuesday and not Monday. I watched her enjoy the liver and onions dinner I picked up from Merritt Bakery and then she asked what I was going to wear on the first day of school.

"You gon' wear your purple pantsuit?"

She knows I can't fit into those pants anymore. I couldn't believe that she still wanted me to wear that same suit. I can't remember the last time I wore it. Years ago, Mama bought me that outfit to wear on my first day teaching at Frederick Douglass Middle School. We went to the Emporium on Broadway and from that day on, she insisted I always wear the same thing on the first day of each and every school year. She said it would bring me good luck. For a long time, that was the uniform that signaled the school year was starting. I remember I lied and said I would wear the pants suit and probably had a fake smile on my face as I said it.

After Mama finished eating, I folded up the TV tray, helped her to bed, and waited for her to get settled under the covers and start her "back to school" speech. Suddenly, the cherry wood-framed mirror over her dresser became very interesting, and I counted the pictures in its reflection as she began to talk. For long as I can remember, we've had that conversation. I show up for her little speech about what I need to do to teach the "younguns," and how to be presentable as their teacher. Mama then tells me she's proud I have such a good career and how all her life she wanted to be a teacher.

In the past ten years, I've grown to staring off into space and saying, "I know Mama." Then last night, like in all the recent years, after going on and on she stopped to ask, "Are you listening Carla? Did you hear what I said?"

Last year, a few months before the end of the term, I started going to work an hour or more before the first bell. I'd sit in the quiet, sometimes with the lights turned off, trying to find strength for my students. The year had been a particularly hard one. Budget cuts were happening and staff members were getting pink-slipped left and right. I honestly thought it would be my last year at Douglass and even told a few people I wasn't coming back. But now, sitting in the auditorium, very aware of the width of my hips in a chair made for a student's bottom, there is no denying that I'm here for another year. All summer long I thought about not coming back. But how could I tell Mama I no longer worked at the school?

I've grown tone deaf to the sound of Vice Principal, Ed Shepherd's words, and my brain starts to count the number of faces in the room. I'm across the aisle from my co-workers, who all sat in the same row. I'm the odd man out. I didn't plan it this way, it just happened. They've all been here at least ten years and there's a new white woman sitting next to them who I heard got recruited to our Special Education department. Cassandra, the young sister with the braids, is back for her second year. I know it's only a prep day, but the holes in her jeans are a little too casual for my taste.

Although I'm twenty years older than Cassandra, we started getting close towards the end of the year; but really, I know we're only work friends. We never saw each other away from school. She's an interesting young woman, but I'm not sure we get each other. So it surprised me when at the beginning of last year's Easter break she presented me with a homemade royal-blue invitation to attend her wedding ceremony at Ocean Beach in San Francisco.

I went. I remember the day being cold and the sky was overcast and gray. It wanted to rain, but she and her intended husband ignored the weather and walked onto the sandy beach in bare feet towards the ocean for their ceremony. They were smiling widely at each other and dozens of friends and family followed them in the required no-shoe attire for the occasion. Since I didn't know her that well, I kept mine on. I thought it was okay not to feel obligated to take my shoes off.

It's been eighteen—no, nineteen years that I've watched Ed Shepherd try to hide his bald spot with fewer and fewer hairs. It's been nineteen years that I've gathered with other teachers to hear a pep talk on how great this year is going to be; each year hearing more and more about budget cuts and how we're the lucky ones because we still have jobs.

Twelve years ago, I believed Ed. Maybe, three years ago, I listened with a hopeful and responsible ear to his favorite part, "You will be faced with the challenge of helping your students learn and grow."

The new teacher, who looks to be in her mid-forties, reminds me of those mid-western women in *Life* magazine who live on farms. I can see her skin has been no stranger to the sun. She's asking a zillion questions. The other teachers are sitting way back in their seats, some with their arms crossed, a few are nodding their heads—I'm not sure if it's to be polite or that they really do agree with him. All I hear is Ed's tired attempt to put a new spin on old problems. After a few more questions, mostly from the new white woman, he sends us off with our halfhearted handclap to his "get out there and make it a great year."

"Well, that was definitely a rah-rah speech, wasn't it?" I say to Cassandra. The replay in my head tells me I sound sarcastic and dry.

"I thought you said last year was it for you." Her head is cocked to the side and has a surprised sound in her voice.

"Did I tell you that, too?" I thought I'd only told the old-timers who I thought would understand.

"You did." Cassandra shakes her head as she stares into her box of measly supplies.

Cassandra's acid wash bell-bottom jeans, tie-dyed tank top, and wide headband remind me of the way people looked in the sixties and seventies, and I wonder what's so different about this generation.

I pick up my box of supplies and look through my own meager rations of pencils, paper, and tape, making a mental inventory of the things I will need to buy from Target.

"Well, I guess there's something I'm not done with, because here I am," I finally say.

Cassandra shrugs her shoulders. How am I supposed to respond to this kid, throwing words back at me as if I didn't mean what I said? That grown woman child poet calling me out Friday, making everyone stare at me is enough. Yes, I'm surprised to be back here as well, but I'm not going to let Cassandra know that.

"Admit it, Ms. Sinclair, you love this job and the children," she says, lifting up her box.

I think she borders on sounding flip.

"You're right. I do love the children, and didn't I tell you to call me by my first name?"

"Oops, I guess over the summer I forgot. Okay, Carla it is."

She turns and bounces off with her box of supplies leaving me to watch her walk down the hallway with her hips swaying and head swinging as if she's listening to a favorite song. *New teachers.*

My room is located in the south wing of the school, past the cafeteria and the faculty lounge. I can't manage a bounce in my step like I saw in Cassandra's, and I don't believe my hips are swaying. Instead, I move through the empty hallways surveying lockers, feeling heavy on my feet and with a slight pain in my hip, wondering why they didn't remove the graffiti during the summer recess.

"Shit."

I look around to see if anyone heard me curse out loud, but luckily, I'm walking through the halls by myself. I forgot to pick up my class rosters, so now I have to go to the main office. You'd think after all these years I'd remember. Well, this year I don't plan on making too many of these trips. The main office is usually a hub of conflict and tension. It's not just a bad place for students to be sent to, it's also not a good place for me to visit too often, either. Last year, two office aides were cut from their jobs mid-year and the remaining aide, along with the secretary, began a war of them against us—"us" being the teachers.

"Hello Mrs. Brown. How was your summer?"

I try to say this nicely, hoping my tone of voice rings sincerity in asking about her time during the summer recess.

"I work—can't afford to do anything special." She continues with digging through a pile of papers.

"Oh? No time for a quick get-away?" I'm still trying to sound upbeat.

She keeps looking down. I stare at the top of her head, noticing the badly colored streaks of grey hair and remember when they weren't there. She's been here almost as long as I have. She started out cheery, everyone's favorite person to go to for help. But now the "Mrs. Brown experience" is something where your best bet is to get in, and get out.

"May I help you?" Finally, she looks over purple reading glasses with an expressionless face, and not even a fake smile to greet me for the new year.

Four, five, six, seven . . . I count the number of lockers lining the walls on the way back to my room, trying to shake off my trip to the main office. Eight, nine, ten...continuing until I see Room 103. When I open the door, I'm delighted to have a desk to set the box of supplies on. Last year, my desk had been moved to the portable classrooms down at the end of the sports field. I had to wait almost a month for a replacement.

I count 35 student desks lined in crooked rows with some stacked on top of each other. When I sit down to imagine arranging the desks into learning pods so students are grouped together in fours, one leg of my chair breaks and I can't stop an awkward plunge to the floor. I'm on my bottom with my legs stretched out in front of me looking up at the ceiling. *I don't want to be here, damn it.* Tears, like hot stinging water flow out—just like last night when I thought about coming to work.

Morning raindrops tap on the window causing more noise than you'd think such a light rainfall should make. The sound of the rain wakes me, drawing my eyelids up from a restless sleep. My head hurts. I rub my temples thinking about the Queen and her poetry: *Sun comes up but we're still under.* Even though my feet are touching the floor I wonder, what am I standing on? After going to the bathroom, I sit on the edge of the bed and through half-drawn curtains watch water fall from the sky. The corner streetlight has darkness behind it, yet drops of water that I imagine are hanging sideways on the window appear to be colored by its light. Lost in thought, thinking, about the mystery of raindrops, eats up most of my getting-dressed time.

Work clothes at the end of the bed are calling for me to jump in and join them—it's the first day of school, they say. I put Mama's jacket on so I won't have to lie about it anymore. It's tight across my hips and the two lower buttons won't fasten without it looking like they'll pop open.

I told her it didn't fit.

Does she really think I haven't missed a year wearing it?

When I arrive at school, the faculty parking lot is only half full. Luckily, I have everything I need and don't have to go near the main office. With this being the first day, Mrs. Brown will be running both the main office and the attendance office like they're emergency-room triage stations, and I don't want to come out with less than I walked in with—especially, not today.

"Good morning, Mr. Jerrod."

My next-door neighbor is dressed in a grey hounds tooth jacket with dark brown elbow patches—his first day and everyday jacket. He pushes his glasses back onto the bridge of his nose and stops with key in hand to look my way, staring as if he's seeing me for the first time.

"Good morning."

"So, what do you think about the upcoming year?" I try to make conversation.

"Would it matter if I thought about it? Would it really make a difference if I thought about it?"

Okay, Carla, don't forget—for the first few weeks of school just say, "Good morning," and don't ask questions.

"Well, I was just wondering."

"Wonder all you want. Who's going to do anything about what I think anyway? Who gets to think around here?"

It's best to just nod at my neighbor and open my own door. Yesterday, after I picked myself up off the floor, I was able to turn a broken room into a classroom. The large windows over the long, scarred, wooden cabinet let me catch just the faint hint of a rainbow lingering over the sports field. It's fading quickly, but I know I see it—I'm trying to let it be a sign that this year will be different.

Student after student walk through the doorway, bringing their disabilities into the room, some obvious and others yet to be revealed, but still they seem eager to be here. They make me believe I want to be here too. All that crying for the past two nights was about what? While waiting for the bell I look at the next class's roster and watch the students choose the seats they want to sit in.

For the fourth time today I write Ms. Sinclair on the blackboard say "Good morning class" and point to my name. As I call roll the many variations of "present" and "here" bring a smile across my face that almost feels real. When I call out, "Rasheed Jenkins," there's no response, only silence. I look up and see a dark-skinned African American boy sitting near the window, staring at me. He's still wearing his oversized coat and his hand is raised, but unlike my other students there's no loud proclamation to announce that indeed, he is here. I meet his eyes with a nod of recognition, repeat his name, and continue on with my list. I think Rasheed's expressive eyes were as loud as any voice I've heard so far today.

CHAPTER THREE

All through September, I've wandered around the inside courtyard during the lunch period or have eaten in my classroom rather than making a beeline to the faculty lunchroom. So far, everything is going well and I want to forget why I didn't want to be here in the first place. I've seen Rasheed many times sitting on the metal bench near the basketball courts eating his sandwich with another boy from fourth period. They appear almost hidden away from the other students. One day, I walked over to make conversation with them.

"Hi Thomas. Hello Rasheed." I wanted to sound casual. "Enjoying your lunch?"

Thomas, dressed in an oversized white tee shirt, said, "Yes."

Rasheed just nodded.

"Do you ever play basketball?"

"Yes," said Thomas, while Rasheed nodded again.

"So what else do you boys like to do?"

"I don't know," Thomas said, hunching his shoulders up.

Rasheed only shrugged. The silence that followed was awkward. I smiled. They squirmed on the bench, looking up briefly to give smaller-than-halfway grins, and then went back to looking down at cracked asphalt growing grass in its crevices. The long silence gave way to a voice in my head that said tell them you will see them in class tomorrow, and leave. Since that day, I've watched at a distance while they sit on the bench. Seems to me Thomas does all the talking. Rasheed nods his head and at times kicks the ground, or buries his face in the sleeve of his jacket when it looks like laughter wants to overtake him.

A restless night of sleeping has left me achy and stiff for most of the morning. I've sat at my desk rather than walking around the classroom as I usually do. I've asked the students to talk about the things they are afraid of. Rocío is in the same desk grouping as Rasheed. She wants to speak first.

"Ms. Sinclair, last year I was afraid to tell my teacher something."

I notice Rasheed is watching intently. Even though I ache, I get up to move closer to the windows near the back of the room where they sit.

"Tell us about it, Rocío." I move just a little closer.

She looks over at Rasheed, which draws my attention to him. He motions his head as if telling her it's okay to keep talking. Her eyes turn to the floor.

"She kept getting me confused and I didn't like it."

"Who's she and what was confusing?"

Rocío sucks her teeth and rolls her eyes. I decide not to correct her because I want to know what this child is trying to tell me. From the look on her face, it must be important.

"My teacher. I'm from Guatemala, I don't got nothing against the Mexicans but that's not where I'm from. I was afraid the teacher would get mad if I told her she was wrong."

Now I know I have to say something.

"I don't *have anything* Rocío, not I don't *got nothing*."

She repeats the proper version, and when I compliment her, a stifled smile appears.

"Did you tell your teacher this?"

"Lots of times. But she kept forgetting I even told her."

She sucks her teeth, but I think twice about giving another correction so soon. Instead, I say, "That was brave, Rocío. I'll make sure not to forget."

She's just a seventh grader, maybe 12 or 13 and already, it matters that people know who she really is and where she's from. I look at this little girl with brown skin and straight dark hair. She could pass for many different kinds of people. This child probably knows more about her family's history than I do about mine.

The rest of the class is quiet. They seem interested in what Rocío is saying so I ask, "What language do you speak when you're at home?"

Rocío turns around to glare at her classmates before she answers.

"Mam. It's not Spanish like everybody thinks. Where I live lots of people speak Mam, so there."

She sucks her teeth again. I make a mental note to deal with that at another time.

When Rocío spoke, Rasheed looked around too, as if underscoring what she said. He reminded me of a protective big brother.

"I've never heard of Mam. Class, how many of you speak a different language at home?"

Over half the students raise their hands and they're all waving to be called on.

Okay.

A look around tells me this is a teachable moment. All the white and African American students' hands are down.

"Class, think about this. How we talk, and what language we speak, depends on where we come from, right?"

"Right," they shout in unison.

Okay, Carla, where are you going to take this now? How are you going to get everyone pointing on a map?

I see Rasheed hovering over his seat—he's looking at me and pointing at the maps, almost directing me to go there. I nod towards him to let him know that's a good idea and move towards that side of the

31

classroom. I stand in front of the map of the United States and say, "I was born here, in the state of California," and point in the vicinity of Oakland. "But my parents came from here, the state of Texas." Then, I move to the world map and point to Africa.

"Many generations ago, my great-great grandparents had parents who lived here."

When I turn back towards the class, I see Rasheed nodding his head at me. I smile back at him and keep going.

"Okay. Let's take turns showing everyone where we were born, and where our parents and grandparents came from. Who wants to go first?"

All the students raise their hands and the room looks like a stadium full of fans waving flags. Fourth period has a lot of talkers. I think how Rasheed, without saying a word, has a big influence on what goes on in this class. Today, I almost thought he was going to say something. When I look in his direction, he's got his hand over his mouth. I'm not sure, but it looks like there is a smile in his eyes. Who is this child, I wonder?

It's two-and-a-half months into the school year and Cassandra's involved in planning holiday assemblies. She asked for my help, but I just can't do it. It's Friday. I may look in step with everyone else, but all the reasons I don't want to be here, not even in my own life stay hidden, tucked away in places where I try not to find them so I can make it through the week. The game of hide-and-no-seek ends on weekends, especially, if I'm alone.

Last weekend, I went out to Mama's. She had the boys and their children over for an early supper; I stayed to clean up afterwards. Mama played with her grandkids on the bed, took a little nap, and used her walker to watch me clean the mountain of dishes in the sink. She seemed in good spirits so I thought to talk about what was really going on, how I'm thinking about doing something—I don't know what, but something different.

In-between sprinklings of when I could get something across, our conversation turned again into a pep talk full of clichés. Mama just said, "Well, Sister, you have to make lemonade out of lemons," or "It only takes one egg to bake a cake," to her favorite, "Well, leave and teach in Brentwood."

I've fallen into a routine at Douglass. Monday to Friday, four classes in the morning; lunch; a prep and then my last class. That's what my day looks like. It must be ingrained now, or I wouldn't be grabbing my bag, headed to the lunchroom like everyone else, without even bothering to see what time it is.

The faculty lunchroom hasn't changed since my first year. The same round, orange tabletops that started peeling from the edges some ten years ago are still here, along with the same blue plastic chairs pushed underneath. At times, I think the room smells of defeat, particularly on a rough day with students, and it's even worse when those rough days are caused by the administration.

Lately, Cassandra and I have taken to eating together like we did last year. I'm not sure why this year she's decided to become my lunchtime buddy. Maybe she's *my* source for borrowed enthusiasm. Then again, I can't help but remember what Mama always says when anyone acts too happy—that they're upbeat from not knowing what they're fixin' to know.

We're sitting at the table sharing our lunch in silence. Mr. Jerrod, I guess to avoid any attempts to bring him into a conversation, has taken to eating in a corner chair hidden behind a newspaper. Last weekend, Mama for the umpteenth time, told me why she wanted to become a teacher, and for the sake of breaking this silence between us, I think to ask Cassandra, "With all that's available to young women these days, why did you become a teacher?"

God, that sounded like a bad talk show host with a dull opening question for an interview, but I wonder why would she choose to be responsible for other people's children—on purpose?

"So, are you asking because you really want to tell me why you became one?" Cassandra bites into a super burrito wrapped in green plastic that I can tell came from the corner store next to the school.

"Not really," I say. "Why do you ask that?"

Never a straight answer from her.

She looks at me with a wise-guy smile, leaning her head to the side.

"I don't know. It just seems when older people ask a question about 'why did you become something,' they usually want to talk about themselves."

Her answer annoys me. Can't I just be trying to make conversation?

"Mmph . . . couldn't I just be curious?" I say.

"No disrespect intended," she says quickly, "but why did *you*? You, first."

Suddenly, my plastic bowl of leftover spaghetti from last night becomes very interesting. I move the fork around as if the task of making sure each string has its share of sauce is the most important thing in the world.

"It was something my mother always wanted to be."

I'm still stirring. A little warm wave crosses over my forehead. Cassandra looks up at me before she takes another bite.

"So, it's a generational thing. She taught, and now you?"

"Not exactly, she never became a teacher. She wasn't able to attend the teacher training schools they had back in her day."

"Oh, I see. So then you became one for her."

"No. It was *my* decision." I'm not sure if I believe my own answer.

God, this child is playing twenty questions. Has Cassandra summed up in so few words something even I'm not sure about?

"And now you don't want to teach anymore?"

She's not looking at me, and barely pauses between bites. Her responses have me wondering if like the poet, she's messing with me.

"You've said it before," she adds.

"I was tired when I said that."

"You sure do a lot of things you don't want to. What's that about?"

She's chewing into that burrito, asking things like why teach special education? Why did I stay at the same school for so long? Why do I continue to teach? I try to say something so she doesn't know how tongue-tied I feel, how her questions have me turned around. This young woman has a boldness I don't know anything about. As much as she rattles my nerves, there's an ease to how she expresses herself that brings up envy in me.

"I hear all that, but I'm not sure I can stay here as long as you have. I give it maybe five years, then I'm going to see what it's like somewhere else." She gives a little bounce in her seat when she says this.

"Like where?"

"I don't know, maybe Hawaii. I would love to live in a place with beautiful sandy beaches so on the weekends I can hang in warm luscious water with my Boo, you know, just chilling. Wouldn't that be fun?" She giggles.

Besides my make-believe-you-are-someone-else trips to The City, it hadn't occurred to me I could just pick up and really go somewhere else. What makes her so confident about leaving? I manage to give a smile at her enthusiasm for this imagined place, and just as quickly my insides twist with sadness. When was the last time I even used the phrase, "Wouldn't that be fun?"

"Okay, your turn" I need a break from being on the hot seat. "So, why did *you* become a teacher?"

"Because I'm good at it." She gets up from the table. "Lunch is over in five minutes. If we don't leave now, we'll have to play dodge the student in the hallways. I'll tell you *why*, later."

As Cassandra walks away, I wave goodbye with a forced smile. Waiting for the bell does mean I'll wade through crowds of students, but I need to sit a while longer. I'm not sure what kind of conversation I just had with Cassandra. Was she being flip with me? She's "good at it?" How does she think she can just go somewhere and get hired? Look at her hair. Those braids look cared for, but I wouldn't call them tamed.

CHAPTER FOUR

A Bay Area storm with thunder and lightning—something unusual for this part of the country—arrived without announcing itself. The weather forecasters missed this one. Huge raindrops are pounding on the rooftop. It's a good reason to stay home and not worry that I should be out doing something, or spinning my mind thinking how lazy I am for not going to church, or having a moment of what Dana calls "colored woman's guilt."

The fact that I show up to work every Monday through Friday is enough of a reason to want to stay inside. I haven't missed a day of school yet, and there've been plenty times I didn't want to put on clothes to match a public face. But if Eve Sinclair's children know anything, we know that not working when you are able to never is an option.

I remember Mama always working for wages. At first, she took in clothes to wash and cleaned other peoples' houses. Then, she worked at the shipbuilding plant in Richmond, standing on her feet all day, which caused her those varicose veins. The plant closed and she went back to cleaning and washing, but finally landed a good job as an account clerk at Clorox. Thirty years later, she retired. Wanting to lie around, doing nothing, is not something Mama would understand.

On many Sundays when I don't take Mama to church, I lay around, but today it's hard to shake this feeling of aloneness and I wonder if it will ever leave. Thoughts of when I left home some twenty years ago creep in. I was twenty-one before I actually moved out—all my brothers had left and it didn't seem right to leave Mama completely alone. After I finished high school, working at the daycare down the street was convenient, and she liked that my job was close to home, but I had this itch that kept saying it was time to go. So, I moved out to go to Cal State Hayward, a total of 20 miles down the freeway. It was a big deal to move away from our West Oakland neighborhood, but still, I always made it home for Sunday church and dinner.

The turkey lasagna that I've eaten for days is warming in the oven for breakfast. On Thursday evening, Dana brought it over saying, "I know you're not cooking. What kind of friend would let you starve?" Then she told me that it looked like an animal got loose in my house and asked if I wanted help to straighten things up.

The heat from the oven has the living room windows steamed up and I can't see out. I'm circling over the thick carpet, moving from room to room in my bare feet, shooting scented mist into the air, trying to find *better*. Most of the time, I trust Dana, even if she is bossy. She's the one who told me to get this lavender mist. "The fragrance is soothing. Try it. You'll feel better," is what she said.

So here I am, drifting around my apartment in Daddy's old faded yellow bathrobe, spraying water into the air. I've done the living room, gone around the plants, sprayed the furniture, went through the kitchen, and I've been twice around the bed.

Dana also told me while spraying to repeat, "I love myself, I love myself." She said, "Shout it, roll on the floor when you say it, jump up and down, spread your arms and legs like you're making a snow angel." There's no snow in the Bay Area, but that's what she told me to do.

Sometimes, she can be real strange, but I love Dana. She's like the sister I never had. Without saying a word, I continue with a few more pumps of her so-called magic liquid. The watery mist hangs in the air and I take a step back so it doesn't get on me. On days like this, there's an itch that keeps happening right underneath my left breastbone and I want it to go away, but it won't. It feels like my soul needs something. I rub, pinch, and scratch, yet that area close to the middle of my heart stays agitated. Dana calls it my heart chakra. Of course, she would say that. She's one of those people black folks call "special." She's definitely counter-culture and not into what everybody else might be doing. She does moon rituals, meditates, chants like Tina Turner, and well...sometimes, I don't quite get her.

Anyway, for now forget what Dana wants me to believe about this itch that won't go away. One time, I told Mama about it and she said that was my soul spot trying to tell me something. Even though I don't think she knows what I really mean, I tend to agree with her. The itch that scratches me is so deep inside that even though I try to ignore its prickling, I can only pretend that it's gone—like now, while spraying this silly water into the air. It doesn't matter if I go to work, hang out at clubs, or walk around trying not to pay attention—it's still here.

My thoughts are spiraling down and my mood is going with them; that's why I hate to be alone. The only thing that stops me from becoming paralyzed and unable to move my life forward is to count.

I started counting when I was a child; it was a distraction from loneliness, or things too big in meaning to understand. When Mama combed my hair, I'd sit with her pointy knees poking my sides, and when she got to my kitchen she'd raise her knees to my shoulders to hold me down because it hurt and I'd squirm. Counting black-and-white tiles on the floor to distract myself from the pain that hair combing caused was how I got through it. When I was sent to the back porch so grown-ups could talk, I'd count the flowers on the curtains. If I was sitting on the front steps at our family home in West Oakland, I'd count how many car wheels went by, the number of shoes that walked by our house, even the geese flying overhead in V-formation. In the kitchen while helping Mama fix food, I counted plates, cups, forks, knives, and spoons in the drawer. I'd count anything where I saw more than one.

A hard rain still pours. From the second floor of my apartment, I can look down on the trees bending over from the weight of the rain and wind. I live at the end of a street lined with oak trees, apartment complexes, and single-family homes. My neighbors frequently come outside, but speaking to one another is not something you can always expect—unless there's a yard sale, and then crowds of people gather to inspect one another's discarded treasures.

The freeway is only two blocks away. It's a constant noise, but over the years that's faded into the background. When I do pay attention to the traffic's low rumblings, I imagine I hear the ocean roaring. I call it an urban river. Only, its more like a steady stream of steeled-off humanity flowing over concrete.

My neighborhood borders on urban, but it's not full blown—yet. Where I live, there are still enough white people and trees left that it's not uprooted barrenness like down on International Boulevard or Martin Luther King, Jr. Way. Mama likes that I live in this area, and she doesn't let an opportunity go by without reminding me how she feels.

"Things are changing so much in Oakland, Carla, I just want you to be somewhere safe," she says. And then depending on her mood she might add, "Why don't you move out to Brentwood with me?"

Through my living room window I can see the wet sky that's not letting up, thinking I've still got time before I have to face my Monday morning at Douglass.

CHAPTER FIVE

I left early for work so I could drive the long way around the lake. I wanted to watch the people who get up for their daily just-past-sunrise constitutional. Dana's been asking me to join her in a new walking program she's cooked up for the both of us. She says it's time to stop driving laps and start walking. If she wasn't my best friend, I don't think I would ever have considered the idea.

"Hi, Carla. How was your weekend?"

I've been sitting in my classroom so lost in thought Cassandra's voice seems to come out from nowhere. She's standing in my doorway. I look at her long flowery skirt and black leotard with an orange fishnet vest over it. If that child isn't a throwback to the sixties I think.

"Oh, I'm sorry. Hi, Cassandra. I was just thinking about something. Why are you here so early?"

"I've noticed how you come early to work, and I thought how peaceful it must be to sit in a quiet room before the day starts."

"Yes, I guess it's nice." I hear my voice drift off at the end.

I'm sitting in my empty classroom because I'm trying to get my scattered mind right for the day and this child is here because she thinks it's peaceful. Cassandra comes in and plops down in the first desk near the door.

"I don't get to do this often. You know I'm still considered a newlywed." She bats her eyes at me.

"Are you planning on staying?" I ask. "What about your peaceful moment?"

"There'll be another. So, do you want to hear why I became a teacher?"

Cassandra crosses her legs to settle in, as if my answer will of course be, "Yes." I don't know how to tell her I wish she would leave me like she found me—alone.

"When I was in high school, I wasn't really a good student. I mean, I made good grades, and was on the honor roll and all. But I have to admit I was more into the social side of things. The boys were so fine that I started cutting school, hanging out and having a good time . . . "

I'm not trying to grab onto this conversation, but she's determined to have it with me. Doesn't she see I'm not really into it? On top of Dana's walking program, I'm thinking about Rasheed and his upcoming Individualized Educational Program meeting a month from now with all the bigwigs. It's been over four months and he's still not talking in class. He won't talk to me or anyone else at school. Ms. Know-It-All, the district's psychologist will be there, of course Ed, and in Rasheed's case, his grandmother instead of his parents.

I call on him to give him a chance to say something, hoping he'll speak. Sometimes, he looks directly at me as if he wants to talk, but then he lowers his eyes, drops his head, and waits for me to take the attention off him without ever saying a word. Ms. Snyder, the psychologist, thinks he has a mild form of autism, or an undiagnosed speech impediment that doesn't allow him to use words. I'm not sure if I agree. When he started the school year, his grunting and head shaking let everyone know he wasn't going to verbally communicate with anyone. But he's very well liked. The students don't seem bothered by him not talking. He and Thomas still sit together during the lunch recess. When I watch them sitting on the bench that's their meeting spot, I can tell that Rasheed is somehow communicating with his friend.

I've read his student folder. It's thick with papers that have barely been touched; they're not tattered or used-looking like I've seen some students' folders. But all those forms and notes don't make sense to me. They keep going back and forth about his inability to use language. All of it reads like a rush to make this child's behavior understandable. The words seem like they contradict themselves. They say his behavior in class is fine, but he doesn't participate in discussions or answer questions. He gets good grades, but won't read out loud. They all end with saying he has a developmental problem that needs to be addressed. Something's not right—I can see that for myself. *Developmental?* Well, I'm not sure about that; he seems to understand all that is happening around him. I remember how he led me towards the map that day when I wasn't sure what to do.

I think Rasheed looks princely. He's tall for his age, stands straight, holds his shoulders back and squared off as if bracing against the world. I wonder if the school, or anyone else for that matter, is able to see this young boy's soul. I just know there's an itch somewhere that he's not able to get to by himself. I hope I'm able to help him.

"…So then I decided I wanted to teach in Oakland. I could have gone to other districts, everyone was after me, but I like the raw challenges we get at Douglass."

Cassandra wraps up her explanation about why she decided to teach middle school students. How much of her story did I miss?

"Well, Oakland and Douglass are lucky to have you." I glance over to see if she's satisfied that I was listening.

"Yes, they are." She jumps up from the student desk and waves as she leaves.

All week long, Cassandra's popped in and out of my classroom looking for advice. What should she do with a student who needs more testing, or with one who's causing problems in class? When should she call the parents if a child won't pay attention to her, and how often can she send somebody to the vice principal before it looks bad on her?

Each time I see Cassandra walking in the hallway with her eyebrows pushed together, she rushes over to ask me a question, and during breaks she comes by my classroom to say, "Uh, you got a minute? I have a little situation here." She just about wears me out with all her *little situations.*

With Cassandra's problems on top and mine underneath, how I make it through the school week mystifies my senses. The weekends don't come fast enough. Yesterday, Otis, my youngest brother, took his latest child to Mama's, giving me a two-day weekend without the disruption of driving to Brentwood to take care of her.

Saturday had been a blur; for most of the day, my bed was my closest friend and don't ask what I did the rest of the time. Sunday's wake-up is coming slow. I feel achy, like I'm coming down with something. Before getting out of the bed, I turn sideways across the mattress and lie on my stomach, gingerly. Under the pressure of my weight, it feels tender. While thinking about Rasheed, I count the lines in the wooden panels on the floor.

In the living room, my stereo sits on the glass bookshelf next to the windows. On the bottom shelf, there's a foot-high stack of magazines I pulled out from the bedroom. Yesterday, I looked through all of them, and with a pen circled pictures. Later on, I will have to bring out some more.

I decide to turn the stereo volume up so loud that Alicia Keyes' voice rises to the ceiling. It makes everything near the speakers vibrate. It's probably too much for this early in the morning, so I turn it down with a remote so tiny and thin, it amazes me. It came with the Bose stereo my brothers gave me at last year's birthday dinner. Mama said the gift was all their doing and that she hadn't helped at all. They handed me a box with a bright purple bow on it and when I tore off the wrapping to reveal the silver toned stereo inside, all I could do was cry.

"Since you won't go to concerts with us, at least you'll have something good to listen to music on," they told me.

We were at Picán's on Broadway, the new southern restaurant across from the YMCA. My three brothers, Mama, Dana and her husband, David, and Mrs. Greenly were all there. I remember ordering fried oysters and the gourmet styled cheesy grits. It was my forty-fifth birthday. My brothers teased me, saying now I had officially joined the ranks of the middle-aged, and that in five years, AARP would hunt me down, relentlessly, to sign me up for its membership.

I like the music loud. It covers up my thoughts. Today, I understand the young men who drive through neighborhoods with music so loud their trunks rattle, and though people stare and reel back from the noise, they don't pay anybody any mind. I decide to turn it back up and the bass bumps on the glass. When Alicia moans at the top of her voice, she sounds tortured. I imagine she's singing about an itch. Many times I put her songs on repeat, playing the CD over and over, working up my emotions. Sometimes, it's my crying song when backed up tears won't fall. I feel backed up today, full with no release—at least not until Alicia started singing.

Little thoughts about my life creep into my mind—I'm so tired of this. All the supposed to's are wearing me down. Cassandra is right; I do a lot of things I don't want to. I feel that so much, right now, I only want to get back in the bed and hide under the covers. This feeling, the itch in my chest, seems to be with me almost daily and now it's become a part of me. I just wonder what it will it be like to say I'm done being here, and where will I go when I die? Will it be restful? Will I see my father resting, too? I guess you're never really sure until you get there. I'm uncertain how I will arrive.

Alicia is singing about someone troubled. "Yes," I say to her, and take a sip of heated cognac, "I keep finding myself down..."

A loud thump on the wall is followed by a muffled, "What the hell?"

If an early morning concert bothers my neighbors, I don't care. How many times do I listen to their sounds late at night? And it's not all music bouncing off these thin apartment walls I hear. From what I can tell, there's not too much concern about me hearing the constant bumping of a headboard on the wall followed by wails of, "Don't stop." Like a rapper dancing in a music video, I throw finger signs at the wall.

"So there!" I shout, and give my own knocks on the wall.

Finally, my neighbors have given up—the repeated thumps have stopped. I guess I won that battle. So, again, I spray the mister into the air. This time I think to let the moisture drop on me. I wait. Nothing happens except blinking from the wetness and the scent of lavender. No amount of Alicia Keyes' singing or me wandering around in half my pajamas is changing anything. One last plod through the rooms, extra sprays over the rugs, two trips into the bedroom to pull another foot-high stack of magazines to the middle of the living room, and all I can think to do is flop on the floor and wait, hoping to find comfort.

When I was growing up, Sunday was for family and church. When Mama became ill and couldn't get to church regularly, I stopped going too, but I remember in the early years those days as being full of purpose. The sidewalks in West Oakland streamed with families; daddies and mamas were dressed in their best, walking their children towards the church that was five blocks from our house on Chester Street.

It was the sixties and the neighborhood sidewalks were even busier on church day than they were during the week. The more well-to-do black families rode in cars, even if they only had a short way to go. I didn't mind walking. From what I'm told, I was the first one to wait at the end of the gate. I would rush everyone else to quickly get dressed so we could be part of the procession. I liked joining in step with the other families on the street.

Our family had a tradition on Sundays. In the early morning, we'd have a thick breakfast of eggs, pancakes, rice and gravy, bacon and sometimes, fried chicken. Mama always cooked a pot of grits, but none of us, except Daddy, ate them. Mama still says she'll never understand how a Southern woman could raise children who didn't like grits. Nevertheless, Sunday breakfast was always hearty and it left our stomachs satisfied. In an unspoken agreement we spent the hours after the meal, and before we left for church, doing things that kept us apart from each other. I guess we were weary from being so close during the week. After breakfast, my three brothers spread out around the house trying to find privacy so they could open the tin cans that held money they earned from doing odd jobs during the week. Each one was careful not to let the others know how much they made. Sometimes they'd be in the kitchen impatient for their turn to use the ironing board to place hot iron creases in their pants and lay down their shirt collars.

After Daddy died, Mama and I shared their bedroom. She said it was too quiet with just her in there. After Sunday breakfast, more than likely, you'd find her behind the curtain that separated our two sides of the room, getting dressed or studying her Bible.

"I'm not one of those people flipping and flapping the pages of the Word, letting everyone know you ain't been studying," she'd say. Most nights, Mama studied her Bible and in church was always quick to locate the scripture called out by the pastor. Then, without fail, she'd raise her head to look around to see who in the congregation was still searching.

And what was I doing after breakfast? Usually, you could find me on the floor in the living room near the couch or under the dining table surrounded by magazines, ignoring my job as the only daughter to wash the morning dishes.

I think back to this particular Sunday morning in 1968. There was turmoil in the air; race riots were either ending or starting in major black cities across the country. I was lying on the living room floor reading an article about a family living in the projects of Chicago. My pre-teen self could care less about the dishes in the sink when I couldn't understand why people were living this way. Mama yelled for me to get to my chores, but I stayed on the floor stretching out as many minutes as I could before she had enough of what she called "my dreamy ways."

"Carla Sinclair, if you don't get to them dishes I'm gon' whup you, you hear? I ain't heard a pot or a pan washing."

"Yes, Ma'm," I said, without moving any closer to the sink that was piled up with dirty pans and dishes that still had food on them.

"And press out your whites," she hollered from upstairs. "You know this is First Sunday."

"Yes, Ma'm," I said, again.

I wasn't interested in what I was supposed to wear to church. I was locked into an article in the June issue of *Life* magazine, about the lives of black folks. I remember the cover had a picture of a dark-skinned boy looking out from the shadows of his front door with a tear coming down his face. His family lived in housing projects 15 stories high. I remember Mama came to the doorway of the living room with a belt wrapped around her hand—counting out loud. I knew by the count of five if I wasn't up washing dishes, my butt would burn from the belt.

"Carla, your brother and me gon' stop buying those magazines if this is all you do," she said counting, "one, two, three, four..."

"I'm up. I'm up." I ran into the kitchen and twisted my hips sideways to get past her.

The belt hit my lower leg, not hard, just enough to let me know she meant what she said. Mama was quick for waving a belt. She stopped as we got older, but when I was growing up, I was always running away from it. She never really beat me, though I'm sure my brothers wouldn't say the same. I can only remember a few times where I really felt the force of the belt, when she was terribly angry about something I did or didn't do.

Mama is maybe all of five-feet tall. I tower over her by at least six inches. Back then, she was barely 100 pounds, but she always seemed bigger. Most of the time, I'd hear her calling my name from another room, shouting for me to stop reading and to do something. I'd stay staring at the pictures in my magazine until I'd feel her shadow, then I'd jump up in the opposite direction of her swing, and she'd miss. Depending on how she felt, she might chase after me, but that happened less and less as time went on. I took advantage of her growing tired and stayed on the floor for hours, absorbed in my magazines.

My oldest brother, Clarence, is the one who got me started collecting all the magazines that came to our house, even though he won't admit to it.

"What you doing with them after you read 'em?" He asked a year after they started coming.

"Putting them over there." I pointed towards the corner near Mama's special lamp.

"You know they just gon' collect dust and make the living room look junky." He said this in a gruff manner so I knew he was getting ready to do something.

"Clarence—don't throw them away." I pleaded as he picked up all of my treasured magazines to carry them to the back porch.

"Stop pulling on my arm," he said. "I'm not throwing them out, girl—we pay too much to do that. Here, when you get done, put them in this box."

And that's how I started. I still have the first ones that date back to the sixties. I keep them stacked in my bedroom. Over 30 years of monthly issues that arrived at the door. The stacks are so high that in the dark you might think they were someone's shadow. When I moved from Chester Street to go to college, the magazines came with me. Four years later, when I couldn't think of anything else but how soon I could get back to Oakland where I knew I'd see people who looked like me, the stacks followed me again. Since then, they go with me every time

I move, lining the walls of each new bedroom, adding the cushion of comfort and familiarity I need. Clarence and my other brothers have moved me more times than I want to admit, and with each move they tease me, asking, "You charging them rent?"

It was after our father died that I asked Mama if we could have the magazines come to the house. From the very first issue, I began flipping through the pages looking for men with butterscotch skin and dark brown hair. Daddy's family has Dutch in them and even though he was a light-skinned man, I remember him saying he wasn't light enough to be accepted by that part of his family. Sometimes I'd replace the name in the article with his, Arthur Sinclair, and read it out loud as if he were the subject of the story.

He died early in the morning. I was upstairs in my bed staring out the window—waiting for everyone to return from the hospital. There was no one walking on the street. Everything looked so dark outside until I saw the lights from our old station wagon with the wooden panels pull into the driveway. Clarence got out to open the gate while Mama, Arthur, Jr., and Otis waited in the car. I heard the front door shut and then the sound of house slippers flopping on the wooden stairs. I knew it was Mama coming to talk to me.

She and my brothers had gone to the emergency room. Earlier that evening, our father said his pain was too much and he needed to go to the hospital. I had been sent to the back porch, but I snuck in closer to see what was going on. I could hear his moans from the kitchen.

He was hurt loading a ship at the naval yard. His injuries stopped him from walking and he couldn't move around. Each time the nurse knocked on the front door and one of my brothers announced she was here, I was sent out the room. Only the boys and Mama were allowed to stay for her visit. I'd go to our screened-off porch in the back of the house to sit among the baskets of clothes placed next to the metal wash bucket and cardboard boxes full of vegetables from Mama's garden.

For two years, the living room had been Daddy's bedroom. He slept in a bed with guardrails and one of those triangle bars to pull himself up. His broken back healed slowly, and the combination of having to lie down all the time and the injuries to his legs never allowed him to walk, again. Mama said it was better for him to be downstairs and not shut off upstairs by himself.

I liked him sleeping in the living room. After school, I'd skip from the bus stop down the street, not waiting to walk with anyone else who lived on my block. I'd rush through doing my homework on the coffee table near his bed so we could read the newspaper together. We took turns reading articles. Sometimes, he stopped what he was reading to tell me an article had too much bad news in it, and that there were better things in the world to know about. I'd pretend to make a frown when he stopped reading. He'd frown back, push up his nose and start a new article. I became attached to him being at home; it was like he waited for me.

The night they took him to the hospital, I cried and cried to go with them, but Mama wasn't having it. It was late, just after midnight, and there was a lot of commotion going on in the house. I didn't know all the uproar was about Mama and the boys trying to decide whether to drive Daddy to the hospital or to call an ambulance. I was the baby, the only girl and just ten years old. I guess no one thought they should give me the details, to let me know Daddy was dying and he would not be coming home.

Mrs. Greenly, who lived four houses down, stayed with me while they took him to the hospital. She sat downstairs and through the upstairs window, I watched the ambulance drive him away.

Mrs. Greenly along with her boys, who are a little older than my brothers, made the trip from Texas with Mama. She was always a handsome looking woman. Back then, she wore her hair slicked back in what people called a "conk." She's Mama's friend, her best friend from what I know of that time, and they're still friends, today. When they came back from the hospital, Mama entered my side of the curtained off bedroom to tell me I no longer had a father.

"Wake up, Carla," she said, although she already knew I was awake.

It's always been Mama's way, when she needs to tell you something difficult, she'll start by saying something you both already know.

When she pulled the curtain back I answered, "Yes Ma'm, I'm awake."

She lifted my back off the mattress so she could wrap her arms around me. She pulled me so close into her small chest that my night-gown wrenched down, bunching around my neck, almost choking me. She held me tight, rested her head on top of mine and cried, her warm tears dripped down onto my hair wetting my face, but I knew they weren't my tears. Aside from washing and doing my hair she didn't touch me much, so when she lifted me in this awkward way, I knew she was attempting to share her sadness. I couldn't look up or see her eyes, so I stared into her thin neck waiting for her to explain.

"Baby, your daddy's gone. He ain't in pain no more."

"Is Daddy *dead*?"

I hadn't yet known anyone to die, but I knew the way Mama was talking that's what she meant. She sounded like the older women in the church when they talk about someone passing on. Before that night, it never crossed my young mind that one day my own mother would sound like them.

"Yes, Baby, his body is dead, but his spirit is living. Don't you forget for a minute he is still watching you."

"Will I be able to see him?"

"Baby you gon' have to see him in your mind or when you get to heaven. He's gone now."

I cried out, "But Mama, he didn't tell me he was leaving—I didn't say goodbye!"

When Daddy was strong, I could expect his "goodbye" to include picking me up and telling me I was his favorite girl. I remember feeling so sad that he'd left without us saying our goodbye.

"It's okay. You can say it at the service."

I don't remember crying that night, and I don't know how long Mama stayed on my side of the room. I just remember looking out the window staring into the early morning darkness, thinking: *That's what I see inside of me—darkness.*

After he died, all the questions a little girl would ever want to ask went unspoken. I learned to be quiet. I watched my brothers not ask Mama anything. I saw the church people come to sit in silence on our couch in the living room. It was hard, but I learned what was expected of me. Two weeks after the funeral, everyone but Mrs. Greenly stopped coming by the house. Relatives from Texas never returned and after that, our house just went quiet. Mama came home from work, we'd eat, and then she'd turn on the Tiffany lamp and sit in the low light of the living room, staring. With Daddy gone, Clarence became the one to enforce quiet if we started roughhousing. He'd come into the room and yell in a whisper, "Mama's tired," and, "Carla, you know better. Ya'll sit still."

The changes that seeped in after his death were subtle; we became used to the whispered silences around the house. No one battled against it, no one tried to stop it. It was the end of all sounds; even our natural voices were quieted. In my mind, I resisted but didn't say anything. I couldn't tell anyone how miserable it felt to be wrapped in the quiet blanket that was our home. My mother and my brothers looked after me, and I looked after Otis. Mama made sure we went to school, I did housework and my brothers did outside chores. On Sunday and Wednesday, Mama and me went to church. That's how I remember those days, but what I remember most is we never talked about Daddy.

After Daddy died, it seemed like Mama stopped treating Clarence like the son he was. My other two brothers were never allowed to go anywhere; I'd sit on the front steps with them as they complained. I don't remember people sitting on the steps with us like they did at the other houses on our street. People waved when they walked by, but it was somewhere else they'd opened a gate to join others on their porch. When Daddy was alive, people always came by, but that stopped when he left. Mama told us not to worry about what others were doing. She had a routine for us to follow except for Clarence, who came and went as he pleased, unless Mama told him he had to go to the park with the rest of the family.

I envied Clarence's freedom and I spent a great deal of time on the back porch imagining how life would be when I got older. When I was supposed to be hanging laundry, I'd daydream for hours, thinking about when I could go where I wanted, have my own money, and there'd be no one telling me what to do. I'd think about going to the clubs on Seventh Street, especially to Ester's Orbit Room or Slim Jenkins Place. That was because Clarence and his buddies talked about it all the time and how famous musicians from Chicago, New York, and Louisiana performed there.

Back then Seventh Street was busy all the time. Black people from around the Bay Area came to shop, get a haircut or a press and curl, and eat at the many restaurants. Clarence said it had a nightlife that beat anything Los Angeles, Chicago, or Philly could offer. I always wondered how he knew that when he had never been to any other city besides Oakland.

At that time, the unofficial mayor of West Oakland was Slim Jenkins, a flamboyant man who owned a restaurant and loved entertaining. There's a retail center now on Seventh Street with blue-sided aluminum walls and sad mustard yellow paint named after him—called Slim Jenkins Court. To see it now, with its empty storefronts sandwiched in by other vacant rundown buildings, would probably make the poor man rise up from his casket and ask, "What happened?"

I knew Clarence went to the clubs, even though he said he didn't. Mama told him to stay away from Seventh Street where all the partygoers went because it could bring him trouble. She had heard about the police stopping people after the clubs let out, and that some were even taken to jail—just for having a good time. Clarence would come in from working one of his many odd jobs, and lean down to kiss Mama on the forehead, almost bending all the way over because she was so small. He'd claim he was tired and that after dinner he was going to bed. I'd sit in my room looking out the window, waiting to see him slip out the back door on the porch. He'd have his hair brushed back and greased down to make waves in it, and he wore the Sunday suit that Mama said hung well on him with his hard-sole, black wing tips.

Sometimes, I'd crouch down in a corner on the porch behind the metal washtub and baskets of laundry. I don't think he ever saw me watching him leave the house, but the next morning, I'd let him know I saw him. I'd break the code of silence at the breakfast table and ask Clarence, "How're your dancing shoes?"

He'd raise a finger to his lips to shush me and then look to see if Mama was paying attention. She usually wasn't. Clarence always tried to act hard with me, he said since he was the big brother I had to mind him. Sometimes, he was nice, especially when he'd let me into his bedroom to watch him count the coins and dollar bills that he'd spread all over his bed. Every so often, he'd flip coins into the air and, if I could catch them, I could keep them. I'd take the money and go to the liquor store just a block away from our house. Clarence knew the man who ran it, and he told Mama it was okay for me to go there. It was the one freedom I was allowed.

The day before Christmas, almost a year after our father died, I remember when I walked into the store and found the magazines had been moved to a rack next to the cold freezer. Normally, I'd buy a pack of Now and Laters and stare at the magazine covers that were beyond my reach, but on this day, I could actually hold them.

I didn't pay any attention to people moving around in the store, not even those who asked me to step aside so they could open the freezer door. The feel of glossy paper on my fingers captivated me. I held the *Ebony* magazine in my hands, slowly turning each page, absorbed in a world I wanted to be a part of. I was pie-eyed with the images of black people smiling, hugging, and standing close together with their arms wrapped around each other. The captions told me who they were, why they were famous, what they were doing. I wanted to experience the noise in their world.

That Christmas, there were no gifts under the tree. We were sitting at the dining room table quietly eating our holiday dinner of turkey, dressing with giblet gravy, homemade rolls, greens, and macaroni and cheese. The silence around the table was so loud in my head that I looked at my family and studied them. Their eyes looked downcasts, with everyone just chewing and chewing. I wondered if they knew that all sounds of living had bypassed our house and gone next door. That was when I decided I wanted the magazines to help me bring life back into our home.

I asked, "Mama, can we order *Jet* and *Ebony*?"

"Order them to do what, child?" she said.

Sometimes, Mama was funny when she'd take your question literally, though I was never quite sure if she was playing with me.

"I mean, get a subscription so they come to the house."

"Ain't nobody got time to read them but you. How much they cost?" asked Clarence. Both of his elbows were on the table, and he was frowning.

"I don't know," I answered, but I knew the few coins I got from Clarence wouldn't be enough to pay for them, "I just know if you get a subscription, they come to your house every month. Wouldn't it be good to have them here? I could read them like I want, and not have to go to the store. The people on the covers are so pretty, everybody looks happy."

"Don't believe everything you see on them covers, girl. Black people ain't all that happy like they trying to get you to think." Clarence shot his objection back at me before anyone else could speak.

"I'll read them with you, Carla," Otis said. "Like you used to read with Daddy."

Otis was a little slower than other boys his age, but whatever made his mind slow to think didn't interfere with his understanding what was going on around him.

"Really Otis? See, Clarence, not everybody thinks it's a bad idea," I said. Otis smiled and nodded his head.

"Arthur, Jr., don't you think it's a good idea, too?" I asked.

I was talking to the one brother who hadn't said anything yet. Arthur, Jr. is the middle boy and he always waited to hear what his bookend brothers would say before he spoke.

"It could cost a lot a money, and money ain't waiting at the door for us to let it in." Arthur, Jr. sounded older than his years. "But it's not good that Carla goes to that liquor store to read them, either. I don't think Daddy would like that."

"It would give me and Otis something to do while you and Clarence are working," I told Mama, excited because it sounded like Arthur, Jr. was taking my side.

"Carla," Mama said, "the good Lord blessed us to have a table full of food this day and every day, but I don't know about paying for some magazines."

"Mrs. Greenly has them coming to her house. She was the one who told me you could get a subscription."

"Well, maybe she should pay for them, then." Clarence growled at me.

"You watch your mouth, Clarence," Mama said. "I've taught you better than to sass grown folks, even if they ain't here to hear it."

"Mama, can we, *please?*" I begged.

I was wise enough to know that bringing up Mrs. Greenly would help my cause. Mama didn't like her children to want something anybody else had, and if Mrs. Greenly thought it was a good thing, she was more than likely to think so, too. Sure enough, *Ebony* and *Jet* soon started arriving rolled up in the mailbox each month, and after a year, I had 24 magazines stacked in the wooden box on the back porch. I think Mama was satisfied and actually proud we had subscriptions. I could tell because when I brought in each new magazine from the mailbox, she placed it prominently on the mahogany coffee table in the living room. She made sure I kept the table dusted and shiny with furniture polish, telling me, "Why would you want to place those pretty people on something dirty?"

Mama's education didn't go further than the sixth grade, but sometimes she'd talk about the colored school she worked at in Texas. She'd tell me how classy the teachers were even if they couldn't teach in the white schools, and how when she visited their homes, there was always reading material on their coffee tables. Before *Jet* and *Ebony*, we only had the newspaper. I was surprised when she said we needed to get another subscription, one for the oversized *Life* magazine, telling me, "It's important to know what white people think, too."

CHAPTER SIX

I've got magazines in two stacks in the living room and I've already looked through all of them. I think I'll need at least two or three more stacks to get through the day. While I lug magazines from the bedroom to the living room, the phone rings—I'm not answering, this is my Sunday. If it's Mama, Otis can handle it if she wants something done. Another sip of cognac and I'll forget I've left Otis to deal with her. After too many warm-ups, the baked chicken potatoes and carrots taste like cardboard. I look at my half-empty brandy snifter and decide to refill it to help swallow these leftovers.

Using the cushions on the couch to help lower myself, I ease onto the floor and begin to move the magazines around. I stack, order, and rearrange according to month, year, or by who is on the front cover. Sometimes, men and women get placed in separate piles, and sometimes celebrities who entice me to join their world get their own stack.

On top the mound of magazines placed next to the couch sits a 1972 May edition of *Jet*. Huey Newton is on the cover in that famous pose I've seen on posters. His legs are crossed and he's sitting in a wide back wicker chair. A black beret pushes out the sides of his Afro and he's holding an African spear. His picture makes me think of a small aquatic park with boats and yachts located in Emeryville that my family visited often. It's an East Bay park with jagged grey rocks separating the water from the shore. Back then, going there was something everyone in the family enjoyed. After our father died, Mama kept taking us there, but it was for a different reason. Whenever she saw tension growing between the police and the young black men who lived in our neighborhood, she'd load me and my brothers into the car to go to the Emeryville park. Even so, she said it was right they stood up for themselves. She said they reminded her of Daddy when he grew up in Texas.

"He didn't take mess from whites either," she told us. "He was the same age."

My brothers didn't like getting rushed to the car; squinted eyes and tight jaws told me so, but they weren't men yet with their own minds and they still did as Mama said. But if Mama saw a threat—like when she'd notice people gathering in anger, or police cars setting up a wall in the middle of the street, she'd stay agitated until we all fell in line. To us, it never made sense, but we knew if we didn't get in the car right away she'd get louder. There'd be tears streaming down her face and her choked voice demanding my brothers do as they were told. Sometimes, she'd holler, "You will not leave us like your father."

One day, before going out to the backyard to hang laundry, I saw Mama watching the boys in black berets position themselves just two blocks from our house. They were the same ones who had begun standing on various corners as protective security from the police and the drug dealers. There were police sirens sounding. I was hanging out the wash on the clothesline strung between the telephone pole and the fence when our neighbors started pouring out of their houses to stand on their porches and out on the sidewalk. There were police cars parked in the middle of the street with the doors wide open. A black boy, small and wiry wearing a blue-and-white striped tee shirt was being dragged by his arm out of a car.

"Leave my boy alone!" shouted Mrs. Camille, our next-door neighbor. She was running down the street with her bathrobe flying in the wind, exposing her nightclothes.

"Leave him alone. Leave him alone!," shouted a growing crowd of women who, like Mrs. Camille, were not yet dressed to be outside. I grew scared when I saw the police put their hands on their gun holsters. Everyone was screaming loudly. Women, police, the other boys in the car, and those in berets on the corner—everyone was trying to tell the other, what to do.

It wasn't a surprise then, to hear Mama shout at us from the side window to get in the car. My brothers had been in Clarence's room down the hallway. I guess they heard all the noise outside because they had rushed outside through the back door.

"Clarence, Arthur, Jr., Otis, grab your sister, and the sandwiches on the counter, and get in the car. I see something getting ready to happen, here."

Normally, we'd all be hurrying to the station wagon parked in the driveway, but the boys paid no attention to Mama. Instead, they ran to the end of clothesline where I was watching the commotion on the corner. Something was very different that day. I'd heard my brothers talk before, out of Mama's range, how rushing to the park made no sense, but I'd never seen them ignore her like that. My eyes were big and my heart pounded so fast I could feel it thump in my chest as I watched the standoff unfold between Mama and my brothers.

"Mama. We don't need to go. That's happening in the street, not in here." Clarence spoke in the stubborn tone Mama said reminded her of our grandfather in Texas. We were all standing in the backyard now, looking past the fence, not paying attention to Mama, who was standing above us on the back porch steps. "Look at me when you talk. All of you turn around here." Mama ordered. "Clarence, I'm not going to lose mine to whites who won't admit they're wrong."

"But Mama," Arthur Jr. said. His voice was high pitched. "No one else is leaving. I see Mrs. Greenly's boys out there. And I go to school with those guys in the car."

"Now look here. They got a right to be mad. I told you they remind me of your father," Mama said.

"We should be out there then," Clarence said, and crossed his arms.

"Uncross your arms when you talk to me." Mama stood so straight her five-foot frame looked much taller and bigger than she was.

"I want everybody to listen."

"Yes Ma'm," Arthur, Jr. and Otis said in unison.

"Yes Ma'm," I chimed in, quickly.

Mama looked in my direction.

"Carla, I'm not talking to you, let me finish here."

Her words stung and I flinched. She had said *everybody*—I thought that meant me, too.

Her hand was placed on one hip and she held the car keys in the other, gripping them tightly and pointing her closed fist at my brothers. Mama's eyes closed, then she looked up to the sky as if trying to find her words to say something. We all stood quietly, waiting for her to speak. My heart was in my throat, and I wanted to cry. The words that told me I wasn't *everybody* had me believing I was in a movie and I wouldn't know the ending until it happened. Boys inside my yard and outside the fence were in a stalemate about what actions to take and all I could do was watch.

In a hushed tone Mama said, "Before your daddy died, he made me swear to keep you safe. He may have been sick, but he knew what was happening in those streets. He was no fool. He knew how far some white folks will go to step on a black man's natural life. He got that from experience."

My brothers nodded. They knew Daddy was a proud man. He didn't talk to them all that often, but when he did, they listened until he was done.

"And what was the last thing he kept telling you boys before he got so ill he could barely speak?"

Mama looked at my brothers, her hands still on her hips. Clarence looked at Arthur, Jr. and Otis, who were waiting quietly for him to answer Mama's question.

"A strong black man is a living black man," he said slowly.

"Yes he did, now didn't he?" She said, "And why?"

Clarence turned away from Mama so she wouldn't see him twisting his mouth into a sneer. This was his way of saying he was through, that it was Arthur, Jr. and Otis's turn to speak. Arthur, Jr. went first.

"Because if you are alive you got possibilities . . ."

"and that's what makes life worth living." Otis finished the sentence we all knew by heart.

"Okay then," Mama said. "Just 'cause your daddy's gone don't mean something he told you all his life don't matter anymore."

"But Mama," Arthur, Jr. and Otis said in unison. Clarence just stood there, staring up at the sky and into the trees. He knew she wouldn't change her mind.

All of us knew, for that matter, that Arthur and Eve Sinclair swore their children's lives would never be caught in the war of hating people because of their skin color. They never let us stay in situations where they thought we'd be humiliated, like the time Mama grabbed me to leave the store when a white sales clerk pretended she didn't hear her ask to unlock the dressing room door.

"Now, you boys—listen."

She wasn't looking at me.

"There are guns out there and none in here. So, I think you and your brothers need to get your sister and let's go."

Mama turned and headed towards the car, not bothering to look back to see if we were following her. When everyone else in the neighborhood was upset, and anger flowed down wooden and concrete steps because the police were acting as if we were the enemy, the park was Mama's safe place to go.

At St. Agnes, the nuns were more concerned that I acted proper enough, no one talked about or told stories that involved the happenings in West Oakland. Sometimes, when I meet others who were part of the Panthers rank and file and have personal stories to tell, it's awkward listening. I try to avoid letting them know how I grew up; I have nothing to share except for what I read or how we fled. I guess I could make something up, tell them we went to the "Free Huey" rally, volunteered at the clinic, or that one of my brothers was a traffic monitor on the bad corner with no stoplight...but I don't say anything.

Warmed up cognac with a twist of lemon on a Sunday afternoon—Mama and my brothers would never, ever understand. In truth, neither do I, but this is what I'm doing. I move the *Jet* with Huey on top and see a pile of magazines with cover stories on black fathers. Last weekend, Mama had me going through her papers and I saw Daddy's name on their marriage certificate and my birth certificate. Ever since then, he's been so much on my mind. Clarence and them may have their reasons for not liking the park in Emeryville, but to me it was a beautiful place to go—I remember when it was fun. I loved how my father painstakingly took time to explain all the sights to me. He told me how the skyscraper buildings in San Francisco were built; why purple flowers could grow out of rocks; which one of the Golden Gate, Bay and San Rafael Bridges was the oldest. We'd imagine what was inside of the orange, yellow, red, and brown shipping containers stacked on top of each other at the Port of Oakland. The colors of the shipping containers always reminded me of a quilt similar in color made by Mama Belle—Mama's mama.

When the park was a good place to go, we'd find our spot and spread the blanket across the grass. Everybody was always calm and we'd laugh at everything. Daddy laid his head in Mama's lap so she'd play in his hair. My brothers walked around freely, sometimes pulling their pants legs up to wade in water too cold for me to even think about joining them—even if I could. I was supposed to stay on the blanket, or at least in watchful distance. I remember sitting with my legs stretched out, laughing when Daddy and Mama laughed, me scratching his hair when her fingers grew tired, passing out the food to my brothers. She'd lie on his chest and they'd forget we were there. After he died, I'm not sure who I felt the sorriest for—Mama or me. We had both catered to our shared man. He satisfied her with special attention. A hug and a kiss when he got home were expected and delivered. A nice cut of meat from the butcher would be handed to her as a gift, or sometimes I'd hear him say, "Let's just you and me go for a drive."

When I came along, Mama was almost forty, and from what everyone tells me, the first time my father laid eyes on me, he named me his second best girl. I'd wait on the porch for him to come home from work so I could get my kiss on the forehead and hear him say, "How's my baby girl?" I didn't mind his oil and grease smell. On Sundays, I'd dress quickly for church so I could sit on Daddy's knee, or drag him to the gate while we waited for the others to get ready. During the week, Mama and I took turns brushing his hair, rubbing his feet, and making sure dinner was ready when he got home. I'd watch how they talked to each other, where they sat and how close, if they kissed or were holding hands. When they were upset, they'd stop touching and the sweet words like "yes, baby" and "honey" disappeared, but I knew they would return.

The Huey cover makes me think of this one day when we were rushed to the park. I'm sure in Mama's way of thinking we had made another successful escape from the massacre of our family. I was sitting on the blanket thrown across the grass. My brothers were off somewhere, no doubt mad, because they were older now—Clarence was seventeen, Arthur, Jr. was sixteen, and Otis was fifteen. Still, Mama made them leave the neighborhood so they would be safe. And even though I was older, I must have been twelve, then, I was left to stay on the blanket to look at Mama's frozen face.

For too many years after Daddy's death, she just went frozen—no smiles, no light in her eyes. At the park, she stared out across the dark grey waters looking towards the bridge. I'd seen her look like this before, with her eyes and everything about her body sitting still. One time, Otis and me peered into the living room, afraid to go in, because we thought she died sitting straight up on the couch. Then, we realized she was only pulled back from everything, including us.

Clarence was the one who said, "She ain't dead. Look at that pin, it's moving." He was right, the gold leaf butterfly pin, the one sent through the mail by Mama Belle, was moving up and down. We all let out a big sigh of relief. Those moments came often, we came to describe them as "Mama's hushed up" or "she's frozen, again." Nothing grabbed her attention; her eyes would be still—staring. I don't know what my brothers thought about it, but I always thought she was thinking about Daddy, how she loved him and the way her life used to be.

This day at the park, I was sitting quietly with my legs stretched over the Gateway market bag full of sandwiches to keep the wind from blowing our food away. I counted the purple flowers that grow in the cracks and holes between the rocks, and like Mama, I stared off towards the bridge.

Sometimes, I broke my stare to watch the other families, especially those who I thought were with their father. This day, there was a family with two boys and a little girl. She kept asking questions of the man holding her hand and was jumping up in his face like a little puppy, pushing on him, punching him in the arm and then grabbing his hand again. Whatever she was trying to get him to do, she kept at it, and I watched how she didn't give up on getting his full attention. I lay on a pillow with my elbows bent, chin in my hands, and watched her go on and on until she was successful. The man finally stopped and sat on a bench with her while the rest of the family went ahead.

After watching that little girl, I began thinking that I wanted to wake my mother up, get her to look at me. I knew I'd better not sock her in the arm or push on her, so I stayed quiet until I could think of a plan. I was worried my brothers might come back to the blanket and interrupt it, but I just had to try something. Countless moments of silence later, I decided to ask Mama a question about the Golden Gate Bridge. It had to do with the color and why they call it golden, when really, it's orange. I'd often asked about this widely accepted error in naming a color, and my brothers would laugh at me every time I brought it up. But this time, I was going to come at it differently, and with all the scheming a twelve-year-old could muster, I started my plan to wake my mother up.

"Mama, how many things you know look orange?"

I sat up to ask my question again, leaning closer to her face so she had to see me.

"Mama, how many things you know look orange?"

While trying to unfreeze her, I wasn't concerned I'd get into trouble. My courage to keep going was boosted when I thought about the little girl who stayed so determined to get what she wanted—it had worked for her.

The air had begun to chill, and Mama whipped her grey scarf around her neck without saying anything and pulled the sides of her work jacket closer to keep out the cold breeze coming off the water. She still hadn't answered my question, but this time I placed my hand on her shoulder and kind of nudged it—very gently though.

"Carla, what nonsense you getting at now?"

Mama wasn't looking at me, but I kept talking, laying out what I thought to be my clever scheme to bring her around.

"I was just thinking about the color orange and things that are orange. You know street cones, tangerines, pumpkins, the bottom of candy corn, all those things are orange."

"Uh huh," Mama said. She still stared off towards the bridges, not looking at me as I talked to her.

"The curtain covering the pantry in the kitchen and the curtains in the bathroom. They're orange, right?"

"Carla, what are you trying to get to?"

Her voice was impatient and I knew I didn't have long before she told me to sit down and be quiet.

"Well, if those things are orange and that's what it looks like, why den they call that bridge golden when it ain't. It be orange, ain't it?"

She turned to look at me with squinted eyes and squeezed eyebrows that made her forehead wrinkle. All of that told me she was irritated.

"I don't send you to that private school to be talking like that. Saying *ain't*, and *it be*, like you was born in Love, Texas."

My stomach stopped feeling so tight and I smiled inside. I knew that would wake her up. Growing up, Mama never let me get away with using slang. She always said when I was caught talking too easy, the only way a colored girl gets ahead, or gets a proper husband, is if she knows how to talk right.

"Carla, my mother didn't go to school, and she had to marry somebody she didn't know," she said, after my plan worked.

I wasn't sure what my mother was trying to tell me about my grandmother. The year before when I was in Texas, I saw my grandparents had a strange way of staying out of each other's way, but I never thought it was because they didn't know each other.

"If your Grandmama had some education, I don't think that would have happened to her," she said. "Now, you don't want to grow up stupid, do you?"

"No Ma'm," I said.

"Well, even with my color I was lucky to find a man that loved me no matter how I talked, but you Carla, you got to speak the King's English proper."

"Yes, Ma'm."

"You not a light girl, Carla. It's going to be hard, you understand."

It took a moment for me to realize she was talking about the color of our skin, and that I might not get lucky like her. Nevertheless, I didn't want to lose her attention so I quickly re-worded my question.

"Mama, I wonder why the Golden Gate Bridge is called golden, when to me it certainly looks orange? Do you know why?"

"There you go. Now you sound like you gon' be somebody," she said. "And you didn't fool me. I know you was asking about that bridge."

I stayed quiet and wondered if she had more to say. Was she really done talking to me? I returned to stare at the water, waiting to see. A while went by, the sun came closer to the water, the air grew colder still and I knew we wouldn't stay much longer. Inside my stomach tightened. I didn't have a back-up plan.

My brothers, as big as they were, had been in the water. Sweaty with wet pants legs, they ran onto the blanket and started digging in the brown grocery bag for the chicken sandwiches and drinks. If Daddy had been there, they wouldn't have dug in the food bag like that. Otis whispered, "She's frozen, huh?"

When they tumbled onto the blanket, Mama didn't move or say anything. I nodded yes, in that way we'd learned to do when she was like this. They sat eating their sandwiches and quietly staring at the water. I wanted to push for understanding about the mystery of the color of the bridge, and then again I needed her to wake up—to not be frozen.

"Mama, what do you think about the bridge and the color orange?" I asked, not sure if she was mad because I was still asking the same question.

My brothers joined in. I think they knew I was trying to unfreeze her because they didn't tease me as they usually did.

"Now that I really look at it, that bridge *is* orange," said Arthur, Jr. "You know, I think my little sister might be right."

"Which ain't often, and I'm not sure she's right now." Clarence was always careful not to lose his position as the oldest boy and the one who knew everything.

I remember frowning at him for his little dig at me.

Otis, my slow brother, tried to help me out, he held up an orange he had pulled out from the grocery bag and tossed it up and down acting like he was studying it's color.

"Looks the same to me."

"All things ain't what you think they are or look to be," Mama said.

Surprised, Otis and I looked at each other wide-eyed with our mouths dropped open.

"That's what I been telling them. Everything's not what it looks like," Clarence said.

"How would Orange Gate Bridge sound anyway?" said Mama, and then her mouth twisted up and she said, "Orrrrange Gate Bridge. Now, don't it sound crazy?"

Clarence and Arthur, Jr. doubled over, holding their sides laughing.

"Orrrrange. Orrrrange," Mama kept saying.

She had gone from a frozen face to twisting her mouth sideways and moaning like a siren on an ambulance. We all laughed hard, and even she chuckled and kept repeating *orrrrange* with her head lifted to the sky, throwing her words into the wind. When she stopped, she got up, started packing and went back to being quiet and we left for the parking lot. I think Clarence was the loudest on the way to the station wagon, he and Arthur, Jr. howled, "Orrrrange" in the air, laughing and shaking their heads. I walked alongside them, waving my hand back and forth, secretly hoping someone would grab it. My father was gone, but Mama unfroze long enough for us to act like family again. I remember, that just for a little while, I didn't have look around to watch someone else's family.

Thinking about the Orange Gate Bridge lifts my mood some. It's still as funny to me as it was back then. My glass is empty and I'm trying to decide if I should get another one when the phone rings. Without thinking, I pick up, forgetting that I'm really not fit to talk to anyone.

"Hello."

"Hey Car. Where you been all weekend?" says a chipper sounding voice.

It's Dana. Shoot. Where have I been?

"Home," I say. "Why? Did you try to call?"

I hoped my voice sounded casual.

"No, I was worried though, I didn't get a chance to tell you we were leaving for Napa Friday night. And then I didn't find a message from you," she says.

"So what have you been doing?"

I've been in the house for two days, moving magazines around, playing sad music and eating four-day old leftovers. Been thinking about my childhood, replaying in my mind my father dying, wondering why Mama is the way she is, thinking about Rasheed . . . oh God, I can't tell Dana all that so I decide to omit everything.

"Nothing much," I say. "Just a slow weekend."

"You didn't go to Brentwood to check on your mother?"

I prop up on the pillow to steady myself. I don't want Dana to know I've been drinking.

"Otis took the new grandbaby to see her. I had the weekend off."

"Good for you," she says.

"Yeah, thanks." Dana has no idea all the trips I've taken this weekend without going anywhere.

"I want us to start our walking program. It's time." Her voice had dropped to a serious tone. *Our* program, I think. This is Dana's idea, but I see she's already got me signed up and delivered.

"We need to start," she adds before I can respond, "it will help me work out some things. I need to finish the book but can't get it right yet, and you know I've been thinking a lot about my brother, Aaron."

"I don't know. I have to think about it. What's going on with Aaron?"

I start to stare at my empty glass of cognac and feel a headache coming on. When I massage the back of my head, I can feel my kitchen starting to go back and I think about going to see Charlene.

"He's getting married soon."

She's always saying he needs to get married, so I don't get the problem.

Puzzled, I ask, "And what's wrong with that?"

"He's not ready."

I look into the receiver as if I can see Dana's face.

"Excuse me, but isn't your brother in his forties?"

"Yeah, 40 some years of not ready."

Her voice is snippy, as if this is a fact not to question.

"Dana, you can't control what he does," I tell her.

"That's what David says. Truth is, I like Clarice."

She continues on, defending why she isn't controlling and how we don't get her intention is only to help.

"Okay, okay," I interrupt. "What is the problem with him getting married, then?"

"That's why I want us to start walking, so I can think about it."

Her laughter comes loud through the phone and I pull the receiver from my ear. Now I know a headache is coming on. I can only roll my eyes upward at her reason for walking.

"Dana Washington, you're a mess."

"I know and you love me. So let's start soon."

"I'll think about it. I have to go. I still have papers to grade."

That was a lie, but it worked.

CHAPTER SEVEN

The lake looks clean today, which is not always the case. In years past, on too many days, if you happened to catch a downwind, it would smell like rotten eggs. A while ago, I struggled to ride a bike around the lake with my nephew; it was what he wanted to do for his special day with Auntie. As I gingerly trailed him on the gravel, we heard shouts of, "It's a body!" fill the air with alarm. Two teenagers in a paddleboat had made a gruesome discovery. Little Art, named after my brother Arthur, Jr. wanted to stop and look. I kept us riding, while others gathered around the edge of the water wanting confirmation right then that a dead person was indeed floating in the water. A day later, the Oakland Tribune reported a woman's body had been found in the lake. The article said she was black, possibly in her mid-forties, and that the police needed help to identify her body and to call this number. They couldn't tell if it was a homicide or suicide. I wondered if the reason she ended up in that murky water was because her life—like I feel mine has—somehow had slipped so far away from herself, she didn't know how to get it back.

Across the lake, a small gust of wind and rays from the sun make thousands of silver ripples shine in the water; they remind me of sequins on a blouse. Each time I try to count them, the wind stops and they disappear, which is what I would like to do right now. Dana's talked me into joining what she calls *our* walking program. She pestered me until I just gave in.

"Just meet me at the Pillars near the new fountain," she said, ignoring all the reasons I gave not to start now.

The Pillars are weathered, off-white columns bridged together with wooden lattices and twisted vines; in the summer little white flowers bloom through the openings. Maybe a mile away, right down the middle of the lake, is the white marbled courthouse. It appears to stand in judgment over all who walk by. The evening sun is unpleasantly hot on my skin. It's like it's coming through a magnifying glass, and it burns. I want to relax, but there's still this tightness in my jaw when I think about Rasheed. I wish he had been there when I conducted my home visit.

"Hold on Carla, I'll be right there!"

It's Dana and she's late. She's striding across the brick plaza in front of the Lakeview Library wearing black-and-purple sweats. As always, her walk is confident and she looks good.

"Sorry I'm late, but you know how it is driving back from The City at this time of the day."

Her hair's brushed back and pinned up in a kind of natural-but-fuzzy French twist, indicating she's been to an important meeting, where, as she would say, it's best to tame her big red 'fro, so as not to scare the client.

In the South, Dana would be called a redbone. Her skin is latte light and her bushy dark red hair is naturally curly. From the Carolinas up to Virginia, there are tribes of black people that look like her. At first glance, they appear to be white, but if you look a little closer you'll see African features, or the thickness of their hair will give them away. When we were young, Mama's dark skin gave her a lot to say about skin color. She says her husband, being such a light skinned man, always tried harder when it came to letting others know he was proud to be from the black race. I think that's true for Dana, too.

She settles into the green patch of grass in front of the fountain spraying water, and joins me to stretch our legs. My stretching is a long way from Dana and her yoga positions. As she twists and contorts her body, she tells me what each pose is called. The only name I can remember is the one she calls the downward dog.

"You're quiet—what's up, Car?" she asks, leaning into her favorite position.

Dana's body is stretched out long on the grass, and her shoulders are dipped towards the ground. Maybe one day I'll be able to do something that looks close to that.

It's true I've been quiet. I stayed on the grass to give her a hug and since then, I haven't said a word.

"I guess I keep thinking about this home visit I made, yesterday."

"Was it for Rasheed?"

"I wanted to find out for myself what is going on with him. His Individualized Education Planning meeting is at the end of the month."

"So, what did you find out?"

"Not as much as I hoped for. He wasn't there, but I spent an hour or more talking to his grandmother. She's smart, in that old-school way black mothers are from that generation. She seems like she still raises children with a heavy hand."

Dana reaches down to touch her toes. I'm lucky to reach my knees from a standing position. Casually, she says, "That's a leftover from slavery, when mothers didn't have time to talk it out. Getting children in line could mean life or death back then. Now, it's a cultural way of parenting."

"I get that. She's no-nonsense. The house was neat and clean. She works two jobs, both minimum wage, and it's service work. So you know she's on her feet all day."

"And where is the mother?" Dana asks.

She rises from her pose to pull me onto my feet. I reluctantly let her, and give in to her obvious hint for us to start walking. When I get up, I feel slow and I'm still sore from the walk we did on Monday. Dana points us towards the trail near Lakeshore Boulevard, and I let my body obey her command.

"Well, to answer your question," I say, "Mrs. Jenkins says her daughter is out on the street. She described it as a place where children and home have no meaning. She's raised these kids since they were little."

"How old is Rasheed?"

"Thirteen. He was held back a year because he wasn't talking to the teachers and they thought he was dumb."

I take the inside path to get closer to the water.

"Lots of grandmothers are raising their children's children. And too many black youth are placed in Special Ed. You know this, Carla. What's got you gripped by Rasheed and his family?"

"His eyes—they're so expressive. That's how he talks to me. The school psychologist told me she thought he was a bright kid, but he should have been taught sign language.

"Is there a history of testing him? What do you think?"

"I'm not sure how much testing has been done, but I do think some trauma happened and that he doesn't want to talk about it, so he avoids communicating, altogether. I know for sure he hasn't received the proper care to help him deal with whatever happened to him."

"How old was he when his grandmother started taking care of him?"

"When he started the first grade, so maybe six? His little brother was just one when his mom left them both and just never returned."

"Maybe he stopped talking because he doesn't have the ability to express the hurt he felt. So how did the third child show up?"

"His mom went into treatment, and after she got out she lived at home with the kids and her mama. That's when she became pregnant with his sister. After she delivered, she went back out, and hasn't been home since."

"Double trauma. It's no wonder that poor baby doesn't talk. He's pissed off at everyone."

"The thing is, his grandmother says he talks all the time at home. She wonders what the school did that makes him stay quiet."

"He talks at home?" Dana says, looking up to the sky. "Now, that is strange—I get it. You've got a bona fide mystery on your hands. I guess I would get gripped, too."

I give her a look that says, "See, I told you."

"I wish he had been there though," I say. "I still tried to find out as much as I could. I asked his grandmother how he behaved at home, did he have chores, did she help him with his homework, and how he got along with his younger brother and sister."

"What did she say?"

"She kept talking about someone named Dub. I wondered if it was Rasheed's father, or a man in the house she hadn't mentioned before. I finally asked who she was referring to, and she acted surprised I didn't know Rasheed's nickname. She said that's what they've called him since he was a little baby."

"So why do they call him *Dub*?"

"I don't know, I didn't ask."

I wonder why I didn't. It's an obvious question and somehow I missed it. Dana starts walking backwards and raises her eyebrows.

"Who in your life does she remind you of?"

"My mother."

She smiles, gets back in step and pushes my shoulder as we continue to walk.

"Uh, you think maybe that's why you didn't ask her?"

I push back on her because I know what she's getting at. Mama raised us to not ask her too many questions and even now, I find myself not willing to pry into her life too much.

"Okay, maybe I was fearful to interrupt or ask questions. She talked. I listened. That's how I learned so much."

"I know, sometimes it's not easy, but find out why his nickname is Dub. It might tell you a lot about him."

Dana's right, why do they call him Dub? Black people are quick to give nicknames to their children, and each one has a story behind why or what it means. Back in the early days, black parents named their children Mister, Sir, Queen, Famous, Precious, Special, and other names of high regard to ensure they would always be treated with respect. But mostly, nicknames come from something about the person's personality, the way they look or act. There's "June Bug," like my father, meant for pretty boy children folks predict will grow up and break a lot of women's hearts. And then there is "Sister," like Mama calls me, reserved for the oldest girl, or the girl child most helpful to their mamas. I once knew a grown man people called Baloney, because he ate nothing but bologna sandwiches when he was young. I remember a family who called their children One Cent, Two Cent, and Three Cent. Mama calls all her sons "Brother," more than she uses their names, and when talking to Mrs. Greenly's boys, she calls them Brother, too.

When people are next to each other and no one is saying a word, it can make time seem like forever. Since talking about Rasheed's nickname, we've passed the courthouse, and now we're on the inside path near Fairyland going back into the park, and we still haven't said anything. I'm thinking about Rasheed and Dana calling him a bona fide mystery—leave it to her to be so dramatic.

The paved path we're on goes through a grove of oak and eucalyptus trees that provide some needed shade from the sun. A young man without a tee shirt, showing perfectly brown skin, six-pack abs, and tight muscles is running towards us, Dana squints her eyes and whispers, "Oowee." He glides through the grove, dipping his head to dodge low-hanging branches, still in full stride, arms pumping hard. When he passes us Dana mumbles underneath her breath, "Testosterone running rampant."

Finally back to our starting point at The Pillars, we stop to talk about the rest of our week; neither one of us says any more about Rasheed. I feel chilled, cold from sweating—it's probably the alcohol I drank last night coming through my pores. I don't want Dana to smell it on me, so I quickly say my goodbye.

"I have to go. It's a work day tomorrow."

Dana looks at me strangely because I say this in mid-conversation, quickly hug her, and head off to my car.

"Are we walking tomorrow?" she shouts.

I turn to shout back at her, "No, not tomorrow."

"Okay. Thursday then. Friday's your appointment, right? And why haven't you been picking up my phone calls?"

Dana's voice trails off with that we-still-need-to-talk-about-some-things tone of voice.

Wednesday was a dreadful day. It rained, the students were restless, and Cassandra called in sick. Somehow, she had gotten a message to her substitute that if she needed anything, to seek me out. It turns out the sub was a college friend of hers, and to me she seemed like a carbon copy of Cassandra. And Miriam, the new hire, came by my classroom to chat during my prep time. Turns out, her schedule changed and she announced, without asking first, that she planned to pop in every once in a while for tips on where to go out. She's nice enough and I see she's committed to her students, but I'm not the one to help her with creating a social calendar for the Bay Area. I told her to try the pink section in the *San Francisco Chronicle*.

"Look at that early moon, Car," Dana says when we meet up on Thursday. "It's so bright and low, it looks like it's using the tops of trees for a resting place."

"I guess even the moon would like a break sometime."

That sounded prickly, but I couldn't help it. Dana looks at me sideways and tilts her head.

"Are we tired, today?"

"Dana, I go to a place five days a week, knowing before I get there that my kids are going to act out. And that's just part of it, then I have to listen to the adults blame or call them animals, so hell yeah, I'm tired."

That comes out with a frustrated and raised tone of voice, and I feel water pooling into my eyes.

"Whoa, whoa, Sweet Pea."

I know she's trying to soothe my rising irritation. She puts her arm through mine to keep me moving along the lake's trail.

"Some things just aren't right, Dana."

I try to wrangle my arm away from her, but she just holds on tighter, keeping my body close to hers as we walk.

"What's going on? Are you PMS-ing?"

"Don't say that. You sound like a man." I say this with a throat full of crankiness.

"Well, are you?"

She looks at me, waiting for an answer. I turn to look across the lake to break her stare down into my face.

"Damn it, no, Dana."

My tears are dropping now. We both get quiet after that last, "Damn it." After a while of walking, and watching Dana's slow-rising moon, she breaks the silence.

"Okay, my darling, precious friend. Let me start over, okay?"

I notice the courthouse standing directly across the long stretch of water where they hold the college boat races. That's a long ways away and I wonder if today I can make it that far.

"I love you, and don't get that twisted," Dana tells me. "So now, how was your day, today?"

A small chuckle that I can't keep in comes out. She's done this so many times before. Dana has a way of rewinding things when you think there is no way out. Maybe it's her tone of voice, or the way she rocks her head side to side, and looks up into the air. She'll turn into a California Valley Girl or become a female version of Mr. Rogers speaking to the neighborhood. I take a deep sigh before I attempt to answer her question.

"I'm frustrated. I feel overwhelmed with everything I need to handle. I got Mama and her health on my mind, and in addition to just trying to teach my other special-ed students, there's this whole Rasheed business."

"Everyone's got a lot to juggle. It can make life hard sometimes."

"I know. Life is hard and then you die, right?" I say, my tone sounded flat.

"Well, that saying may be right for some, and Car, this might be a surprise, but I have to tell you it doesn't have to be true. I don't want to see you do hard time, that's all I'm trying to say."

Hard time? Is this what I'm feeling? Caught in the worst prison possible, sentenced to break open every rock? Dana has no idea.

CHAPTER EIGHT

Maybe if I put darker curtains up, I'll stop waiting for dim light from the morning sun to peek into my bedroom window. I've just been lying here in the bed, hoping to find comfort on my newly bought foam mattress topper. I wanted it to be the cure-all for my restless nights. Despite my efforts, the jury is out—the sun and I are still greeting each other. It's not like me to take time off, but I guess a doctor's appointment on a Friday is a legitimate excuse for a three-day weekend.

The phone's ringing—it's either Mama or Dana, but I'm pretty sure it's Mama. I was so caught up with arranging Rasheed's home visit that a week's gone by and we haven't talked. It's early morning I know she's probably trying to catch me at home.

My message machine is old school. It throws voices into the air so my ears catch Mama's voice.

"Hi, Sister. This is your mother. When you get a chance, give your mother a call. Love you."

I hate to screen her call, but I've lost my don't-worry-Mama-I'm-okay voice; today, I just can't fake it. Besides, this is not something she can understand. Falling apart when there's work to be done is not Mama's way. She instilled in her children a work ethic—she expected us to work and we knew it. You went to school every day, no matter what, picked up your clothes off the floor, made your bed, washed dishes, and by all means made sure the house was clean before she got home.

Another hour of just lying in the bed goes by and I force myself to call Mama back so I can focus on my afternoon appointment. I sit up straight to brace myself for the conversation and realize my head is starting to hurt.

"Hi, Mama."

"Hello." She sounds like she didn't hear me.

"Hi, Mama."

"Is that you, Carla?"

Her voice is weak as if I called too early and it takes me into more of Dana's colored girl's guilt . . . how can I be such a bad daughter?

"Yes, Mama, it's me. I was in the shower when you called," I lied. "I have a doctor's appointment today, so I got up early."

"Well, I wasn't sure if I'd hear from you, it's been so long. I was worried, thought you upped and moved, quit your job and didn't tell anybody."

"No, Mama. I still work at Douglass."

"Mmph," she grumbles. "Maybe you *should* quit and come to Brentwood."

"Why's that, Mama?" I know what she's going to say, so why did I ask that?

"The schools are nice, they keep them up better here and you don't have to deal with all those problems. Look at the fit you having with that boy who doesn't talk."

"Kids got problems everywhere, Mama. Douglass is like any other school, it has its share, but I'm still there."

"I watch the news. I know what's going on. It's not like it used to be when we lived on Chester."

I let her words hang in the air without a response.

"So, how are you doing?" I ask.

I need to shift this conversation. Mama is always telling me what to do about my job.

"Well, I'm doing okay. You know it's hard getting old—you'll see when your time comes. Things are hard right now, baby."

Her heavy sigh comes through the phone and I feel my stomach twist.

"How's your new home-health aide working out?"

"She's another no-cooking one. I tell her how to do it, watch her real close when she's in the kitchen, but it never tastes right. I'm not eating much these days."

"Mama, you have to eat. You can't go long without eating."

"I know, but that girl don't know how to cook. She gives me my medicine and all, but I still have to tell her everything to do. I don't know why it's so hard to get good help. My house stays such a mess."

Mama's messy house looks like two dishes in the sink, an immaculate living room that no one sits in, a half load of laundry, and maybe small bits of paper in her trashcans. She's always looking for a new "girl," as she calls the home health aides who come and go as quickly as a revolving door turns.

"I liked that first girl, but she got married and quit and you know the last one was stealing from me."

As Mama talks, I stare through an opening in the curtains, and look at the pile of clothes so thick I can't see parts of the rug. I need to wash and vacuum. I say a few *uh-huhs*, *I knows*, and *really Mamas*, while she tells me her problems with the home aides. My mind drifts from our conversation and I've started to count the flowers on the bed sheets when I hear a sign the call will end right away.

"What time is it? I haven't taken my morning medication, yet."

And just that quick she says, "I love you," and hangs up.

I love you too, Mama.

Well that's done. I need to put myself into the shower and try to wash off some of this funk that's not just coming from stinky armpits.

The shower stings, instead of me doing the it's-way-too-hot-dance that steamy water like this calls for, I stand under the flow letting it pelt my back and watch it go down the drain, imagining I am going down with it. In the end, I'm water-whipped. Carefully, I lift a leg at a time over the tub and stumble-walk towards the bed. On the way to the bedroom, I glance at the door mirror that reflects my dark, round, naked body and cringe at the sight of the overweight woman in it. I think about those Rubensque paintings of white women lying naked on a fainting couch, pudgy and dreamy eyed with protruding stomachs hanging over their sides. I wonder if they had fibroids, too.

It was at least a year ago when the hard mass in my lower abdomen let me know something was growing inside of me. I told Dana about the hard lump and she made me promise I'd schedule an appointment to have it checked. Then, she went into a lecture about me changing my diet. I think I counted the whole time she talked.

"Fibroids are a sign your life is not what you want it to be, Car. Many women grow them when they have an excess of self-doubt, or stifle their creativity, and when they give and give but don't know how to receive," Dana said.

Later on, I went to Marcus Book Store on MLK Boulevard to pick up a book to learn more—minus the lecture. The book read like Dana talks—her voice jumped out at me from every page.

A few months ago, I was sitting at home, unable to make myself leave the house, mindlessly surfing through the TV channels and ignoring Mama's caution about not letting the idiot box take up all my time. I stopped on the PBS station and caught a show with a black psychologist as the guest. It was in the middle of the program and she was talking about black women growing fibroids. She said the same things I'd read in the book so I almost flipped the channel, but when she started speaking about unhealed grief passed down through generations of women, I got curious. She said the experiences of slavery had cast black women into the role of beasts of burden, and our true feminine energy had to be buried in order to survive slavery, and that even today it's still guarded.

To me, the white interviewer looked stunned when she heard her guest say that. I thought this because her reaction was delayed, and when she did speak she stumbled over her words.

"I see, I um, don't think I've, um, thought about women's health in that way, um, so this is common, you say?"

It was obvious the interviewer was flustered, but the doctor didn't seem to miss a beat. I thought she was classy. I remember she brushed her hair back behind her ear, reached across the little table between them to pat the interviewer's hand, and kept right on talking.

Oh, shit. Did I just run that stop sign? I guess so from the way that driver is giving me the middle finger and shaking his head. *I'm sorry,* I say in his direction. *I've got things on my mind. You see, I have this doctor appointment, my mama's not doing well, and I have this job that wears me out,* to explain my bad driving to him. I give a little wave of apology, and promise myself that I will pay more attention.

When I get to the doctor's office I'm surprised there are so many people in the waiting room. Don't they have to work? These magazines set out on coffee tables to distract you from how long you have to wait aren't very well taken care of, I think. Many of the front covers are torn off, and the pages are dog-eared and wrinkled. I would never treat my magazines that way.

"Carla Sinclair."

The woman shouted my name so loud she sounded like a gym teacher calling roll.

"Present," I say, dutifully.

I'm gestured through the door with a wave of a hand and ushered towards a chair next to the blood pressure machine. When I start to sit down, the nurse tells me to stand on the scale. I already know what it's going to say. My clothes have fit tight for some time now. The scale confirms my weight is 40 pounds more than I want. The nurse takes my blood pressure, which she says is high, and then my temperature, which is fine. Then, only saying, "This way," she directs me down a stark white hallway to the examination room. It's chilly in here. The table inside reminds me of a massage table, but this one has stirrups sticking out like padded mechanical hands with fingers forming a circle.

"Panties off, please and place this across your abdomen and legs. The doctor will be in soon." The woman leaves me in the room, alone.

I pull off the fat jeans and the cotton panties I'm wearing. It's so cold in here I'm glad to keep my top on. I scrunch down so my feet fit in the stirrups with my knees up. My legs fall sideways allowing a cool breeze to pass over my private parts. There are square tiles on the ceiling with small black dots that look randomly placed, which makes them hard to count.

A woman enters at the same time that she knocks on the door.

"Hello Ms. Sinclair. I'm Dr. Richards. You haven't had an exam for a while."

She's right and I think she's no-nonsense.

"I've been so busy with work I couldn't get an appointment scheduled. I took off for this one. I didn't feel comfortable with my previous doctor, I guess I didn't realize how much time had gone by," I say.

"It's important you have regular appointments. We can't help you if you are not here."

The doctor's face is literally covered by the folder she's holding, which I guess are my medical records. When our eyes meet there is no understanding look about why I delayed making an appointment. The doctor is quiet. I'm quiet. She washes her hands, pulls on purple latex gloves, and goes directly to my lower body where she tells me to move even closer to the edge of the examination table.

"I see your previous doctor ordered an ultrasound. I'm going to need to do a physical exam where I insert my fingers into your vagina so I can feel your uterus." "Okay." I try to match her disconnected demeanor.

"First, I am going to lubricate your vagina so the speculum will slide in smoothly."

The cool liquid feels like KY jelly, and the sensation reminds me of preparing to have sex.

"I am now inserting the speculum to expand the walls of your vagina. This will allow me to see your cervix."

Will she just do it? Her step-by-step announcements make me think about a terrible lover who made known every action he was doing and what direction he was headed in. I don't remember his name. It was a two-night stand after way too much drinking that started on a Friday night after work. I don't think I ever told Dana about that one. When he loudly proclaimed he was heading down to the honey pot, I knew he had to go. It took a while to get him out of my apartment after our sex-by-the-map escapade. He slept for hours and hours into the next evening.

Unceremoniously, the doctor pulls out the device that opened the walls of my vagina like temporary scaffolding for a retrofit on a freeway column.

"Now, I'm going to palpate your uterus. I'll put one hand inside of you and one on your stomach."

Even with all the forewarning, I still flinch when she puts her fingers inside of me—it feels like she has her whole hand in there. She pushes down on my abdomen with her other hand, and the sensation causes me to count the tiny dots on the ceiling even faster. She finally announces she's done and I feel her withdraw her fingers. She expertly tosses her gloves into the trashcan and then walks closer to speak to the upper portion of my body.

"I was able to feel some small tumors around your uterus. Have your fibroids caused any complications with your cycle?"

"No, just some tenderness when I lay on my stomach."

"I see. These tumors are usually benign. I've seen some shrinkage or stabilization with proper dietary changes, but surgical removal is more expedient. They can also develop from high levels of cortisol due to stress. Have you been stressed?"

Really? If she has to ask, then she's not looking at me.

"Some," I say.

No way am I going to tell her that I feel like taking myself out, that killing myself has begun to feel like the solution to everything. She'd probably have me locked up if I told her what I really felt.

"Here is a schedule for health education classes on women's health and stress reduction that I highly recommend you attend. You may get dressed now."

She hands me a wipe in a foil packet for the sticky gel left down there and leaves the room.

"Well, thank you very much."

I sarcastically say this to no one, wipe myself with the moist towelette I was given, and get dressed.

When I leave the hospital's entrance, the video store across the street draws my attention. I go inside hoping a movie will distract me from thinking about these things growing inside of me, or about having to go to somebody's recommended health classes. I think I might pick up some Courvoisier before I go home. Why is this store always so slow? I don't want to go to some class so they can lecture me. Between Mama and Dana, I already have enough lectures.

The pony-tailed young woman in front of me lets out a big sigh. I know how she feels. She looks back and forth at the clerks standing at the registers who seem to be moving at a snail's pace and she shifts from one foot to the other. I try to ignore her, but when she bends down to look at the candy on the lower shelf, and her butt crack peeks out of her underwear, I find myself staring. It isn't pretty. I notice she doesn't have a tattoo there like so many young people do nowadays. The other people in line have stone faces. Maybe they're pretending not to see what they see. I don't see any wide eyes or smirking—not even a whisper about what we all see. *What's the use?* If it doesn't matter to them, why should it matter to me? I point my head towards nothing and form a stony face like those around me.

CHAPTER NINE

On Mondays, my students come in either flying happy about the fun they had over the weekend, or they greet me with long faces and lots of sighs. This Monday was no different, but the day was full of interruptions and it went by fast.

I got distracted during lunch by an unplanned meeting with Cassandra and forgot to eat. She kept popping in with one of those situations that lasted through the afternoon. Lately, I've noticed her situations are coming up more often. Ms. because-I'm-good-at-it still doesn't think she needs any help. This time she's organized students for a talent show—the maintenance person said he didn't know anything about it, and turns out the floor is getting waxed the day she planned for—the bigwigs got involved, and well, now she's trying to figure out what to do.

This poor tuna sandwich has been in my desk drawer all day. I hope the Miracle Whip didn't go bad. I kiss it up to God and decide to eat it, anyway. I don't want to go into the IEP meeting totally starving. Last night, I was headachy from thinking so hard about it. I told myself I wasn't going to do this, but here I am at the last minute, looking for Rasheed's papers.

"Eating at your desk again?"

It's Miriam standing in my classroom's doorway.

"You startled me," I say. "Didn't anyone tell you it's common courtesy to knock, especially when there are no students?"

"Oops. I forgot. Sorry." She does a fake knock on the wall.

"I'm trying to get ready for an IEP this afternoon."

I've wondered who Miriam's people are, but haven't asked her any questions. She looks to be in her late forties. Her dark facial spots and wrinkled skin lets me know she's spent a lot of time in the hot Texas sun. She still makes me think of those rugged farmwomen I saw in *Life* magazine.

"You mind if I eat my sandwich while you work?"

Before I can answer, she drops her portly body down at a desk. We have the same prep time, and in the last couple of weeks she's taken to stopping by. Maybe she has grown weary of the faculty lunchroom.

"Go ahead, but don't expect much conversation right now," I say.

Her sandwich must be store-bought because the plastic wrap crinkles loudly as she unravels it. It's distracting and I can feel the frown on my face.

Miriam scrunches up her shoulders.

"Sorry," she whispers.

I try to ignore her, but she wrangles my attention away from the papers when she offers half of a green-looking sandwich with tentacles sticking out of it. I shake my head signaling, "No, thank you," and bite into my warm tuna sandwich pretending it tastes good.

There are so many students' papers piled up on top of my desk—I see Rasheed's name on a few of them and click my tongue like Cassandra. His papers weren't too deep down in the stack of mismatched papers piled on my desk. I could have had my hands on them already, if I had only looked earlier instead of stressing an hour before the meeting.

"Thank goodness, I found them," I say out loud, more to myself than to Miriam.

"Found what?" Her voice sounds muffled with a mouthful of sandwich.

"Rasheed's papers. I thought it was going to take the whole hour."

I sigh relief and lean back into my seat.

"Can I look?" Miriam asks.

Why not? Most of the people in the meeting will be white like Miriam, so maybe I'll get an indication of how they'll respond. I hand her a stack of Rasheed's work and wait to see what she will say.

She inspects Rasheed's assignments, carefully looking at the front and back of each paper.

"He spells and writes well, his letters have the same deliberate style and all his words are in-between the lines. His papers aren't wrinkled up, either."

"His grandmother pays attention to his homework. She's probably shown him how to keep his papers neat," I say.

"I just went through one of those meetings. I can help you get ready," Miriam tells me, still looking at Rasheed's papers.

I've taught at Douglass for 19 years, she's here not quite two semesters and she wants to help me get ready. Am I just imagining that she thinks she knows more than me?

"Rasheed tests well, does his homework, pays attention in class. He's a good student," I say.

"That may be so, but still, he's in Special Ed. His ability to succeed will have limitations," Miriam tells me.

Her tone of assumed authority brings heat across my forehead. Miriam can't understand how race and skin color complicate a student's "ability to succeed." But I will give her credit. I've watched Miriam fight for her students. I even saw her take on Ed when he rushed to punish a few without having all the information. I've also seen how he listens attentively to her and will usher her into his office to take a seat. When I approach Ed, I have to follow him around the main office or down the hallways to get his attention.

"Why did they schedule the IEP? Do you know what his problems are?" asks Miriam.

It's been three months—I think I know a few things about my students.

"The problem is, he doesn't talk at school," I say, "He doesn't speak, and shakes his head to answer, "Yes" and "No."

"Is he deaf?"

"No. Miriam," I say tersely. "He would be at a school for the deaf—not at Douglass."

What I'm not saying is that he's a dark-skinned boy—almost blue-black—I can only imagine the amount of teasing his skin color has brought him.

"All my IEP's have been helpful," she says. "The district psychologist will be there, and you know Ed is really helpful. Just show them his work. When is it?"

"This afternoon."

Miriam sees me look at the clock. There are only 20 minutes left to get ready.

"You're a good teacher, all the students love you. I know you can help him."

I hope this second look at the clock announces to Miriam that it's time for her to leave.

"I think I'll go check my mailbox," she says.

With Miriam's exit, I can return to what I was doing. Halfheartedly, I move papers around, thinking about what makes someone just go silent.

The summer I turned eleven, Mama decided I needed to spend it under the watchful eye of Mama Belle. No amount of crying and sad looks changed her mind. The night before I was to leave, I had gone into our walk-in pantry to put bags of flour and corn meal back on the shelf when Mama called her mother.

"I know it's ten years since I been home. After June died, it's been just the children and me, and I got to work. I miss ya'll too, but I can't move back to Texas."

I knelt down in the corner so Mama couldn't see me and listened to her phone conversation. I had hoped to find out why all of sudden I was being sent away. I'd spent summers at home with her working long days before, my brothers looked after me, and everything was just fine. We'd be there when she got home, the house was clean and sometimes, I even tried to cook dinner. I didn't understand why this summer had to be different.

I was young, but I knew what Mama thought about Love, Texas—she wasn't ever going back. In rare moments when she talks into the air, not really at me or anyone else, she says she'd fled that red dusty town with only one regret—leaving her mama.

"Mama, I 'preciate you taking Carla this summer. She's eleven now and I was surprised her cycle come during the winter. I can't be at home, and them boys in the neighborhood, well I know you'll look out for her."

Then there was a lot of silence on Mama's side of the conversation. Mama mostly said a few *mmms, yeses,* and lots of *I knows.* While I stretched my ears to hear everything, my brother, Otis, walked into the pantry and almost got me found out.

"Ooh, I'm telling—you listening."

He was older than me, but I took advantage of his slow ways and covered his mouth, showing him a chocolate bar hidden high on the top shelf behind the grease can, hoping to buy his silence. He took the bar and walked out grinning back at me, understanding it was a bribe for acting like he didn't see anything. It wasn't long after quieting Otis down that Mama ended her call.

"Bye, Mama. Ya'll have a good time. Call me when she gets there."

That summer while in Texas I could tell from the way Mama Belle and Grandpa Clarence didn't talk or stay in the same room too long—something wasn't right between them. They weren't like Mama and Daddy, who talked all the time, laughed and were always hugging on each other. Every morning, Mama Belle cooked a big breakfast with lots of meat, grits and hand-rolled biscuits, and Grandpa would come in and eat by himself unless I was up to eat with him. He didn't say much, but I could tell he was glad for my company. Sometimes, he'd place a piece of bacon on my plate when he saw I'd eaten through mine, or he would tell me about what he was going to do for the day.

He'd finish and leave his plate on the table for Mama Belle to clear away and if he didn't go out to the field, he went to a leaning shed built under a huge tree for shade. And there he'd stay for most of the day until it was suppertime. Inside, he had a chair, a table, wooden boxes, and he was always looking through rusted-out tools. I'd stare through the curtain door and think how lonely he looked. He'd see me, but he never acted like he wanted me to come in.

A few weeks after I returned from my trip, I overheard the neighbor who shared our driveway tell Mama she saw a difference in my behavior since I came back from Texas. I was still mad about going and had begun to say as little as possible, just "Yes" and "No," and if I could get away with it, I'd just nod my head.

"She's just growing up, that's all," is what Mama told her.

Who knows what Rasheed experienced to make him act the way he does? Not talking could be his revenge, maybe he feels wronged—and he isn't forgiving or forgetting it. I haven't forgotten about the trip that was forced on me, and I'm grown. A knock on the door draws my attention away from daydreaming It's Ruth Snyder, the district psychologist. Why is this a day for continuous interruptions?

"Ms. Sinclair, aren't you joining us for the IEP session?" Ruth's eyes wander around my empty classroom, but she has yet to look at me.

"I saw your name on the list of attendees. It starts in five minutes."

"I am planning to attend Ms. Snyder."

Like her, I say my words into the air without making direct eye contact.

Her navy blue skirted suit looks very professional, and I think about it being a big-ticket item in her closet brought out for days like this. For a moment, I wonder if my orange Sunday pantsuit will carry the authority I need for the meeting.

"I'm placing Rasheed's work in a folder and will join you shortly." I answer in the best professional tone of voice I can muster.

For the entire walk down the hallway, I hold onto a sigh that doesn't come out until I'm standing in front of Conference Room A—I hope they didn't hear me inside. When I open the door, I see Vice-Principal, Ed Shepherd; Ruth Snyder; the Douglass academic counselor; and a teacher I recognize as a transfer from the feeder elementary school. Ed's sitting at the end of the conference table and the three white women are all sitting on one side.

Rasheed's grandmother, Mrs. Jenkins, sits alone on the other side of the table. I nod a greeting to everyone and sit next to her. I already know what picture this must be painting—us against them. Mrs. Jenkins is dressed in her service uniform. She's wearing a brushed back ponytail, a style most women use when they don't have a lot of free time. The condition of her hair—dry and dull—her uniform and the reason she's here make me think her hairstyle is the least of her worries. Her crossed arms and tight lips are an obvious clue she's irritated to be here.

Ed starts the meeting with the required introductions. As the other women talk, they have yet to have their eyes fall directly on Mrs. Jenkins.

The meeting started at 4:00 pm. I can honestly say this is one of the most frustrating meetings I've attended in a long while. It turns out, the former elementary teacher in previous years had Rasheed in her class and that's why she was asked to attend.

"I experienced the grunting and shaking his head as aggressive behavior. It was disturbing to me and the other students," she reports.

I know what she's talking about. He does grunt, but I wouldn't describe it as aggressive. The academic counselor announces that

Rasheed has been placed in Special Ed classes since the fifth grade with no progress shown on his part. This is so frustrating. I've yet to hear Rasheed's strengths talked about—just the fact this boy is still attending school is an accomplishment. Finally, someone talks to Mrs. Jenkins, directly. The district psychologist starts out in what I hear as an apologetic tone.

"It's a shame the school system didn't identify his condition earlier. He might have learned sign language, so he could communicate in a more socially acceptable manner. I've seen this happen before, when low-income parents aren't able to help their children due to a lack of insurance or unintentional neglect."

Oh no, she didn't use the word, "neglect."

From the corner of my eye, I notice Mrs. Jenkins stirring in her chair. Anyone can see Rasheed is not neglected. His clothes are always clean, even pressed neatly; from what I can tell, he doesn't come to school hungry like so many other unfortunate students do. He is respectful and he definitely has home training.

The word, *neglect*, has Mrs. Jenkins pressing her lips even tighter than before. She's leaned her head to the side and now is clearing her throat. A firestorm has started. I can feel the heat getting ready to come.

"My grandson has not been neglected," she says slowly and deliberately. "I take good care of him. He does his homework and his grades are good."

Ruth Snyder sits straight up in her chair, her eyes have grown wide from what I guess is her reaction to becoming a target for the anger that has entered the room. The other two women nervously look at each other shuffling their papers, but say nothing.

"What I want to know—and I want to know, today—what have you people done to make Rasheed stop talking at school?" demands Mrs. Jenkins.

Her voice is loud and she's pointing her finger across the table, glaring at the women. Through the glass window in the conference room, I can see Mrs. Brown's shadow hovering nearby as if she is acting as security.

Ed waves Mrs. Brown off and taps his pencil on the yellow pad in front of him.

"Now now, Mrs. Jenkins. We know you're concerned about your grandson's welfare."

I guess he said that to take some of the heat off the women across from us. Mrs. Jenkins snaps her head in his direction to glare at him, too.

"Every year, since the fourth grade, it's been the same thing; Rasheed can't talk. My grandson talks and I want to know what you've done to him." Mrs. Jenkins crosses her arms.

Everyone gets an earful about her displeasure with the treatment of her grandson. At one point, I try to calm Mrs. Jenkins down, but she brushes me aside with a wave of her hand saying, "Don't you get into this."

I'm supposed to be *in this*. I care about Rasheed. Why doesn't she see me as part of it, too?

I just have to make myself part of this. While I'm talking, Mrs. Jenkins has a stare-off with the others in the room. I'm not sure if anyone is even paying attention to what I am saying. I pass around his papers so everyone can review his work.

"As you can see, he has excellent penmanship and is able to carry out a complete thought with his writing. I want to bring attention to the fact that Rasheed has above-average test scores, and even though he is not verbal, he has become a leader in my fourth period class."

The psychologist, Ruth Snyder says, "I am very well aware of his test scores, Ms. Sinclair. However, Rasheed is still failing in verbal and social development categories."

Mrs. Jenkins shifts her hips.

"You don't know what you are talking about. The whole neighborhood loves my grandson. What kind of tests are you giving him?"

"They are standardized tests widely accepted in school systems." Ruth's tone is so terse and hard sounding it surprises me.

"To *whose* standard? They don't tell you much if you don't know he can talk."

Mrs. Jenkins leans across the table with her elbows pointed in the direction of the psychologist who is challenging how she is raising Rasheed. The two women are just looking at each other saying nothing, but to me, their eyes are screaming.

At this point, Ed pushes his remaining hair over his bald spot and jumps in.

"All things will be considered, Mrs. Jenkins. Thank you for coming. Our recommendations will be sent to you by certified mail."

On the way to the parking lot, I see Mrs. Jenkins walking towards the bus stop. For a moment, I'm seriously thinking to offer her a ride, but her words, *don't you get into this*, still ring in my ears. I don't know if she sees me as the enemy, and her telling me to stay out of this has my stomach twisted. Why would she say that?

Instead of taking my usual meandering way home that includes a lap around the lake, I drive down Harrison Street to take a straight shot home.

Sitting in my car, my hands have yet to come off the steering wheel. I'm literally waiting for them to stop trembling. It takes a while, but my wits come back enough for me to walk to the elevator.

Which key opens the security gate? Shit. Hold on, keep it together long enough to get inside—don't lose it now.

My neighbors who share a wall step out when the elevator door opens. They don't speak and look right past me. I have no desire to speak to them either and I step to the side so they can pass.

I immediately throw my purse, coat, and keys on the floor, adding to the mess that's already there. Clothes are scattered in the living room, three days of dishes are in the sink, and the bedroom—I don't want to even look at it—so I just close the door.

White walls with artwork surround me as I plop onto the couch and let my feet dangle over the armrest. My paintings all have images of black women working with bundles on their heads, like the women in Africa carry. My neighbor on the first floor who frequently knocks on my door to borrow something once told me I needed to be careful with what I put on my walls.

"All these images attract hard work to you. You'll end up carrying other people's burdens."

I stare at the walls thinking about what my neighbor said, and honestly I'm not sure if she is right or wrong. I think I should straighten up, but I just lay on the couch with my legs still hanging over the armrest, staring blankly at nothing and watch the room light dim as the sun goes down. The phone rings four times but I just let it ring and ignore them all. Mama, my neighbor, and twice I hear Dana's voice. In my head, I give each one an answer.

It's completely dark. I've been sleep for a while in this funny position and my back aches. I feel tired and still upset about the IEP meeting. Why did Mrs. Jenkins tell me to stay out of it when things got so heated? *Oh God.* Doesn't she know I only want to help? My work clothes aren't that wrinkled and since I'm dressed anyway, I might as well go to the club down the hill. One more night on my couch in this miserable state . . . well, I just need to get out and try to shake this mood.

The club down the street is five minutes away, including time for parking, and I don't have to worry about running into anybody—not too many black people go there anymore. The Manhattan Club, or the Lucky Lounge as it's named now, has been gentrified. It used to be an R & B place. After work, it would be filled with black couples and singles, and on Ladies Night, it would be wall to wall. The bartenders now are all young and white with piercings and tattoos. They're friendly, but clearly different from the smooth-talking black men who used to bartend there. Now, the club attracts bohemian whites looking for urban culture, as long as there aren't too many black people. I think about Dana's husband David who knows a lot about the clubs in Oakland. Even he's said it saddens him to see so many of them gone. It seems as the clubs have disappeared, so have the black folks.

I wonder how many people know the first blacks to migrate to Oakland came through the waterways, going all the way down to the Panama Canal and through Central America just to avoid driving through the Gulf Coast states. They learned this route from black merchant marines. They moved into shotgun row houses, rented rooms by the week, or stayed with family members who had already bought homes. Often, the men travelled first and their wives and relatives joined them as soon as they could. I know Daddy stayed with his uncle for two years before Mama was able to join him. I'm not sure which was harder for them, getting here—or trying to stay.

The new owners of the nightclub changed the old ruby-red carpet to wooden floors; put in little round cushioned chairs and tables with ample room between them so you can't hear your neighbor's conversation; and placed red leather benches along the wall. They have too many neon signs behind the bar for my taste. As usual, I sit at the end of the oversized bar that's more than half the length of the club, and face the doorway so I can see who walks in—just in case. I order a Courvoisier with a water back.

At least the music is still good. That's *Down on the Boardwalk* playing. I sing the words softly, the melody is comforting and I start swaying my shoulders. The curly-haired bartender wearing a retro shirt with a black stripe off center is new. He must think I'm smiling at him; the other bartenders know to serve my drink and then leave me alone. He's coming towards me swaying like I am—I hope he doesn't want to make conversation. I pretend to be fixated on something and look into my over-sized brandy snifter as if tea leaves are telling my future. The

Temptations sing black culture into the air, but when I look around, I'm the only one of us here. I laugh. We can be heard but not seen.

It Was Just My Imagination came out in the early seventies. Everybody was singing or playing it. You could walk down the streets of West Oakland and at the same time, you'd hear the smooth sound coming from cars waiting at corner stops, when you passed by houses, and on the small transistor radios people held close to their ears.

Mulling over a brandy snifter and reminiscing about the old days is pretty much all I do when I come to the Lucky Lounge. But it's better than staying alone in my apartment, where my thoughts turn to questioning if I even want to stay around. A day like this one doesn't help with the answer. *Aggressive*—there's nothing about Rasheed that is aggressive.

I keep my head lowered, raising my eyes only occasionally to see what's going on. Thank goodness, the bartender got the message. In the doorway, much to my surprise, there's a tall, dark-skinned, full-lipped, confident-walking black man striding in. He looks around, sees me, and gives a slight nod of his head before he goes to the bar. Up until now, I had been slumping, but I rise up to straighten my back and wonder if he's going to come over.

Maybe 10 minutes go by, which seems like forever. I'm caught in that game of looking and not looking, obsessed with trying to figure out his next move. For a moment, I think he's never going to give me another look. In the Bay Area, I've learned not to expect that all black men want to date black women, but he nods again in the way some of us do when we see each other, smiles, and walks over to sit on the empty stool next to me. He's in a dark-blue uniform that he wears well. It doesn't look like a police officer's or a fireman's. I guess the Red Cross on his shirt pocket must mean he's some sort of emergency worker.

"Hi. I'm Clyde." He gestures to the bartender to come over, the same one I've been avoiding all night.

"Carla. Carla Sinclair." I reach out to shake his hand and can't help noticing how firm and soft it feels at the same time. He orders a Scotch and water, looks at my almost empty glass, and with a facial expression, his eyes ask if I want another one.

"Courvoisier and a water back."

His stare into my eyes is so intense I have to look away to break his gaze. Our handshake is still held in mid-air and I wonder where this is leading. Clyde places his other hand on top of mine. It's clear he wants to spend time with me. I smile, pull my hand back from his two-layered greeting, and he looks over my head to take another glance around the club.

"So why, in the heart of Oakland, are you and I the only black people here? I thought Oakland was supposed to be the Atlanta of the West."

He's observant, quick to the point, not afraid to ask the obvious. I like that. Already, I want to know more about this man named Clyde who doesn't need to use his last name. His leg touches the outside of my upper thigh. Is that intentional or is he just getting comfortable on the barstool?

"I can tell you're new," I say. "Oakland's changing—we leave or get pushed out. The old places get new owners, everything changes, including who works where. Black people fled to the suburbs and you-know-who wants to move in again." I look to see how Clyde responds to my Dana-styled history lesson.

He leans his head back to take a long drink and shakes his head with his eyes closed. I know he understands what I'm talking about. It's not a new story.

"What's this area called?"

His eyes are still wandering around the club and he keeps looking over his shoulder.

"This is the Grand Lake area." I tell him "So, where are you from?"

"Oklahoma City."

I don't know if Clyde is a conversationalist. He hasn't settled down after his initial look-me-in-the-eye-and-hold-my-hand greeting. He seems a little on edge. He finishes the rest of his drink, slams the glass on the bar, drawing the attention of the curly-head bartender. His quick action startles me and I jump a little.

"Yeah, that's what I'm talking about, let's do it again," he says loudly in the young man's direction.

The barkeep brings another Scotch and water. I start wondering, *how old is Clyde?* That move, just then, was a youngster's move. I ignore what it could mean, and instead, I turn to listen to him talk.

"I can't claim Oakland. I've been here less than three months. Back home, I worked for the Feds in the Bureau of Alcohol, Tobacco and Firearms. I was with them for over 15 years. When the bombing happened I was there. That day was nothing pretty." He takes a big swallow of his drink.

"I've never met anyone who was actually there."

"I was on vacation, didn't go anywhere, you know just hung around the house. If not for that, I would have been in the Federal Building with my coworkers when the bomb went off." He downs his third drink.

"Did you know anyone that got killed?"

He nods yes.

"I rushed down when I heard it on the news and was part of the rescue. Nightmares started happening and they wanted to send me to a shrink, so I thought it was time to leave."

"Why Oakland?"

"A frat brother hooked me up with this EMT Company, the best one in Oakland. My family, friends, even my dog are back there."

I remember calling Mama that day to see if she was watching the television and all she could say was, "Dear Lord, pray for all those people and little babies killed. Carla, you stay home—no telling what's gettin' ready to happen." I went to work anyway because I knew my students would show up. The image of the fireman carrying a burned child in his arms flashes through my mind, but I break myself from the memory of that day to turn to Clyde.

"So, how are you doing settling into Oakland?" I ask.

"I'm good. The nightmares are less frequent. I left because Oklahoma City forgot black folks were in all that mess, too. We lost people—plenty—but you'd think by the media coverage we weren't there."

Clyde's attitude shifts and I hear agitation in his voice.

As he gets into the story about what happened to him in the aftermath of the bombing, there's no question now—he's a talker. I'm a good listener and I play my role well—lots of *mmms, really's* and *you-don't-says*. That's all he needs to keep going. I don't think he's asked a single question about me yet. Was I born in Oakland? What kind of work do I do? Am I married, do I have kids? In less than two hours, he reveals that he's been through two divorces, has three children, and pays child support to two different women who he claims give him a hard time. He went to the Million Man March, graduated from Howard University, keeps in good shape, and sometimes eats vegetarian.

Clyde's bought me two maybe three drinks and they have me feeling woozy. While he talks I hold my chin in my hand, with my elbow on top of the bar and hope I don't appear drunk.

Halfway into his life story, our bodies have begun to lean into each other and every once in a while he touches my face to tell me how pretty I am. Daddy used to tell me I was pretty and like then, I'm melting under his attention. His touches are more frequent now, his hand lingers on my back, and when he makes a point, he surrounds my shoulders with his arm and stares into my face. He moves in for a kiss, but I offer him a cheek—it's been a while, but I'm not ready for that.

The look on his face says, "Why not?"

I ignore it. My look tells him to continue holding court and I'll listen. He shrugs his shoulders and turns toward the bartender. "*Garçon,*"

Clyde calls out. "My lady friend is ready for another drink. I'll have a Scotch and water. What's yours, again?"

"*Garçon?* Do all black fathers teach their sons to call a waiter that?" I jokingly ask.

Clyde lets out a huge sigh, shakes his head and reminding me of my brother, Otis, when he was young—says, "No, no, no."

"I made me. I did this—all by myself." He sounds rattled. "Nobody gave me nothing but hard work."

He proceeds to go on and on about the problem with black fathers. I want to tell him that the apple doesn't fall far from the tree, since he's not with his children, but I know it will only inflame our conversation. One fire today is enough. So instead, I interrupt his monologue.

"You asked what I was drinking. It's Courvoisier and water back."

I catch my slur before it comes out. It's obvious I don't need another drink but it's the only thing I can think to re-route Clyde's sudden change in attitude. I'm still surprised at his reaction. It was a harmless joke and now he's gone on to tell me what's wrong with Sisters.

"Clyde, I'm not trying to say anything like that. It was just a curious question. My brothers use that word, but you've taken it all over the map as if I've done something to you."

"Yeah, right." He slams the latest empty glass again onto the bar and asks for another.

How many does that make? I've lost count.

"I'm going to the bathroom. There's definitely a timeout needed here." I'm not sure I can make it off this stool without falling.

"*Time out?* Woman, don't treat me like a child," he shouts and brings the attention of the bartender our way.

"Oh, God. I mean we need a breather—let's take a break is all I'm trying to say."

In the mirror behind the wooden bar with too many neon signs, I see surprise written all over my face. I think if I stay longer this could get real ugly. I slide each leg off the red leather barstool one at a time, not looking at Clyde as I get up to leave.

Okay, steady girl, the bathroom is to the left.

When I try to push the door open, my head bumps into it with a loud thud—the door swings out. *Did anyone see?* I don't think so and from where we're sitting, Clyde can't see around the corner.

My thighs shake over the bowl and my low crouch turns into a plop down on the toilet without the benefit of a seat cover. My stomach has twisted—this is not good. How did everything go wrong so quickly? I'm shaking my head in disbelief that I'm hiding in the bathroom. It's time to end all this foolishness, as Mama would say, and go home, but really the thought of dealing with Clyde is enough for me to think about making this small stall my home. I don't even know him. And oh, God—all the touching that went on. Why'd I let him do that? Rub my back, grab my face, oh, and the way he surrounded me with his arms…what was I thinking?

You weren't—that's the problem, Carla.

I finger my eyebrows to bring them down. I didn't see this coming from Clyde.

The walls of the bathroom stall provide a tall shield from everyone and sitting on the toilet tucked inside this make-believe panic room there is a sense of safety. There's no bathroom tissue, another good reason to stay longer while I air dry. I'm in no hurry; maybe Clyde will get the message and leave before I come out. I read the graffiti on the stall door, but on a closer look I see it's an HIV prevention message. The toll-free number for testing looks like a number for a booty call.

There's nothing on the ceiling to count so I start with the tiles on the floor. The bottom of the stall blocks my view so I have to repeat myself, often. I search through my purse, satisfied that at least I remembered to bring it with me, and find my mirror to smooth down the edges of my hair so it looks neater. Oh God, if Dana saw me now she would be all over me, asking what am I doing. Then she'd probably go into her psychobabble and ask why I overlooked all the red flags just to have some affection.

Two women come in just talking away with each other, one of them sounds upset. By their voices I can tell they're white. One is complaining about the date the other one fixed her up with.

"He only talks about himself and he won't keep his hands off me. This is your fault. He's cute, but please, is there something else to talk about besides him?"

Her friend listens to her rant on and on, she finally says, "Just find your happy space and tell him what you want or don't want, that's all you have to do."

I quietly laugh, so they can't hear me, and my mouth silently mocks her words.

I'll just go out there in my "happy space" and tell Clyde—your father's probably sorry for what he didn't do, you drink too much, and you got problems—right, it's just that easy.

Women keep coming in and out, not knowing that I've never left this stall. I overhear conversations about their lives, their dates, even a sad tale by a woman who just got fired from her job. For maybe an hour I've sat on this toilet, letting the stall make me believe I'm safe, and whatever Clyde's problems are they can't affect me in here. It must be getting late. No one's come in for a while. I need to get out and go home, my knees are wobbly but I can stand. I leave the safety of the stall, smooth my edges down in the bathroom mirror and get up the nerve to leave. Before going too far, I peek around the corner, to make sure Clyde's gone and then walk towards the bar. Thank God he's not here. I'm doing my best to walk a straight path to the Lucky Lounge's door and get to my car.

The night's quiet, in the way early morning hours can be, when everyone else is asleep. No one is walking on the sidewalk and only one car passes by, no lights cast a glow through the windows of peoples' homes. The only beacons are streetlamps and porch lights trying their best to ward off suspected intruders. I feel sick, and it's not just from too much Courvoisier. When I roll down the window for some air to collect myself, the freeway roars like an angry ocean. Oh God, my head hurts. *Damn it, Carla.*

CHAPTER TEN

The main entranceway to Frederick Douglass Middle School reminds me of the plantation home in *Song of the South*, an old Disney movie. Uncle Remus, the lead character, is a white-bearded slave whose job is to take care of the master's children during a summer visit with their grandmother. In one of my magazines I read that the NAACP—and even some white folks—protested against it showing at the Paramount Theater down on Broadway. That was in 1946. I think it was around the same time Daddy came to Oakland and Mama came two years later. Sometimes, I wonder what they thought about that and if they were involved in any of the protests.

Then again, on days like today, as I make my turn into the teachers' parking lot and see the building's tall, dull-white circular pillars and green lawn stretching as far as the sidewalk, it reminds me of the White House. I arrived early this morning, so it's fairly quiet, the hallways are empty, and I can make the long walk to Room 103 without dodging hundreds of children or having to listen to banging lockers or the hallway monitors constantly shouting, "Stop running!"

It's taken me a whole semester, but I've finally regrouped from when my chair broke and I sat on the floor crying about not wanting to be here. Somehow, I've been able to ignore my hopeless feelings for the sake of the children. I made my classroom hands-on with plenty of projects they can touch and hold—it's a far cry from the activities at the Exploratorium in San Francisco—but it works. I can see the students are interested.

Our latest project is a saltwater tide pool with yellow-finned and blue colored fish, as well as seaweed and anemones I brought from the local fish store. I went to Alameda beach for the sand and broken seashells and placed everything in a toddler's size swimming pool. Rasheed spends more time than any other student looking and dipping his hand into the water of our pretend tide pool. I think today, when I see him in his usual place at the back of the room, I'll ease over and share my fascination with one of the anemones or something else that draws my attention. Then, I'll casually ask what's his favorite thing in the tide pool. I'll act nonchalant, no pressure, hopefully with only curiosity in my tone of voice. I want to create a shared moment between the two of us. Maybe I'll hear an unguarded and unmuffled, "That one." Who knows—a long time ago, my plan worked with Mama when I tried to get her to talk to me.

A sea of wild-eyed fourth-period students run into my classroom bumping into others trying to leave. They're pointing towards the hallway.

"Fight, Ms. Sinclair, fight! There's a fight in the hallway."

My stomach sinks with the feeling of ice weighing it down. Don't ask me how, but I have a premonition that Rasheed is somehow involved. I hurriedly wade through students crowded around the door, almost tripping on one child sitting on the floor to the side of door. What is she doing down there? Oh my God, what is going on here? I don't know if she needs help, but I look in her eyes and she's not crying, so I keep moving fast towards the water fountain where a circle of students are gathered in front of the lockers.

"I'm a kill you!"

The threat is coming from a student who is struggling to be let go by the hall monitor who is grabbing him by the waist. The front of his white tee shirt is covered with bright red spots from the blood dripping down his mouth.

"I'm gonna get you, man, you dead now!"

The monitor meets my eyes and says, "Don't worry; I got him."

The boy's elbow and arms are flailing, his fists are balled up and waving around. The way the monitor is holding him, both legs are lifted off the ground and all he can do is kick wildly in the air.

The blood rushing out of his mouth startles me. It's a lot—he's taken a hard hit to the mouth. I turn my attention to Rasheed, who is standing a few feet away but out of kicking range.

"Did you hit this boy?" I demand.

Rasheed doesn't say anything, and he doesn't need to be held back. He's leaning against the metal lockers with his mouth puffed up and lips tucked under. Like the other boy, his fists are clenched tight.

"Rasheed, *did you hit him?*"

"He was teasing him," a small voice says.

Was that in Rasheed's defense? I look to see who was talking and I'm surprised to see it's the East Indian girl in my fourth-period class who doesn't like to bring attention to herself.

"Yeah," a few other students say all together.

My morning plan to act casual and nonchalant with Rasheed is out the window now. I'm turning into someone I don't recognize, but I can't stop myself. I hear my voice getting louder and I'm looking Rasheed straight in his eyes.

"Tell me why you hit him, Rasheed. Why did you hit him?"

I keep repeating my questions over and over, and I move closer to where I'm now towering over him.

He's standing by himself with a half circle of too many eyes staring—waiting. I catch myself.

What am I doing?

When I look behind me, all eyes in the circle are on Rasheed. Why didn't I remove him from this audience of onlookers who now, because of my demands, are also waiting for the boy who never speaks to say something?

Here I am standing with both hands on my hips and obviously angry, something I think I'll regret for a long time.

With that many eyes I should have known there wasn't a hell's chance he would say anything. Disgust washes all over me. I knew better. Another monitor arrives and grabs Rasheed forcefully, holding his arms back. Both boys are roughly guided towards the main office. I'm torn whether I should go with them, but 34 other children are waiting for class to start.

I try to get the lesson started, but my students are still upset and I can't get them to calm down. What happened in the hallway isn't over. They don't want Rasheed to get in trouble, because apparently the other boy started the fight.

"Ms. Sinclair, it's not fair. All the time they tease us," says Roshanna, who sits in Rasheed's desk group.

"I'm glad he hit him," she says.

"Yeah, I went past him and the hall monitor saw that kid messing with Rasheed from behind and he didn't do anything," another student says.

"Ms. Sinclair, I saw it, too. He followed Rasheed, calling him dummy-mummy, pushing on him," says Manuel, who wears a full back brace for his scoliosis.

Okay. I hadn't arranged for this period to go this way. I wish I could put things on pause and call Dana. She's much better than I am when something that happens makes sense but it's not right.

"Maybe Rasheed was provoked, but he should not have hit him," I tell them.

"He was being really nasty," Manuel says.

I don't feel like I'm doing too good of a job in this teachable moment. The bright red blood, the memory of me standing with my hands on my hips yelling at Rasheed, demanding an answer, are enough to keep me unsettled, too. I stop talking. I stop trying to explain what they saw and just listen. Hands are jerking and waving in the air, students are sitting on the edge of their chairs, their outrage at what happened not allowing their bottoms to remain fully seated. They've witnessed violence and need to say something about it. At least half of the class still wants a chance to say what's on their minds.

Thomas, who's slumped over his desk, has held his hand up for a while, just barely though, as if he's not sure he wants to be called on. When I do call on him, he eases from his chair to stand and looks down at the floor. His chin is dropped, and I think he is biting his lip as he speaks. All we hear is mumbling. No one can understand what he's saying, and a student on the other side of the room tells him to talk louder.

"Thomas, can you speak up?" I ask. I don't want to repeat the mistake I made in the hallway. Rasheed's look, his stare that said, "Are you really doing this to me," hasn't gone away.

"Thomas, do you want to come up here and tell me what you saw?"

He vigorously nods his head up and down reminding me how Otis responded to Mama when he was hurt or angry. I tell the rest of the class to pull out their readers. Students look at me with disappointment, only 15 minutes of class time are left. They know it's over for the rest of them. Thomas's seat is in the far corner of the room and he walks slowly to the front, dragging out the time. Everyone has closed their backpacks and looks away from their readers to watch Thomas's lone processional to my desk.

The chair by my desk is made for adult bottoms. I notice his feet barely touch the floor. I also notice he's wearing what I call the unfathered son street uniform—saggy jeans with no belt and an oversized white tee shirt. He's probably seen more fights than his years. That's why it surprises me to see that his lower eyelids are wet when he sits down.

"Are you okay?" I ask him.

I ease the tissue box closer to the edge of my desk and at the same time take a look around to see what the other students are doing. All the heads that had been propped up drop quickly.

"Thomas, can you tell me what made Rasheed so upset?"

He nods yes, but doesn't say anything. I wait a moment, touch his shoulder to reassure him, and leave my hand to rest on the edge of the desk next to him.

"It's okay to tell me." My voice is low.

Thomas wipes a tear off his face with a baggy sleeve, revealing his thin tiny arm, confirming that he is much smaller than most boys his age. He squirms in the oversize seat and sighs. I think he's too young to be sighing that way. Then, with worry lines across his forehead, he tells me, "Calvin say Rasheed ain't ever gone be no home boy's niggah."

"Excuse me?"

I know that sounds as lame as if the bank teller had told me I was overdrawn when I had just given her my whole check. I'm not sure I heard what I heard.

"He say he a nigger ain't nobody give a shit about."

His words surprise me again and the cold wave in my stomach turns to frost. Thomas is looking at me. I believe he's expecting me to help him keep talking. I'm not sure what to say.

"Did the other boy push him?" I finally ask.

He nods yes.

"Rasheed, he kept walking. He didn't step at him. I was behind and…"

More tears well up and he gets quiet, trying to hold back a snivel that won't stop.

"What else, Thomas?" I say gently, thinking, *Oh, God* what else could there be.

His head rises up and he turns around to see which classmates are trying to listen. His mumbling is back so I lean in closer to hear his whisper.

"That boy he say Rasheed's mama a junkie cuz he so black and a dummy." He looks even further down and says, "I'm sorry. I know I was supposed to look out for him."

"Oh, Thomas . . ."

Trouble bigger than his years.

"It's not your fault," I say to him.

His stone face doesn't let me know if he believes this. From the beginning of the year, I've watched Thomas take on the job of protecting Rasheed. They are an odd couple. Thomas is constantly pulling his no-belt sagging jeans up and Rasheed is always neatly dressed in fitted and pressed khakis and usually a shirt with a collar. I think I understand why he feels so bad and why the offending boy's words cut through him like a knife.

What he said about Rasheed's mama could just as easily been directed at him. Thomas lifts his nose, takes a deep breath and a long sniff into the air to stop the water that's pooling in his eyes. The class is silent. I don't ask Thomas to go back to his seat, and he doesn't ask to be relieved. We sit, but are no longer looking at each other.

I don't know what to make of this. The offending boy may not be as dark as Rasheed but would surely be called dark-skinned. Where did he learn to go for the jugular and hurt Rasheed with those kinds of words?

As soon as the bell rings, my sixth-period class rushes out, barely saying goodbye. Obviously, they're anxious to be somewhere else. I don't blame them it's been a rough day. In slow motion, I organize papers to take home for grading. Water from my eyes drops and a wet pool forms, smudging the ink when I wipe the paper dry. My mind won't stop replaying the morning's events. I've seen students fight

119

before, even broke up a few that started right in front of me, but this business of "Are you a niggah or a nigger," and picking on someone's skin color, picking on his mama—all of it has my stomach twisted. On my way down the hallway, I stop in front of the locker where Rasheed stood with his hands balled up in a fist. It still has blood splattered on it. For a moment, I just stand, replaying the confusing scene through my mind.

"Why are they taking so long to wash it off?" Cassandra's voice startles me.

I was so absorbed in staring at the blood on the locker that I didn't notice her near me. I can still see Rasheed standing there and me with my hands on my hips.

"Who knows?" I shrug my shoulders, feeling helpless about the situation.

"I have Thomas in my sixth-period class. He told me what happened."

"Did he tell you everything?" I ask Cassandra without taking my eyes off the lockers.

"Pretty much. It's so sad. He really feels he let Rasheed down. I know they were tight."

"Ed needs to know what started the fight." I say, finally turning to look at Cassandra's disheartened face. "So he can help the boys handle the emotions that drove them to this."

"Carla are you for real? Oh, please—I might be new here, but even I can see that Ed wouldn't know where to begin."

"But what else is there Cassandra?" I'm surprised that my voice reveals so much frustration. I have to try something.

"What else for what?" Miriam says, joining us at the lockers.

Cassandra rolls her eyes and sucks her teeth to head on her way, leaving me to respond to Miriam's uninvited question. I don't know what's going on between these two. We both watch Cassandra walk down the hall, then Miriam turns to me.

"Whose blood is that?"

"Didn't you hear about the fight this morning?" I ask her.

"Is this where it happened?" She sounds excited.

I don't bother to answer her question, which has an obvious answer.

"Mr. Jerrod in Room 104 told me at lunch that he saw two gang-bangers in white tee shirts following Rasheed down the hallway before the fight broke out. Was it self-defense?"

"Yes, it was."

My voice doesn't give her any room to question whether it was self-defense or not. I think Rasheed was defending his soul—someone had messed with his itch.

"Do you know what started it?" Miriam asks.

I look at her and her eyes seem caring and not just searching for the drama of the situation. But I really can't talk to Miriam right now. There's something I have to do.

"Look, I have to catch Ed before he leaves."

A terrible feeling is coming over me. I have to see Ed and I hope I'm not too late. Why didn't I go with Rasheed when it happened?

"Are you okay?" asks Miriam.

She places a hand on my arm in an attempt to console me, but it just makes me want to get out of here even sooner.

"Yeah, really I have to go. I'll see you later."

I walk quickly towards the main office, my mind swirls with what Miriam has told me.

Two gangbangers? Thomas said he was behind Rasheed when the teasing started, and he's wearing a white tee shirt. He's probably the other boy Mr. Jerrod is calling a gangbanger. He doesn't know how wrong he is. Do I know what started it? How would I even begin to tell Miriam why Rasheed had to defend himself? More and more, Cassandra's, "Oh please," makes sense. Ed wouldn't know where to begin, neither do I in trying to make him understand. It's like two different worlds, the one white people live in and the one these black children live in, and to avoid the collision we all stay quiet about what's burning underneath.

The designated rows of chairs for the vice-principal's office are empty. Mrs. Brown's not paying attention to anyone standing at the counter and she ignores my, "Hello." I don't know why I keep speaking to her since she's made it clear that I shouldn't expect an answer in return. Ed's door is slightly open, so I walk past the counter and knock on the wooden doorframe to get his attention. He's on the phone.

"Where are the boys?"

His face frowns up. Well, at least he doesn't wave me away, which he often does. Maybe the boys were still trying to get at each other in his office. Maybe at least one of them shouted out the reason for the fight, and Ed heard them, but based on what Thomas told me, I seriously doubt it.

I sit in one of the chairs in front of his desk and wait for him to finish his conversation. Is any part of his office different than when we first started working at Douglass? Bookshelves with memorabilia from his alma mater in Texas are still in the same place when he first set up his office. He was in his late twenties then, and I was about the same age, or maybe a few years younger. We had decided then to change the school, the world—together. In our early years, we took everything on—the curriculum, keeping the school clean, motivating parent involvement, and together, we went through numerous tough school battles about budget cuts that never seemed to have students come out as the winners.

He hangs up the phone, searches through a stack of yellow papers as thick as a book, and hands me one. It's an incident report. His signature is on the bottom and in the name section he's written Rasheed Jenkins and the other boy, Calvin Williams. The top of the page says Five-Day Suspension.

"What's this?" I ask. "How can things be settled like that in just a few hours?"

He should have talked to me first. I keep asking Ed why—why didn't he seek my counsel with the situation? My voice rises with each question. For a second Mrs. Brown, again, acting as security peeks into the open doorway. Ed's leans back in his chair to answer another ringing phone, shaking his head no. During the conversation with his higher-ups, I wave the yellow paper at him, mouthing my disbelief at this decision. When he hangs the phone up, I try to tell him that both boys' grandmother's work—why not give them in-school detention? Ed signals he's done talking about it, runs a finger over his bald spot, and gives me a shoulder shrug. I know I'm about to be waved off. If I don't push back, things will just stay the same.

"So Ed, is this it?"

Oh God, that was a feeble sounding pushback. I wanted to tell him that this is the wrong way to handle the situation, don't kick them out, they'll be home alone, their grandmothers will worry, let's think of another way—like we used to. I was almost out of the door when Ed says, "Carla, you know the rules. There's zero tolerance for violence here, and that's that."

I turn around to stare at him the way the Queen stared at me. It takes everything I can to hold back my growing disappointment in Ed and not point my finger to ask what's he's been feeding his twisted soul. He looks away from my eyes and swivels back and forth in the chair. When did he stop caring? The Ed I once knew would have found another way. A few years into our careers we had a moment together in the student cafeteria, we were just two adults watching other people's children, and he told me what it felt like to be a latchkey child. I told him the story of my father dying, and how I understood what coming home to an empty house felt like. When did extraterrestrials grab his heart and place it inside a lock box on the mother ship?

"Look, it's not me. It's the rules," he says.

Maybe Ed heard my thoughts and that's why he repeats his decision.

I decide not to say anything and turn around to leave his office shaking my head, at Ed, at me. I can't tell if my feet are on the ground. He didn't even say he was sorry, or that he understands, or that we'll come up with something.

My plodding has returned, it alerts me that my feet are touching the ground, but the pain in my hip that starts slowly before it screams, joins me for the walk to the teacher's parking lot. I imagine myself in a Spike Lee movie, walking alone down a long sidewalk or a thin hallway in slow motion, disconnected from a world that's moving fast.

I almost forget that I'm supposed to meet Dana at the Pillars. I think about going home before driving to the lake, I have enough time to change out of my work clothes because I know Dana is going to be late. The effort feels like way too much. Besides, I don't want to see the condition of my house any sooner than I have to.

It's not yet spring. Underneath the grass, the ground is probably still wet from this morning, not fully dried out from a hot sun. Nevertheless, it calls me to lie down. I hesitate—I have on my work clothes. I lean over to touch my knees and drop into an unceremonious flop onto the ground. I look around to see if anyone saw my not-so-graceful fall, but I can tell by the way the walkers keep going that no one's given me a second look or thought.

The late winter sky is crispy blue. There's a lone puffy cloud, radiant from the sun, and it catches my attention. It's not moving or, if it is, it's moving so slowly I can't tell. I imagine it's waiting on its posse to show up, wondering when help will come so it can shield us from the rays burning down, or bring rain to wash away all the muck—I think it needs help to do its job. A flock of geese fly in formation by my cloud, heading to the other end of the lake. They're so high up all I see are black shadows. They're moving way too fast to count, and it's frustrating to even try.

"What's up, girl?"

Dana's voice breaks my fixation on the cloud and my inability to count the geese. Her hair is in cornrows. She's always doing something different; wearing it bushy, twisting it back into French braids, and even once in a blue moon straightening it. I've watched her hairstyles change over the years and I've secretly envied her freedom. My press and curl doesn't give much variety. Truth is, I stopped a long time ago imagining that my hair could look different.

"Where are your sweats?" Dana asks.

She's in a black running suit with a lime green stripe running down both sides of her pants. I'm in a pair of brown corduroys that swish when I walk and the black down jacket Arthur, Jr. passed on to me last year.

"I haven't done laundry yet." I point at my walking shoes. I don't want to talk about why I'm still in my work clothes or about the events of the day.

"Believe me, I understand," she says, "How was work?"

The top of my body collapses closer to the ground and I mumble, "Good question."

"Were you screening calls again last night? It went straight to your answering machine," Dana watches my effort to stand up. She extends a sympathetic hand to help me off the ground. I'm concentrating hard on getting up and not sure what to say about my workday.

Once I'm straightened out, I ask, "Can we forget the warm-up stretches and just start walking?"

Dana gives a Tiger Woods fist pump into the air and says, "Let's do it."

We start walking on the pathway that runs along Lakeshore Avenue towards the trail of low wooden stumps left behind when diseased trees were cut down. To me, they look like tables waiting for chairs to be placed around them. Every once in a while I say a stump number out loud and Dana looks at me weirdly. She sets the pace fast, stretching her long legs almost twice as far as my one step. I have to slow her down.

When we get to the first stoplight, she nods that she understands she's walking too fast and slows to match my pace, occasionally, bumping into me. That last bump felt on purpose.

"Okay, who goes first to say how their day went?" Dana asks.

"Can't we just walk?" I sigh loudly. I don't want to get into it.

"That bad?" She gives me another sympathetic look.

I nod.

Dana throws her arms up in the air and pats her head repeatedly like Chicken Little, saying, "Well, I'm so preoccupied that it could take our whole walk to tell you about it. I need to talk with my brother and I don't know how I'm to start."

"I thought you already did that."

"No." She winces with her shoulders up, "Not yet."

"*Dana…*"

"I know, I know. When I try to talk to him all we do is argue."

"You keep saying it's important."

"I don't know what to say about it, Car, that's why you should go first."

"I don't want to say anything about my day."

We sound like middle schoolers, going back and forth, not grown women. I finally decide to go first. Otherwise, we're going to stay here all night.

"Rasheed had a fight at school, there was a lot of blood, someone called him the "N" word, said he would never be a *niggah*, and talks about his mama, then, another boy tells me what happened and cries at my desk, and Ed gives out a stupid five-day suspension."

I say all this without taking a breath or a break between my words.

"And I don't want to say any more about it," I add.

Dana looks over at me as we walk. Her eyebrows are up and she has a wondering look on her face. "The boy who doesn't talk?"

"Yes, Rasheed."

Dana moves closer as we head towards east 18th Street near Merritt Bakery. She rubs my back, landing her hand on the shoulder nearest her as we keep walking. Her touch is comforting, but I don't want to go into all that happened today. I'm still not sure how I lost it like that. And then how do I explain walking away from Ed's office without fighting for Rasheed?

"I mean it, I'm done. That was my day."

"Okay then," Dana says with a little laugh. "Fight, blood, students suspended at Fredrick Douglass today," she repeats my words sounding like a Channel 2 newscaster. "A good sound bite for the 6:00 news. Concise, but not much detail."

We make it past the 18th Street pier where people sit during the golden hour to watch the sunset. She hasn't asked another thing about Rasheed or said anything about what's on her mind. Once we slow down, the walking is okay, but I'm still feeling heavy on my feet. Dana isn't stretching out her long dancer legs anymore to hurry us around the lake. We're not even close to 14th Street, the halfway mark, and even though I was the one who wanted to slow down, I'd like for this walk to be over. If I nudge Dana into the conversation about her brother, it can be a distraction from how far it is back to our cars and thinking about the circumstances of my day.

"Isn't it your turn?" I give a small push on her shoulder.

"Oh, my day? I thought you'd never ask." She feigns surprise like a southern belle.

"You're a mess."

"I know. I needed you to help me start talking." Dana smiles.

"He's getting married soon, right?"

"For the third time. He's just going to make the same mistakes with this marriage."

"Why do you say that?"

"Because he thinks since mother and father have died so has their influence over him. But he's wrong."

I knew this was going to be deep, but I remember I wanted the distraction.

"Wasn't he the one taking care of them?" I ask Dana. "He's probably glad for the break—I mean, not glad they died—you know what I mean."

"I know what you're saying, Car. But sometimes, I feel my colored guilt creeping in because I wasn't there."

"That was a big year for you."

"Yes it was. I was up for tenure and he kept telling me to stay put, that he had it covered. He said he didn't want to end up taking care of me, too. He even joked that I needed to put my psychology degree to work on other people besides the family."

"Well, you do give out a lot of sessions for free," I say.

She turns towards me to frown at my little dig.

"I'm not talking about how he took care of our parents, he did a wonderful job."

"Well what are you talking about then?"

"I've got to do it, soon."

"Do what, Dana?" Now she is the one frustrating me. "You keep talking around it."

"Sorry, I guess I'm anxious. I'm talking about the inheritance our father left him."

I lean my head over and squeeze my left eye down. I know I must look puzzled.

"What's the problem there? Isn't running the law firm pretty lucrative for him?"

Dana stops walking to look at me and then doubles over to laugh. What's so funny about that? Aaron makes good money. I watch her bent over and think my friend has lost it.

"What, Dana? I don't understand what's so funny."

She stands up, still laughing.

"Car, girl that was a good one. I'm talking about his emotions, not the law firm."

I pull on her to start walking and try to break up this comic relief in the middle of the walkway at my expense. Inheritance and emotions, my friend never disappoints.

"Okay Professor Washington. What theory, now?" I ask.

"You know I have one," she says.

"I'm almost scared to hear it."

Dana always has a theory about this and that—sometimes they're interesting and then other times, I think they are just flat-out strange.

"Well, you know I've been looking at the concept of emotional intelligence for my book—but I put my own little twist on it. Want to hear it?" Dana asks.

"I thought you'd never tell me."

My answer is sarcastic, but we still have a lot more walking to get around this huge lake. Walking is definitely different from driving a lap or two.

"Just like the money, houses, furniture, and things that our parents leave us in a will, they also leave an emotional legacy. Good, bad, and ugly emotions get passed on to you, whether you want them or not—a quick temper, flightiness, moodiness—we inherit all of these things and more from our parents. Aaron doesn't understand this.

"Okay," I say.

"He gets angry when he thinks I'm going all psychobabble on him."

"He's probably not the only one," I say underneath my breath, and look at Dana to see if she heard me.

"He has to hear me out, though. It's the only way things will change," she says.

"Have you said anything to him about this? You could make it sound like a question on the *What's Your Legacy* game show."

"Oh, now you're the one being funny," Dana says. "Well, I'll take ten for what your mama and daddy left you."

This is the first time I've found any humor today.

"But seriously, Carla, I have to find a way for him to get this—to understand why his wives don't stay. This will be his third, you know."

Dana's degree sometimes has her coming up with ideas that I don't know if anyone but her gets.

"I told you the story about my parents, how they were forced together, that it was a marriage without love, right?"

She says this so casual I look over at her.

"You did." I tell my brain to get ready. "And?"

"They were steeped in the traditions of the black bourgeoisie. I mean, really old-school ways. My mother acted like it didn't matter that there was no love between them, but I know it did. She buried her pain imitating the cult of *ladydom*, and you know my mother was from the St. Louis projects. Paula Giddings, a black researcher and historian, wrote about it. This was in the 1930s—when the elite men of white society required their wives to follow a rulebook for acting posh and privileged in ways that set them apart from the regular rich white folks."

"What's that got to do with Aaron?"

"That's how my father saw himself, an elite black man of high society. That's who my grandparents wanted him to be. Mother knew nothing about that way of life."

"Again I say, and...?"

"Aaron's doing the same thing as our father and it doesn't work with women now, if it ever did."

"Dana, I don't know what hurts more, my brain or my feet, trying to keep up with you."

I know the answer to that—both.

"I've been rattling on and on, Car. Thanks for listening. I still don't know what to say to Aaron, but at least I'm getting my emotions out."

"So do I get a fee, then?"

"You definitely got jokes today," she laughs.

I draw her attention towards the library parking lot where we can see our cars.

"Well, only a few hundred more steps to make your point."

Dana grabs her head, faking surprise we are so close to the end, and continues to talk about her brother's situation.

"I met this new fiancée last year. She's not going to go for any of that, and soon she'll be gone, too. He chooses thinking women and God forgive them if they actually want love to show up in their marriage."

"Dana, that's heavy stuff. If it was me, I don't think I'd want to hear all of that, either."

"Mother told me what it was like to be married to my father, I've tried to be subtle in telling Aaron, but two weeks ago when I brought it up, we got into an argument, and Car…the conversation went to pieces. He got defensive, I got upset, and there you have it. He hung up on me."

After that, we fall silent. Loudly, the swishing noise made by my corduroy pants, competes with the hum of passing cars and the buzzing in my head. I don't know what to tell Dana about Aaron. I barely know what to say to myself. We cross the red brick walkway in front of the Lakeside library to finish the final steps with our arms locked. I think both of us know we have some things to deal with.

CHAPTER ELEVEN

All last week, I held back my anticipation of Rasheed returning to class after his five-day suspension. I've imagined him in his princely way taking the empty seat that is only his to fill. I've missed seeing his eyes surveying the rest of us, his head giving approval or not, his hand over his mouth, holding back words when something wanted to push him beyond his inability to speak, or desire not to speak. The silence from his absence makes me realize how loud a presence he really is.

During my morning classes, I found myself thinking how his return will go. I'll meet his closed smile to welcome his return, let him know I'm glad he's back in class, and we'll move on from the interruption. The doorway streams with students rushing in, shouting greetings to me, they seem excited. Do they remember Rasheed comes back, today? Everyone's almost settled in—class is soon to begin—but there's not yet a bright yellow coat walking through the door.

Finally, Rasheed enters with slow and measured steps. As he walks through the doorway, he slides his eyes past me, offering only a green backpack for me to welcome. He takes the long way to his desk, avoiding his normal route through the middle of the room. I think it's intentional to avoid passing by me. He heads down the narrow path next to the wall and students are slapping his coat with, "Hi Rasheed," and "Glad you're back." He sits to join the others, pushes the hood off his head, but the huge jacket stays on like a protective armor—not to be removed.

I tell myself to focus on the other children. They need me to pay attention. It's time to start. While calling roll, my eyes look towards Rasheed, believing that all we need to do is make eye contact and everything will be okay. I write the lesson on the blackboard and then turn around to see if I can catch his usual watchful eye. He's not looking at anyone. Not at the children next to him, or at his classmates who are asking questions. He didn't even raise his head to see who came up front—and definitely, he's not watching me. I don't think things are going back to the way they were.

Oh God, have I lost this child?

The bell will ring in about five minutes. Still Rasheed's head is bent while he draws on paper, exposing rowed waves of shiny black hair, the neat rows tell me he wears a stocking cap to bed. At the bell, students scramble to gather their things, and rush into the hallway with bursts of freed energy. Rasheed again walks the long way to the door, looking only at the floor, never at me. He leaves my room, making it clear our chance for re-connection will not happen—with no clue or hint it ever will.

There's a paper left on Rasheed's desk. He's left papers before. At first, this one seems just forgotten, jagged pieces torn off. But as I continue looking at his doodling, paying more attention, I realize he was communicating with me. Maybe it's a note telling me its okay, he forgives me, and just couldn't let me know, that he needed to show the rest of the students he was still in charge of his life. I walk towards his desk, straightening the squared seating arrangements, delaying the moment when I will know if indeed it is a message left for me.

Oh no . . .

The drawing is a cartoonish man with a wide clownish smile and a tongue sticking out. Off to the side of his head there's a word bubble, what's written inside has been scratched over in ink. I can't read what it says. The tongue's colored entirely in black ink, and the smile is obviously meant to be fake it's so out of proportion to the face. I lift the drawing into the light to see if I can read the crossed out lettering. The first word is "I" and the next is "hate," everything else is not readable, but there's no mistaking the first two words. *I hate* what?

While teaching, I ignored the hangover I've felt since the morning, but now, walking through the park, there's no mistaking the fuzz in my brain and wooze in my stomach. Last night, I went out in East Oakland and stayed at the Continental Club near the airport till everything closed down. After yesterday's walk, Dana and I went in different directions. She went home to David and I went home to an apartment I can barely stand to look at. I knew I was going to go out—staying home is risky. I'm too afraid how these thoughts about leaving—my job, the students, my life—will finally play out.

The headache in my temples won't rub out and the Tums I keep in the desk drawer don't help with the disgust I feel about everything. My interaction, or lack of, with Rasheed still has my chest feeling tight. The closest bench to sit on is full of graffiti, but it will have to do while I wait for Dana. There's an older black man, sportily dressed, with two small children feeding pigeons gathered around them.

It's cold. Easterners laugh at our warm California winters, but those funny looking blue-winged birds with triangle shaped heads are cold, too. The one string of hair that marks their oddity blows in the wind and they huddle together. The birds in the estuary depend on the array of crusty hot dog buns, dried bread, and whatever people see fit to share with them.

When the children's scattered breadcrumbs run out, the flock of birds snuggles close for warmth, and almost on cue, I pull my jacket tighter trying to match their efforts against the wind. Am I like them? Looking for a warmer climate, only to be fooled? Ending up in a place where harshness is just a gust away, required to hope that this time, it will be different. It makes no sense for me to wonder this, but are black folks like these birds, migrating to look for a warmer, less harsh way of life?

My desire to go to sleep is so strong that my eyes stay closed. Except for my head that keeps rocking, I'd probably be dead asleep. A firm pressure on my shoe opens my eyes. It's Dana, and she's standing over me like a fitness trainer. Her swept-up ponytail makes her seem much taller. I rub my jaw to loosen the hold it has on my face. The tightness and numbness that set in after I saw Rasheed's picture haven't left.

"Wake up, girlfriend. We're walking, not sleeping," Dana orders, with her hands on her hips.

The bright glare from the clear sky makes me rub my eyes.

"Just thinking," I say.

"Right—with your eyes closed. Someone needs to get more sleep, that's what I think."

I just shrug my shoulders and stretch my arms upward, as if I was trying to get out of bed.

"Aren't you the one who calls sitting with your eyes closed, day-dreaming in the shadows?" I ask.

"I say that all the time and I still think you need to get more sleep."

Her tone is playful, but I catch her tone of authority. Her matter-of-fact statement lets me know her opinion whether I'm sleeping enough is not up for debate. Dana says I'm responsible for when the sun gets up and not the other way around. I haven't told her wakeful nights are times for thinking about something my best friend wouldn't understand.

"Remember when David caught us sleeping at the A's game?" I ask.

The question I hope moves the subject away from my sleeping problems and the way things turned out with Rasheed. I don't think I'll say anything about that to Dana.

"Oh yes, he was too through with us," she says. I know it's one of her favorite stories. Hopefully, the distraction will work.

As she breaks out into laughter, her bushy ponytail flops in the air, and she has a good laugh at the thought of us falling asleep at the biggest sporting event of the year.

"How much did those seats cost, again?" I say to lead her on.

"I think it was five or six hundred—a piece. It was the World Series makeup game after the '89 earthquake. You know they weren't cheap. He was so angry."

"And it was the A's and the Giants." I let my voice drop to underscore how mad David was at the two of us.

We both shake our heads. Dana goes on to say, for the hundredth time, how David's extended display of sulking lasted a week or more, how he could not believe that in a luxury box full of Who's Who in the Bay Area, we both went to sleep.

"Girl, it took a lot of punani to get that man to calm down and talk about something else."

She uses her shoes to pull my legs from the bench, trying to get me to stand. I get up slowly, grabbing her reached out hand that helps me get up.

"And what were you so involved in you needed your eyes closed?" She asks this question with a head dip and raised eye, and her voice in that familiar I-expect-you-to-tell-me sound.

I don't feel like telling her what I was thinking about, even if she is giving me the big-sister attitude, so I say, "Just daydreaming."

"Car, your daydreams are always about something important. So, what's up?"

I sigh.

"Really nothing, just thinking on the birds at the lake and how black folks came to Oakland to start over."

It's not much of the truth, but I did think about a bird, and me—the black person who wants a chance to start again.

"Birds and black folks. Remember when Disney cartoons had magpies talking like black people?"

"When I was growing up, we didn't own a TV," I say.

Across the long stretch of water, I easily see the courthouse. Oh God, that seems too far of a distance, especially with this headache. Dana drags my arm to start down the trail. She's still talking about watching TV and old shows like *Good Times*, *The Jeffersons*, and who knows what.

"Hello, in there," Dana says.

She's pretending to knock on my head.

"Car, you still here? We're past the courthouse and you've been sleepwalking the whole way, ever since I asked you about watching TV."

I look around and see we are going past the Park and Rec building and the mother of all oak trees in Oakland. We are past the halfway mark and I don't remember getting here.

"Guess I got lost in another daydream," I say, sounding irritated and huffy.

"When's the last time you had good sex?"

Her question comes out of the blue and her voice is not quiet.

"Dana!" I almost shout. "Why are you asking me that?"

I look around the trail, lined with twisted manzanita trees, to see if anyone is walking close enough to overhear her ask about my sex life. A Mexican family some 20 yards ahead is preoccupied with keeping their children walking. The couple behind us wearing matching blue sweat suits and holding hands quickly passes by us, oblivious to anyone but each other.

"Just thinking. The other morning I got up and fried David some chicken wings. I thought about making him some fish and grits, too."

"Please, I don't want to hear about your Jill Scott moments."

My frown shows annoyance. She smiles, shakes her body as she continues walking, but she doesn't go any further trying to get me to talk about my sex life. We're back to walking quietly, my insides feel heated and bursting with things I haven't told Dana. It's all getting backed up—where do I even start? I count the little lights strung on wire 12 feet in the air. This keeps my head looking up, but when they turn on, we both look at each other with surprise. It's at least two hours before darkness falls.

"The days are longer," Dana says. "Every time they come on, I think about little rays of light shining on Oakland."

As we're walking, Dana smiles and waves at most of the people we pass by. She seems to be in a good mood. I imagine the lights are a prod to say something about what's been on my mind.

"How crazy would a person be if everything around them is a mess, except for stacks and stacks of magazines and they don't throw them out because it means they're throwing black people away?"

Her almost six-foot frame looks down at me and her eyebrows squirm. I can only imagine what she's thinking.

"And does that person have years of *Ebony* and *Jet*'s so old they're losing color?"

"Yes. They have *Black Enterprise* and Oprah's *O* magazine, too."

I know it's silly to talk like this about something so important, but I couldn't get it out any other way.

"Are you asking my professional opinion?" she asks.

It's hard to tell the difference between Dana's professional opinion and a Dana truism. I'll just have to wait to see which one of her shows up. I turn my head to the side so she can see my eyes when I nod yes.

"I know it sounds crazy, but I feel close to them."

I've ended the silly game of speaking in third person and now I feel exposed that my real feelings are coming out.

"Mmm, I see." She moves closer to me as we continue to walk.

"I move them around by similar covers, and I put men, women, and celebrities in different stacks. They never stay in the same pile for long."

"And what are you thinking about when you're moving the magazines around?"

"I'm not sure. I just like the covers to be in some kind of order."

Why doesn't she just say, "Yes, that's crazy behavior, Carla?"

"You know this big fancy degree I have?" she says.

"Who doesn't?"

"Well, I need you to hear what I think could be happening."

She stops us walking and we move away from the trail to stand near the side of the Park and Rec building. Dana's looking directly at me and I return the stare.

My head hurts. I shouldn't have walked this far.

"All right Carla, be mad if you want, but to me it sounds like OCD—obsessive compulsive disorder."

"OCD? Oh please."

"Yes, the way you describe compulsively moving them around, fear of getting rid of them or breaking your routine, all sound like symptoms of OCD."

"It's not that, Dana."

"You asked for my professional opinion, didn't you?"

"Yeah, but that's not it. It's black people in the garbage smiling back—that's what doesn't seem right."

"Smiling in the garbage? Recycle or better yet, donate them. Think how many art projects will be made. I see vision boards everywhere."

"Dana, I don't want to get rid of any. None of them."

A cold wave hits my stomach. I'm not sure if it's from anger or fear that I've exposed some of my real thoughts to Dana.

"You've carried them around with you for years. What do they represent? What are you holding on to, Car?"

"Oh please, Dana, don't psychobabble me. No wonder Aaron hangs up on you."

I don't care how she might feel that I brought her brother into the conversation. My outburst causes a loud silence between us, but there's no denying that came from my mouth. Dana looks at me with no expression. I can't tell if I hurt her feelings. I only wanted to talk about the magazines. If she hadn't gotten so serious psychoanalyzing me, maybe I wouldn't have done that. The silence between us is screaming. As we start walking again, we are on separate sides of the trail, not looking at each other. I try to count the small fish swimming in the shallow water. Eventually, Dana walks back close enough to have the outside of our arms touching.

"Sorry for what I said about Aaron."

"You might be right. Maybe that is why he hangs up on me. Car, are you still wondering about crazy?"

"Maybe."

Really, I don't know what I'm wondering about right now.

"Actually, I was thinking how there's so many ways people look at the word—especially, our people. I mean there's *crazy*, as in "That nigger is so *crazy*, don't even think about messing with him or her.""

"Don't use that word—I hate it."

It makes me think about what Thomas told me on the day Rasheed had his fight. I hated hearing it then and still don't get the difference if it ends with an "a" or an "er."

"I'm just making my point," Dana says.

I need a break from walking, my stomach is catching up with me, and before Dana can say anything, I slump on the nearest bench on the trail towards Fairyland. Her mouth drops open with surprise that I stopped walking with no announcement of my intention to sit down.

"Okay, let's take a rest. I can see you need it."

She moves to stand on the side of the bench stretching her legs. My mind flies away, waiting for her to get to the destination of all things she considers important. Two young men with sagging pants are feeding ducks. One keeps a toddler from falling into the water, while the other has a child's little fingers grasping onto his hand.

"Where was I? Right. *Crazy* can also mean your nose is so wide open from being in love you can't see straight, or too many times it's someone with odd behavior and everybody just walks around them because they're scary to be near."

"Do you always have to give multiple choices?"

"*Crazy* is also an impolite, incorrect, and very rude way to refer to a person with a mental health problem and then again…"

Is she finally finished?

". . . it could simply mean something is not making sense." She peers into my eyes.

"Are you done?" I ask sarcastically.

"Yes, I am. Now, which *crazy* were you talking about?"

"As in it doesn't make sense to get rid of my magazines."

"You're making a big to do about this. Throwing away a magazine doesn't mean that you don't care or that black people don't matter anymore."

I stare right past her at brown-winged birds flying off and diving with their heads first into the water looking for something. I count the ones sitting in the middle of the lake on the buoys. Dana's responses didn't get to that itch. She's my best friend, but she doesn't get it.

"So Carla, what's up?"

"Damn it's cold."

She rolls her eyes and nudges my shoulder. I feel teary but don't want to cry. I'm not sure how to get started. Dana sees the water in my eyes and with alarm in her voice she asks, "Has something bad happened Carla? What aren't you telling me?"

"I'm not sure how to say it." "Are you sick? Is that why you went to the doctor?"

"No, I'm not sick. It was for my fibroids."

Dana's sits on the hard bench and turns to place her closest arm around my back.

"Oh. You had me worried. Are they pushing you to have surgery?"

She pats my hand. I feel circled by her but it doesn't feel soothing at all.

"No, that's not it," I drag words out, slowly. "I'm not sure what makes sense anymore."

"Tell me about it. There's a lot going on in the world that can be considered crazy."

"It's everything...."

"Well, are you going to tell me what *everything* is? I'm here, Carla, why else would I sit in this cold ass air on a bench with you?"

"Today was Rasheed's first day back after his suspension."

I thought I wasn't going to talk about this.

"He wouldn't look at me and he drew a picture and left it on his desk; it had the words, "I hate," written on it."

I feel myself sinking, again, as I think about losing Rasheed—about it all.

"I know you're either real sad or real angry about the whole thing. But every child is not going to be saved. You tried, Car."

"You know, sometimes I think about dying—not being here anymore."

"You spend a lot of time going out to your mother's, that job is working your last nerve, and I can understand why you'd think about leaving."

"No, I mean . . . I mean . . . I really want to be gone from everything."

"I know how you feel, Car. A lot of women just want to run away and be done with it. Society is not making it easy on us."

I just look at her—didn't she hear me say I want to die? An awkward silence comes between us. Does she even get what "I want to leave" really means?

"Dana, remember the poet? Ever since I heard her poem about the damn pot liquor, twisted stomachs, empty souls, it won't leave my head. She named feelings I didn't know I had."

"Yeah, she stepped on lots of toes with that one."

Why is she ignoring the obvious? I'm telling her I want to kill myself and she's talking about other peoples' toes. Damn, Dana, not you, too. Why aren't you listening to me? Do I have to spell it out? Haven't I said it?

I look out across the lake, paying more attention to small waves rippling across it. I'm done with trying to have Dana understand. I can't get up. My legs feel like Jell-O so I sit and listen, only saying a few meaningless words. This is so far from how I imagined it would go when I eventually told her my real feelings that I'm numb about what to do now.

"I've done a lot of research on who we've become, what it means to be a triple B, a black Baby Boomer."

The feeling that I'm floating won't let my legs move and is moving up into my arms. I imagine my head has disconnected from my body and is hanging, suspended in the air, looking down at my friend.

"Pretty good huh? Black baby boomer is a tongue twister."

She goes on not paying attention to see if I am listening. My mind stays drifting in the air where I can pretend I'm not really sitting next to her.

"In the United States, baby boomers were born from 1946 to 1964. We make up 30% of the population, almost 70 million people; over 9 million are triple Bs."

Dana's acting like Mama, Ed, Clyde, the doctor, even Rasheed—who's made it obvious he isn't going to give me a chance to say something to make things right between us. I'd hoped she would point her researcher, or even that she's-my-best-friend mind on me, to help me to dig out all the bones that feel twisted.

"Dana, Dana." I interrupt. Her statistical rant is making my head hurt harder.

"Sorry. You know me and numbers. Car, we're different from white baby boomers sandwiched between their parents and the generation after them. And right now, you're like a bad salami sandwich."

"Dana!" I raise my voice the best that I can with this headache. "What is your point?"

Now, I'm angry. I so need to go home. My stomach has turned back into the knots of the morning. I'm mad at myself, because I don't know how to get up and just leave. All night I tossed over, even cried about, how to tell Dana. She's the one person I thought would see me, help me to stop spiraling down, and she's telling me about black people being discriminated against. I know that—everyone does. What happened to her saying she'd be devastated, if one day she learned I had taken my life?

She continues with her crazy explanation.

"What's important is back in the early forties, black people had grandparents, maybe even parents, who could tell them something about slavery. That's the bottom side of the sandwich—the top is a whole generation that knows little to nothing about Jim Crow, lynching, cross burnings, marches, bombings, red-lining."

"Dana, I don't feel good. I think I should go."

I finally find my feet to stand and turn towards the path that will take us back to our cars. The sun is setting yet I can still see a small blue patch through the clouds and the evening fog that's rolling over it. Dana hasn't missed a beat as we walk—she's still giving me her opinion why I feel so bad—*overwhelmed*, as she says.

"Why are you telling me this Dana?"

How far to get to our cars is all I can think about now, as she answers my question.

"Because we're just like the mystery meat they call salami, shredded up culture, manipulated, and shaped to enter white institutions, with little care for what it meant to our emotions to even be there. I'm sorry, and Lord don't strike me down, even to our parents what mattered the most is that we were there—not how we felt about it. And to make it worse, we're the ones who remember what everyone else wants to forget. But without knowing our emotions, it's like your stomach's processing that sandwich without enzymes to break it down."

What do you say when someone compares your life to a bad sandwich, says you don't have enzymes to break it down? Dana is the one talking crazy.

The walk back to the car is a blur. I've been staring at the waning blue patch in the sky and Dana's been talking the whole way. I can't take this anymore—the urge to flee from my friend grips me and ungraciously, I pull my door open without looking at her. I turn to say, "You don't get it, do you?"

Everything inside wants to scream, "Dana you don't know anything, I'm dying right in front of you!" Instead, I jump in quickly to start the engine and I'm gone. As I pull off, I see her standing in the parking lot with confusion written all over her face. I hadn't hugged her like I normally do. I just couldn't. I can't pretend anymore that I'm listening, marveling at how smart she is, not jealous she has David. He's there for her and I have nothing to land softly on when my world spins out of control.

Damn her. In all that talking, not once did she think to say, "I'm so sorry Carla. I had no idea you were feeling that way, but now that I do know, you can count on me." Instead, her newfound information about black people was wrapped in a lecture, something she's so sure would help. That was supposed to give me what?

CHAPTER TWELVE

The heat's been off all day, and now my apartment walls are holding on to the Bay Area chill. Daddy's old robe will help warm me up along with this fifth of Courvoisier I picked up after our walk. My legs feel weary and sinking into the couch brings attention to the ache in my hip. Whether to open the curtains or keep them closed feels like a really big decision. I want to look out the window and watch the nothingness as night falls. But if neighbors walk by they'll look in—they always do—so I decide to close the crack between the curtains with a safety pin.

If the kitchen had a door, I wouldn't have to see all this. The only thing not a mess is the glass cabinet holding my brandy snifters. They're lined up in an orderly fashion and they look acceptable, but I don't think the small ones are going to work tonight. I want the huge one like at the club so I can swish my drink around and dip my face into the glass. A quick swirl and down goes the first, the cognac is sweet and then bitter, but it's the warmth in my chest I'm looking for. I don't remember pricking my finger on the safety pin; I wonder if sucking the blood makes this a Sacrament?

I can take only one more trip to the bedroom because bending and carrying magazine stacks to the living room is making me dizzy. I had better sit down. This should be enough pillows to make a chair on the floor. The ache in my hip feels nauseating. When I used to sit on the floor next to Daddy, it didn't take this much. Why did I get down so soon? It'll be too hard to get up now.

I guess the hall light will just have to stay on. I've got everything I need—the bottle is close, the magazine stacks are high enough for a good armrest, and these pillows and dirty clothes work well for a seat cushion. I should have made a toast before I drank half of my glass down. With my hand lifted ceremoniously in the air I say, "Here's to the people who think they know so much—which includes you, Dana Washington."

That Dana, to her everything's a theory, and oh please that salami sandwich bit, she really got ridiculous with that one. She makes me mad when she does that. It's never about me, or whenever it is, she's telling me how to live my life. Are you doing what you should be doing? Have you talked to Aaron, Dana? No, and you say it's so important. You know what I think? You just don't want to be bothered if it's not pretty or wrapped up in one of your fancy theories.

During the week I planned how I was going to do this, and so far my plan is working. This first stack has my favorite magazines. They're old, but this one I remember has this man in a car advertisement who except for the golden-brown hair, looks a lot like Daddy. I like the way he leans against the car with his arms crossed and a wide grin. He looks satisfied. *Daddy, I remember you looking like that. You left before I could learn how to cross my arms and feel what it's like to have satisfaction written all over my face.* I'm tired of people not telling the truth. I always have to guess. Mama and Clarence knew the truth, that you were dying, but they didn't say anything.

My legs start kicking up and down and thrashing around, magazines that were neatly piled up on each other scatter across the carpet. Some get their covers torn off as I kick my heels on top of them. Oh God, I'm breathing so hard, all that movement has me hot and sweaty. The smooth glass against my cheek feels cool, but my face is warm from these hot tears.

Daddy, everyone had secrets from me, I watched, tried to see what was going on, but they always sent me to the porch, told me to leave the room. You never did that. If I could be Otis right now, I'd roll my head on the floor like he did when he was confused. *Do you remember him doing that when he didn't understand what you wanted from him? What should I do now? I know I missed the chance to soothe you, Daddy, and I did it again with Rasheed.* I saw how sensitive he was, how he cares about everyone even if he doesn't speak. The fight couldn't erase that, could it? No...I just had to let him know I was the one in control and demand he speak to me right then.

I need to listen to music, and something that can't be played on that fancy Bose. My old vinyl albums are on the bottom shelf, and crawling to the other side of the living room will be worth it. The needle on the turntable may be old, but it works for me, because this is the sound I need to hear now. Oh, Aretha...please tell me what to do. *Call Me,* my tears fall every time I hear you sing that you don't want people to forget about you.

Dana says, "Call me," and then she sashays away without a care in the world. I've been trying to tell her my secrets. How could I be friends with someone for so long and she doesn't know what I'm doing? She acted like telling her that I'm through and I don't see the use anymore is something I say every day. She doesn't get it—she really doesn't.

David's home—gotta go—that's what you always say. Well, here's a toast to you, Miss I'm-a-phone-call-away, Miss use-the-oil-and-breathe. Can you tell how mad I am now, Dana? Can you hear me now?

Well, Miss just-a-phone-call-away, sometimes I need you to hear what *I'm* saying. Maybe I don't have it like you and David, but my father loved me—his only daughter. I had sweetness with him and damn it, I miss it.

And then Mama went frozen on me. You went frozen, forgot you were a big part of our family, or maybe you didn't want us anymore after he died. Well, this next drink is for you, Mama. Let's just pour it on top of the heat that's already in my belly.

I miss Daddy and after all these years it still hurts to know I needed to fight somebody to have our last goodbye. Mama, you and Clarence caused that, because neither one of you wanted to tell me the truth. Did it scare you to tell me he was dying?

Remember that time I was sitting at the kitchen table finishing my dinner, and you and Daddy were kissing in the pantry? I heard what you said. You told him he was like honey, like music that made you sway and dip. I heard everything, Mama—only a curtain separated that little room from the kitchen. When you came out you pushed the back of my head and told me, that's my man, and don't you forget it. I was only eight. I didn't have it backwards—did you? What was wrong with you? Don't lie to me Mama, after he died you took it all away on purpose, didn't you? You were supposed to keep it going, you know Daddy would have wanted it that way. These tears I'm crying, they're not for you, Mama, they're for Daddy, and I'm going to see him soon.

I remember the day before he died. I was curled up on the floor near his bed reading the newspaper out loud. His eyes were beginning to close more often, but when they opened they fixed on me. The next day I ran home from the bus stop to sit on the floor next to him. I knew something was different, so I didn't try to read the paper. I just kept looking at him, hoping to see his eyes sparkle again.

Mama, I told you something was wrong, and you didn't pay any attention to what I said. Clarence, while you were in the hallway taking off your work shoes, I told you too. You shushed me and said he was probably just having a bad day.

I stayed by Daddy's side, pretending to read but watching him closely. I kept thinking somebody should be doing something. Wasn't the nurse supposed to come and help with his pain? When you came back, Mama, you fell asleep holding his hand, and then you whispered, "Carla, he's going to be okay." Then you got up and left me to stand guard and watch for death to come. I wanted to scream—he's not okay—Daddy is leaving! But I stayed quiet. I saw his sweetness slipping away, while Mama you pretended not to see. I was on the floor, leaned against the bed where he lay with his eyes closed. When he touched me on the shoulder he could barely speak. "Baby, go tell your Mama I need to go to the hospital," is what he said. That's when I ran to the bottom of the stairs and called out to everybody. Mama, you and Clarence had no right to keep me from Daddy's last goodbye.

I should have fought to go to the hospital. But when the ambulance came and the two men with a stretcher rushed in, Clarence, you shouted at me to go upstairs and stay out of the way. Mama, I called out to you—didn't you see my eyes asking if I could stay? I didn't know what your look meant, and then you turned back to Daddy. I should have been in the car when you and everyone else left for the hospital. What was Clarence trying to protect me from—a goodbye?

Daddy you needed me—saying goodbye was how we always did. I know you were looking for me. I wasn't too young to understand—I knew. Oh, God...I know you looked for me. Did you tell them to go get me when you realized I wasn't there, and they just didn't listen?

My body easily sways to Anita Baker singing *I Apologize*.

I apologize Daddy, believe me I do.

The cognac has eased me into a place where I know what I know. I sway with the music and see Mama in the glass saying, "Your daddy told me to tell you children..." I think she made all that up. She never told us how much you loved us. Mama's been so afraid of everything. She never listened when I reminded her that you always told me, "Baby, you and your brothers be happy. It's there... just choose what's gone bring it to you, and stay away from what won't."

Daddy, I'm not happy. I chose wrong.

I can't stand to look at how puffy my face is from all these crying songs. It's late, I hurt, I'm tired. This Vicodin for cramps caused by these damn fibroids has been sitting in the medicine cabinet for months. Take two every six hours for pain—well, pain is what I got. I turn the bottle over and over, shaking the little white, oblong pills inside. The sound reminds me of the gourds women play in the drumming circle at the Berkeley Flea Market. I grip the pill bottle and shake it up and down, harder and louder. There are more than enough pills here to end my biggest pain.

What I want now is another drink, and to sway with this music that takes me back and leads me away. What becomes of the broken hearted, who has love that's now departed? That's your record, Mama. You don't even know I took it home with me, and been playing it over and over in honor of Daddy.

Oh God, I long for everything to be different. My mind won't rest. Mama, your prescription for loss—don't talk about it, just work hard to be acceptable, is that you telling me to drink the pot liquor, no matter what? Damn that girl and her poetry. How dare she push thoughts into my head.

My magazines are all neatly stacked against the bedroom walls, the special stack I made just waiting for me. All week after work I dug through the earliest editions looking for pictures of Daddy. Some magazines smell like mildew and the covers are fragile, but I was careful to put the ones I wanted into a tight stack, ceremoniously laying one on top of the other so that I could sit on them. I wanted Daddy in one place, easily available like when his sickness forced him to lie in the living room, and every day he waited for me. The brandy has me wobbly but with some shifting I'm able to sit on top of the stack.

So now what, Carla? How will you say goodbye?

I have a full drink in one hand and the bottle of pills in the other. I feel like a little girl sitting on a bench, my legs move up and down and kick the magazines, first hard and then softly, causing my body to rock back and forth.

I'm sorry, Daddy, just so sorry. When you died, Mama said you told her to keep us safe, and she did. The boys never got involved with the trouble in the streets—even though they wanted to. I had magazines and I looked for you all the time in the pictures. I went to school and became a teacher. Mama says you'd be proud of me. Daddy, I never got pregnant. I looked but I never found a man I thought could be like you. I'm sorry I didn't bring you any grandchildren, but Clarence, Arthur, Jr. and Otis brought you seven; five big boys taller than their daddies and two girls you'd love to pick up so you could plant kisses on their foreheads like you did with me. We sold the house. I know Daddy, that was your gift to the family, but Mama couldn't stay by herself and none of us wanted to live there. We kept it nice, but we just couldn't stay, and now I can't stay here any longer either. You know what that feels like, don't you?

Every day you'd ask me if I'd done all my homework. I'd say, "Yes, sir", and then run to get the newspaper so we could read it together. But now, Daddy, I haven't done my work. It's too, too much. The sweetness in everything is gone. Mama didn't want to talk about you, and down here without you, I won't ever know about your dreams. I didn't help a boy in my class who needed me, and I know he's watching. I can't find the will to fight, Daddy, I want to rest—like you.

Shit! I start to throw my glass, but stop myself. My other arm feels like it's lifting on its own and the hand holding the pill bottle throws it across the room. It hits the wall, rattles to the floor and rolls underneath the end table. I smell terrible. Is this wet spot on my robe, a spilled drink? I remember stumbling into the living room but how did I end up with my arms and legs spread across the rug? The sweet aroma of Courvosier is gone and now it stinks. My mouth is so dry. I start kicking everything in reach—pillows, magazines, and furniture. I hit a lamp and it falls over and breaks. I want to scream, but my stomach's heaving up and down so fast that I can't. I needed to break more than a lamp damn it, nothing has changed!

Clarence was right. Don't be fooled. Black people ain't all that happy. I don't want to look at you magazines, get away from me; leave me alone! I rip a cover off, and then another one and another one and throw the crumpled papers at the closed curtains. A page with Daddy's likeness on it makes me stop. My cheeks are wet and salty. Teardrops roll off my face and onto the page, causing it to wrinkle.

What now, Daddy? I tear the picture out and crumble it on my face, rubbing, mashing and grabbing at my cheeks and at the paper. My sobs come faster and the paper gets wetter. *I'm sorry, Daddy, I'm mad and tired—you left because you said it hurt too much. I'm hurting every day and I'm ready to let go, too.*

I look at what's left of the picture in my hand and try to smooth out the man's wet face with my fingers. The pill bottle is still where it rolled under the table. All I need to do is crawl over there to get them back, put them in my pocket so I'll have them when I'm ready to try again. I don't know what happened—I'm supposed to be gone.

It's already morning. I can see a faint sun shining through the curtains. I'm not going to make it to the afternoon if I stay here alone. I could call Dana but what if David doesn't let her pick up the phone? It's still early. I've never felt so scared of me like I feel right now. A cold sweat is breaking out and my stomach's turning. I don't know what to do—I feel like throwing up.

I make it to the bathroom and vomit up the remnants of last night from my belly. The tile floor hurts my knees, but there's no choice, my body is out of my control and brown liquid is forcing its way out. I hug the cold bowl to keep from falling over, and dry heaves won't let me get up yet.

Now, nothing is happening. My stomach has stopped trying to turn inside out, sweat dripping down my face stings my eyes, but I'm afraid to move because I'm still queasy. The morning sun coming through the window is hot on my back, and the cold air from the bowl is cooling my face. What a crazy night. My eyes open to caked-up shit under the toilet rim, the sight of it and the stench of vomit make me pull my head out of the toilet so fast that I fall back against the wall. Oh God, I don't know what to do. A sunbeam from the window lands on my chest and sprays warmth across me, lulling me into sleep.

I must have been asleep and curled up on the floor a while. My neck feels stiff and oh, my hip. Truth is, everything hurts. I feel something stabbing my side and realize I've been lying on my cell phone. I need to leave the bathroom. It smells horrible in here. The side of the tub serves as a crutch, and I lean on the edge to push myself up and off the floor.

Oh no, look at this mess—I tore up my magazines. My favorite lamp, the ceramic one is, is shattered to pieces. Carla, sit down and think. What now? What are you going to do? My fingernails scratch up and down my neck, it hurts, but the pain lets me know I'm alive.

Oh God, I wanted to kill myself, and I tried—look at the shambles in my living room. But, there has to be a part of me that doesn't want to go, it's not natural, but the itch in my soul, the pain in my bones; how do I live with that? If I leave, I'll see Daddy, maybe, and if I stay what's going to be different? What will Mama say if I kill myself? And my brothers will be so mad. They would never understand what happened. I had convinced myself this would set me free, I'm not as sure as I was last night. It hurts to even be thinking that way now.

I feel sick to my stomach and sick in my mind, for the first time I want to call someone—I need help. Maybe Mama's right that I could use more than one friend, someone besides Dana to call. I'm so upset with her, but she's the only friend I have. I look at the pill bottle under the table as I move to the kitchen. While drinking a glass of water I keep eyeing them. My hand slips into the side pocket of my robe and I hit the speed dial.

" Uh, hi David, I'm sorry, but is Dana awake?"

"Car, are you alright? It's so early, I almost didn't pick up the phone."

"I'm okay. I had a rough night. I need to speak with Dana."

Through the phone I hear him say, "Babe, wake up babe, it's Carla. She sounds real upset."

"Car? What's going on? You okay?"

"Kinda sorta, Dana. Can you meet me in Albany in thirty minutes?"

"I'm still in the bed, but I'll get up. You want me to come get you?"

"No, no that's okay," I say quickly, "I'm fine, just meet me there in the parking lot."

"Okay I'll see you in thirty minutes." Dana says.

A quick wash up and brushing my teeth is the most I can handle. I need to leave soon before I change my mind. Take the back streets I tell myself, the freeway has too much speed and a dip over the guardrail would be too tempting. The ride down San Pablo Avenue takes me away from the Oakland sun into an early morning fog that eerily hovers close to the ground. It's too early for the usual crowd of people who wait on the sidewalk for a table at their favorite breakfast places, and only a few people are heading into the McDonalds. Even though I washed my face, a look in the side mirror tells me my eyes are still puffy. There's nothing I can do about that now.

I see Dana's already in the parking lot, sitting with the top up on her convertible. As I get closer she looks like she's dressed for winter. I still don't know if I'm ready for this, but I park alongside her, turn off the engine and a deep sigh comes out. Dana gets out to greet me at my car, gives me a weird look and a tentative hug.

"Let's walk to the artist colony before we start talking," she says.

"Alright," I say and stuff my hands in my pockets for warmth.

We take the upper trail that leads us up a hill and then forks off to the right. Along the way I notice a few people in sleeping bags in the bushes. They don't stir as we walk past their makeshift homes. At the bottom of the hill, the goddess statue that stands some twenty feet tall, made of mix-matched painted wood and steel, has her arm extended out, her hand invites us to join her near the edge of the Bay waters and the small pond surrounded by driftwood paintings and rock statues.

"Let's sit here." Dana points to a bench sized rock. Her raised eyebrow and wrinkled forehead tell me she wonders what's going on. I join her to sit down, and she pushes closer so our hips touch. As we sit in the low fog, my mind races with images of alcohol, my crying songs, talking to Daddy on a stack of magazines, the pill bottle. I don't know which one to talk about, or how to begin.

"I'm glad you called," she says, "I thought you were mad at me."

"I know it's early for you to be out on a Saturday."

"It's okay."

I don't say anything and she doesn't push so we sit quietly on the hard flat rock, staring across the water. Even through the fog I can see all three bridges, just like when I was young. The Golden Gate Bridge is still orange, but it doesn't matter anymore. As the waves wash in they bring me a little closer to myself, soothing dark thoughts, then just as fast as they wash out to rejoin the deep ocean waters, they carry me away again.

"You know I love you Carla, and David loves you a whole lot, too."

"I know that's what you guys say."

"Last night David cooked, he grilled so much food I thought we were having company over, but he said it was for the week. That man loves you like a sister, he told me so, and the entire time he was cooking he kept asking me about you."

"Why would he talk about me?"

"Because he loves you . . . and I told him about how upset you were with me on Friday and I didn't know why."

"I was really tired and you were talking so much. I didn't understand what you were trying to say."

"I'm sorry, I know I get carried away sometimes."

"It's alright, I'll get over it."

"I was in the Papasan chair, the one he wants me to throw out, waiting for him to finish the dishes, and I was thinking about you."

"Damn it feels cold," I say.

"Yes, I think it was you who wanted to come out here." Dana nudges my arm.

How do I tell her what's happened? She didn't get it last time I tried, so what makes me think she will now?

"Look Carla, I can see you're not saying much, so I'll just talk, okay? I told him what you said about wanting to leave, about not wanting to be here anymore. He said he thought the same thing when he had his big depression. You remember that time don't you?"

"Some. You didn't say much about it, Dana."

She gets off the rock to stretch her legs out, bends over to touch her toes, and reaches her arms far up into the air. I wonder if she feels uneasy. I get off the rock to walk around and start counting the paintings, and the piles of stones stacked on top of each other. I need something to calm this burning feeling inside. Dana follows me to the edge of the water. She seems to watch the waves ripple on top of each other, and then stands in front of me so we're face to face.

"David and I went through a lot during that time. I'm supposed to understand depression, Carla, hell—I'm a psychologist—but when it hit so close to home, I felt helpless. Yesterday, when you told me how you felt, I didn't want to see it."

I think there has to be point where waves meet each other. The ones coming in and the ones leaving have to bump into each other, don't they? Have Dana and I finally bumped into the feelings we never speak about?

"I don't know what to say Dana. I'm afraid you won't get it and then I'll have nothing, and I'm scared to go there."

"The truth is, I pushed David so hard he had to leave our home. I didn't want you to leave me too. Sweetie, I'm really sorry."

My eyes fill up with water.

"I don't know what to do, I can't be alone right now."

"Car, I'm here. I'm not leaving you alone this time."

Her arms reach out and for the moment I allow myself to sink into them and feel my best friend holding me. My mouth tightens to hold back a rush of tears. I can't believe she won't rush off before I can really get things out.

"So let's just sit while you figure out what you want to say. I have a few things I want to talk about, too. Are you alright with that?"

Dana's voice sounds gentle. I nod yes and tears slip out. We both are crying. It's quiet near the water. No one else is around, and the only sound is the slow rush of waves and a few hungry seagulls that keep flying over us, squawking for a meal. Their squeals sound strangely spine-chilling, and I start to feel nervous when I realize maybe both of us will finally get real.

Dana breaks the silence.

"Well honey, you smell like a brewery. How much did you drink last night?"

I sit up straight, breaking Dana's full arm hug around my shoulders. Her voice is still low and sweet, but her question not only makes me feel embarrassed, it makes me angry to think that after I tell her I can't be alone the first thing she wants to tell me is I drank too much.

"More than I want to say," I snap.

"Where'd you go? And I bet you went alone."

"I was at home, Dana."

I start to sob. I get off the rock, needing to put space between us. A surge of cold waves rushes into my stomach—an explosion is getting ready to come.

"I drank the whole bottle, okay? I wanted to leave, to kill myself. I was done. The pills threw themselves. I threw up. I saw my own shit. A sunbeam saved me. I fell asleep on the bathroom floor, called you, and nothing makes sense any more. That's where I was, okay!" I scream. My swinging arms pound fists into my thighs and my feet stomp the ground.

"Well, I see that fit of temper has been a long time coming," Dana says when I finish.

She just looks at me, acting all nonchalant with her legs crossed.

"Dana!" I scream, again. "What happened to 'I don't want to upset you like I did with David'? Didn't you hear anything I said?"

"You just told me something big, and I'm glad you said it that way. I think you've been holding on to that anger for a long, long time."

I throw my arms in the air with all the frustration of trying to open a can with no opener. God, is this really my friend?

"Want to stomp some more? I'll do it with you."

Dana stands, walks towards me and grab my arms. I try to pull back, but she grips them tightly and then starts to stomp her feet, hard, first one, then the other. I let her guide me into stomping the mess out of the ground. We keep doing this, stamping and cursing, until I pull away to cover my face and sob loudly. We're both breathing hard. I feel exhausted and unable to move, Dana takes my arm and leads me back to our perch on the rock.

"I brought tissues. I thought we might be needing some."

"Dana, I keep thinking that if I die, I can finally rest."

I take a tissue to wipe my nose, and she hands me another one before I rub my eyes with the same snotty tissue. My nephew's scull cap is pulled down over my eyes, I don't want to see or be seen. Through the cap Dana holds my head, her hands are squeezing down tight, it feels like a grip on my sanity.

"This is a start. What else do you think about—besides killing yourself?"

"Oh God. Dana, I think about everything. My mind doesn't stop."

I can't stay in this hold, or breathe, so I tear off the cap and look to the sky as if something up there will help, but all I see is fog and clouds.

"I know it's hard. But tell me about it. I'm not going anywhere. I know you spend a lot of time going out to your mother's, and that your job is working your last nerve. I've been listening."

I drop my head from looking at the sky to fixate on the rocky ground.

"Every time I think about my father, I just get sad," I eventually say. "It's like I feel so young about it. I know it's been years, but I miss him."

"I'm so sorry, Carla. I know you loved him dearly. What else are you thinking about?"

"I think about Mama. She's not dying but she's so weak now. Rasheed makes me think I shouldn't teach anymore. Everything just seems so messed up."

"I know, honey, it all feels hard. I'm sorry I didn't try harder to find out what was going on. I was scared you'd think I was just being bossy or pushy."

"You are bossy," I sniff through tears.

"You and David make two, so I guess I must be."

Dana pulls the electric green vest I bought her tight to her chest, protecting herself from the chill. She smiles and nods for me to continue.

"After our walk I was so mad at you, yesterday I told you I wanted to die and you gave me some damn statistics and talked about a silly salami sandwich."

"I knew you were upset, but I'm sorry I didn't hear you wanted to die, like I did with David. Maybe I was blocking it out, didn't want to believe that you, too, wanted to leave."

She raises her eyebrows and gives me a humble look.

"I'm so sorry girl," she says. "But I'm here now. Tell me what else you think about."

"Last night I was thinking about my father. I was sitting on top of magazines talking to him as if he was there with me, and I remember crying a lot and thinking how I was going to die that night."

"Carla, where are these thoughts coming from?"

She's back into questions. This time they feel helpful.

"I miss my father. I didn't get to say goodbye to him. What I know about him you can put on one piece of paper. He died when I was ten."

"I remember you told me that."

I begin to cry again. A familiar silence comes between us. We watch the foamy waves leaving lines of yellow bubbles on the sand until my tears stop falling.

"You miss your father," Dana says. "From what you've told me I can tell you two had a very special relationship. I imagine it was hard for you to not say goodbye. But what are you feeling about that?"

"Lost, dumb, and stupid."

"Why *dumb* and *stupid*? You were just a child."

"Because I looked for him in those stupid magazines, pretended he was in the stories, and I never asked Mama any questions. She didn't want us to talk about him."

"Oh…the magazines. Now, I see. I'm sorry I didn't get it."

"How could you? I never told you how I looked for him. Dana, when I was coming up, he was my world—he gave all of us such sweetness. There's nothing like that in my life anymore. I want him to know that I'm sorry I didn't fight to say our goodbye. I wanted to tell him that I was tired of waiting."

"Waiting for what?"

"To die so I can see him, again."

The sobs return and stay longer than any other time since we came to the water. When the crying begins to loosen its grip I look up to see a small, rounded opening in the fog where the blue sky shines through. Dana hands me more tissues.

"What do you know about your Mama?" she asks.

I look at her sideways—the question doesn't fit. It's Daddy I want to see.

"I miss my father, Dana, not Mama."

"Didn't you ever wonder who your mother was before you came along? She's the one who picked him, you know."

That thought just causes more confusion. I never thought about Mama picking Daddy. I don't know who picked who or even why they picked each other.

"They met in Texas, you know that. He was June Bug and she was Eve, everybody knew they were going to be together, and that's exactly what happened. Dana that sums it up—she doesn't say anything else."

"Your Mama's pretty tight-lipped. Mine told me everything, including some things I didn't need to know."

"I've been with her all my life. It's Daddy who was ripped away from me. Ten years wasn't long enough to know all the things about him. And like I said, Mama isn't saying much."

"Car, you can change that if you want to."

"How?"

That was Daddy's favorite saying. It's strange to hear Dana say it too.

"She's a lot older now, many elders want to talk about their days back when, but few people have the patience to sit and really listen."

"I don't know if she'd go there. Remember I told you how depressed she acts."

"And who's the depressed one now?" Dana's expression is deadpan.

"I'm just sad, real sad," I say in my own defense. "I've told you my reasons."

"Car, sweetie, what if you are depressed?"

I move away from Dana to stare out at the bridges thinking, I'm sad, and I have a right to be. I wanted to end the pain I felt.

"You wanted to kill yourself last night. But you're still here."

"But for how long?"

Dana comes up behind me and surprises me by grabbing my hand and twirling me around. She takes my other hand and starts swinging our arms back and forth like little children.

"If you get to where you're thinking about sooner than your time, David and I will find you and you will have no rest." Dana acts like she is singing.

"I can't be with you two, forever."

Dana rocks me side to side. For a while I ease into her gentle pushes on my shoulders and now she's humming some song I don't recognize.

"David will come looking for you," Dana says, still in a sing songy voice.

She encircles me with her arms until we're standing with our chins on each other's shoulders. I can't tell who is holding who tighter.

"What a picture," I say. "The wonder boy in angel wings followed by a black beatnik with a halo."

"A *beatnik with a halo*—is that how you see me?" she laughs.

Dana keeps on laughing as she dances out of our hug and pulls on my arm to steer me back to our seat. My legs still feel weak from last night and I'm nauseous, even though I drank almost a half of bottle of pink stuff before I left. Does all this humor, laughter, mean that we've made up, and that I'm past the point of asking why I should stay? I love Dana. This is the way we always talk, messing with each other and joking around, but my sadness is still here. I don't know if this is enough to make me want to stay.

"Get your mama's story, Carla. Your father's bound to be tangled up in hers."

"I know Mama." I shake my head and pull on my jacket one sleeve at a time, as if that helps me make my point. "What if she only talks about herself?"

"She won't." Dana tries to assure me. "He has to be in there."

Dana's eyes are wide and she has a wise guy smile.

"Ask her how they met and what their lives were like when they got together."

"That's it?" I think that sounds too easy.

"Be patient. Don't rush her or interrupt once she starts to talk."

"Excuse me—isn't that the pot calling the kettle black?"

"Okay, I deserve that. But remember, her story may be hard to hear. When was she born?"

"They were both born in the thirties."

"As children in Texas they saw more than a child ever needs to see."

She pauses and looks up as if waiting to develop her next point.

"Back then, segregation defined black people's lives, so the true story of a black person from the south can't be told without bringing up the Jim Crow laws."

Dana breaks into her lecture tone of voice, giving example after example of what it was like back then, and what Mama and Daddy would have experienced. I don't have the will to stop her. That's my friend's way, so I wait until she's finished.

"I forget how much of an egghead nerd you are, Dana. Yesterday, I tell you I want to die, then I tell you—again—that I want to die, and you're prepping me with a history lesson so I can go talk to my mother. Who's off here?"

"Back to your Mama. How much do you know about that time in her life?"

"Not much, probably nothing—like I keep telling you, Dr. Washington. She didn't, doesn't, won't say anything about Daddy or her life before they were together. At the house on Chestnut Street there were all these pictures of the two of them over the fireplace, along with my brothers' football and baseball trophies. She has my father's best picture on her dresser now."

"You know what I think," Dana says.

I just look at her, since she's going to tell me what she thinks no matter what I say.

"I think your mama really loved your father. They had a bone love, the kind of love everyone calls crazy—remember how we talked about that kind of crazy? Now that I think about it, Carla, you've never told me about the suitors in her life."

"She's never had another man."

Dana turns to look me in the eye. "Are you *sure*? You never know what she's not saying."

"Eve Sinclair with another man? Oh, please." I look right back at her.

"Sorry, I wasn't trying to be disrespectful, but that's how my mother made it through her hapless marriage."

"How do you know that for sure?"

"Because she said so." Dana waves her hands in the air. "I told you, she treated me like a girlfriend. She didn't keep anything a secret."

"I don't know if that was a good thing."

"Well, maybe not, but don't let my experience stop you. If you get her story it will probably help the both of you."

"Yeah, maybe. Have you talked to Aaron?"

"No, not yet. I haven't found the right time."

"Dana, it's been months. What's going on with *you*?"

"Today is your turn. We'll get to me, later."

The blue opening in the cloud has grown larger, a sign it won't be foggy all day. The air is starting to warm up and it feels good.

"That's an idea," I say faintly, but I'm trying to think how that can happen. "All that driving back and forth, and I'd have to stay a while if I want her to talk to me, and then I have to go to work. It's way too much."

"Take off from work. Take a week. You have such good attendance you should be getting one of those gold stars you give your students. You can take the time, you have to girl—this is about your life."

I thought she had forgotten why we were here in the first place. And I can't imagine showing up at Douglass as if everything were fine. Even a week at Mama's would be better than going back to work right now.

"Or, if you want, you can stay with us. I don't think you should be alone, Carla. It sounds like you are still trying to work things out, and sweetie, I'm concerned."

"I'm going out to Mama's, I don't have anything to lose in doing that. Maybe it will help."

Walking back to the cars, lots of maybes are running through my head. Maybe I will stay long enough to learn something about Daddy that I never knew. Dana wants to follow me home to help me pack. I know it's because I told her about the pills—she's probably afraid I might still take them.

"I'll be fine Dana, promise. I'll be in and out."

"I'm going to follow you home anyway. I won't come in, but if you're not out in ten minutes, I'm calling in the troops and busting that door down."

True to her word, Dana follows my car home. She ignores my "I'm okay" sign at the turnoff that would have taken her to her house. When we pull into the lot, she parks in a visitor space and gets on the phone. She's probably calling David. I try to quicken my step, but it feels more like I'm dragging myself to the elevator. It's the best I can do to hurry things along to get in the house, pack a few things and leave. When I open the door, I pay no attention to the pile of clothes and crumpled magazines on the living room floor. Seeing the empty brown Courvoisier bottle makes me want to puke again. The pills are still under the end table, but I'll leave them there. I need to shower again since Dana says I smell like a brewery.

Standing under the hot water, I think about Dana's idea to get Mama's story. I love Mama. My brothers have been there for me, but Mama, even in all the ways she went frozen, still made sure we had a home, food on the table, and knew school was always important. I don't know what her story is, but just maybe I'll learn something that helps me understand what's going on inside my head. What's Dana call it? An *emotional legacy*? Am I afraid like she says, scared to hear Mama's story? I don't know if I should hope for something different. Damn Dana, she did it again. I'm off going to do something I know nothing about.

When I return to the car, Dana is still sitting outside. I wave her off and she throws me a kiss before she heads out of the parking lot. I call Lois the Pie Queen and order a salmon croquette dinner to pick up on the way to Brentwood. The order's not ready yet so I stare at the many pictures with celebrities on the walls of the restaurant. The same woman is in most of them—I imagine that's Lois and began to wonder what's in her story that's not shown on these walls. I better call Mama and let her know I'm coming.

"Hi Mama. I'm on my way out to Brentwood."

"That's good baby but I thought you said you were coming earlier."

"I did?"

"Yes last week you said you be here early so we could have breakfast together."

I don't remember telling her that, but who knows what I said or did last week.

"I'm getting a late start but I'll be there soon."

Before driving through the Caldecott Tunnel I decide to open my sunroof. It's dark inside the tunnel and I remember to turn my lights on, the air flowing in feels cool and breezy. I feel my senses waking up, and when I come out on the other side the sun shines through, spraying heat on my chest and on the top of my head. It makes me think how just this morning it was a sunbeam that let me know I was still among the living. All of this helps my hangover, makes me think that going to Mama's might help. For the moment, I'm hopeful something different is getting ready to happen.

CHAPTER THIRTEEN

It takes three different keys for four locks to open Mama's door. At seventy-five years old, I guess this is what she needs to feel safe living alone. I take a few deep breaths, before walking in and think I'm ready.

"Hi Mama," I call out as I make my way down the hall to her little den, "I brought you some of those salmon croquettes you like so much."

I notice the walker is positioned just so, next to where she's sitting in her blue leather recliner, she must have gone to the bathroom and left it that way. Her varicose veins are so bad she has trouble standing or walking too long.

"Girl, you know your mama's starving. Just maybe, since you brought me one of my favorite things, I'll forget that you so late."

I lean over to kiss her slick thinning grey hair, and remind myself not to get too close since I only took a quick shower to wash off the funk from last night.

"Well, that's a good thing then." I ease away, hoping she doesn't smell the alcohol coming from my pores like Dana did.

I sit myself on the small loveseat next to the closet and listen to Mama talk about her new church. Her room is pleasant enough, with lots of sun coming through the windows. She has all her pictures of the family on the bookshelf. Mama Belle's quilt lays on the armrest of the loveseat. A huge television dominates the wall. It's a wonder to me that in her later years she's taken to watching so much television, when we grew up without one, and she was always giving cautionary words about not letting it take up all our time.

"You think we can get the boys to go with me on First Sunday? It's coming up soon," she asks.

"I don't know, Mama. When's Clarence coming in?"

"Didn't I tell you? He's already here."

"No. I missed hearing that one."

"You know, Sister, I like these croquettes, but next time, bring me some bread from the Merritt Bakery. The little flat dinner rolls—you know the ones that are buttery on top."

"Those rolls are so full of butter, and all that white flour is not good for you."

"Well I guess this fried fish isn't good for me either, you think?" She chews and smiles because of all her children, I'm the one who can't deny her any little pleasure she wants, and she knows it.

"All right, you got me there. Flat biscuits next time," I tell her.

"I'm talking about rolls, not biscuits, Carla. Have you heard from your brothers?"

"Okay Mama, rolls. No, maybe they'll come in tomorrow morning and we can fix a breakfast."

My brothers stopped going to church a while ago and it's never for sure if they will come for a Sunday morning service.

"You know Clarence came by himself on a two-week special assignment, he's not here with his wife."

So Clarence is here. A cold wave hits my stomach as I think about how he pushed me upstairs the night Daddy went to the hospital.

"Actually, Mama, I wanted to spend some time with you. Thought maybe we could talk about some things I've been thinking about lately."

"You was always a wondering child. What's on your mind now, baby?"

Now that I'm actually sitting with her I wonder if I can really do this. I take a deep breath to calm myself and pretend that I'm talking with Dana.

"I ran into Mrs. Greenly at the Acorn Center on Seventh and Market. We talked about the old days in the neighborhood, and it got me to thinking."

"Really? I talked to her just a few days ago and she didn't say anything about seeing you."

Uh oh. How do I make right this lie I just told? I haven't seen Mrs. Greenly in months. How could I forget that she and Mama talk all the time?

"Mrs. Greenly must have forgot," I say quickly. "It was a while back and we didn't get to talk long. She was doing errands with her son so she had to leave fast."

There's quiet in the room. Mama's looking at me, but I can't read the expression on her face. I don't know if she believes what I told her, but I'll wait to see what comes next.

"It's hard when you get old, Carla. Your mind leaves, so you can't remember things when people rush you, it just makes it worse trying to remember."

My stomach unknots and I tell myself not to make up something to say because I'm nervous about the real reason I'm here. It only makes this harder.

"So baby, what you been thinking about?"

She puts her plate down on the TV tray next to the recliner.

"Dana was telling me the story of how her parents got together, and it made me realize that I don't know much about you and Daddy. It just got me to wondering—how did you two get together?"

"I already told you about that, I'm sure I did. Maybe you just didn't hear. You know you kids don't listen to much that I say these days."

Mama adjusts herself in the chair with a frown as if she's in pain and points towards her glass of water. The sunlight coming through the sheer curtains makes me think it's still early in the afternoon. If I'm patient she might start telling me her story before she gets sleepy.

"Carla, what kinds of things you want me to tell you?" she asks without looking at me.

"Lately, I've really been missing Daddy. I miss how you two were together, and all the fun you had before he got sick. Nobody knew him better than you."

She smiles when I say this, even pats the arm of her chair some. Like Dana told me to do, I've asked the question. There's nothing else to do but wait to see what she does.

"Your daddy and me was something else. I know I said my memory is bad, but some things you never forget."

"I know what you mean, Mama. Can you tell me what you remember?"

"There's a lot to those memories, that's for sure," she says.

"I have time if you want to tell me. Remember I said I was staying the week with you."

"Yes. I was so happy to hear you say that. That's nice you won't be in such a rush to get back home."

"Nope, I'm here. So, Mama, what was it like for you and Daddy?"

"Well, I remember when he left me to come to Oakland, my life went rocky and flat like planting fields turned over. But I knew he was working on something. I was like a seed in the ground, waiting for when June Bug, your Daddy, would tell me it was time to come."

"That must have been hard. How were you able to wait like that?"

"For sure my life went flat, but in planting season you can't tell from just looking at crumbled rows of dirt that one day those fields will be full of life. Everything is underground, waiting to be taken care of by the sun, water, and the people. I knew he was going to take care of me, and me him."

Mama is looking out the window. She seems to be lost in thought, even though she continues to speak.

"He left to work in the shipyards, but truth is he wanted something else. It was the forties and lots of coloreds were leaving Texas, headed for jobs supposed to be in California. Everybody was trying to start a new life. June's uncle had already been in Oakland a few years. He was a settled man, known around the town pretty good from what your daddy told me. That's why he was able to leave and get set up so fast. June's uncle was a friend to a famous boxer. I remember his name was John Henry Lewis, and he was a world champion living right there in West Oakland. Black men had real jobs—they were firefighters, railroad workers and porters—men who made real money, owned they own homes, ran businesses, and all kinds of things. Your daddy wanted to be part of that."

"Didn't he want to find a job in Texas so you two didn't have to be separated?

Mama shakes her head.

"I got me a modern daughter who don't know what things were really like. That's your daddy's fault. He didn't want them stepping on your dreams like they did ours."

I think about how Daddy made me turn the page when I read him the newspaper. If the story was bad and he didn't want me to know about it, he'd say change it. I don't remember Mama and Daddy saying how they felt about whites. When I was young what I learned about the differences between whites and blacks came from watching what happened in our neighborhood, when I attended St. Agnes parochial school, and my magazines.

"Daddy was always sweet, but I know it was hard during the end of the Depression and harder on black folks. Billy Holiday's *Strange Fruit* came out during the time you lived in Texas, so Mama, I know."

"Well, why you ask couldn't he get a job then? Your daddy wasn't going to live a sharecropper's life. That I knew. He had finished high school. He was a smart man but couldn't pay for college. Most of the jobs in Texas were tied to working for the white folks and it was far and few between those who treated a black man fair. He didn't have no money to start something of his own, even if they had let him."

"I'm sorry, Mama. I know Daddy was proud and always did good by us. But I was wondering what it was like before you had all of us kids."

"Baby, those times were hard." She turns her face away from me. "When your daddy left all I could do was wait for him to tell me when to come. I waited, that's what I did."

I can hear the irritation in her voice. I don't want to sound naïve about what they went through. Dana, for one, talks about these things all the time. Maybe I don't want to believe that this kind of racism hit so close to home.

"What do you want to do for dinner?" I ask. It's been a little over two hours since she ate the salmon but I know it won't be long before she'll need to eat again.

Maybe a break would be good—for the both of us.

"What are you cooking for dinner? You did say you were staying the night. We got to eat before it gets too late for my evening medication."

"I am staying the night, but I forgot about dinner." I feel sheepish that I'd asked about food and hadn't made any plans about what we'd eat.

"There's a chicken thawing in the kitchen. I know my daughter." She smiles. "I'm gon' nap some while you cook dinner. Will you turn my TV on for me?"

Mama's kitchen is as immaculate as always. I think about all the pots and dirty dishes sitting in my sink and stacked up on the counter. I decide to cook the chicken on top of the stove, smother it with mushroom soup for gravy and open a can of cream style corn. While in the kitchen I think about Mama starting to tell her story. I think I'm sitting with a strange woman I'm just meeting for the first time. I wonder if we'd be friends if she weren't my Mama. Her way of storytelling feels like I'm listening to a slow drip from the faucet. How could she have been so sure Daddy was going to send for her? Sometimes people drift apart and find other interests. But she never stopped believing.

"This looks good, Carla. Got me a good nap in and woke up hungry. You're right on time," she says with a pat in her foot.

"You're welcome Mama. You've been sleep for almost two hours."

"Child when you get my age, napping and sleeping is what you do."

I sit my own tray next to her and watch television. Dana said don't rush her, so I eat slow, watch an episode of *Perry Mason* with her and listen to Mama tell him how to find out who's done it. When it's over she wants me to make some sweet milk tea. I think this means she's done for the night, although it's just early evening, but when I set the cup and saucer down she starts talking again.

"Well you know, Carla, I believed him when he said he'd send for me. Even though he was a June Bug on the outside, his insides weren't like other pretty boys folks called by that same name. There's men who jump from woman to woman, those are the trifling ones. But mine wasn't one of them. From the day he asked me to be his girl he was strong and steady. I was eleven and he was twelve. From that point on he started making plans for our life. June Bug wasn't his real name, you know."

"Of course I do," I say, noticing the impatience in my voice.

"Since I can remember, your daddy was called that. When we got older I'd tease him, saying it was strange calling a grown man a month and some kind of crawling critter. I always told him I wondered why folks put those two words together to describe a good-looking man."

Her smile tells me she's proud her husband had been such a handsome man, a man so good looking women stopped him on the street to tell him that his eyes and hair were pretty.

"When he told me he was leaving we were sitting out by the slow muddy creek a half field from my house. It was his graduation day from Carver High School. He'd been telling me all year that as soon as he got his good job he'd take me away from that red dusty place."

"How did he tell you?"

"Child, do you want to hear this story or you just going to keep asking questions? When I get to talking, let me talk or else I'll forget where I was."

"Okay, I'm sorry. Keep going." I settle back in my seat and let Mama tell me her story.

"I'm going to tell it to you just like it was happening today. That's the only way I can get it out. I remember he told me while we were staring at a full moon so bright, it looked like blue rings were circling the outside of it. We were happy. I was proud of him for graduating.

"That night he told me, 'Eve, I can't stay here no more.' His arms held me tight and I was staring at the moon, feeling good and snug in his arms. I didn't know why he wanted to leave so soon so I asked him what did he mean. We'd only been sitting out there for a while. I thought he wanted to go to the graduation party at the church.

"He squeezed me tighter and said, 'No, Eve, I mean to be leaving Love, Texas.'

"Then June looked in my eyes. He was trying to say something, but his words got stuck. He kept trying until finally he told me he couldn't stay here no more, he said he got into a situation with them Anderson boys that morning and he had to leave the next day, that he had already bought his bus ticket.

"I rose up straight like a tree. I felt so scared for your daddy. Carla, you ain't ever seen what I know, how bad mad white folks can get. I saw one lynching and it was by accident. My daddy was driving home from the next town over. He'd gone there to pick up seed and took my brothers and me with him. From the back of the truck we saw men out in the field, they didn't see my daddy's truck because he turned off the lights before we passed them. It was so many and they carried torches and was hollering all kinds of things at that poor man who was already strung up dead. I just couldn't see that happening to my June. When your daddy saw how troubled I was he pulled me back into his arms

176

and told me he had plans to stay with his Uncle Charles in Oakland. I jumped out of his arms again and asked him, 'Where is Oakland?'"

"He pulled me back closer, tighter and told me, 'Don't worry, baby, I'm sending for you when I get settled.' He told me we'd get married and start having our babies just like we had been talking about.

"I just knew something would change after June got his high-school certificate. Love, Texas was a hard place to live if you were a colored man with ideas on making life better for you and your family. Texas lynched so-called uppity colored men, and your daddy was seen that way. So even though I didn't want it to, I knew this day would come.

"Your daddy and me always sat in the dark near the creek. It was peaceful like there. After a long time sitting in that quiet, I asked him a whole bunch of questions. I wanted to know why didn't he wait, told him that next year I'd be finish with my schooling and we could leave together. I wanted to know who was going to look after him, how was he gon' get along. Maybe his uncle would get him a job but who was gon' take to his care.

"'I'm staying with my uncle,' he told me. 'I'll be all right. He says there are opportunities for a colored man there. Oakland's got an unofficial colored mayor, his name is Slim Jenkins. My uncle says he knows him real good and he can help me get a job.'

"I told him I didn't want to be in Love if he was leaving. I tried not to cry, but tears started coming down my face. Your daddy knew he had to go. He lifted the tears off my face with his finger and told me so.

"'One more year in Love, Eve, and there's a chance I might not be living no more. You know how it is when a colored man tries to do better for himself. These crackers ain't gon' let it happen.'

"What he said was true. I saw for myself how they treated a colored man, who tried to start a business, maybe buy a piece of land. He was sad about it. Then he told me something I also already knew. He said them Andersons were the same boys he'd swum naked with in that creek, and now they want him to look down when he talk to them, say 'Yessuh boss,' and act like he was still a boy. He said, 'They grown up to be men, didn't I grow up to be a man, too? I'm not going to let them get the best of me, just ain't gone happen.'

"In Love, it seemed white folks were only okay if you didn't try to do no better than be a sharecropper. As June got closer to his graduation day I saw it for myself. The white boys were egging him on, trying to get his goat so maybe he'd lose his temper and haul-off and hit one of them. A grown colored man couldn't hit a white man and live to tell it. It didn't matter what they did to make you want to. Now, if you were a boy and you hit one of them, they might, just might, overlook it, saying that boys will have their fights. A colored boy growing up wasn't a threat to the whites and those who had their own way of keeping the races separate. But when a colored boy like your daddy started growing into his man body, became strong, hard working, and let others know he was intent on finishing his schooling, doing something for himself, their whole attitude changed.

"I remember a day in town when we were picking up supplies for June's daddy. I saw them Anderson boys with their own daddy come up to the counter and step right in front of June, knowing full well he'd been there first. They turned their backs and started making small talk with the shopkeeper. June just waited it out. He pointed his finger for me to go outside till he was finished. I went. I knew he didn't want me to see him go though the indignity they were putting on him. June always said he didn't want me to see what he had to do to stay alive in that town.

"So that night when we were sitting by the creek and he told me he was leaving, I knew why all right. I came to accept it and I took the white and blue church scarf wrapped around my neck and put it around his, tying it real slow and placing it under his shirt.

"'I'm not gon' have you look at me the same way our mamas look at our daddies. I want it to be different for you and me, alright?' June said to me and he kissed me so gentle like.

"You see, I hadn't known any other life. We lived on a farm, a sharecropper's farm, and that's what Daddy and Mama did to put food on the table. It was harder on June when his family moved there from Alabama. He said it hurt him so to have his daddy pack them up and drive that old wood sided truck with all their belongings down that rusty dirt road to their new place.

"When I first saw June, I was tending the black-eyed peas in Mama's garden on the side of the house. I saw this rickety old truck with furniture tied up on the back of it. Your daddy was standing in all of it. I waved, thinking it was going to be nice to have a new colored boy move here. Even though I know he saw me, he didn't wave back. He had the most disgusted look on his face I could imagine a person his age can make. It was hard back then.

"You see it wasn't easy like you have it now, Carla. That's why I don't understand why those children keep acting up so much in Oakland, killing and fighting each other."

"It's not easy now either, Mama. It's gotten complicated." I think she doesn't have a clue about how things really are. "The schools have changed and it's hard to get good jobs."

"Complicated?" she says huffily. "Don't they have the same schools where you grew up and your brothers went to? Seems they should still be able to teach what's right and wrong even if the parents don't. Isn't that what you do in that special class you teach? I don't see what's so hard about that."

And then she's silent. I wait, for what seems a long while, sitting and wondering if she will speak again.

"Mama." I finally whisper in a low voice to get her attention.

I don't know if she's stopped talking because of what I said, but things aren't all that easy now like she thinks. But, maybe I still shouldn't have said something.

"Mama."

It's dark so I have to lean in closer to see her eyes. She's fallen asleep in the lounge chair. Each breath is releasing with a low sounding snore. I know better than to wake her so I pull Mama Belle's quilt off the armrest and cover her up with it. Mindlessly, I watch *Court TV* while I think about why she said things shouldn't be complicated when everything I know says they still are.

CHAPTER FOURTEEN

Last night, when I laid down to rest on a blowup mattress in Mama's living room, it felt like trying to sleep in a rowboat rocking on water. Every time I turned over, which was often, I ended up on the edge of the bed. The rising sun finally greets my already awakened eyes, and I think to slip out for a walk. Maybe that and some coffee will move out this melancholy I feel. I keep wondering what part of Mama's story will help me decide that my own life is something to stay around for. What can I learn from Eve and June Bug that makes a life worth living?

Moments of people watching, drifting in thought, and sipping on two lattes turns into almost two hours, more time than I had planned to be gone. Now I'm worried that I've been gone too long and fumble with the keys while trying to open Mama's four locks. She'd have even more if Arthur, Jr. hadn't told her there wasn't enough room on the door. Mama says that those who are up to no good will get frustrated and leave. Her security system makes me smile, and I relax some thinking about it. Surely the home aide has helped her to get up this morning. As soon as I open the door, I smell something burning.

"Carla, is that you?" Mama shouts from the back room she calls a den.

"Yes, it's me."

"Make sure you lock the door, and do all of them."

The source of the smell is in the kitchen. A pot of eggs on the stove has burned all its water out and now the eggs are frying with the shell still on.

"Eve, you doing okay?" I say when I peek my head into her den.

"You ain't that grown yet to be calling me by my first name," Mama says, just as I expected she would. "Did you lock the door?"

"I did," I say, and before she can ask I tell her I did all four locks.

"Have you been trying to cook?"

"I got to feed myself. You were gone and I sent that no-cooking girl home. I can do for myself you know. I'm making egg salad."

A Negro spiritual that sounds ancient is playing from the boom box sitting next to her chair. It's a sad sounding song. I wonder what that kind of music says about Mama's mood. The closet doors are shut, and the gold linen curtains are drawn open so she can see out. The waste paper basket is empty, a glass of water is close by, and her ever-present saltine crackers sit stacked up and ready in their individual plastic wraps—just in case, as she says, no one brings her food. Everything is in order, just as she likes it. The home health aide must have done all this before she was sent home.

"I called for you, but you were gone."

Her eyes are halfway closed and she's swaying her head to the music.

"I went for a walk and coffee. Sorry I was gone so long. How's your morning been so far?"

"Every day is the same, not much difference in what I do."

She sounds dismal and matter-of-fact. Her lips barely move to form a faint smile and she's got one foot tapping like they do in church when everyone says God is speaking through the choir. In the background a tambourine is working double time and Mama starts to clap to match its rhythm—this is definitely church music. *I'm a stranger*, the chorus goes, *don't drive me away*. I remember this song well. It cautions you to be careful how you treat the stranger at the door—she could be your mama. The melody is rocking and the singing's good, but I wonder if Mama's trying to tell me something.

Outside, a couple with silver hair make their way past the window, holding hands, I wonder what their life is like. I don't know what to say to Mama about her day so far, so I settle into the small couch and join her, quietly listening to the music. A man's deep voice that sounds like Paul Robeson is singing. I recognize the song as *Sometimes I Feel Like a Motherless Child*. Is this Mama's crying song, like Alicia can be mine? I can't help myself. I have to interrupt her listening session.

"Mama, why are you playing all this sad music?"

She doesn't look at me when she answers.

"I'm having feelings, old ones I thought would just stay away. You been prying out the story about your father and me, and now them feelings are back again. We both hoped Oakland would be our chance, but he was gone too soon to tell."

"Do you want to stop talking?"

"Well, yes and no. Remembering brings up feelings, some good, some bad. Some stories are not for telling, Carla, but I see it means a lot to you so I want to try. It keeps you here more than I'm used to so it must be important."

"I don't know Mama, I guess it *is* important to me right now."

"I suppose that's a good thing. I knew you would be asking one day. You always were the nosy one in the family."

"I learned that from you. I'm going in the kitchen to make you that egg salad. I'll let you finish listening to your music, and then if you feel like it you can tell me more of the story. How's that?"

"Okay. I just need to sit for a while longer."

If a few plus-size people happen to be in Mama's two-hip kitchen at the same time they might need to turn sideways to get around each other. Her senior apartment is small. It's two bedrooms, but definitely smaller than the Chester Street house. Aside from the burned pot on the stove, Mama's no-nonsense kitchen is so like her; clean and practical. As she would say, there's no need for a lot of frilly gadgets, since you can whip eggs with a fork, and a spoon will do for most anything else. That mama of mine is not an easy one to do for. I can hear the music playing and it's still sounds sad, now someone's singing about wanting to hear her mother's voice again. Her mood seems as sad as this music. She doesn't know that just a few days ago I tried to kill myself, and I don't think I could ever tell her about that night. Did Mama ever feel like that after Daddy died, did she think of leaving us to go join him?

The gospel tape is off and now she's watching Judge Judy, one of her favorite shows. If people are stupid enough to go on television airing their business, Mama always says, then they get what they deserve.

"Judge Judy don't take no mess."

"Here you are—an egg salad sandwich and some rice pudding."

"Did you put pickles in it?"

She doesn't bother to look at me she's so captivated by Judge Judy, who's chastising a young married couple for suing each other for nonpayment of rent.

"And did you put a little mustard in it?"

"I know how to cook."

After Daddy died, Mama was always at work so I did most of the cooking and keeping the house, all two floors. I think about how the house I grew up in had way too many small rooms.

"That Judge Judy, she's a pistol," Mama says. "Those people ought to know better."

She bites into her sandwich and takes a moment from the TV to give me a wink and nod of approval. While she eats I count a few pictures on the bookshelf, stare out the window looking for a distraction, and try to work my nerve up to ask if she wants to start back with her story. The morning's sad song recital weighs on my mind, and I'm not sure if she wants to continue. I watch as the judge finishes her ruling and cross my legs, hoping to appear relaxed and not as anxious as I felt while in the kitchen.

"They look young. Maybe they don't know any better," I say.

"When me and your Daddy were young like that we didn't act stupid. How you gon' take each other to court while you still married? Just seems ridiculous to me."

Maybe this is my opening to ask her.

"Mama, I was wondering if you felt up to telling more of your story?"

"All morning I been thinking about it, can't get out of my mind how much hope your father had after he left and we were finally back together."

"What was Daddy hoping for?"

She looks out the window and sighs, "He wanted to be called George."

"George?"

For a moment Mama is quiet. She leans back in her chair and stares at the ceiling. I wrap myself in Mama Belle's quilt and settle in on the small couch. I wonder if Mama is going to go frozen.

"Well, Carla," she says slowly, still staring upwards, "*George* is what they called those Pullman Porters who worked on the railroad. Some say they were the butlers of the railways."

"Daddy wanted to be a *porter*? I didn't know that, I only knew he worked on ships after he left Slim Jenkins' restaurant."

"His uncle helped him get that busboy job when he first moved out here, but he never wanted to stay there. He had his application in for the railways, but it just didn't come quick enough to feed his family. That's why he worked at the shipyards."

"Why a porter? Seems like after living in Love, Texas he wouldn't want to wait on nobody white."

"Carla, the waiting on wasn't what he was after," she says, shaking her head.

"Didn't that job mean you had to wait on white people, feed them, clean up after them, run their errands and have to cater to their needs?"

Mama is sitting lower than me in her lounger chair and when she looks over her glasses she reminds me of Mrs. Brown from the main office at school. Again she shakes her head. By the time she finishes her story, there's probably going to be whole lot of those looks thrown my way.

"Carla, your Daddy was a proud man."

"I know, Mama."

"It's true them porters dealt with white folk's ways on those long trips. They was almost living together when they went across the country."

"Why would he want to do that then?"

"The whites who rode the train said they couldn't tell the difference between one porter from another, so they just called all the colored men George. But still, it was the respect that came with it, that's what he was looking for."

"Respect from the whites?"

"Yes and no. That's every black man's secret want, to be respected by whites. Respect is any man's want. They don't need it from whites to survive, but I think they still want it."

"So that's why he wanted to be called George?"

"What your father liked and wanted was the respect those porters had once they came home. They were held up so high in the neighborhood. That's what meant something to him. Everyone treated those men real special."

Mama dips her spoon in the rice pudding before she finishes her sandwich and goes quiet. I try to remember what I'd read about the Pullman porters. I remember seeing men in their porter's uniforms, wearing tall round caps, and walking through our neighborhood. It seemed they couldn't walk too far without someone stopping them to talk. Mama bringing up the porters makes think about a time when

Daddy had two porters over to the house. The living room was full
of neighbors sitting in chairs, the couch and some sat on the floor;
everyone was listening intently to stories about their trip back East.
Often, the room filled with laughter, and people shaking their heads
in disbelief at the ways of some white folks.

"The men started this union." Mama voice interrupts my thoughts
bringing me back from the memory of when laughter filled our house.
"They called themselves the Brotherhood of the Sleeping Car Porters.
They stood the tallest down on Seventh Street, or when the train pulled
in at the station on Wood. Your Daddy wanted to stand with them."

"I remember reading about them, but this is the first time I've heard
Daddy wanted to be one. What else don't I know about?"

"You sound like somebody was trying to keep something from
you," she says, shifting in the chair so she can lean forward, "Carla,
back then we tried to raise you children up, send you to school, and
just prayed the world didn't hurt you too much along the way."

"I don't know Mama, I wish I'd learned more about you and—"

"I told you it wasn't easy like it is now." She rocks forward in the
chair, a signal she wants to get up.

"Back then you never knew when something awful would happen
because a white person thought you stepped out of your place."

She motions for me to help, which really means watch her push and
pull the walker as she struggles to take a step. Once in her bedroom, I
fluff the pillows and fold back her favorite comforter. Mama releases
her grip on the handles of the walker to lie down, and with her eyes
closed she turns slowly onto her side to face the middle of the bed. I'm
tired enough that now it's my turn to lie down, and on the other side
of the bed I ease softly onto the mattress and rest my head on a pillow
next to her. Mama's complexion is ebony smooth, and it's still dewy
looking. The skin around her eyes looks thin. At times I've known her
eyes to look tired, but for seventy-five her eyes are fairly clear. It's been
a long time since I've looked at my mother like this, and I feel lost in

it. It startles me a little when she reaches over and gently touches my face, strokes my cheek with her fingers and smiles.

"I thought you were asleep," I say.

"I felt your eyes on me. I was just thinking."

"About what?"

"The things we been talking about—your daddy and how you loved him so much. I know you miss him, Baby."

I don't remember the last time I heard that kind of tenderness coming from Mama, or felt so close to her. I wonder if this is leading her to tell me more about her life.

"I do, and I know you do too," I say.

"I know, baby. It's been too many years that he's been gone. But, nothing you can do about it, that's just what life gave us."

She gives me a little pat on my shoulder as if to console me, and her eyes become fixed, almost staring past me.

"So Mama," I say to break the trance she seemed to slip into, "Daddy was your boyfriend, and you two loved each other, but he was forced to leave Texas before you could get your plans together."

"I see you trying to inch me back, and I can tell you've been listening. That's good."

She pinches my arm and extends her lips into a wide smile. I think she's glad I'm still into the story with her.

"Well, let's see. One night . . ."

Mama props herself up on the pillows and rests her head back as if her mind is returning to Love, Texas.

"I had been down at the creek, thinking about June, and when I came home my daddy wasn't too happy about me wandering around in the dark. We had words about that and whether or not June was really gon' send for me. You see, my father didn't know anything about love; it wasn't something that folks got to experience much. Not too many was lucky like June and me. Marriages just happened for girls whose parents wanted to see they got a husband as soon as they could. Even my own daddy was looking for me to marry so he could get help in the fields.

"I didn't pay too much attention to his warnings about them Anderson boys getting at me because they couldn't get at June. I told him I had been at the creek, thinking about when we were going to get married and what living in California was going to be like. He was sitting on the porch when I walked up, sucking on his pipe and blowing smoke circles in the air.

"'After all this time, you still think June got you in his plans?' he said. 'I don't think you should count on that as hard as you are. When a man up and leaves, it don't mean he thinking about you.'

"I told him it was just taking June a little longer to get settled and feel like he was ready to start a family. I told him June wrote me every week and that I wasn't worried about him sending for me and that he shouldn't be, either. Well, it came out in a sassing tone before I could catch myself. I didn't like him talking about June in that way and he struck a nerve in me.

"But one thing my daddy learned on that plantation where he lived before Love was that women were to stay in their place. I seen him whup Mama like he was beating on a man whenever she questioned him or had a different kind of thought about what he was doing. June used to tell me that my daddy did that because he couldn't do it to the white men who made him feel less than a man.

"But June was a different kind of man, even as a boy. He'd be sweet, bring me fruit from town, or pick some wild flower and tell me he wasn't sure which was the prettiest. I knew I was in his plans even if my daddy didn't know it.

"After I had words with my daddy on the porch, I went inside and crawled on the pallet alongside my brothers' bed. Back in those days the three of them slept in a huge wooden bed and I used the floor. It was hard down there but I was comfortable. Mama and Daddy slept in the only other room with a sheet curtain that separated them from us.

"The curtain that acted as a door to their bedroom kept us from seeing, but we could hear plenty. When Daddy came inside, I heard him telling Mama that I'd been sassing him. His voice was loud, I don't think he gave it any mind I could hear him. He told her I better mind how I was living in his house and that just because I was waiting on a man who up and left didn't give me the right to talk to him the way I did.

"My mama tried to quiet him, but I could still hear him say how it was his house, and he wasn't going to have a daughter live here and disrespect him like that.

"That next morning Mama wakes me and says, 'Eve, you got to go get water so I can start making breakfast before your daddy and brothers get up.'

"It was cold and I was moaning, trying to rub my eyes awake. I didn't want to get out from under the covers until Mama lit the stove to warm up the house, but she pulled on my arm to get me up, whispering not to wake the others. She told me I needed to stop worrying about how cold it was, and start worrying about not upsetting my daddy anymore. I looked at my brothers who were still sleeping. They weren't bothered one bit by the noise we was making. They were such hard sleepers and nothing ever woke them before they was ready. I started to tell Mama that I heard what Daddy said the night before.

"'Shush, child,' Mama said. She held my cheeks to quiet me, worried that I would wake Daddy up. She whispered that it was payment day, and that Mr. Carson would be coming in the afternoon and hopefully not too late. She told me to help her make a big breakfast so maybe Daddy wouldn't get too agitated or more upset.

"And then we heard, 'Belle, what's going on?'

"At the sound of Daddy's voice, Mama and me froze. We looked at each other quiet-like with our eyes saying we hope he goes back to sleep. We waited to see if we would to have to face his crossness from the night before, and from being waked earlier than he wanted to. I'd forgotten about payment day. Any other troubles that happened that day would be dealt with hard, mostly because of the anger my father was going to have to swallow when he met with Mr. Carson. I looked at the curtain waiting to see Daddy's tall and wide-body appear, with his brow crunched down in that riled up look both me and Mama feared, but it didn't happen. The house stayed quiet. I got up to put something warm on, my shoes were by the door and I threw on Daddy's big field coat to stay warm.

"'Wait a minute. I'm going with you to the water pump,' Mama whispered.

"I was surprised she was coming along since getting the water was my job. But she grabbed her coat and closed the door, holding her finger to her mouth to keep me quiet. She kept looking back to make sure Daddy was still asleep and not looking out the window. The air was cold and the ground wet with morning dew. I felt coolness coming through my worn out shoe so I stopped near the tractor to fix the paper inside. 'Sister, I came out here because I need to talk to you and it can't wait 'til later,' Mama said, while I fixed my shoe.

"When I finished, I stood up and told her that I didn't mean any disrespect, and Daddy was just upset because I wanted to leave. She shushed me again and pointed towards the water pump. We walked, not saying anything to each other, and when we got there I lifted the wooden bucket while she worked the pump. She just shook her head from side to side in that worrisome way folks do when they want to say something that ain't coming out easy. She was pushing down strongly on the handle, waiting for the water to start flowing out. She wasn't talking, but I knew she would say something when she got her thoughts together. I waited, watching for the water. It took a long time to come out, which meant the well was going dry and Daddy and my brothers would have to dig another one soon. Finally, the water started pouring out, and my mama told me what was on her mind.

"'Sister, I'm not mad at you,' she said. 'And your Daddy, well, you know how he gets when he's upset. Don't you worry though, I know how to handle my husband, but Sister, I don't need you bringing a whole 'notha thing for him to think about, 'specially on this day, you hear?'

"We went quiet, pumping the water and still looking at the porch to see if Daddy was awake and watching. My mother talked to me woman-to-woman that day. Reminded me it wasn't my place to tell her about her man. I'd only seen them kiss once, and afterwards I saw her wipe her mouth. But she said she loved him, no matter what, she knew he'd keep her a home. Mama Belle was all of fourteen when my daddy showed up at her home, asking her father if he could board with them for a few days while his truck got fixed. She told me when she saw the rusted holes and brick-hard clay in the tire wells, she knew it meant he worked the land.

"Anyway, that's how they came together; and after two weeks of meeting each other she was married and sitting alongside him in that truck, heading to Texas.

"'Mama, wait a minute. I know I'm supposed to listen, but I can't believe what I just heard: Mama Belle and Grandpa got married after knowing each other for just two weeks?"

"That's what I said, didn't I?"

"She went off with a strange man no one knew? How could that happen?"

"Now, Carla, see you looking at it like back then is now. Women, colored and white, were married off all the time. It was the 1940s, and most folks worked the land. Finding a wife, like I said, was getting somebody to help."

"Maybe so. But it's still hard to believe that really happened. What about love? Did folks have that?"

"Most was put together and it took a while, maybe a long while, for them to know each other. My mama didn't get to know what her husband would be like in a family way, since his family wasn't around.

He beat her when he'd get so riled. She tried to calm him but he didn't want to hear nothing she had to say. Yes, Carla, I watched my mama get beat, that's something you never had to worry about. All that made it hard loving him. But I guess she did—me and your uncles got here, didn't we?"

"You didn't love him."

I'm not sure if I'm asking a question or making a statement. She speaks about her father like he was a stranger.

"Maybe sometimes I did and sometimes I didn't."

She says this with her lips pursed together, like someone trying to decide if they really like something or not. What's that supposed mean? I loved my daddy so much I never thought it could be different for Mama. I wonder if I should ask her more about that, then I tell myself not to push. Dana told me I needed to let her tell the story like she wants.

"Mama Belle should of left him," I couldn't help but say.

"Baby," Mama says like I'm a little girl and not the forty-plus year old woman I am. "And where was she gon' go? A colored woman, no woman back then for that matter, could just up and leave. Go where? How she gon' take care of herself and her children? It just wasn't done like that. Women found a way to make it with what they had been married to."

"That doesn't seem right, I feel sorry for Mama Belle." I sound like my students.

"I told that girl, what's her name, not to come back. That you would be cooking dinner."

"You did?"

I see Mama's the one changing the subject, so I guess she's done talking.

"Yes, I did. Surprise me with what you make. I think I need to rest a while. Will you turn my TV on?"

While I'm in the kitchen, preparing smothered steak and squash for dinner, I think about everything I've heard so far. It all makes me feel heavy. I let my hand with the cleaver drop hard on to the steak. I'm pounding the red meat harder and harder and making so much noise that Mama calls out to see if everything is all right.

"Everything's fine." I holler towards her room. "Just tenderizing."

"Well, don't forget we still got to eat it."

Mama Belle died not knowing love, at least that's what it sounds like to me from how Mama is telling the story. Did Mama Belle ever want to leave—I mean *leave* leave—in the way I've thought about doing?

After dinner, I help Mama to bed, turn the radio to the program she likes to sleep with, and try to settle on the couch in the living room with just Mama Belle's quilt for covering. The sun has long passed over Mama's ground floor apartment, and there's no need to turn on a lamp because there's light coming in from the street. It would be nice to hide in the dark, but the constant glare of car lights keeps me from sleeping. Like this hard couch, the light is not comforting.

Why does Mama still keep a plastic cover on the couch when all her children are grown? I remember when I was a girl I'd sweat in the warmer days of summer, and the back of my legs would stick to the plastic when I'd get up. The passing headlights shine like a spotlight on the family pictures hanging on the wall. I start counting the photo collages Mama chose to hang in the living room, remembering when we hung them on newly painted walls.

There's Grandpa Clarence, Mama Belle, my two uncles Clarence and Otis on Mama's side, Mama and Daddy, me, my brothers Clarence, Arthur, Jr., Otis, and Mama's seven grandchildren. There aren't any pictures of Daddy's side of the family, only of him. And there's not one picture of just me and Mama. There are three of her and my brothers, but not one of us together. Mama, you've always loved your sons, haven't you? Why aren't they here for this download of sadness?

The number of cars passing by has slowed down. It must be early in the morning with everyone already where they're supposed to be at this time of night. Still, I can't sleep, and my mind is full of thoughts. I got to Mama's on Saturday afternoon and all week it's been non-stop, tending to her needs and waiting for her story to leak out. I feel exhausted, it's only two more days before I go back to work, and I can't tell if she is even close to finishing her story.

With all the windows closed the house is hot. I think I'll get a glass of ice water to cool off. I'm almost naked, wearing just a bra and panties, but Mama's asleep so I tiptoe into the kitchen just as I am, not bothering to cover up. The water soothes my throat and I rub some of it onto my neck and chest.

That Dana—she's the one who got me into this. It was her big idea to take the week off. "Don't worry I'll check on you," she told me. And where is she now? What's she doing while I carry out her plan? I have a mind to call her, so I quietly go back into the living room to get my phone, and return only to start pacing in the kitchen. The next thing I know my finger pushes Dana's speed dial number and I'm waiting for someone to pick up.

"Dana?"

"Carla?" she says, with surprise reeking in her voice, "Do you know what time it is? We're asleep."

"Truthfully, I really don't care," I say, pacing back and forth. "Because of you I'm listening to a sad, sad story, sleeping on a too hard couch or a blow up mattress, cooking all the time, and all you have to worry about is your precious sleep. Well, wake up."

"What? Wait a minute let me go to the other room."

"Make it quick then."

I hear her tell David everything's okay and she'll be right back. Well, I don't think everything's okay.

"Do you know it's after two in the morning?" Dana asks.

"Like I told you, I don't really care. I haven't heard from you in six days. You said you'd help me through this and where have you been?"

"Car, I'm sorry. It's been a busy week and David and I went out last night. He wanted to hear music at the club. I'm so sorry. I've been thinking about you though. How is it going?"

"Oh, now you want to know? That's not why I called anyway."

"Then why are you waking me up?"

"I want you to stop telling me what to do when you aren't doing anything about what you're supposed to do."

"What are you talking about?"

"You really don't know?"

"Car, please, it's late. I'm sorry I haven't called. What is it?"

"Aaron. Have you talked to him?"

"It's late, Car, I promise we'll talk later about that."

"See, that's what I mean. You're all in my business and you haven't done a thing about yours."

"It's complicated."

How many times have I heard her say this?

"And you don't think this is complicated? Listening to Mama talk about her life, scared I'm going to say something to hurt her feelings not knowing what's coming next?"

"I know."

"Only you know about that night, only you, Dana—and David— since I know you told him. Hearing Mama's story is supposed to help me stay, but damn it, I don't see why I'm the only one trying to find truth that's not in a history book or whatever damn books you read. You're not dealing with anything real. *I'm* the only one who is."

I ramble off everything that comes to my mind, how she doesn't know how to be there for anyone—how she leaves people hanging, all the while listening to see if Mama's waking up. It's hard to keep my voice low when I feel so mad at Dana.

"Look sweetie," Dana interrupts, "I'm sorry, really. What do you want me to do?"

"*Sorry* is a sorry word. Talk to Aaron, stop saying it and do something!"

"I promise. I'll call you in the morning, Car."

"Me? Damn it, you need to call Aaron," I almost shout. "You haven't been listening. Call Aaron, that's what you can do for me. You promised to call me, you know what I am going through—and you couldn't even do that. See what it feels like to tell the truth, or to listen when it scares you to even get close to the conversation."

"I think…"

"Just do it," I interrupt her. "After I hear all of Mama's story, I don't know what's next, but right now I'm saying everything. I'm done just listening and done watching everyone—including you—act like no one sees the craziness around us."

Now there's phone silence between us. I'm breathing hard, I can hear sniffing on the other side—is she crying? Oh well, what's it matter now?

"Dana, what are you afraid of?"

I hear her breathing loudly in the phone and there's a moment of silence before she speaks.

"That I don't know what to do or say to help."

"So you just make up stuff?"

"Not all the time, Carla."

"Yeah well, a lot of time it feels that way."

"I'm sorry…"

"There you go again."

"All right, but I feel so bad that you think I don't care about you."

"What about Aaron—do you listen to him?"

"That's not fair Carla. I listen."

"Did you hear me say I wanted to die? That I don't want to stay here any more?"

"You told me about the pills, and all that alcohol. I asked you to tell me where you had the pills. Didn't I meet you at the water? Can't you see I care?"

"Before that Dana. I tried the best way I knew to let you know, and still you always left me to go to your precious David."

"Carla, you're not being fair. He loves you, too."

"You hide from being real with us, always saying David needs you—well me and Aaron are family too. We need you."

"What do you want me to do?"

"You love Aaron, right?"

"You know that I do."

"Well, act like it then. Talk to him. Leave those silly things out like salami sandwiches, rolling on the floor, and those other things you always tell me. Get real—not bossy—if you can help it."

"I'm not bossy."

There's silence and I just stare at the phone shaking my head.

"Okay. Sometimes, I am."

So she's finally admitted to something. Just hearing her say that calms me down.

"It's been a hard week, Dana. But somehow I'm getting through it."

"I'm glad Carla, and honestly, I didn't forget about you."

"Well don't forget about Aaron either."

"When you get back, let's walk the lake."

I'm almost naked, standing with bare feet on a cold kitchen floor. I've told my best friend off and how she should love her brother. Maybe I haven't been the best at loving folks either, loving on magazines instead of talking about my father. Haven't I tried to earn Mama's sweetness by being the extra good daughter, or doing more for my students than anyone would dare. I think about Rasheed and slap my forehead. Haven't I failed, too?

"Okay," I say to Dana's suggestion and soften my voice. "I'll see you at The Pillars on Monday."

CHAPTER FIFTEEN

"Help! Help me!"

My head bolts up from the couch to see who is calling out. I think it's Mama, so frantically I throw the quilt on the floor and rush to her bedroom door. She's still sleeping. No one else is here, but I know I heard something. Oh God, was that me screaming for help? I get back on the couch and lean my ears towards the back rooms, hoping my cries didn't disturb Mama's sleep. Not a sound—that's good. I must have fallen asleep after talking to Dana. That was me who called—I can't believe I did it, but I did. I could become another statistic, like that black woman found dead in the lake, and Dana would probably go look in one of her books to find out why it happened.

Had I been dreaming? I reach for the glass of water on the coffee table. My throat feels dry, and my face and neck are dripping wet with sweat—what was I dreaming about?

I remember I was dressed in my whites. A long, braided rope looped around my ankle and it was tied in a thick knot like the kind you would see on a ship. It was attached to a pointy rooftop of some building and the rope would only let me go so high. My arms were flailing like I was trying to swim in the air but the rope kept stopping me from going higher. My arms flapped harder, my hands stretched out trying to grab onto something and then the rope snapped loose. I was tumbling upwards, first head over heels and then rolling sideways. Finally I righted myself, so my head led the way up. I wasn't sure where I was going, I flew higher and higher into the sky and then, I guess that's when I screamed.

Remembering my dream is unsettling, and I feel the need to move around to shake off its effects, so I slip out of Mama's house for an early morning walk. The sidewalks look like freshly poured cement and the houses are definitely designed by the same person—the same one who built all those similar looking peach colored strip malls you see when you drive anywhere outside of the city. My head is hurting from all the craziness last night, and Dana crying about how people expect her to know all the answers. And my dream—I still don't know how to make sense of it, unless it means that soon I'm going to be free of all this.

After walking a few blocks, I decide to sit on a bench at the edge of a little park. Four kindergarten-aged children are playing and running in the grass, squealing their heads off, not caring about who hears their loud noises. It's pretty early for them to be out, but I see their parents are close by. Two couples, in between looking over their shoulder at their kids, are casually laughing and drinking coffee. How did they get to a life so simple that they just get up, get their coffee and take the kids to the park? When Daddy was alive, I guess we did that too. I keep watching the families play with each other, and when the fathers lift their children onto their backs and pretend to be horses galloping across the grass, tears fall down my cheeks. I remember when we had fun like that. It's not fair that it all went away and we became the house that was so serious no one knew how to laugh anymore.

The parents gather their children and walk past me without saying good morning, or giving a head nod. I overhear one of them say it's almost eleven o'clock, and that jars me into remembering Mama is expecting all of us to go to church today. Not to her regular one in West

Oakland, but to her new church home in Brentwood. I don't think the choir is very good, but she still goes, probably because the only other black woman in her building, who lives on the second floor, introduced her to this church. My legs start moving a little faster towards Mama's street. The swiftness makes my headache come back but I know if I slow down if I'm not going to make it on time. When I turn the corner towards Mama's building, I see Clarence's sky blue SUV.

"Well, look who's here."

That's just like Clarence—he could have gotten up to let me in the door.

"Clarence, why did you put all the locks back on?"

His head and eyes point towards Mama, who is sitting in what she calls her parlor chair.

"Oh." I understand.

"Still, you could have opened the door."

He throws a kiss in the air in my direction, thinking that will make it all better.

"That's not letting you off the hook. Are Otis and Arthur, Jr. coming?"

"They're supposed to, but we haven't heard from them yet. You see we're still waiting."

It's 11:15. I'll have to shower and dress fast to be ready on time. Mama's dressed in her white suit, the one with gold brocade on the shoulder and she's wearing Mama Belle's gold pin on her heart. Her white hat is sitting on the coffee table next to her Bible. Oh God, I forgot it's First Sunday. If she doesn't go, she'll be disappointed.

"Mama, how you doing?"

"I had to get dressed by myself, cause my daughter wasn't here to help me."

"I went for a walk and lost track of the time. I'm sorry." I hope my apology will help to keep her in a good mood.

"You sure have been walking a lot lately," she says.

Her forehead is raised and I plant the expected kiss on it, while giving Clarence a frown as I pass by him on my way to the bathroom. I shower quickly and pull out the whites I leave in Mama's closet just for times like this. It's a three-quarter-length dress with a white button-down jacket. Mama bought it. For some reason she always thinks I need to wear a jacket. The dress is A-line. She says my hips won't ever outgrow it.

"Twelve o'clock service is starting soon. I'm gon' lose my seat. This new church don't know that's my seat yet. You know I like to sit in the middle row near the windows. Otis and Arthur, Jr. just being trifling."

"Then let's you, me, and Clarence go. They know where the church is, don't they?"

This is not the first time they have held us up. I'm tired of waiting on them and Mama thinking we can't go unless they are here.

"It's First Sunday, Carla. Mrs. Williams upstairs has all her children every time on First Sunday. What I'm gone look like having half my family show up?"

"Like a woman who came to church."

"Watch your tone—you not that old to just say anything to your Mama."

Clarence walks past and leans his head close to my ear, "Yeah, you ain't that grown."

He laughs quietly, heads into the kitchen and leaves Mama and me to look at each other while we wait for her other two sons to arrive.

"I think your brothers don't want to go to church no more," she finally says to end the stare off. Mama starts rocking in the chair that's not meant to rock and gazes out the window.

"Last month, I asked them to go to First Sunday and they made up all those excuses why they couldn't come."

"Arthur, Jr. had to let two employees go so he's short with help to run the print shop." I say in his defense.

"What about Otis? He has time. Those boys just don't care."

"That's not so Mama," I say, "Clarence is here."

"Yeah," Clarence shouts from the kitchen, "I'm here."

"Yes Brother, and I'm not forgetting about that. But I was counting on everybody, all my sons, coming with me to church today."

A cold freeze shoots through my stomach. There it is again. Why does "everybody" never include me?

"Excuse me, but I'm here and I'm your daughter. Am I included in that everybody?" Warm heat crosses my forehead. Ever since I can remember, Mama's *everybody* has only referred to her sons.

"Carla don't act sensitive, you know I mean you, too."

I hate being called that. *Black* and *sensitive* is like oil and water mixing–they don't. People, even your own mama, will get on you for being that way.

"You don't ever say my daughter, when you talk about everybody." I'm surprised to have heard my voice say that.

"I don't need to because you're always here. It's those boys I'm never sure about."

"But everybody should mean me, too," I complain.

"Carla, stop it. You know what I meant."

"No, Mama, I don't if you never say it."

"You trying to say something again?" Her voice sounds annoyed. We've had this argument before with no ending to it.

"Say what Mama? What am I saying?"

I feel my voice rise and my knees start to tremble. To make them stop I change my position from standing to sitting on the living room couch.

"I was supposed to treat you different," she raises her voice back at me, "You don't know how hard it is when you have a girl child, and only one at that. I *had* to make you do things different than your brothers."

She turns her head away from me and goes back to looking out the window—she's ignoring me now.

"You sure did that and you're doing it now. Why aren't I everybody?"

I feel out of my body, not sure these words are coming from my mouth. I think about that day in the backyard when she was trying to rush us to the park and her everybody didn't include me.

"Whoa," Clarence comes from the kitchen and jumps in. He looks me directly in the eyes, "Carla, you and Mama need to stop before it gets out of hand in here."

"Out of whose hands Clarence?" Mama turns her head. *Uh oh.* Now she's on to Clarence.

"I only meant to say…"

Mama talks over Clarence so he's not able to finish his sentence.

"Well, I know your sister. And I don't think she gon' get out of hand with me."

She looks in my direction, then at Clarence, and she says to him, "Are you fixing to?"

I'm not sure what is happening. But I notice Mama's bookshelf has four shelves, the books on top are all the same height, except three stick out higher than the others.

"It's 11:45, Mama. If we are going, we need to leave now." Clarence says. His voice has regained its authority.

Mama looks out the window and sighs. I shrug my shoulders at Clarence and shake my head. I know what that means. All of Mama's sighs have different meanings. This one says she's done arguing with me. She's done waiting on Otis and Arthur, Jr. She's just done talking about it.

"I'm staying home, going to my bed," she says in a matter-of-fact voice.

"We can still take you," I tell her.

"No. I *said* I'm staying home. Don't worry me about it no more," she says sounding bad-tempered.

Now Clarence is the one shaking his head and looking up at the ceiling.

"What about next Sunday? I'll still be here," he says.

"Maybe you will but it won't be First Sunday. You go on now, Clarence. Carla, I want you to stay and help me get ready for my nap."

"Yes, Ma'm."

I still know when to say yes and do as I'm told. Clarence stays in the living room while I walk alongside Mama and her walker to the bedroom. The bed is made and everything is neat and in order. In silence I help her out of her Sunday dress and hang it in the closet. She reminds me to close the sliding door. She never likes to look at an open closet.

"Carla, bring me my Bible. It's sitting on the coffee table."

Clarence is still here and it doesn't look like he's leaving anytime soon. He's got Mama Belle's quilt folded across his lap and his gaze is dreamy, like he's caught in deep thought. I don't interrupt his moment and pick up the Bible to take it back to Mama's room. She's already under the covers.

"I'm gon' take a nap. I'll eat my crackers for lunch."

"When you wake up, I'll have some soup ready for you," I say. "Mama, do you want anything else?"

"No."

Back in the living room I sit next to Clarence on the couch and nudge his shoulders. He nudges me in the same way. It's like we're kids again, sitting next to each other, worried that we made Mama mad. We sit quietly, tracing the quilt patterns with our fingers and pulling on the tattered edges. I start braiding the loose strings, making a neat row of plaits on my side.

"Carla, I'm sorry," Clarence says while looking down at the quilt.

"Sorry for what, Clarence?" His voice sounds young, not like the grown man I know to be sitting next to me, not like the always-telling-me-what-to-do big brother who I learned to fear.

"I see it's difficult. That woman can make you forget you've grown up. When I heard you asking why aren't you everybody, it got me to thinking."

"No, she's not easy. What were you thinking about?"

"About you."

"*Me?*"

"I know I was hard on you and everybody else. I thought I was supposed to be, with our father gone so early."

I nodded.

"Clarence, you're like two different people now that you've grown up. I remember the big brother who scared everyone away—and especially boys from coming around."

He laughs a little, rubs his forehead with his hand and looks at me with a sheepish grin. "I was something, wasn't I?"

"Yes, you were." I grab his arm, holding on to it and expecting him to say more.

"Mama was tired, frozen all the time after Dad died. I just felt that it was on me to protect the family."

"Did you really think we were in danger?"

"Just from life, Carla. Things happen when you're not watching. Someone had to watch out for us. Mama was so afraid that we'd be hurt or killed, or something. I had to let the world know the Sinclairs weren't to be messed with."

"Are you talking about how she made us run to the park when trouble started?"

"Some. Whenever we got back, the boys on the block would ask us where we were when things went down. How come we weren't out there, standing with them."

"What did you say?"

He looks down and twists the edges of the quilt in his hands.

"What could I say, really? My mama made me leave?" he groans deeply, ending in a high pitch tone. He sounds hurt by it all.

I always believed my brothers wanted to join the Panthers to express their outrage when we saw the police mistreat our neighbors. As I think about it now, I didn't really feel the danger from the streets. My brothers were always around me so I felt protected, unaware that others were in a fight for their lives. Running to the park didn't allow me to see what actually happened when the crowds gathered and the police came. By the time we got back from the park, all would be quiet. It didn't occur to me then, that, for Clarence, it wasn't really over.

"Why do you think Mama was so scared?"

"It had to do with what she saw in Texas. It was pretty nasty back in those days. She was afraid for us."

"Clarence, how come nobody told me what was really going on? I feel like you all had a different life than I did, even though we lived in the same house."

He turns to hug me and his eyes are moist as he wraps his arms around me, drawing my body into his chest. I lay my head on his shoulder and it feels strange. I don't remember this ever happening—sure, we've hugged throughout the years, but not like this. I feel so small, like the little sister that I am, protected in his embrace.

"When I went to Texas for basic training, white people on the base may not have been as violent as the police were back home but their attitude came through all over the place. You still had to watch out for yourself."

"I'm so sorry, Clarence."

"Dad made me promise that I would keep his little girl safe. That's why, even though I didn't want to, I ran with ya'll to the park whenever Mama said it was time to go."

I give him a kiss on the cheek. "Clarence, you're a good man and a good brother."

"Mama sent you to that private school to get you away from the battleground in the neighborhood. We were so proud of our little sister.

Maybe we didn't let you know that enough because we were too busy being protective of you."

"Remember how you didn't want me to get those magazines?" I say.

"I know, and look at how many you got now."

"Dana says I should get rid of some of them because the stacks have taken over my bedroom."

"Is she still married to my boy David?"

"Yeah, going on ten years now."

"We used to hang pretty tight when we lived on Chester. His family lived a few blocks over on Peralta. They had that Victorian that always looked like it needed paint."

"I didn't know you two were that close."

"I haven't seen him in a while, but back then he was my brother from another mother. And you think our mother is difficult? Boy, let me tell you he had it rough."

I knew David had gone through a difficult period when he and Dana first got married, but having it rough, that's not how I think about him.

"Let's go into the kitchen so I can start making Mama's soup."

I don't want Clarence to leave yet. What he's told me so far makes me wonder what else I don't know about David—or him for that matter. I put on some water for coffee and gesture for Clarence to sit on the stool near the counter. I didn't have to egg him on to tell me more about David. He just sits down and starts talking.

"Everyone called his father Slim. He played the alto sax in this band and well he had real talent, he was, you know, local famous. David being his son made him a celebrity and since we hung together it made me one too. Boy, did the women love us." He loudly laughs. I put my finger to my lips and point towards Mama's room.

"Sorry, I forgot," he whispers.

"So why do you say David had it rough? To me he's always been the Wonder Boy."

"Yeah, he's pretty special. Everybody knew that, even back then. But his mama, oh man, his mama used to do some things—and publicly, so everybody saw."

What things I think to myself. Okay, if Clarence is telling a story I guess then like Mama I have to be patient and let him get to the details on his own.

"Me and David," he says, looking like he's lost in his thinking. "Man, those were some good times."

I guess Clarence is in those good time memories, because he's awfully quiet now. I go about cutting up celery and tomatoes to make the soup and let him have his moment, but really I'm dying for him to get to it. When I look over at him, he's rubbing the edges of his coffee mug and making circles around it. Okay, do I say something?

"Clarence." I say his name to snap him out it. "What was so hard for David?"

"I was thinking about how dark-skinned David is and something that happened to him."

"And he's pretty handsome, too—don't you think?"

"Well, I don't know about all that, but his mama is real dark, and his father was a light and bright man, almost the color of Dad."

"So?"

"So his mama was jealous of the groupies that came around the club trying to get next to his dad. She'd make a scene inside the club and out if she thought some light skinned woman was trying to get to him. It didn't matter who was there. Every time she came, that's what she thought was going on."

"Really?"

"Yeah, she had it bad. I remember one night when the band took their break and went outside for a smoke, she stormed after her husband, screaming and cussing him out. He tried to calm her down, but she wasn't hearing anything he had to say. David and I had stepped out for a smoke, so we saw everything."

"I didn't know you smoked."

He lowers his head and rocks it side to side. "I was trying to look cool, but no more for me. When have you seen me with a cigarette? Anyway, she hollered at the crowd waiting in line that she didn't give a flying fuck what they thought, and she just kept cussing at David's father, telling him he was no good for anything. Then she said something I think really hurt David, cause he teared up. I pretended like I didn't see it, but I did."

He's quiet after that. I look over and he's staring at the floor. I wonder if he is counting the lines in the tile. I'm not sure if it's okay to ask him a question, but I ask anyway.

"What did she say, Clarence?"

"It was hard stuff, Carla. Man, she was hard."

He goes quiet again and I realize I'm listening to another slow-dripping faucet of truth. I cut up the carrots for the soup. He'll start talking again when he's ready, like Mama did.

Clarence eventually clears his throat, stands up, and stretches his arms upwards. He rests his hands clasped together on top of his head as if trying to hold himself down.

"David's mother stood screaming in front of everybody, the band members, people standing on the sidewalk—and there were plenty out there—she screamed she had married David's father to get a light baby and that he couldn't even give her that. That his baby was so dark she didn't know how to dress him."

"No Clarence," I say, honestly shocked. "She didn't say that, did she?"

"She did. David father's tried to move away but she followed him back into the club, shouting how was she supposed to love something blacker than her."

"Oh God, that's unthinkable." All at once my heart and soul shiver imagining how David must have felt when he heard his mama say this.

Clarence returns to tracing the round edges of his coffee mug and staring at the counter top. Some time goes by before he continues David's story.

"After that, David and I didn't hang the same anymore. He just drifted away and I went into the service," he says, letting out a huge sigh.

"I better go now, Sis," Clarence says.

I watch my brother add his mug to dishes already in the sink, and I remind myself to wash them before Mama comes into the kitchen. Clarence puts his arm around me and we walk towards the door, stuck together like Velcro. Before he steps out he gives me a long hug.

"I love you little one," he whispers. "Be strong."

As I put on all four locks, I wonder if Dana knows that part of David's story. Clarence's sadness about what happened to his friend lingers thick in the air, and I think about the loss of his friend, and the reasons why it has weighed on him for all these years.

I decide to check on Mama and peek around the corner into her bedroom, being careful not to let her see me. She's awake, listening to a Sunday gospel program. I can tell she's enjoying it by the way her feet are moving under the covers. Well, that's a good sign. I don't want to disturb her, so I tiptoe away from the door and go back into the kitchen. While I finish preparing lunch I think about how there is so much hurt underneath everyone it's a wonder anyone wants to stick around to see their life through. My heart still aches for David. How could he ever forget what his mama said?

I'm afraid to go into Mama's room—she hasn't unloaded her feelings about the morning yet and I have no idea what that's going to bring. But I know she needs to put something in her stomach so she can take her afternoon medication.

"Mama, are you ready to eat?"

"What did you make?" she asks.

I set the bed tray down and offer her a spoon.

211

"Homemade vegetable soup with big chunks of tomato in it, just like you like."

I decide to go on the offensive and make the first attempt to talk about what happened this morning.

"I'm sorry you missed church today," I say softly. "Why didn't you want us to take you?"

She dips her spoon into the soup, blows on it, and sighs before eating.

God, there's a lot of sighing going on today.

"When your father was alive we went to First Sunday as a family. You remember. It used to be all of us."

"I remember."

"He wasn't big on going to church, said he worshipped the Lord twenty-four hours a day and didn't have to do it in a church. But he promised he'd always go with us on First Sunday, and he kept that promise as long as he could, so it has special meaning."

Here's another thing I never knew. In all the years of going to church with Mama I never knew Daddy had made that promise.

"Do my brothers know that about First Sunday?"

"I shouldn't have to tell them that to get them to go church," she says.

"Maybe if they knew they'd want to go more because it's a family tradition that you and Daddy started. They'd understand why it's important."

"Mmph, maybe," she says, and continues eating her soup.

Now do I ask her why I'm not part of everybody, why she favors her sons— or do I let that go? Clarence is gone—what if it gets heated again and he's not here to stop us? Besides, she hasn't finished the story yet. If she gets mad it will never be finished, and I'm too far in not to get the rest of it. She left off telling me how her daddy was upset because he didn't like her tone of voice. Boy, does that sound familiar.

Mama finishes lunch and tells me how much she enjoyed the soup. She even raises the bowl to drink the last bit of broth, wipes her mouth and smiles at me. She likes when I cook for her. She seems to have shifted into a better mood.

"You know, I think I want to get up and sit in the living room for awhile," she says.

The kitchen's not clean. Oh God, that will only start another problem. Maybe I can get her to go into the den so she won't see the mess I made.

"What about sitting in your recliner? It'll be easier on your back and you can put your legs up."

"Yes, you're probably right, my back is a little achy today. And it seems like these veins popping out my legs trying to get the best of me. I think I will go sit in my chair."

Whew. I help her with the walker and we make the trek to the den. She plops down and makes the recliner rock back so the leg rest sticks out. I sit on the loveseat waiting to hear what she wants next. There's always a *next* when it comes to taking care of Mama.

"Maybe we should get back to the story I've been telling you. Are you going back to work tomorrow?"

"That's a good idea, and yes, I have to go to work tomorrow." I'm surprised she's offering her story without any prodding from me.

"If you get me a glass of water, we can get started."

I get her the water, go in the living room to get Mama Belle's quilt and reposition myself on the small couch. I throw the quilt over me and wait. Mama sips the water slowly, clears her throat and sighs. I wonder if Mama's sighs, or anybody's sighs for that matter, always means they're thinking about something sad. I tell myself to get ready for whatever truth is about to come.

"Let me see where I was," Mama says. "I know I told you me and my daddy had words, and when I went to get water for the morning breakfast your grandmother, Mama Belle, followed me out to the pump. That's right, now I remember where I left off."

"It's good the water's real slow today. It gives us time to talk," My mama told me.

"I didn't know what she wanted to talk about. I knew it had to be important for her to make the hike to the pump. She looked so serious that I became worried. Mama leaned close into the pump and put my hand on the handle, so it looked as if it was taking the two of us to lift the wooden handle up and push it back down.

"'Sister,' she whispered to me, and then she told me that I was gon' have to leave Love real soon or I might not like what was going to happen. I told her not to worry, that the Anderson boys weren't looking for me like Daddy thought. She told me it wasn't about them Anderson boys. She wanted to tell me something about my daddy. We kept pretending to pump the water and then she said that he was planning to marry me off to an old colored man that lived across the creek and she couldn't stop him from doing that.

"I remember an ache just grew inside of me. I tried to get Mama back on my side. I needed her to believe June was going to send for me soon. I reminded her that she had seen the letters coming every week. That he hadn't forgot about me. I don't think she listened to what I had to say, 'cause she just kept pulling and pushing on that old pump. She said her father had done the same thing to her, and she believed my daddy was getting ready to do it to me. And that was that. We walked back to the house, being careful when we came in not to wake Daddy and the boys. She said Mr. Carter coming out meant the day was going to be hard enough. I remember working alongside her in the dark kitchen. Our only light was from two candles and we moved around quietly. A big breakfast was going to be important that day.

"After we just about finished cooking, Daddy swung the sheet curtain open that separated his bedroom from the rest of the house. He went to the face bowl, not saying a word to anyone. I'd already filled the white bowl with the water we carried from the pump. I put a clean washrag next to it and the special smelling soap Mama kept in

214

the corner of the kitchen cabinet. When he finished washing up he spoke to Mama and the boys, but said nothing to me. He didn't even look at my face when I placed his food in front of him.

"After he ate he told Mama and me to get the house ready for Mr. Carson's visit, and that Arthur and Clarence, Jr. should bring the tractor to the side of the house. Otis was to be on the first lookout. We put on our Sunday dresses and made some lemonade. All day we stayed in the house, dusting, straightening things up, and taking turns sitting in the chair by the window. We spent all day trying to make things look extra nice so just in case Mr. Carson came inside, he'd see we were taking good care of his property and all. Outside, Daddy and the boys walked around fixing things that needed fixing. One year, on the day before payment day, Daddy had the boys hurry up to paint the porch steps white. He said Mr. Carson liked coloreds who took concern with how his property looked.

"Daddy was standing at the door, complaining that things still didn't look right, when Otis shouted that a black car was coming up the road. When Otis hollered the alarm that Mr. Carson was coming, Daddy rushed to sit in one of the porch chairs and was acting all easy like when that car pulled in. Mr. Carson had a work truck that he drove most times he came to check on things, but on payment days he drove his shiny black car, wore his matching suit and tie and tried to look all official. Your Grandpa Clarence told all of us to come to the porch so we could pay our respects to Mr. Carson.

"It was late in the day, and that wasn't a good sign. The gate was already open and Mr. Carson pulled right up to the porch step, just like he always did when he was driving that black car. He got so close the car almost touched the porch before he turned the engine off. Daddy dipped his hat at Mr. Carson before he stood up to meet him. Mr. Carson, he got out and told Mama Belle how lovely we looked and that the boys were looking strong—he told Daddy that he had some good field boys.

"A young white man with a whole mess of hair was sitting in the car on the passenger's side, resting his foot on the dashboard, just a wiggling it and staring. He didn't say hello to any of us. Mr. Carson and Daddy walked towards the water pump at the end of the yard, but they didn't go too far. They thought we couldn't hear, but we could. Clarence sat on the wooden porch with a knee to his chest, acting as if he was doing something else. Arthur and Otis were leaning on the railing near Mama. Seemed like we all were straining our ears to hear what he was saying. We just had to watch and wait. I remember the wind picked up and clouds were moving in, and to tell you the truth, baby, I knew nothing good was fixing to come.

Mama stops talking, she looks to the window where a late afternoon sun is creeping in and pats the side of her leg and begins to hum with her eyes closed. Her humming is a low moan yet it sounds soothing and I allow myself to relax in to it. I don't feel to ask any questions even though I'm sure her story is far from done. I pull Mama Belle's quilt up to my neck and close my eyes.

"You see, Carla, my Daddy had so much on his mind that I don't hold it against him for what he was trying to do."

Her voice causes my eyes to open. How long had we been sitting in quiet? The sun has passed over and the room is filled with grey light.

"Fieldwork was hard and being a sharecropper was even harder. I know he hoped that when I married, my husband would work the fields with him, and not live way off in California."

"Why were you and Daddy willing to move so far away from your family?"

"Like I said, baby, I'd been there all my life. A sharecropping life was all I knew. But it was real hard on your Daddy to move there from Alapaha."

"Alapaha? Where's that?"

"It's in Georgia, Carla."

216

To me Daddy had just been from Georgia. Did I know what town he actually came from? Suddenly I'm feeling more ignorant about everything. How could I not have asked to know more about my father?

"Yes, Alapaha is a small town in Georgia. Lots of blacks lived there. You see, even though it had been a plantation before, it was a prosperous one so June and his Daddy were used to living on the seconds handed down from the whites. When we got to know each other better, he told me that when he got to Love and saw his new home was just a tattered old house on stilts, with no shade trees and only crusty red dirt for a front yard, well, he just wanted to run away."

"So going to California was how he ran away from being forced to live there."

"Those Anderson boys made him leave, but I guess you could say that even if I wasn't looking at it that way. Maybe all that money I spent on your schooling did pay off," Mama smiles after her wisecrack and I smile back at her.

"If that hadn't happened, I think we still would have left," Mama says. "You couldn't live your dreams, with white folks having their foot on colored folks' necks and all. And the lynchings—seem like every day you heard about a black man strung from a tree. I grew to be glad that June left."

My hands are gripped tight in my lap. Mama's shoulders have slumped in the chair and I can see her saddened feelings.

"My daddy's father, Jesse Luther Adams, grew up on a plantation in southern Georgia. He was born in the 1880's or somewhere around then. When I was a little girl he visited twice, and I heard him tell stories about slave masters and overseers in Georgia that scared me more than I can say," Mama says, shaking her head.

"Great Grandpa Jesse was born on a plantation? How's that possible, Mama?"

"Carla, do your math. My grandfather Jesse was 103 years old when he died back in 1990. Remember it was in the paper, 'cause he lived to be over a hundred."

"I remember. He received a letter from the President, didn't he?" Okay so that means he was born in 1887."

"No one is sure how old his daddy, Alexander, was when Jesse was born but everyone thinks your great-great-granddaddy was born around 1869. And folks still stayed on plantations then. Just because Lincoln signed that paper didn't mean everything happened right away."

I guess nothing happens right away.

The day is getting ready to leave us and we haven't eaten dinner yet. Mama says she's not hungry, but she'll eat a sandwich so her blood sugar doesn't drop too low during the night. I think we're both tired and we eat in silence. I help Mama get into bed and go clean the kitchen, because otherwise I know the home health aide will tell her how I left it a mess. Finally I can lie down on the couch and hear myself think.

Grandpa Clarence left Georgia, came to Texas to stay in Love for the rest of his life and never wanted anything else. Great-Grandpa Jesse was born free but lived on the plantation. No one knows when my great-great-grandfather Alexander was born, but they know it was also on a plantation in Georgia. I wonder what their children knew about their lives, how they felt about things. I guess this is Dana's theory about emotional legacy and what we inherit, whether we know it or not.

One more night of car lights coming through the window and I can be back in my own bed. I've been at Mama's since last Saturday. It was only that Friday that I wanted to be gone from the planet, soaring the heavens looking for my father. It was Dana's idea to come here, but she couldn't make me listen. I'm the one who was willing to hear Mama's story, hoping I'd learn something sweet, something that would convince me life is worth living. I can't say I've heard it yet. It's all been so painful. My own huge sigh comes out to join every other sigh I've heard all week.

No telling what condition my students and classroom are in. I haven't talked with Dana since she made me so mad. And then there's Rasheed. Oh God, what kind of life am I going back to?

CHAPTER SIXTEEN

To get to work on time, I need to leave Brentwood at what seems like a hellish hour to join the rivers of people who do this every day. Before I leave I check on Mama, who is awake, so I lean over the bed to give her a kiss on the forehead.

"Baby, thank you for staying so long," she says. "I want you to come back to hear the rest of the story. Promise me you'll be back next weekend."

"Okay Mama, I'll be back, promise."

She wants to finish it. Maybe she feels undone, in the middle of something. I didn't know it would turn out this way. This past week we've both gone through something, and as anxious as I feel about it, I want her to finish the story too.

Despite the traffic, I get to school with plenty of time. I've been gone for a week so going into the Main Office is unavoidable. Mrs. Brown gives me her usual grunt when I say good morning—that hasn't changed. My box is filled to the top with stacks of papers, announcements, and notes from other teachers. It's more than I want to deal with right now. As I stuff a week worth of paper into my bag, Ed walks by, gives a nod, and walks away. It's still early so, the walk down the hallway is event free. Well, at least you can't see the blood on the locker where Rasheed had his fight, but the patch of beige colored paint doesn't match very well.

"Good morning, Mr. Jerrod."

"Morning." He doesn't bother to look up or provide any morning pleasantry.

That confirms that at Douglass business is as usual. When I open the door to my classroom I find the desks rearranged into rows, with the maps tightly rolled up instead of hanging on the wall where the students can see them. I can't let the condition of it bother me. It was probably a rookie substitute who only knows one way to teach. I've got to turn it back into what the students are used to, so quickly I go about changing the desks into the four student cubes they were in from the beginning of the year.

Fifteen minutes before the first bell, Miriam sticks her head through the doorway.

"May I come in?" she asks. Miriam asking permission first—now that's a change.

"I missed seeing you, Carla. Are you okay?"

"Oh, I'm fine. I needed to help my mother out, she's getting on in her years." Over the past several months Miriam and I have become friendly towards each other, but not so friendly that I can tell her the truth.

"I see you put the classroom back. Your students sure didn't like it the other way."

"I bet they didn't. Uh, Miriam, there's only a few minutes before the bell. Can we talk later?"

"Oh sure, I didn't mean to take up your time. Welcome back."

Okay, that felt different. Normally, I'd find myself waiting for her to leave. I take the stack of papers from my bag and place them on the corner of the desk. I'll have to look through them later, as the students are already starting to trickle into the room.

"Ms. Sinclair, where you been?"

"Hi, Ms. Sinclair."

"Ms. Sinclair, that sub, he was horrible. Glad you're back."

One after another, the students greet me, each one letting me know they had missed me. I'd only been gone a week. My lesson plan for today is an assignment to write about how last week went for them. It turns out to be well received and all the students want to read their stories about the horrors they endured while I was gone. After third period, I feel a familiar cold wave in my stomach—Rasheed's class will be here soon.

I tell myself it's okay, whatever happens happens—I can deal with it. I just have to be patient. In time I will win his trust back. The room fills up with fourth period students, all welcoming me back. Manuel wheels himself to my desk and asks for a hug. When the bell rings, it's clear to me that Rasheed will not be in class today. I wonder where he is. I tell myself to put it out of my mind, take roll and start with the class assignment.

When last period ends I look at the stack of papers on my desk that still needs sorting, but Dana's left me a voicemail that simply said, "four o'clock, still walking?" That's enough of an excuse for me—the paperwork can wait until I get home. I have to admit, I want to see her. No matter what goes down between us she's still my girl.

If I know Dana, 4:00 is probably going to be closer to 4:30, so I take my time walking to the parking lot and driving to the lake. Cassandra catches me sitting in the car and spills out her plans for her husband's surprise birthday. She's so giddy about her plans she doesn't fill me in on what happened while I was gone.

"I still have to pick up party supplies and decorations. I'm thinking of a navy and light blue theme. You know, keep it manly. Even though it's not until Friday, I have so much to do between now and then. Will you come, Carla? You know my Boo likes you. He says it's good I have an older friend and that we should hang out more often."

"That sounds fun, Cassandra, but I told my mother I'd be back to see her this weekend. She's expecting me on Friday."

While Cassandra goes on and on about all the fun I'll be missing, I'm thinking about Clarence and me sitting on Mama's couch. Sometimes I got so caught up in Mama's story that I didn't even notice when it got dark. I'm remembering Mama's tears and her sad gospel music.

"Cassandra I better get going. I'm meeting someone soon."

"Okay, glad you're back. We missed you."

My drive to the lake is just enough time to shake my thoughts from the weekend, although I have to admit I'm a little anxious about seeing Dana. A parking space that's close to the Pillars shows up quickly on Lakeshore and I'm relieved I don't have to walk half the lake to get to where I'm going. In front of our usual meeting spot there's a small gathering of people. When I get closer, I see their wide circle has formed around two boys who look about Rasheed's age. They have that same princely way about them, and they're playing chess. It's like they're holding court, and their confidence in this center of attention as they play their game brings a smile to my face.

"Hey Carla, over here. Look this way—hey, it's me!"

The loud voice draws my attention—and a few other people—away from the boys. Of course, it's Dana. I give her a wave to assure her she is in my sight and to get her to lower her voice. Dana's got the top down on the convertible, and she leans to the passenger side waving her free hand.

"Hey girl," she shouts. "Be there in a minute. As soon as I find a parking space."

A minute turns into ten, and, finally, in her customary long-legged way Dana strides through the library's brick yard still hollering, "I'm coming!" Why does she think I don't see her? When Dana arrives she glances into the crowd of people and then positions herself directly in front of me. Like two teenage girls we look each other up and down, give a few neck rolls, then satisfied that neither one of us wants to keep the argument going, we laugh and hug. Dana holds on to me for a very long time. It feels like Clarence's hug before he left Mama's.

"I'm sorry," we say at the same time, and we both start laughing.

"Car, you know I can't stay mad at you."

"Me neither. Like Mama says—I only got one friend—so I better keep you."

"Let's skip the warm-up and start walking," Dana says, "I have so much to tell you. But wait a minute, how are you doing? And tell me the truth."

"Well, I'm not going to lie, Dana, it was a tiring week. Mama's story is intense—oh my God, has she been through some things. Maybe it was a good idea to go, but I'm sleepy, I missed my bed, and . . . as you can see, I'm still here."

"Girl, I see you and I want you to stay. I love you. David loves you."

She grabs my arm and places it over her bent elbow. Her gesture feels comforting and reassuring.

"I'm trying, Dana. I'm really trying."

We hug each other again.

"And before I forget, I'm going home with you after our walk and you, Miss One, will give me those pills. The Wonder Boy backs me up on this. He says don't make him have to come over there and get them himself."

"Okay, okay, let's walk," I say.

Dana's got a Cassandra-bounce going as we take the trail towards the tree stumps. I start to count them, but stop myself when I feel the cool breeze brushing my face. I look at Dana, she smiles and grabs my arm again, and for a while we walk like this. I don't see shiny sequins on top of the water today, but ripples crossing the lake flow in a rhythmic motion, each one with just enough space before the next ripple to show its own fullness. I'm not counting, just watching the beauty they bring. Two women are walking towards us, the way they're holding hands and gazing at each other I think they must be in love. They remind me of David and Dana when they're together. For a moment I try to remember if I've ever known that in love feeling. The women smile at us as they pass by, and Dana and I smile back.

"Love simply walks like it wants to," Dana says cheerily.

"So, Dana, I think we should talk about the night I called you. It's been weighing heavy on my mind."

"Me, too. I've been waiting to tell you what I did afterwards."

"It was pretty late and I remember how I sounded."

"Well, I'm not mad anymore. It hurt, some, but Car, I admit you were one hundred percent right," she says.

"That's a relief. I'm not mad, either. But Dana, you still need to call Aaron. I don't know any more about holding onto things until they back up inside of you. You should have seen how sad Mama was, remembering all those things from her past."

"I did it already! I called Aaron and we talked."

"Sure you did," I say sarcastically. "You've been running from this for months and now—poof— just like that it's done? I don't know if I believe you."

"Really, I called him," she says.

Disbelief makes me stop walking to look her in the eye.

"I'm telling the truth, Miss gotta-stare-me-in-the-eyes-to-see-if-I-really-did-do-it," Dana says, with her hands on her hips and her eyebrows dipped, as if to say this is the truth.

"That morning I talked with David and he was on your side. It took a minute, but Car, I understand now what you were saying."

"Nice to hear somebody else is getting real besides me."

My hand rises for a high five and she meets me in the air. The trail seems extra busy today and we're standing in the middle of the stream of people trying to get by, so I start us walking again.

"I thought you would like that," she says. "It took me all day to work myself up to it. After David left the house I did everything I could to put it off. Girl, I mopped floors that were already mopped and dusted where there was no dust. I was even getting ready to organize my closets, and you know my closets are always neat. Then David called from the golf course and interrupted my procrastination. All he said was, "make the call," and then he hung up."

"So, how did it go?"

She sighs, and is quiet for a while.

"It's hard to remember, it felt so emotional."

I shake my head—Dana's supposed to be writing a book about emotions, but when it comes to her own feelings she doesn't know what to say.

"What was so important you just had to tell Aaron?"

"Carla, it's a whole story, and I don't know if you want to hear it. You've just listened to your Mama's story, and I know that's been hard."

"Well, I guess I'm getting good practice at hearing hard stuff."

We've just passed the courthouse, which means we've got at least thirty more minutes of walking time left. If we take the inside path, it might be a little longer.

"Dana, I know I've been in a bad way, but now you get to have your turn. I'll listen."

She looks at me and then looks down. We're walking at a much slower pace and Dana's moved much closer to me. This time I grab her arm to hold it and she leans her head over as if to whisper.

"My mother became pregnant with me through her panties. There was never any penetration. She told my grandparents that she didn't know who the father was, but that was a lie."

I don't say anything but I must have surprise in my eyes because she steps back to nod her head a few times as if to say yes, that's really what happened.

"Maybe six months or more into her pregnancy she was still living in the St. Louis projects with her parents, when one day the father of the baby, or I should say—my father—showed up with his parents. They came to take my mother and me to live with them in Virginia. His parents said the Jeffersons came from a long family line, and their son would not be the first Jefferson to create a public scandal by having a bastard child showing up later and claiming to be his."

"How do you know all this?"

"I've told you, Mother treated me like I was her girlfriend. I knew everything about her life, and I mean everything."

"Okay. I'm sorry for interrupting." I remember my lessons from listening to Mama and Clarence tell their stories.

"It's okay, I know how it sounds. They told my mother's parents that the child, which meant me, would grow up in its proper station in life and that my mother would be well taken care of."

"And her parents just let her go?"

Dana looks at me with a lowered eyebrow which I know means to be quiet. But it's so hard. Here's another story of a woman just being sent off with strangers.

"My mother's own father was adamant he would take care of his daughter and her child. He didn't want her to leave —but my mother's mother said she had to go and be with the father of her child. From then on her life was dictated by the lifestyles of the black bourgeoisie, a way of life she knew nothing about. When I told Aaron how our parents got together he was so quiet, it surprised me that he was actually listening and not getting angry with me. He even asked what happened to Mother when she moved to Virginia. I was so glad to hear him ask that, because it's the next part that I wanted him to know.

"In Virginia, Mother lived in an expensive two-story house in a very posh white neighborhood where they were one of only two black families. It's where I grew up. Anyway, she spent most of her days inside unless our father escorted her somewhere. He ran the family's law firm and was hardly ever around the house. He'd take her out for public appearances—they were always going to some society function because my father was the heir to the family business and his father made sure he stayed well connected. But when they returned home, he ignored her. He stayed in his office and they slept in separate bedrooms.

"The only people Mother talked to besides me were the maid, the butler, and the driver. My father never tried to see to her needs. He left that up to the servants. And sex was nonexistent, Carla. My father told her when she moved to Virginia that would never be part of the deal. She felt so alone and trapped. I guess they must have done it at least one more time because Aaron is here, but Mother always told me she was starved for attention and dreamed about running away."

When we get to the estuary where the birds wait to be fed breadcrumbs, Dana suddenly sits down on a bench and pauses. I sit down next to her and wait to see if she wants to keep talking.

"What do you think so far?" she asks.

"I don't know what to say, Dana. It's a sad story of someone's life."

"That's almost the same thing Aaron said."

"Did he ever get why you thought it was so important for him to know all this?"

"Not at first. It took quite a bit of explaining what our parents' lives had to do with him now. You know he's ten years younger and in many ways he was protected from their affairs. Mother had little to do with his upbringing, Father saw to that. Aaron thought ignoring women at home and letting servants tend to your wife is what made a marriage. How could he not? That was all he'd ever seen. When we were young we rarely played together, because Father kept us apart. Aaron is successful and a good provider, but Carla he doesn't know how to love his wives. He doesn't make any kind of emotional connection with them, and so they leave. That's why all his previous marriages have failed."

"All those failed marriages must have made him sad."

"Not really, Car. He just said it was their loss. But during our conversation I had to tell him that each of his ex-wives called me after they divorced to tell me why they had left. They all said he was a nice guy and they were calling out of concern for him. And I feel guilty that I never told him what they said until now. I just couldn't let it happen to him again."

Dana lets out a deep, chest moving sigh, and it makes me think of how Clarence sighed when he told me about David's mother and how Mama sighs a whole lot while telling her story.

Once we get back to The Pillars, the crowd has thinned out, but the boys are still playing chess. I want to watch them a little more, and Dana joins me. We have to pull ourselves away from the boys' intense concentration on their game, so we can head to our cars. On the way Dana still pushes to follow me home.

"Look, I'm not going to say anything about the condition of your apartment. I know you haven't been there."

"It's a mess, Dana. Really, it's okay."

"I want to go in with you and besides, David told me to get that pill bottle. I'll leave as soon as you hand them over, unless you want me to stay."

"Thanks, but there's something about this mess that is for only me to do. You know what I mean."

She nods.

"Sometimes cleaning is part of putting yourself back together," Dana says and places her hand on my shoulder as we walk to the cars.

When we get to my building, we have to wait for the elevator to come down to the lobby. The door opens and there are my loud and oversexed neighbors. I start to frown, but instead I give them a pleasant hello—to my surprise they do the same. Dana follows me down the walkway. She's not talking. Maybe we're both anxious about what we will find in my apartment. I put the key in the first lock and look at Dana.

"You sure you want to come in here?"

"Car, it's all right. Let's go in," she says.

When I unlock the deadbolt and open my door I gasp.

She puts her hand on my shoulder. "It's okay."

Dana steps inside first. When I walk in my shoulders rise up and I cover my mouth with both hands. Oh God, I'm so ashamed. The apartment smells of stale alcohol, the floor is covered with shredded magazine pages, pieces of the broken ceramic lamp are scattered around, and something must have spoiled in the refrigerator.

"Maybe I do need some help."

She gives me a small hug and it eases my embarrassment.

"I promise I won't say a word."

The pill bottle is on the floor underneath the end table. Dana drops to her knees and crawls under the table in order to get to it. She shows me the bottle and stuffs it into her pocket. She doesn't say anything and I just shrug.

"I'll clean the bathroom. I don't expect you to deal with that," I say.

She starts picking up the balled up magazine pictures from the floor and tells me she will vacuum. The toilet had been flushed, thank God for that, but it still reeks of alcohol and vomit. I think about the ray of sunshine that warmed me that day and how I fell asleep on the floor. This bathroom is going to require rubber gloves.

Dana opens all the windows, even the ones in the bedroom, and leaves the front door open. She doesn't think I can see her, but on the sly she's holding her nose. With the both of us cleaning it still takes an hour or more to make it not be the place where I wanted to die. It's not a deep clean, but it'll have to do. After we finish Dana turns the Bose to KCSM and we end up on the couch, sitting, quietly listening to Winton Marsalis. His horn is full of emotion and speaks what I feel, but can't say.

"Car, if you want me to stay I will. Or come home with me."

"I'll be alright. I want to be in my own bed. I've been on Mama's couch and the blowup bed all week."

"Still, I'm going to wait till I see you in there."

I know there's no way to change her mind. Dana is going to stay until I get into bed.

"Okay, but then you go home. I've got school tomorrow. Really, all I'm going to do is sleep and get up for work in the morning."

I'm too tired to even think about looking at the papers in my bag. They will have to wait. I take one of the most soothing showers I can remember in a long time. I didn't need the water so hot that it scalded me. The shower was just warm enough and I triple soaped myself up, as if I removing layers of gunk from my skin. While I was in the bathroom Dana changed my sheets and made the bed.

"Oh, my bed," I say, and ease into it, pulling the covers over my head. Now this is a love affair I've missed. Dana gives me a little forehead kiss goodbye and says she'll use her key to lock up. I don't hear any locks turning. I smile and let myself drift off to sleep.

The phone wakes me from my deep sleep. Where is it? It must be in the living room. This time of the morning, it must be either Mama or Dana. I have to get ready for work. I can't believe I slept all the way through the night—the sun's already up. I stumble over a stack of magazines close to the doorway, pause to look at them and pick up the phone before it goes to my answering machine.

"'This is your wake up call," Dana says with merry and bright in her voice.

"Dana? What time is it?"

"Seven-thirty. Doesn't school start at eight-thirty?"

"If you hadn't called, I probably would have overslept."

"I thought you might, so here's your wake up call. Now get up."

"Girl, you're a mess, but thank you."

"Hey, I can't walk today. I'm going out of town until Friday," Dana says, "there's a conference in Seattle and they want me to come in early."

"Okay, call me when you get back. I'm dressed and out. Thanks again."

"David says don't white knuckle it. Call him if you need to."

Ten minutes before the bell rings, I arrive at Douglass. No quiet time for me today. I throw my bag under my desk and write today's assignment on the board. The day goes fast. Students are still excited to tell me about their week while I was gone. At the end of each class I let those who didn't get a chance to share their paper yesterday read today. Each one has something in there for me about not leaving again. Teaching the babies . . . I know I do that well.

I'm concerned that still Rasheed has not shown up. It's the second day he's been absent. I look at my attendance book to see if he had been here last week. The sub's markings show he was here up to Wednesday. If he's not here tomorrow, even though I want to avoid the main office, I'm going to have to talk to Ed about looking into why he's not coming to school. I could ask one of his classmates, but a cold wave streams through my stomach when I think about how he ignored me the last time. Since no one has said anything about him there must be a code of silence about Rasheed going on right now.

When I look in the long cabinet underneath the window, it's clear my students need supplies; we're out of colored paper and drawing pens. After school I'm going to have to go to Target to pick up what we will need for the next assignment, and maybe I'll pick up a chess set. Rasheed could become interested in learning how to play, just like he became so involved with the tide pool; and if he doesn't other students might.

I'm in no hurry and at this hour I decide to avoid the freeway. I don't want to chance getting caught in a sea of traffic, so I take San Pablo Avenue to El Cerrito to get to the closest Target. The last time I drove up San Pablo, I was on my way to meet Dana at the Albany Bulb. Am I deciding to stay around? Last night I can really say I slept all the way through until morning. I'm still cautious though. One good night's sleep doesn't mean the rest are going to be that way.

Wandering around Target is like a taking a drug. All the merchandise makes me feel intoxicated—I want to buy everything—it's at least thirty minutes ago that I finished picking up what I needed for school. The woman down the aisle near the housewares department looks familiar, and isn't that Cassandra pushing a cart alongside her? How do I know that other woman? She's short in height with a big bust line and wearing a head wrap—oh God—it's the Queen, the poet from the Black Dot Café. Her words have haunted me for months. What are those two doing together? Before I can decide if I want to avoid them, Cassandra waves and pushes her cart in my direction.

"Fancy seeing you here," Cassandra says. We lean in to hug and at the same time look into each other's carts.

"Buying supplies?"

Her voice sounds knowing, in a way that only another teacher might understand. I nod yes. There's no hiding my intentions here. The shopping cart is full of construction paper, cotton balls, glue, colored pencils and two chess sets.

"We're making clouds."

She picks up the construction paper for inspection and gives me her nonverbal approval of the colors I've chosen.

"It was either buy them or beg the administration," I say.

We both shake our heads.

"Anyway, I'm here for my Boo's birthday party," Cassandra says.

My attention is divided between Cassandra showing me her choices in party supplies and paying attention to the Queen. She still looks awfully young to me, but her eyes don't have that same eerie stare I experienced at the Café. Finally, Cassandra realizes that in all her excitement about the party, she hasn't introduced us.

"I'm sorry. Latiste, this is Carla Sinclair. We work together. Latiste is a fierce spoken word artist. You be throwing it down, don't you 'Tiste."

I give the Queen a tentative hello. She reaches out her hand to shake mine. I recognize the same thin hand that pointed at me that night.

"We've met before. I've seen one of your performances," I say.

"How cool is that?" Cassandra chimes in with her bubbly nature.

"Actually, we met before that, Mama Sinclair," Latiste says.

Mama? I don't remember when or where, except at the café, and I can't say that was an actual meeting, given the way she was messing with me. I'm thinking twice about meeting her now. Latiste turns to Cassandra.

"I would like to talk to Mama Sinclair alone for a minute. Do you mind Cass?"

"I still have a few more things to get," Cassandra says. She turns her cart and bounces away.

"May we sit and talk?" Her head gives a slight bow. I guess always the performer is her style.

"Yes, let's do."

Our eyes lock on each other; I guess we both know we have something to talk about. I look around the store and say, "The only place to sit is in the food court near the front entrance."

We head in that direction, not saying anything, and find a table in the corner. I push my basket to the side and squirm a little bit to find my comfort in the chair—and from being in the presence of the Queen. She pulls her long flowing skirt back and sits softly into her seat. As she looks at me, her posture is erect and her hands are folded on the table. The Queen's eyes are calm and she gives me a thin smile. We just look at each other. Is this another one of those who-goes-first games? I decide to start. This girl has been on my mind for too long. I lean across the table to keep my voice at a whisper and ask her the question I've needed to ask for a long time.

"Why did you do that? Why me?"

She doesn't lean forward or try to whisper as I have done.

"I didn't intend you any harm. My performance called for someone in the audience to receive the question I asked. When I saw you in the café, I knew the poem was for you."

I look at the people sitting down next to us to see if they are listening, but un-boxing their pizza and situating their food is more important than two Black women having a conversation.

"The poem was for me?" My whisper raises some. "You don't know me."

"I know something about you."

"What do you mean?" I ask.

"I was at Cassandra's wedding. I don't believe you saw me, but I watched you as you walked along the beach."

I scan my brain to see if I can remember seeing someone who looked like her, but nothing comes up.

"Why were you watching me?"

"Again, I meant no harm," Latiste says repeating herself.

I can't think of any reason why I deserved her attention that day. I remember I stayed in the back while I watched the ceremony, and left as soon as it was over. I didn't even attend the reception.

"Honestly, this sounds a little strange, and I have to say—a little eerie."

"That day we all were connecting to the earth in celebration of our love for Cassandra and her husband-to-be. If you remember, there were all ages and types of people there, and everyone took their shoes off, except you."

"Cassandra and I had just met, I didn't feel obligated."

"The earth and the land we stood on was our common connection. You breathed the same ocean air as we did. I knew, since you didn't remove your shoes, that you were not free."

Her voice was low and steady as she told me this, her hands remaining folded in front of her. In the same manner she continues.

"Our people are not yet free, Mama Sinclair. The mamas will lead the way, and not alone. Fathers, brothers, and uncles will lead too. You teach the babies, yet you are not free in your mind. I know that your spirit suffers—how could it not?"

Okay. Am I sitting here with a brown-skinned Yoda? Where's Cassandra? She should be done by now. I agreed to talk to the Queen because I needed to know why she had singled me out, but this is a whole lot more than I expected.

"Latiste, you don't know me. That night you called me out without even knowing me."

"Have you not felt twisted with your emotions? Waiting, wanting, needing something to feed your soul? Sister, I see you."

Her words are unsettling. She continues talking. I'm doing my best to listen, but my mind is jumping back and forth about what to do. I can leave this impromptu conversation. I came to Target to shop, not have my soul read by someone I don't know.

"We do know each other."

Carla what are you going to do—stay or leave. I let out a sigh that is so deep my chest rises. She reaches over to touch my hand.

"I know this is hard. The truth of who we are, who we are becoming, is hard."

I look over her head and around the food court to distract myself, but I notice I don't try to remove my hand from hers.

"This situation is not true for our souls. For generations we have had love beaten and torn out of us, and now it's the only thing that is going to save us—loving ourselves—loving each other is our new pot liquor. Many are seeking a different way of being. I think you are one of those. Does not your soul itch for something else?"

"Honestly, this sounds like a performance for an audience of one." I say.

"My performances come from my heart, that is from where I speak. Once I spoke from a place of despair. My heart had simmered out and I was trapped in my own mind. Some may have called it depression, but that inferno was much more."

"You are way too young to have all that inside of you," I tell her.

For the first time I see her laugh.

"My Being started a long time ago and what I carry inside is more than just me. The Ancestors gave us more than a physical body. We carry their Spirit."

"Your words can be haunting," I say.

She nods, spreads her skirt out a little more and looks at me. The people next to us have left their table littered with boxes, empty cups and dirty napkins. I return to Latiste and her gaze.

"Decide your life, Mama Sinclair. The possibilities are endless. Your gifts, your talents, are vital to our people—all people. I know this to be true. Otherwise you would not have heard my words that night at the Café, you would not have felt uncomfortable, or wondered if all would stay the same. "

"I don't know what to say right now. I feel many things."

She's right, I've spent almost an entire year trying to decide my life and it's ending, looking for something to let me know I can leave.

"There's joy mixed in with pain. Remember the Ancestors on your journey to find your answers. I bring you these messages from all women before me who had the Sight. I honor you, Mama Sinclair."

Before I can respond, a voice interrupts.

"Hey did you two get something to eat?"

It's Cassandra, with two huge shopping bags and it looks like she can use some help carrying them.

Latiste and I look at each other. Is our conversation over?

"Carla, I wanted to say in the faculty parking lot that I'm so sorry about Rasheed," Cassandra says, "but I was so caught up with planning the party I forgot. I know you tried hard to help him."

I look at her, puzzled. What does she mean? Sorry about Rasheed? A freeze comes into my gut. The two days I've been back he hasn't been there and he was out two days the week I was gone. No one has said anything about him, not even his classmates. Oh God, I'm afraid to ask.

"What do you mean Cassandra? I don't know anything."

Her face drops. It must be something terrible.

"Tell me—what happened?" I demand.

"I thought you knew. He's been expelled. Didn't you see the expulsion papers? All his teachers got the notice."

The papers in my bag. I never got around to reading them. I'd planned to but forgot.

"What happened?"

She sighs before starting. I feel my emotions grip.

"He was accused of stealing something from the sub. I think it was his wallet. He said Rasheed went into his desk and took it, that he had seen him open the drawer."

"Rasheed *stealing*? " I cry out, "Wait a minute—if it was the top drawer on the right side, all the students go in there. That's where I keep extra pencils and pens for when they need one."

"It happened on Wednesday. The substitute eventually found his wallet, but Rasheed in the meantime just lost it and started throwing things around the room. When Ed Shepherd was called, Rasheed wouldn't leave the classroom so they had to carry him out. Oh girl, I'm so sorry. That poor child just wasn't able to find his way at school, no one really knows what he's thinking."

I know what he's thinking. Oh God, I want to scream.

"Thank you for telling me. I forgot I have to be somewhere. I'll see you at school Cassandra."

I say good-bye to Latiste, who has her hands crossed over her chest and nods. I don't know what to say—nice to meet you, nice talking ... my words are stuck. Then like Latiste I just nod, and leave. I had been feeling lighter, but now the same old heavy plod comes back as I walk to my car. Expelled? Hitting the steering wheel, I shout, "Damn, damn, damn!" My eyes sting and my chest heaves up and down. When will it end? I'm tempted to get a fifth of Courvoisier, but don't think I can handle getting out of the car. I've got just enough sense about me to get home and nowhere else. Once in the house, I throw everything on the floor, clothes and all, and crawl into the bed.

Rasheed's expelled. Is this the end? It can't be. If I'd been there and not wallowing in my own pain, this would never have happened. He didn't want to leave the classroom, the one place he knew he could find something that could make his life better. I saw how he dressed, how he kept his papers neat, and watched everything going on. That boy likes school, maybe he didn't talk—but damn Ed for kicking him out. He's so tired; maybe he's the one who should leave.

Okay Carla, what are you going to do? You can't stay in this bed under the covers like nothing has happened. "Decide your life," Latiste said. Decide something now Carla, don't stay under. Dana's no doubt at dinner with the conference organizers or some official group. She said I should call David if I needed too, and right now I need to talk to someone.

Shit. It went to his voice mail.

"David, please call me, this is Carla. I need your help."

I don't know how my voice sounded, but hopefully he gets it's important. Where is he? It's early evening, so maybe he went out to dinner too. I get up to wash my face and move through the apartment to distract myself from watching the phone. It will never ring if I keep staring at it. I decide to clean the refrigerator out. It's still is a mess and I think I smell more spoiled food. I'm bent over, tossing out plastic bowls that had turned into science projects when my ringer goes off. It's just one ping, signaling a text or voice mail. It's a text from David. "Got msg call in 15."

For a long 15 minutes I sit on the couch, with my phone in hand, waiting for it to ring.

"David?" I sniffle.

"Car, what's going on? Are you okay?"

"Yes. No, I'm not okay. Rasheed got expelled."

"The boy who doesn't talk? Dana's told me about him."

"I feel so bad. I've been so deep in my own stuff that I forgot about him. I was gone all last week. If I'd been there this would never

240

have happened. I feel so bad, and I'm scared, real scared, David, about what I'll do."

I start crying in heavy heaves. David shouts into the phone, "Car, Car listen to me. I'll be right there. I want you to meet me at the bottom of the stairs. You need to get out. It's still daylight, we can go somewhere and talk. Did you hear me Car?

"I heard you. I'll be downstairs. Please hurry, David."

"Don't worry, I'll be right there."

I wash my face and brush my hair. I'm breathing easier. He said he would come, that he's on his way. Not in an hour or what about tomorrow, he's on his way now. I look into the bathroom mirror. "Thank you, David."

I decide to walk down the two flights of stairs to avoid running into any of my neighbors. Once outside the gate I find a tree to stand near for cover and shelter. It's not raining, but I need to feel sheltered right now. A few minutes later David's classic blue Mercedes pulls up. I start to get in, but he gets out of the car and comes around to give me a hug—a long one. I drop my head onto his shoulder and start crying again.

"Let's go to Tilden Park in Berkeley. It'll be good to get fresh air. How's that sound? You should eat something, too."

"Okay. Thank you."

David drives to Nellie's Restaurant in Jack London Square's warehouse section to get soul food to go. He comes out carrying two big bags. His jacket and tie are off and he looks pretty casual now. I think he's gotten too much food.

"Dana's gone. I got extra for tomorrow so I don't have to cook," he grins at me as if he read my mind. "Okay, let's go to the park."

That's what my father used to say whenever we were headed for a family outing. David avoids the freeway and takes the side streets to Berkeley. We drive through the homes that line the street as we head up a hill towards Tilden Park. At the intersection instead of turning right like most people, he goes to the left.

"A while back I found this special place. It won't be crowded and there are picnic tables."

Once in the parking lot David opens the trunk and pulls out a blanket and a large black pea coat. He places the coat around my shoulders.

"It can get chilly up here."

We walk into a clearing surrounded by pine trees towards a cluster of tables. We're the only people here.

"How about this one?" he asks.

"It's fine."

David lays the blanket over the bench and we sit next to each other in silence while he unpacks the food—greens, fish, yams, corn bread and two small peach cobblers. Eating helps calm my insides. There's a breeze blowing. It rustles through the trees as if they are whispering. I imagine them saying, "Now what are you deciding to do?" I pull the coat tighter around me and fasten the top button.

"Thanks for the coat. Aren't you cold?"

"No, I'm a warm-blooded American boy. I never get cold."

I glance at him sideways while he eats. This is why Dana loves this man so much, and why she's always talking about his gallant ways—he is that. I can't imagine how his mother didn't see him for who he is. *Shame on her for hurting him that way.*

"Carla, I already know a lot about Rasheed. Remember who my wife is—she tells me everything. So, what has happened to make you so upset?"

What I know isn't much, just what Cassandra told me at Target and from the expulsion papers—when I finally read them. They had Ed's signature, but the incident report is in someone else's handwriting. It said that the teacher and students were endangered by Rasheed's willful defiance, that he tore tissues from a tissue box in a violent manner, then threw the box at the wall and kicked the box multiple times. When the student was asked to leave the classroom he refused and had to be physically carried out. The part about stealing the wallet was crossed out, but I could still read what it said. I tell David all of this, and the whole time I'm speaking he holds my hand and looks at me with concern in his eyes.

"They carried him out of the classroom? Man, he didn't want to leave, did he?" David says.

"I feel so bad—I should have been there, and not so broke down."

"From what I know you couldn't have been there anyway, Car."

"I hate that I wasn't there to protect him." Then Thomas's deflated body in an oversized chair flashes through my mind. Had his tissue box become Rasheed's dangerous weapon?

"Car, I think I know how you feel," David says, "We didn't know each other the way we do now, but two years into my marriage I began to feel like a backed up sewage plant. I got so depressed that killing myself seemed the only way out."

He says this so matter-of-factly that I'm stunned. There's no shame in his voice, no need to look away. He must see the look on my face, because he says, "I've done a lot of work to accept that's how I felt then—and I no longer feel that way now." He wraps his long arm around my shoulders.

"You know Dana's told me some about your depression."

So she's still calling it depression, even if I'm not. I manage a small smile at the thought of "tell it all" Dana.

"That's my baby." David grins, and I grin with him as I think about Dana and her special ways. He gives me a gentle squeeze and returns to his food. I think this is our moment; it's just us. The whispering trees speak louder, dare I ask about things I don't understand about him? I push the whole Rasheed mess to the corner of my mind and look at David.

"Why did you move out? Dana never said much about it. I mean we talked, but it always seemed like she was leaving something out."

He takes a long swig of his juice in that way only men seem to do; then clears his throat.

"When we got married, something was already going on with me. I thought it was just pressure from work." He takes another drink and continues.

"I was happy to marry Dana, but I ignored what I was feeling. I was tired all the time, my thinking was confused, it got harder and harder to hide what I was feeling—sometimes I felt like I'd been hit by a truck."

"I know what you mean," I say and think about the times when I haven't been able to get out of the bed, stuck underneath sheets and covers, unable to lift my head off the pillow.

"Back then I cried a lot, but you know I couldn't let Dana see that, I was supposed to be a man's man. Even I didn't understand it. The face I put on for her, and the rest of the world, wasn't real."

"But why leave the house?" I ask.

"I was hurting her, Car. I'm not proud of that but it's true," David says this and rubs his hand over his moustache and mouth, stretching his face downward as if he's trying to stop tears from forming.

My eyes get big. I don't want them to but is he saying he hit Dana?

"To this day I regret it, I knew what I was doing, but I couldn't stop myself. And no, I never hit her Car. I just needed to be left alone. She was so concerned, and rightfully so, but she wouldn't leave me be. I know I was a mess, and that's why she couldn't—I was irritated all the time and on weekends sometimes I wouldn't even change my clothes. I'd just sit in the dark, alone. I didn't want Dana to see me like that. I didn't leave her, I went away so I could get better."

"She always says you came back new and improved."

"I was better, am better. I took meds for a while, after I found out my depression was organic. I resisted taking anything at first, but in the end I believe they helped."

"So the medication did it?"

"Yes and no. The meds were a part of it, but there was something else I hadn't expected. I met these brothers who were in a weekly support group to talk about what was going on with them. They taught me how to breathe through the madness I was feeling."

"Therapy?" I ask.

"Sort of. But even more they were a group of brothers who just knew how to get real. I learned that I hated everything about me. My skin color, my wide nose, my nappy hair—there wasn't anything that I thought was right. To this day I love them brothers. They helped me get to the other side of that. Where I am, who I am, what I am is just fine."

"But David, you're the Wonder Boy. Everybody's so proud of you. You know that, don't you? Even Clarence says so."

He gives a wide grin and says, "Clarence, my man, I haven't seen him in a long time. We used to be boys together, is he good?"

"He's good, and as old as he is, he's still in the service. He says they'll to have to retire him because he's not leaving. He loves to travel."

"That's good. I'm glad he's happy."

He pauses, turns to look at me with squinted eyes and tilts his head—I'm not a mind reader, but I think he's trying to see if I know.

"Did Clarence tell you about my mom?"

He rubs his hand over his close-cropped hair. I wonder if that's a nervous gesture.

I nod yes.

"A few days ago. He was at Mama's place. I'm so sorry, David. You're beautiful—I mean, handsome."

He smiles and rubs the top of his head again, grabs his chin and fakes a model's pose.

"I'm okay, really. I worked that out with my group. My mom didn't know any better than to hate my blackness—I mean what she said hurt and I carried it for a long time, but I understand where her thinking came from. Dana tells me that Rasheed is a dark skinned boy, and you know that's not been easy on him. Maybe not talking is his way of fighting back. That's power. Backasswards maybe, but deciding not to speak is powerful. Dana says you think he can talk though."

"I was trying to win his trust, show him that I was here for him. Then that fight happened and now this incident with the substitute that got him expelled. God David, I should have been there."

"It's not your fault. Something bigger is happening."

"You make it sound like we should just accept it. That there's nothing we can do about how bad things have gotten."

He shakes his head no as he finishes his drink, and it's awhile before he speaks.

"You're wrong, Car. That's not what I'm saying. When we rush in and rescue, before we have a plan, or have decided what we can and can't do, sometimes it makes it worst. Let's say you find Rasheed tomorrow. Then what?"

"I'll help him get back in school," I say, crossing my arms to defend my answer.

"I'm on your side remember, but there's a lot to think about here. Is the school going to take him back? Should he even be back at the same school where they've already labeled him a problem?"

"I'll help him get into another school then," I shoot back, "I have to do something."

"I'm just saying Car, decide what you can do. Maybe you can't do everything. A lot of these kids are mad because we're stressed out around them. Too many of us act like a broke down vehicle, running today and busted tomorrow. Look, if you try to find him that's okay, but Car, you got to get it right. If you do find him, I'll help you. And I won't leave you out on a limb. I promise I'll help."

"I'm still trying to find a limb, David. I don't know what to decide, I don't know where I'm standing. It all feels so hard."

"So what's the rest of your week look like?" he asks.

"Work and going to Mama's on Friday."

"You still getting her story?"

He looks at me and smiles as if to say, yeah, Dana again.

"I wish I'd had that chance," David says, "My Moms left the state and she doesn't stay in touch. Sometimes I wonder about her story, how she got to where she hated herself so much that she taught it to me."

"I'm learning a lot. There's a mixture of joy and pain in my mother's story." There's Queen again, all up in my head and thoughts.

"Here's a plan. You go to work. Afterwards we walk, and then we'll go to dinner and talk some more. It's two days Car—we can do this."

What ever made me think I wasn't thought of as "we" with David, or even questioned that Dana saw me as part of her family? It makes me smile to think when they married Dana told him I came along with the package and he said yes to both of us...I love this man. There's silence between us. It's a comfortable silence, and for the moment I'm okay with not knowing what will come next. David turns quickly towards me with his finger pointing in the air as if he had just remembered something.

"You know, another thing that helped me through my depression was a poem by Langston Hughes. One of the guys in the group shared it with me. It's called "Mother to Son." It may sound crazy, but I used to imagine my Moms tucking me into bed at night, kissing my forehead and reciting that poem like a performer. She was pretty dramatic, you know."

"So I've heard." He nudges my shoulder and we both laugh.

"The part that I always remember goes something like this—*Boy, don't you turn back, don't you set down on the steps*—meaning don't give up, life's not easy, but you just don't give up."

David was true to his word. On Wednesday and Thursday evening, we met after work to walk along the shoreline at Alameda beach. It was his idea to walk someplace different. He said the change of scenery would give me a new outlook on things. It was an effort to keep up with his long legs. I think he knew this but he kept pushing me to stay the pace.

On Thursday, when we were almost back to the car, I stopped to look across the water and noticed how calm the waves seemed to be rolling in and out. I thought about Cassandra's wedding, and how everyone looked so happy strolling along the beach in their bare feet. I took off my shoes and socks, and started squirming my toes into the sand doing a little twisty dance. David scratched his head and asked me what was I doing. I smiled and said my silliness came from hanging out with his wife.

Before we got in the car, he said he wanted to show me a breathing exercise that he uses when stress starts to grab him. We stood in the parking lot, ignoring the strange looks given by passersby. It was simple enough. He said to breathe so that I could feel my chest and abdomen move up and down, then look around and name whatever I see. It might be trees, buildings, chairs, flowers—whatever showed up in my line of sight. I wondered, but didn't ask, if I should count what I see. When David dropped me off at my apartment, he gave me a forehead kiss and said, "Remember to breathe when listening to her story."

CHAPTER SEVENTEEN

Once I'm out of the tunnel, I notice all the trees lining the freeway and the houses comfortably tucked underneath. A little further down, where the turn off goes towards Livermore and San Jose, traffic begins to slow to a crawl, I start to feel anxious about getting to Mama's on time. She's been unrelenting that I come this Friday, she's called three days in a row to make sure I get there by dinnertime. I don't want to be late, but there's nothing I can do about it right now so I slowly breathe in and out, and watch the stalled river that surrounds me.

As I turn left onto Deerview Drive, I look directly at Mama's windows. The living room and her little den both sit at the end of the street. When she moved here, my brothers and I tried to convince her a place in the back would be much better, with less noise and no car lights at night, but she said she needed to see what was coming her way. I smile as I undo all the locks, thinking that at least she feels safe.

"You surprised me sitting in here—what're you doing Mama?"

"I'm enjoying all my pretty things. Remember this lamp? I've had it for over sixty years."

She smiles fondly at the bronze-colored floor lamp with its Tiffany glass shade.

"I didn't realize you've had it that long."

I look at the lamp with a new appreciation for how long its been in the family.

"It was the first nice thing we bought when we lived on Chester Street. June and me dressed up like we was going to church and went to the downtown Emporium. I had seen it window-shopping. I told your Daddy I wanted it, and he said we could buy it. It was his idea to get all dressed up like we were going somewhere fancy. We walked into that store just like the white folks and paid cash. Those sales clerks sure were surprised when we pulled out that money."

"I bet they were. I hope you like Marie Callender's for dinner, I picked up some take-out so you wouldn't have to eat late."

"That was good thinking, baby."

I place the bag on her small, rarely used dining table that sits off in the corner of the living room. Mama shared that memory so easily that I think she must be ready to get back to her story.

"Let's eat at the table," I say. "I'll set the fine dishes and silverware and it will be like we went out to dinner. How 'bout that?"

"Mmm. That sounds nice," she says. "I'll just sit here until you call me."

All of Mama's nice tablecloths and napkins are kept in the large wooden sideboard. She only brings them out for special occasions. The gold tablecloth and matching napkins will look nice alongside the good dishes and silverware from the china cabinet. The plant, even though it's artificial, will add to my table setting, and now all I have to do is place the food onto serving dishes.

"It's ready."

Mama makes her way to the table, pulling her walker with each measured step. She looks at the table and then at me.

"You remembered what I told you about setting a table. The forks and knives are in the right place, but you forgot the crystal water glasses."

I wanted it to be perfect, but I let that wish go and head back to the cabinet. Instead of the crystal glasses I return with two golden goblets. Mama Belle sent them through the mail, and I remember when Mama opened the carefully packaged box how we all crowded around to see what was inside. When I place them on the table Mama gives me an approving look.

"There, everything looks so nice, Carla," she says. "You know, one day all this is going to be yours."

She says this as casually as if remarking that the weather will be cloudy all day. After Mama says grace we eat in silence, just chewing our food and not saying anything. It reminds me of how quiet our meals were growing up.

"Why do they always put these little dried up peas and carrots next to a meat loaf? A meal like this needs okra or greens or maybe fried corn, fresh from the cob."

"You're right, greens would be good. I remember how you used to make a mean fried okra."

"Yes, I did make a good okra, didn't I?"

And then silence returns. Okay. That was a bit of conversation. Be patient, she's just warming up. The meal is pleasant, even though not much more is said than the comment on the food. Afterwards I decide to clear off the table right away, put everything back into its place and wash the dishes. The sun is setting. There's still daylight but Mama decides she wants to get into bed. I assist her by pulling the floral comforter back, and then she asks for Mama Belle's quilt. I can't help but wonder how she'll begin telling her story again.

"How's that? Are the pillows comfortable for you to be sitting up like that?"

Her eyes seem heavy. I don't know if she's sleepy or wakeful.

"Yes, that's good, Carla," she says. "I don't feel like watching TV. That Judge Judy got on my nerves last time. She didn't have to be so mean to that young black couple. Seemed to me she was making fun of them for having so many kids, and you know I don't like no one making fun of someone's children."

I wonder if she is giving me an opening to ask about the story, since she doesn't want to watch TV.

"Well, how about getting back to the story? Do you feel like doing that? You don't have to if you're not ready yet." I say, hoping I sound as casual as she was in telling me that someday I will inherit her dishes.

"I know I wanted you to come so I could finish, but I don't remember where I left off. Do you?"

Okay. This is another test to find out how much I've been paying attention. I look up at the ceiling, pretending that somehow it's helping me to draw down what I remember.

"Well, you left off with Mama Belle walking with you to the well. She told you that your Daddy was going to marry you off, and you were really upset to hear that. I remember you said it was cold and the two of you went inside to make a big breakfast and you talked about it being payment day. You said everybody was tense about what time some man, I think the landowner, would show up."

"You been listening, that's good. I couldn't remember where I left off. Okay, let me see. It was payment day, that's right. And you're right, early that morning Mama did warn me that Daddy was thinking about marrying me to that old colored man across the creek. All right, I got it. You ready?"

She looks at me for my answer. I nod my head and sit next to her on the bed. Like her, I lean back on the headboard, as she stares off to find her story again.

"It was always strange to watch Daddy stand with his back so rigid, holding his hat and talking to this man who waved his hands and always pointed his finger when he talked. I used to imagine Daddy picking up Mr. Carson and turning him right side down, shaking him like you would a chicken whose head just got chopped off.

"They were standing close to each other, Mr. Carson was doing all the talking. Then we heard him call Daddy 'a good field boy.' He said it a few times, and sometimes he just said 'boy.' Clarence raised his back and shifted his position on the porch when he heard Mr. Carson call Daddy a boy. Mama whispered for him to steady himself and not to cause nothing extra for Daddy to deal with.

"My daddy ignored Mr. Carson calling him a boy and didn't react like Clarence, just said the crop was the biggest ever and how he was thinking about getting a mule to help with the work. While Daddy talked, Mr. Carson stared up at the sky, which had turned red from the setting sun, and pulled out a long cigar, lit it, and puffed smoke into the air. And then he asked Daddy who owned the land he was working on. At that question, we all leaned a little further towards their way to listen better.

"'You do, sir, everybody knows that,'" Daddy told him.

"I knew Mr. Carson asking that meant no good and wondered what he was up to. Carson laughed, and slapped Daddy on the back like he had just told a joke. Then he got real serious and dropped his voice. We could barely hear him but we all heard what he said next.

"'So it won't bother you none to pay for the use of my land, right'

"I saw a confused look on Daddy's face, like he was wondering what Mr. Carson was getting at. He said he'd been paying all those years to work the land and had a paper with his mark on it. Well, that Carson didn't say anything to that. He reached inside the pocket of his fancy suit, unfolded a piece of paper, showed Daddy his mark, and started reading. It seemed like he raised his voice so there wasn't no guessing by us on the porch about what it said. The paper said we owed five hundred dollars for the use of the land, and Daddy had three months to pay it. None of us understood what he meant. Daddy said he'd been paying for the seed, fertilizer and all, and five years before he had bought that tractor from Carson. To him and to us, it didn't make no sense that now we had to pay more. My Daddy twisted his hat into a rope. When I saw him do that I was feeling like it ain"t no use, because the more he talked to that man, the worse it was getting.

"This paper says you got to pay for the right to sole use of my land. Nobody but you been working it for twenty years, right?'"

"Mr. Carson said that it was just business, and he didn't want to lose money from letting Daddy be his only tenant. Daddy was just nodding and shaking his head. I changed position on the porch to sit on the top step alongside Clarence. I didn't like how that man in the car was staring up and down at me, but I wanted to hear, so I stayed where I sat. None of us had ever heard of that kind of payment before. Daddy's shoulders dropped. He hit his hat on his leg as if he was dusting it off, and turned to walk back to the porch. Mr. Carson walked along side of him and pointed to the young man.

"'Clarence, this here is my son, Harold, my oldest, and he's come back home from school to take over my business. He will be calling on you for payments and any other things concerning my land. You deal with him from now on instead of me.'"

"Daddy gave that young man a nod and kept on walking up the stairs into the house, not looking or saying anything to us on the porch. Payment day was over for Mr. Carson. He and his son backed out, sending up red dust as they drove off. For them it was done, but we knew it wasn't over for us.

"I knew when Mr. Carson left, we were going to have a stormy night. Daddy was spitting mad, he kept saying five hundred dollars, over and over again. He kept asking how was he supposed to get that much money in three damn months. He took out his anger on your Mama Belle, said he'd made a mistake marrying a don't-know-nothing woman in the first place. Finally, my brother Clarence got him to calm down.

"Well, when I got up that next morning and saw Mama washing her face, she was touching it gentle like. She had a black eye and bruises on her arms. It was too much for me to look at, so I left the house as soon as I finished washing the morning dishes and went to see June's mama.

The Sinclairs lived more than a few fields away, and the walk took almost an hour, but I didn't mind. I didn't want to see Mama's pain, even though I was still carrying it inside of me.

"I was glad June's mother was by herself, so we could talk without the men around. She saw the worry on my face and asked if everything was all right. I told her what had happened the day before, and she said that a lot of folks were hurting from what happened on payment day. I wanted to know if she had heard from June—told her I didn't know why it was taking so long for him to send for me. She looked out the window and said not to worry, that she knew June loved me and would have me for his wife. It helped some hearing her say that cause my own Mama and Daddy didn't believe it.

"We sat and talked for a good while, she made me some sun tea and told me about June's ways and things I should do to be a good wife for him. It was the late afternoon when I started walking back home. I didn't know it, but it was going to be the last time I'd walk that distance to June's mama's house. At home, I saw Mama on the porch, at the furthest end from the door, and two of my brothers were standing close to the gate down by the well. Otis was on the porch with Mama. All them outside was a sign Daddy was having a fit about something. As I walked past Clarence and Arthur, Clarence said, if he was me, he wouldn't go inside right now. I asked why, but both of them dropped their heads and stared into the ground. I asked them again what was going on.

"Arthur punched Clarence in the arm and told him not to tell me nothing. He was like that with me. I never understood why, but he always took Daddy's side about things and talked to Mama like she wasn't his mother. Sometimes I think I never should have named my second son after him.

"Clarence walked up to me so close I could smell the sweat on him.

"'Daddy says you got to get married now,' he whispered in my ear. "He don't have no other way to get the money Mr. Carson asking for.

That farmer across the creek said he'd give him some money if ya'll get married next week.'"

"My knees buckled like they had turned to jelly. I looked across the yard towards Mama. She was rocking in the chair; the quilt she made from old baby clothes was wrapped around her shoulders. The air was hot and I couldn't imagine she was chilled. I just stared at her, not saying anything, but I think my mouth trembled when I saw what she was doing. She was leaned over so far the front of the rocker was almost touching the porch and she was pushing her hands into the air like people do when they want you to go away. I was confused until Clarence explained.

"'She telling you to go. Don't go in the house, she want you to leave.'"

"Arthur added a warning too, said if I went in there Daddy might hog-tie me to the bed until the wedding happened. I knew if Arthur said something it was real serious. Mama held her heart. Her head was dropped, shaking side to side, and she kept waving, rocking, touching her heart and waving back at me again and again. And then she just hung her arm out in the air with her hands flat and wide open, pushing them towards me. My whole body got hot, hotter than the heat around me. Then I just felt froze, couldn't move, didn't know what to do.

"By then, Daddy had seen me at the gate, and yelled for me to get in the house. Clarence, he pushed on me to wake up. Then he pushed on me harder to leave.

"I started walking slowly, then sped up some, but I was afraid to run from him. When I got out the gate, I starting running though, was running so fast I lost a shoe. I ran the other way, not the way I'd been earlier to June's house, but towards the fields going west. I could hear Daddy yelling.

"'Girl, get in this house, right now.'"

"I didn't look back. I just kept running to the end of the dirt road and turned west, like June and I always talked about. At the end of the road, I cut across the fields. I knew Daddy's old truck with patched up tires couldn't make it across a field already been turned over, so when I got to the other side I was a good distance from the road he had to take if he was coming to get me. I kept going west. I was further than June and me talked about, and didn't know where I was, and I was scared Daddy was coming. I couldn't let him find me so I dropped into the ditches on the side of the road and kept running.

"I was so tired I had to start walking, but I never stopped. The sun was setting and I knew daylight was going to be gone soon. I kept walking, dodging water in the ditches, careful to peek around first when I had to cross over a road just in case he was driving down that same road, but thank you Jesus, we never saw each other. By that time I had no shoes, I had kicked off the one still left a long time ago because it slowed me down.

"I had it made up in my mind that I was gon' walk all the way if I had to, there was no going back for me. But one time when I came up from a ditch to cross the road I see a car, a fine looking station wagon with wood panels, parked alongside the road, and people were standing next to it. They was Black people, a tall woman dressed in overalls, and two boys that looked to be about three and five years old.

"What you down in the ditches for?' the woman asked. 'Honey, you okay?'"

"I'm wary still because I'm now on the top road, and I think my Daddy is still looking for me. But she's smiling at me, so I don't get scared of her. I was afraid to tell her the truth, but something told me I had to trust this woman, cause I didn't see no other plan.

"'Honey, you look like something scared you to your early grave, and where are your shoes? Are you in trouble?'"

"She said it kindly, and I felt embarrassed when I looked at my feet and dirty clothes. When she looked at my bloody feet I could see her face turn with concern, so I tell her I'm going out West, had to leave right away 'cause my daddy wants to marry me off, and I already got a husband intended. I told her he was in California, and that I was going to meet up with him. She looked at me with her head sideways and had a thumb hooked around her overalls, and told me that I had a long time getting there if this was how I was gon' get out West. I dropped my head and went down to my knees, and started crying because I knew she was right. She walked over to me and lifted my arms to help me stand up.

"'We got something in common then, cause I'm running there too, but I got me a car.'"

Mama's lips have gotten dry, and she's having a hard time talking. I get her a glass of water from the kitchen, and she drinks all of it down as if her thirst hadn't been quenched all day.

"Thank you. It felt like I was still running in those ditches. Can you bring me another one?"

When I get back she drinks some more, and says, "And the next thing I know, I was on my way to Oakland, riding in a big fancy car."

"Mama, who was that lady?"

She takes another sip and I think I see a faint smile coming through her lips.

"Well, it was no other than Mrs. Greenly."

"*Mrs. Greenly*? Really?"

It's a surprise to learn this, I knew they came out about the same time but I had no clue this is how they had met each other.

"If not for her, I can't say if you would have had the same daddy that you did."

I smile at Mama's logic, but I know what she's trying to say.

"Her and her two boys had left Alabama and she was driving to California, headed to Oakland. Can you beat that?"

"Mama, she was your guardian angel."

"My God has never left me alone. Mrs. Greenly stopped on the road to let her boys pee and that's how I came up on her. She offered me a ride, told me not to worry about gas money because she hadn't planned on me anyway. She told me if I could put up with her two knuckleheads, I was more than welcome, so I jumped into the backseat and that was that, I was on my way to Oakland.

"What was Mrs. Greenly doing out there?" My mind feels gripped by this incredible turn in Mama's story and I realize I'm holding my breath, so I let out a big sigh and try to sit up a little straighter.

"Well, she had started on the low road from Alabama to get to California, but going through Texas the whites got meaner with each town she went through. She was a Black woman alone with two boys and a fancy car that brought a lot of attention. She said she had met a black man who worked at a filling station right outside of Dallas, who told her she better get to the high road along Route 66. So she started driving north hoping just to get through with out any troubles, and that's how we met up."

"God, Mama, didn't it scare you to travel all that way with a stranger."

"I was no more afraid than if I had stayed and let my Daddy marry me off. I could see Mrs. Greenly was special, a kind person, and I had no fear. I was on my way to see your father. It took us four days to get there. I didn't know how to drive and she had to rest some along the way. We found different places to sleep, mostly underneath the trees on the side of the roads where no one could see us parked. I stayed awake to be the on look out and watched the boys while she slept."

I have to get up and move, because my shoulders and neck have stiffened, I can tell I'm still holding in my breath. This story just seems unbelievable, but Mama has no reason to make it up. I stare out the window for a moment trying to feel my chest and abdomen move up and down, Mama's not saying anything, I think she's waiting on me to say something. When I turn around she's looking at me, anticipating my question.

"Did you run into any trouble? How long were you on the road?"

"We were blessed and didn't have any problems. The biggest problem was I was barefoot and didn't have proper clothes for how cold it got in those mountains. Mrs. Greenly gave me a blanket to cover up and one of her boy's shirts that was way too small. I wrapped my feet in it to keep them warm. She was sorry she didn't have more but she had to leave in a hurry."

"Why was she in such a hurry?"

"Well, at first we rode not saying anything, but after a while we got kind of easy with each other and started telling about our lives. You know, about our troubles and why we were going to California in such a rush. After a while she got real talkative, I guess to keep her awake while she drove. Riding with her was like riding with a history book. She had all kinds of stories to tell. She even told me how her she came to have so much money and was able to buy that car."

"Mrs. Greenly was rich?"

"Yes, she was and still is well off. She came into money from the sale of her daddy's land in Alabama. She was feisty about herself back then and laughed as she told me how her father outsmarted the white folks."

Mama slaps her knee and laughs out loud.

"Are you going to tell me what's so funny?"

It's a relief to see her smile and laugh. Up to this point everything has been so heavy.

"If you get me some sweet milk tea I might," she says in a teasing tone. I rush into the kitchen fill the kettle halfway and put the burner on high to hurry it along. I wonder what could have Mama so tickled. After telling me about running through the fields, and how she feared her daddy would find her, it's hard to believe that she found something to laugh about.

"Okay, here's your tea, so now tell me."

"It's a bit of a tale, you not tired of listening are you?"

"No!" I spread across the bed and bend my elbows so I can place my chin in my hands. Mama smiles at me as she watches me get into position to listen to this part of the story.

"Well, Mrs. Greenly came from people who were mixed with the Indians. Her daddy had married a woman from the Creek Indians that lived in Alabama. I could tell by the way she talked about him she was proud that he had come from freemen who weren't slaves. Well, being a freeman, he was able to be a tenant farmer and not a sharecropper."

"What's the difference?"

"A tenant farmer can buy the land they work, while a sharecropper could never wish for that. Her father, I think his name was James, had this land that he worked for years and saved up enough money to buy. It was far from town, so most time she said people forgot they were even out there. It was right before the Depression and he was doing good. When the Depression came poor whites got sorely mad about any colored man doing better than they was and would get pretty ugly about that fact. Mrs. Greenly's daddy was prospering, his land grew big crops but when he brought his crop to market the locals were beginning to make trouble for him about that. One day a white man in town made a big to do about him having no right to be living that well when whites couldn't do the same. She said he made a big scene in the packing store with a crowd of people watching him. The man even threatened that if her daddy didn't leave he might not be alive much longer. He told him to get the hell out of there."

"He couldn't just do that could he?"

"Back then lots of colored farmers were losing their land so this wasn't no different from what was happening. So the next day Mr. Greenly came to town to sign over his deed to that fellow, he took what little money the man gave him, then packed up and left. He took his family to live back with the Indians. Well come to find out, as Mrs. Greenly told it, her father knew who this white man was, they'd been friends since they were young boys running and playing in the woods. Seems they put their heads together and concocted a plan to fool the townspeople into thinking like many other coloreds, he was being driven out. But Mr. Greenly's friend, who must be another one of God's angels, kept that land for the Greenly family, it was a secret between the two of them."

"Oh my God Mama, is that a true story?"

"Yes indeed it is," she answers with a look of satisfaction on her face. "Her father never could move back there but some years down the road the white man sold the land for what it was worth and from what she said it was valuable land. He gave all the money to Mrs. Greenly. Her father had died many years before it was sold and her mother wanted to stay where she was, so Mrs. Greenly got all the money. She said she bought that fancy car because it was something her daddy always wanted and said it was the least she could do for him."

Unbelievable. We look at each other smiling and Mama's nodding her head sipping on her tea.

"So, I still don't get why Mrs. Greenly had to leave in such a hurry. Was she in danger because she got all that money?"

"Well, she had received a letter from her sister in Oakland who told her to come to California right away. So she says she packed up what she could in boxes and headed out west. We laughed about being two women on the road with a purpose. I was headed out to California to get with your father. Mrs. Greenly said looking for a man wasn't anywhere close on her mind. Said she wanted be to be herself and stop pretending."

Mama's lids are lowered and her eyes look slanted as if to say, "If you know what I mean."

"Are you saying Mrs. Greenly is gay?" I want to say more, but she interrupts before I can get my next question out.

"Yes, I know that's what you kids call it now. I was surprised, I never met anyone who was, but it never mattered none. She was kind to me Carla. I'm not here to judge folks. She's a good woman, been a good friend all these years. And I will never let anyone speak of her otherwise."

"But didn't you say when she found you on the side of the road that she had left her husband?"

"Oh, that didn't mean nothing, people had all kinds of reasons for getting married. It was her husband who helped her."

"Then why did she have to leave?"

"That's Mrs. Greenly's business, Carla, and it's not for me to tell you all her business. Back then folks didn't have time to care about things like that and wasn't no colored folks beating up on people for how they lived. You just didn't talk about it."

"Okay, I get, it but you still haven't said anything about when you finally got to Oakland. Daddy must have been glad to see you."

"I think I'd like some water before I get started on that part. You've had me talking for a while you know. My throat is parched."

In the kitchen I think about calling Dana. She would love to hear Mrs. Greenly's story. I can't help but laugh thinking about it, but I know it would be hard to get her off the phone and Mama is on a roll with her story.

"Mmm," she says as she takes a few sips. "Thank you."

"So, are you ready?"

Mama nods her head.

"By the time I got to Oakland, your daddy had already been there for two years. He wasn't alone all that time, though, remember he stayed with his uncle's family, and they had brought June in just like the rest of them. It always gave me comfort to know he was being cared for, but I couldn't wait until I was the one who was looking after him. June's people lived on Linden Street, and when I saw the house he had been living in I knew he made the right decision to leave Texas. It was two stories high and painted white with a pretty green trim, with a metal gate that curved at the top met the sidewalk with neatly trimmed grass behind it. It was a beautiful house. Mrs. Greenly asked if I was sure I had the right address. I looked at the envelope and it was the same numbers on his letter so I knew that was it. When we said goodbye we hugged each other real tight, I knew I had found "me a good friend and we promised to keep in touch with each other.

The door was made out of wood and stained glass to peek through. It was so sturdy looking that I knocked real hard, to make sure they heard me. A tiny woman about my size wearing a flowered apron answered the door.

"Well, I'll be,' she said and looked me up and down. 'June talked about you so much I feel like I already know you."

"She wiped her hands on the apron and pulled me in for a big hug. She told me to call her Mama Lorraine and said that June was at work. She asked where were my bags and I told her I didn't have any. I wanted to tell June why I only had the clothes on my back, before I told anyone else.

"The women folk received me like I was a long-lost daughter. They told me your daddy was working a late shift at the restaurant and would be home at eight-thirty. There was a lot of excitement. I was getting introduced to so many people—June's cousins, uncles, his nieces and nephews, even the neighbors stopped by. I mostly stayed in the kitchen with the women telling them about my trip. I still didn't say anything about how my Daddy wanted to marry me off; I just said he wasn't happy I left. They understood though, said when you love a man like I did you just have to go and take what comes with it.

"It was almost 8:30 and I was getting nervous. Then a great noise came from the front, it was the men greeting June. I could hear them teasing him that his woman was in the kitchen waiting on him and he better hurry up and get in there. When he came through that kitchen door, filling it up with all of his six-foot body, I almost fainted. Oh we hugged, I cried, and I think he even cried some. We just kept rocking and rocking back and forth, looking at each other's face and kissing right in front of everybody.

"When all the ruckus calmed down, I went into the same bedroom with June. I saw the women turn their head, pretending they didn't see me go in with him. He went over to the tall dresser and from the top drawer he pulled out the same blue and white scarf I had given him at the creek, and wrapped it around my neck. As I was telling him what happened I started crying into his chest. He brushed my tears off my face just like the night he had to leave.

"We talked into the early morning hours. June got mad about all that had happened, but I kept telling him everything would be all right now that we was together. The next day we woke up to a big breakfast, the same kind I used to cook for you and your brothers. The long table must have had ten people sitting around—all June's family. We kept looking at each other, grinning, and under the table he never moved his leg from touching mine. Mama Lorraine asked questions about my trip, so I told her a little more about why I left so soon and how Mrs. Greenly saved me. June's uncle, who seemed to be a quiet man, called for everybody's attention and made an announcement that the next day there would be a big celebration.

"On Saturday, we got up to another big breakfast and afterwards June left with the other men. I wandered through the house. It had so many rooms, and the floors were all shiny wood with rugs spread everywhere except the kitchen, which had real checkered black and white linoleum. I knew one day we would live in something this fine. In the sitting room there were family pictures on the fireplace, on the coffee table and there must have been a dozen or more hung in the hallway. Mostly I sat with the women in the kitchen, helping them to chop up vegetables and make sweet potato pies.

"In the afternoon the back yard filled up with family and neighbors. Men June worked with even came with their wives—it was such a beautiful thing. A few hours in, June's uncle wanted everyone's attention and he gives me a proper introduction. Then in front of everyone, June gets down on one knee, shows me a gold ring with a stone on top and asks me to marry him. I said yes, but he said he couldn't hear me. I was crying so hard I had to say yes again.

"After all the fuss about me and your daddy was over, and the food was eaten, the women cleaned the kitchen and sat at the table. The men went to the porch to have their cigars. I went out on the porch with them and sat in June's lap and he was kissing on me while the other men talked. I stayed on the porch all night with the men folk and never went back into the kitchen.

"The next morning, the breakfast table was real quiet and not much talking was going on except folks asking to pass a plate of biscuits, the syrup or pass the chicken. Just small talk and things like that. I didn't know June's people, so I thought this was the way they normally were, that the excitement of me being here had worn off and they was back to their usual. After breakfast we all went to church and came home for the Sunday supper and it was still quiet around the table, except they talked about the sermon and the preacher.

"I felt so good about being there, I told Mama Lorraine and her sisters I'd wash the supper dishes. They didn't say anything to me, I didn't pay it any mind, just thought they was resting. But when no one came in the kitchen to keep me company, I begin to wonder if something was wrong. It was only that night I learned why all of a sudden they were acting cold towards me.

"We were upstairs in the bedroom. I was sitting in the chair next to the window and June was laid across the bed. When I asked if something was wrong, he got up to bring me to lay down with him. I knew he had something to say by the way he sighed. I was worried what that meant, but I knew June was always gon' tell me the truth about things, so I just waited till he was ready. We laid on the bed holding each other. He was quiet but not sleeping. I played some in his hair, but then I just couldn't take it no more so I asked him if he was upset with me.

"He said, 'Now, baby, you know it ain't no different with us. It's just like how we use to sit on the side of the creek and talk about our dreams. I'm glad you here. It's the women folk—they got it in their mind you not right for me.'

"I had only been there three days and couldn't think of anything I'd done to make them think I wasn't gon' take good care of June. It was hard for him to say, but finally he was able to tell me. He said the women didn't think a self-respecting woman would have stayed on the porch all night with the men like I had done. It was hard to believe he was serious, but I knew June wouldn't lie to me. He said it was his uncle that told the women I was acting like the pool hall girls or the ones who go to nightclubs and all the time push themselves up against the men.

"What?!" I'm in disbelief.

"I know baby," Mama says with a whole lot of sadness in her voice. "I didn't want to believe it either. Back home, it was just me and Mama, then Daddy and my three brothers. I was use to sitting out on the porch with men folk, so I didn't think no different in what I was doing. I was just so happy to be there. That night I started crying in his arms, and he rocked me and kept telling me it would be okay, that it would just take a while for them to get to know me. Well no amount of cleaning their kitchen, cooking or going to church changed their minds. When June and me got our own place they never came to visit, when we went to the family parties at his uncle's they still acted cold."

"Mama, I'm so sorry."

"That's why we didn't have family around us after your daddy died. They came when he was sick, but when he was gone so was they. I knew it made you sad we didn't have big parties with family like the other children. I wanted them to like me for you and your brothers. But it just never worked out—they never let it turn around."

So that's why no one came to see us. I remember sitting on the steps watching people coming and going into the other houses wishing they'd stop at ours. Mrs. Greenly came over, every once in awhile a few church people stopped by for Bible study but we didn't usually have visitors. I wonder if those women gossiped in the neighborhood about her.

Mama's eyes have lowered. I wonder for a minute if she's sleeping, but then see tears sneaking out from under her closed eyelids. I feel so sorry for all that has happened to her and my father. For once I really understand when people say, "They did the best they could."

She pulls the covers back and gestures for me to get in bed with her and places her arm across my shoulders to hold me. In a whispered voice that sounds tired she says, "Carla, you my only daughter and I love you. Don't ever forget that, no matter how I act, Mama loves you."

"I love you, too."

"I think I'm done telling you this story about me. Next time you come, I want you to tell me about you."

CHAPTER EIGHTEEN

I wake up with my eyes closed to the morning sunlight, and I'm very aware Mama still has her arm around my shoulders; her body is leaning into my back. I think she's held me all through the night. I hate to break her strong hold, it's comforting, but I have to get up and make the commute to Oakland for work.

She's done telling her story, at least done with all she sees fit to tell her daughter. Mama's worked hard. After all the sighs and tears, she deserves this restful sleep. She didn't have to tell me all that she did. I think, remembering what the Queen told me at the food court that evening, there is definitely joy mixed in with the pain of her stories. I feel like for me this is just the beginning of a wrestling match between the two, and I wonder which is going to win—joy, or pain?

When I ease out from under her arm to place my feet on the thick pile rug on the floor; she stirs, but doesn't wake up. I'll call her during my lunch break. In her bathroom I wash up quietly, and try not to look in the mirror, fearful of what it will reveal back to me. Finally daring to look, I see it isn't as harsh as some previous mornings. My eyes are pinkish from not sleeping well, but there's no denying I still see Mama's reflection looking back at me. Even with all her hardships she found her way West, and found the joy she wanted for her life. My hair is a mess—it needs Charlene time. I'm doing my best to make sure it's presentable for work, but all the while I'm thinking, what will be my direction—where do I want to find my way to?

As I drive into the parking lot, I see students gathered in a slew of small circles on the sidewalk, mingling and talking to each other. I wonder what stories their mothers and fathers could tell them about their lives before they came to exist. I wonder if these young ones, when and if their time comes, will even want to know. I start to get out of the car, but one leg doesn't want to follow the other, so I sit not yet finding the will to stand up. Is it the so-called depression Dana's named for me that's got me stuck to the seat, or am I just completely numb after hearing the heartache of my mother's life?

I've noticed today how the students seem to just trickle into class, many have their shoulders slumped over, and when they sit down, I hear them sigh. Maybe, like me, they've got emotions that were stirred up over the weekend that they can't talk about. They go about their reading assignment without having too much to say. Like I plan, at lunchtime I call Mama. She complains the aide can't cook and makes little mention of her telling me her story, other than to say she's glad I stayed the night.

At the end of sixth period, Dana sends me a text. We are supposed to walk the lake this afternoon, but for some reason she wants me to meet her at Scott's Seafood Restaurant instead. I smile. I wonder where she got the idea for a change?

Scott's Seafood Restaurant in Jack London Square sits opposite a grey-bricked plaza. I've gone there for dinner a few times for functions hosted by David's organization and for a few retirement parties. I decide to wait for Dana on the wharf, alongside the restaurant. The waters underneath are quiet, not many waves lap against the pylons that go deep into the bay. It's surprising the water is this calm, when I can see storm clouds creeping around the Golden Gate Bridge.

COLETTE WINLOCK

Down the way is a statue of the adventurer Jack London, perched on a cement base, an image of his wanderlust soul captured in bronze, trapped forever to remain in this Square. I read in the *San Francisco Chronicle* that Oakland's adopted prodigal son was actually born in San Francisco.

"I didn't know if you got my text." Dana interrupts my thoughts. "Why didn't you text me back?"

Dana knows I can't text while I'm teaching.

"I got your message, that's why I'm here. How did it go with your agent?"

"Good. He's got the publishing company working on a tour. But I'm not finished yet and oh, I'm feeling the pressure."

She gives me a quick hug.

"What's left to do?" I ask.

I point towards the path to start us walking alongside the Port of Oakland's thick green. I don't want to stand still. I need to move—I feel agitated.

"How are you doing? David said you went to your mama's this weekend. Have you gotten to hear more of her story?"

I feel a wave of heat across my face. The wind's cool but suddenly I feel hot, and my jaw tightens like I've seen Rasheed's do when he's upset or excited. How am I doing? I remember how I felt at Mama's yesterday, how I felt when she lay motionless—staring out the window. I remember how I needed to take a break.

"Mama's story is done," I snap at Dana. "And I'm mad."

"Mad about what? Oh, I know, about what you've learned from her story. I'm sorry."

"Yes, that, but I'm angry with you too."

"What did I do?"

Dana sounds surprised, which agitates me even more. I stop walking to face her directly.

271

"You didn't tell me about how I'd feel after hearing her story. All along you've been talking about Black people this and that. 'Get her story, Carla, it'll help,' but you never once, not once talked about afterwards—about what to do with these feelings.

"Dana, I heard things that just hurt me to my heart, so many fathers' dreams—including mine—got crushed, and no one really knew what freedom meant. Just yesterday I found out that Mama had to leave her home to save herself from getting married off and having a life like her mother's."

I blurt out whatever I can remember. It seems like the wind is blowing my words past Dana and into the water. I say any and all the things inside of me—Mama's story, Clarence's truths, how my father wanted to be called George, Daddy dying and I didn't get to be there—how I feel so naïve about it all. Dana's standing in front of me, not touching or pushing me as she usually does. She's not trying to explain anything—she's just listening. As I speak my lips are trembling like Jello. My chest heaves up and down. Angry words are directed at my best friend. I don't know when they'll stop. I continue with my tirade, letting my arms and hands wave around.

"I didn't know how anybody ever really felt. I had to make things up to understand what was going on."

A rush of feelings that had been pushed down are spurting out and spilling over. When a couple walks by and gives us a backward look as if to ask *is she okay* only then do I realize we're standing in the middle of the walkway. Dana moves closer to me, in a protective way.

"You want to sit down?" she asks.

Huge pools of tears flow from my eyes, I nod yes and she guides me towards a bench close to the water and away from the walkway. Three trees surround the bench, giving us privacy from the rest of the world. I start sobbing uncontrollably. Dana's hand is on my back, but she's not rubbing or trying to soothe me—she's just here.

My thoughts race with pictures gushing through my mind. Am I having a nervous breakdown, becoming one of those women church people whisper about? I see Grandpa twisting his hat, speaking to the white man who is wronging him, Mama frozen at the gate, then running and hiding in watery ditches to keep her freedom. I see how I've skipped quietly along over the injured parts of my life—Oh God. Who am I crying for? Me? Mama? Daddy? Mama's daddy who saw no way out? Mama's mother who threw her heart out so her only daughter would leave to be free?

I don't know how much time has gone by, but when I look up from my hunched over position and see Dana's face, it's wet with tears. She's been crying with me.

"Hey," is all I can say.

"Hey," she says back, and reaches her other arm around to hold me.

"I don't know what happened."

My voice sounds faint, my head hurts and my body feels lashed upon. I feel Dana's arms are keeping my spirit from flying off into nothingness.

"You were having your feelings, some big ones at that. I was waiting for you to call me everything but my real name. I'm sorry, Car. I couldn't tell you how you were going to feel, what emotions you'd have, only you knew what needed to come out."

"It all feels so huge. I don't know who I was crying for."

And I'm still crying as I try to tell her what I saw in my mind, what pain I felt with no place to put it.

"Please hear me, Car, and I'm not trying to get all academic or talk about the book. Your tears came from some place you don't know but can feel. I believe you are grieving for our people. Those are the tears from the ancestors."

"What are you saying, Dana?"

She hands me a crumbled napkin from her jacket pocket and I try to dry up what's running from my nose. My face still feels wet.

"Honey, some of us are more in tune to the unspoken feelings of others. Imagine all the enslaved people who were sensitive, who felt the spirit of others, and who looked for truth even when it was painful. You're like them."

Dana's not looking up as she does in her lectures, and honestly, I've never heard this before, from anyone.

"It's your nature, Car. You're sensitive."

"I hate when Mama says that about me."

"I mean it in another way. We've been told *sensitive* and *black* don't go together. Your sensitivity makes you special and it can put you in harm's way. If we were in a society where people understood your gift, and didn't try to shame it out of you it'd be different for you."

I let go of a deep breath.

"Dana, I don't want to feel this."

She gently grabs my face with two hands and turns my head, making me look at her.

"I can tell you this, after sitting next to you and watching you cry with your chest jumping up and down—you are well past the pain passed on to you that isn't yours. Do you hear me?"

I sniffle and wipe my nose. I hear her words like never before. *Well past the pain.* In this moment I like how those words sound. The truth is I know I've been walking around with something that's making my belly swell up, as Mama would say.

"I don't know what's going to happen to us, to me, to our people . . . the injury just feels so great."

I can't say anything else. Like Mama, I'm exhausted—spent. Dana guides me off the bench, and with her arm wrapped around mine she helps me to walk back to our cars. When we get there, she won't let me drive home and tells me to leave my car in the parking garage.

"Do you know how much overnight parking is going to cost? I can't afford that."

She pats my shoulder.

"Don't worry, I got you covered. Remember who I'm married to, I'm sure the Wonder Boy won't miss the money."

"I feel exhausted," I say and sigh deeply.

"I know you are. I want to make one stop before I take you home. There's something we need to do first," she says.

She gives the parking attendant a bill, waits for the change, and alerts him that my car will be staying overnight. Dana says something about my having suddenly taken ill. She's right. I don't feel well. I just want to go home.

Instead of getting on the freeway, she drives down Broadway. The streets have emptied as Oakland's downtown always does after work hours, but when we go past the Burger King on 13th Street, I see homeless people gathering around the corner as they do nightly. Many of these people have been out here for so long they now look familiar. At the red light a woman close to my skin color stares at me from her perch on the concrete bench on the corner, she's dressed in layers of coats with a tattered and dirty-looking green blanket for a head wrap.

As Dana waits for the light to turn, the woman and I stare at each other. As we stay locked into each other's sight there's no expression on her face and probably none on mine. I think to turn away, but can't make myself to do it. When the light changes Dana drives through the intersection, pulling us away from each other, the homeless woman waves and the corners of her mouth turn up. She's smiling and nodding. I nod back, but I'm not able to return her smile.

"Dana, I want to go home."

New tears are rushing out as I plead with Dana to take me home.

"I'll get you there soon, I promise. I need you to trust me on this, okay, sweetie?"

She drives past 20th Street—that would have taken me home, but I don't feel able to object to this errand she wants to make.

"Where are we going?"

"Over to 55th and Martin Luther King, there's a shop that has some things that will help you when you get home. Just lay back. How about taking my jacket to keep warm? Do you want the heat on?"

She reaches behind the seat for her long coat and places it over me. I think about Mama with her feet wrapped in a child's t-shirt to stay warm. I must have drifted off to sleep because I don't remember Dana getting out of the car. She gets back in with a brown bag that she softly places on the back seat. No need in asking her what's in it, I lean my head on the window to go back to sleep. When we finally arrive at my apartment, she sits me down on the couch, goes into the kitchen, and brings me a large glass of water.

"Drink all of it," she says, and leaves me alone.

Now she's got the linen closet open and is looking for something.

"Where are your white sheets?" With her head deep in the closet her voice sounds like an echo.

"In the dirty laundry."

I feel swept up and not really sure what she's doing.

"These mint green ones will do. Green represents new growth so they'll be okay," she says, and goes into my bedroom.

She changes the sheets, takes my glass from me, comes back from the kitchen with it filled up again and then heads toward the bathroom. Our eyes catch as she passes through to the kitchen again and she points towards my glass—silently ordering me to drink. I listen to water pouring into the tub and then Dana arrives to carefully guide my body into the bathroom. She starts taking my clothes off. Young is how I would describe this feeling, not embarrassed or shy because she's doing this, but years away from feeling forty-six. The only light in the bathroom is a soft glow from candles she's placed on the top shelf, but I can see the water in the tub is white and something is floating on top. Dana reads my look and answers my unspoken question.

"Milk and fresh lavender buds. They'll help soothe you."

The water in the tub isn't too hot, but it's warm enough that after stepping in I sit down and my back collapses and hunches over, my bones feel deflated. Dana sits on the side of the tub and pours water over my shoulders and arms, slowly refilling the cup each time that it empties. The stream of water down my back causes me to let out moaning sounds. She pours water over my head that messes up my press and curl, I don't say a word about this or flinch. I have completely turned myself over to Dana's care. She offers me a teacup that doesn't look anything like sweet milk tea.

"It's chamomile, a soothing and relaxing tea. Just try it."

I lean back to slowly take a sip while she places one of my oversized towels into the water and then folds it to lie over my breasts. The warm wet weight of the towel is comforting, and my lips taste the salty tears dripping down my cheeks. Dana leaves me to be alone in the tranquility of the warm water, the warm towel on my chest and glowing candles. I release a huge sigh, close my eyes, and more tears start to stream. After awhile I smell an odd fragrance drifting into the bathroom and Dana appears waving and looping a ceramic bowl with smoke coming from it that fills the air.

"White sage," she says. "It helps clear any negative energy lingering in your house. I had her put eucalyptus in it to help you breathe deeper."

She pours hot water from the teakettle into the tub to warm up the water, and I realize that I'm not even considering getting out right now. When I finally do get out, Dana shows up again with one of my big towels to dry me off. Still I feel no hint of shyness for this intimate action. By my arm she leads me to the bed, the smell from the sage is light, and I can feel myself breathing slower and deeper. The way she tucks the blankets tight around me and then lays another on top of me, I feel like I am grounded to the mattress and my body sinks in for what I hope is my deserved rest.

There's warm moisture on the sheets. I think maybe my cycle started during the night, but when I reach down to touch the wet spot I realize it's something else.

"Oh no!"

I exclaim so loudly it brings Dana running to the bedroom. She must have stayed the night on the couch.

"Carla, what's wrong?"

Dana's eyebrows are standing on her forehead and her eyes look in a fright. I didn't mean to scare her like that.

"Oh God, I wet the bed, what is happening to me?" I ask, thinking that in addition to peeing in the bed, I'm probably going to be late to work. "Dana, what time is it?"

"Slow down, sweet pea. I called the school and told them you had a bad case of food poisoning, and the bed can always be changed." She strokes my forehead to calm me down.

Her resolve that everything is okay allows me to fall back on the pillow. Then I remember Dana wet my hair in the bathtub—oh God, it must look a mess.

"Let's get you up for a shower. I'll change the sheets and we can talk about what to do for the day. I cancelled my appointments, so I'm here."

I don't want to see the mess on top of my head and intentionally avoid looking in the mirror. While in the shower I hear the front door close and I wonder where could she be going? I make the water not too hot, just warm enough to fully place my body under the stream. This bathroom hasn't seen shampoo for a long time. Charlene always takes care of that, so this bar of soap will have to do. The shower stream licks my face and there's no difference between the water and my tears. When will I stop crying?

When I finally get out of my long shower, Dana's still not back yet. On the bathroom counter are two bowls; one is labeled *lavender oil* and the other says *yellow rose petals*. Oh God, look at my hair. Mama would just shake her head. A wrapped towel helps to hide it from myself.

The phone rings. There's no way I can move fast enough to catch it anyway, so I listen to Mama's voice when the answering machine picks up her call.

"Sister, it's your mama. When you get home give your mama a call. Love you."

I smile. She's been saying that for as long as I can remember. Today I answer to no one in particular, "Yes, that is my mama."

The sheets have been freshly changed and when I get in my bed they draw me back to sleep. It's the scent of food cooking that awakens me.

"Something smells good, what are you making?" I say, standing in the kitchen doorway.

"Hamburger stew, the ultimate comfort food. Am I right?" Dana laughs. "I got grass fed beef and the vegetables are organic."

I laugh, too. I'm the one who taught her how to make it—it's Mama's special recipe. She says she's the inventor and one day she'll get a patent. Two bowls later, Dana says, "Let's go for a walk. The air will do you good and there's a new place I want to show you."

"Is it new like that artist gallery in Albany?" I ask cautiously—I've learned from experience that Dana's versions of "a new place" are always something to be suspicious about.

"No, but I'm sure you'll like it and there's nothing scary about it." She places the dishes in the sink, returns and lifts my arms up to get me off the couch.

"Now, get dressed like you going walking," she orders.

"I think you're enjoying this."

"In more ways than one," she says. "But most of all, I'm enjoying seeing my friend coming back to herself."

She hugs me and I melt into it, more grateful than she knows for someone to have caught me and help me find my sanity. My nephew's baseball cap with the big T on the front will have to do; dealing with my hair right now feels overwhelming.

With the top down on Dana's car we go towards the hills of Montclair, up Snake Road and further than I remember ever going, even with Daddy. After he died Clarence drove us through these neighborhoods during the Christmas holidays to look at how people decorated their homes, but we never came this far.

The sign leading into parking area says Sibley Volcanic Park.

"Dana, does that sign mean volcano like I know the word to mean?"

"Yes it does, right here in Oakland, it erupted a few hundred years ago. It surprises me how many people don't know about this or use the park. Come on, let's go for a walk."

Moving feels good although my body aches, particularly in my rib cage. I didn't know crying can make you hurt like that.

"My ribs hurt," I tell Dana.

"I bet they do, that's from all that deep heaving."

She exaggerates her breathing, making her chest rise up and down imitating me. I push on her shoulder to make her stop.

"Car, you've been enduring and prolonging a lot of grief, and yesterday it said, 'I want the hell out.' It's actually a good thing. Remember— you are well past the pain."

Well past the pain. I still like how that sounds. We are high enough on the mountain that the cool breeze sings through the redwood trees making the air feel crisp and clear. The trail is covered with piles of pinecones, I'm not tempted to count them, but I do wonder where the heck is Dana taking me.

"So what do you think?" Dana waves her arm, introducing me to a deep canyon some fifty feet down from where we're standing.

"Looks like a path going in circles."

"It's a labyrinth. Let's go down there and walk in it," she says, the excitement in her voice is that of a girl getting her first bra or going on her first date.

"I've seen pictures of those, and there's a teeny one at the lake. But are we going way down there?"

I stare down the cliff at the bottom that is not at all close to where we are standing. I can see dirt trails going down the steep hill. I don't know about this.

"Girl, we're not climbing down that cliff. Over here is a paved road that leads to the labyrinth. You don't always have to do hard."

She's right. I only saw the hard way to get there, as if there were no other options. I laugh out loud about this new information and Dana laughs with me.

"You know what a labyrinth is for, right?" she asks.

I start to react to her assumption that I don't know anything about this, but instead I say, "It's your job to seek out all the unknown places in life, remember?"

"It is my job, isn't it?" She cheerily grabs my arm to walk down to the canyon and she begins the mini-lecture I knew would be coming.

"The labyrinth actually has African origins, but the Greeks get all the credit. Some people mistakenly call it a maze, but it's not supposed to trip you up like a maze is designed to do. The Africans saw it as a representation of one's life journey. It may surprise you but their belief is life is not to be as difficult as so many people think. It's a spiritual meditation with eleven circuits, paths that may look different and crazed, but really it's all just one line from where you enter to where you come out."

All I do is smile at the information she's shared—I know she means well. I have to admit, walking the labyrinth is peaceful. We follow the trails silently, in and around, until we walk ourselves back out from where we started. The sun is high, and there's not a cloud up there blocking its warm rays.

Dana pulls out a blanket from her small backpack with a Native American pattern on it. She unfolds it and ceremoniously spreads it under a tree so we can sit down. She lays out food and water, and then pulls out a grassy looking wand with string wrapped around it and lights the end with a lighter. She starts waving it around us and in the air. It smells almost like marijuana and my eyebrow goes up.

"It's not what you think. It's another kind of sage to purify the energy around us."

I smile, again. That's my friend. She sits cross-legged on the blanket and bends over into a yoga pose. The air up here is so clear it feels light as I breathe it in. For a while, we sit saying nothing. Dana offers a fancy white cheese with green stripes running through it with crackers made from rice. I eat slowly, thinking about how Mama said she wants to hear my story and wondering what parts of my life I will tell her.

"How are you feeling now?" Dana asks.

"My insides have calmed down. Only these sore ribs remind me where I was at yesterday. I didn't think I would ever stop crying. I even cried while in the shower this morning."

"You could keep crying for a while, Car, but look, you're still here. You passed through it."

"I did, didn't I? Oh God, Dana, I wasn't sure for a while, but you know—I'm not leaving. I hate that I thought I had to kill myself to make all these bad feelings stop. I've been thinking about what you said yesterday, about me being sensitive to other people's feelings."

"There are highly sensitive people of all races in the world, and most of the time they are given support to handle this gift, maybe special classes or even a counselor with who they can talk to when the feelings of others begin to get overwhelming."

"But Black folks don't see it that way, you know that."

"I know," says Dana, "so many things about us haven't been given support. You can't be smart, you can't listen to opera, you can't cook your greens without meat, you can't, you can't—it's all so harmful. But not being sensitive to your feelings or emotions is one of the worst things I think slavery created."

"I don't know what to say, but I hear what you're saying."

"What are you thinking about doing now? I know it's only one day but having a North Star will help you get to where you want to go."

"North Star?"

"Harriet Tubman, remember her? That's how she found freedom."

Dana's mention of Harriet reminds me how she always looked to the stars to lead herself and others to freedom. I get lost in thought, thinking about people experiencing freedom on the inside, the kind that can't be seen, maybe Mama and Daddy felt that way and that's why their love never faded even when freedom on the outside wasn't there. Dana's knock in the air to say, "Hello in there," brings me out of my daydream.

"I think," I say slowly, "that my North Star is Rasheed. I know I'm meant to help him, I think he's one of those sensitive people you're talking about."

"He could be—I can't wait to meet that boy. He's got to be your spiritual son that landed inside another mother."

"Maybe he is that child to me, but you know when you have that feeling something is undone and you just can't let it go of it."

"Yes, I know that feeling all too well," Dana says.

"Well, I wish I had been able to do another home visit. If I just could have seen him away from the school, I just believe I would have learned what's going on."

Dana hands me another cracker with the odd-looking cheese on top and digs two bottled waters from her backpack. She hands me one and stares me in the eye.

"What?" I ask.

"Carla, what's stopping you from doing another home visit?"

"Hello, remember he's been expelled," I say, annoyed. How could Dana forget that one piece of important information?

"You know how to get in touch with his grandmother, don't you?"

"Mrs. Jenkins. Uh, yes, but…"

"But," she says over me, "if she gives you permission to come by, there you have it—home visit off the grid."

Her hands stretch out like a magician who has just completed a sleight of hand trick, and in this moment I get it too.

"Oh my God, I don't need the school's permission if Mrs. Jenkins says it's okay. Why didn't I think of that? I missed the obvious."

"Your mind's been preoccupied, but now you know."

She keeps talking about what people don't know, how we don't think critically and that's why she does the work she does. As she talks I eat the crackers and cheese, and watch a couple take their silent journey through the labyrinth when I begin to notice a familiar unsettled feeling creeping in.

"Dana," I interrupt, "you don't know how people feel about everything."

The look on her face is one of surprise. She doesn't look away, but instead tilts her head as if she's trying to understand what I mean. I pick up her bottle of water off the blanket and hand it to her.

"Drink and listen," I say, "you've been talking a long time."

"Yes ma'm," she says with a little smirk that lets me know she's playing with me.

I shift my legs on the blanket so they're in front of me, raise my back up and take a deep breath, realizing there are some feelings I've been holding onto for a long time.

"Dana, I love you like a sister, and the way you took care of me yesterday, and even today, I don't think my own Mama has ever taken such care with me."

She smiles.

"You're welcome, Car. I love you like a sister, too."

"I don't want to seem ungrateful, but you don't listen very well. I'm the one who is always listening. You act like you know what everybody should do and feel. How could you? Who have you talked to, I mean really listened to?"

"I think…" she begins, but I interrupt before she can finish.

"I'm not done. Drink some more water," I tell her.

She sheepishly obeys my command. She's still playing. I take a drink myself, a long one before I continue telling her what's on my mind.

"After listening to Mama, I know there are many more crazy stories out there that people just don't want to talk about but have feelings about. Don't you think I'm right about that?

"Yes, I would agree."

"Well, for your book, whose stories have you listened to?"

"It's more of an academic book. There are a few case studies, but I focus on achievement, the civil rights movement, religious beliefs, living patterns, family migration patterns and economic status. It's a snapshot of all the things that have impacted the lives of Black Baby Boomers. The agent says the publisher likes that it's not too heavy."

Mama says that book smarts will never get an egg fried right—you learn by doing it and right now my friend's eggs look pretty ragged.

"Dana, listen to what you just said. Where is the emotional inheritance you've been talking about? Where are the feelings of that salami sandwich you say we all are supposed to be? You need to put some real lives in there, with some real emotions and feelings. I think you're scared to hear what they might say."

"Are you getting ready to go off on me, again?"

"No. But look at your talk with Aaron. You wanted to tell him something so bad, and you did, but how much time have you spent listening to how he felt about it?"

"We're supposed to talk soon. He's been busy and so have I. He hasn't called so I thought I'd let him have time to think about it."

"Dana, Dana, Dana," I say to get her attention. "Sometimes you have to be patient and let the story leak out, remember?"

"I know I said something like that, but my book and Aaron aren't the same thing. Aaron is family, it's always harder with family and, yes, I'm scared to hear what he feels about all that I told him."

Dana's head drops. I don't want her to feel bad, so now I'm the one to place my hand on her back and just hold it there while she keeps her head down. I think she's quietly crying. The sun has passed over the canyon and it's getting cool sitting in the shade. I tell Dana to stand up so I can repack the bag. That's all I say for the moment. She walks towards the labyrinth, not going inside, just looking at it with her hands on her hips.

Everything is packed, I walk towards the labyrinth to stand by Dana and she does a little jelly move with her body like she's shaking something off her.

"Car, I know what you were trying to say, I'm not mad."

"So what are you going to do? What's your North Star, Dana?"

"I've been rethinking what's missing in my book and you know—and don't get all fanatical about this—but you are right. When I think about it, there aren't any emotions directly from what people feel about those times. There's so many of us I got caught up with the numbers and not the feelings. So my North Star is a focus group on emotions—the publisher will just have to wait."

I high-five her and she squeezes my arm. We both smile and walk back to the car in silence. I still feel tired, but the adrenaline running through me makes the walk easy. I'm laying a plan in my head to call Mrs. Jenkins, tell her my interest in Rasheed's education, and ask if I may have another visit to her home. I'm pretty sure she'll say, "Yes." We seemed to make a good connection, maybe not at the IEP, but definitely when I had that first home visit.

CHAPTER NINETEEN

The water at the lake is perfectly still, there's no wind in the air and even though it's late afternoon, the sun still sits close to Oakland's small skyscraper buildings. I'm early. It's almost an hour before Dana and I had planned to meet. The fountain is spraying water into the air and drops of mist land on my skin. The cool wetness feels good. It reminds me of spraying lavender water around my apartment.

I laugh to myself when I think about how last weekend David and Dana showed up, unannounced, carrying a mop, gloves, dusting cloths and throwaway bags and told me it was time to clean—what could I say? Dana said, "A good girlfriend is one who'll let you know when you need to get some Brillo pads." I love those two. I enjoyed going to church with Mama on Sunday—even though her choir still sounds awful. I'm glad I took the time to buy a few new albums from Reids Records in Berkeley. I didn't know I'd like reggae music so much. The little diary I'm using to write down my feelings seems to be helping. I laugh again thinking that if Ed or anyone from the school ever read it I'd probably get fired.

To my surprise, Dana is walking across the brickyard on time. Actually she's a little early.

"We need to make this a fast walk so we can get ready for the group," she says as she sweeps me up from the concrete step I had been sitting on.

"Hi to you, too," I say while trying to catch up to her pace.

"I know, I know, I'm sorry. Hi."

All through our walk, she talks about tonight's focus group, how hard it was to find folks to attend, how she wants to set up her living room and what food we have to prepare. She makes me promise a million times that I will show up early.

When I get home I freshen up with a birdbath, change into my orange church pants suit and, like I promised, arrive at Dana's house early enough to help her set up. We move chairs from the dining room into the living room to form a circle around the huge papasan, Dana's talking chair, as the centerpiece. We place TV tables near the chairs for the food and snacks so people won't have to leave the discussion to fix their plates. The paper plates and napkins match, and the little plastic cups aren't the kind you buy at Walgreens. The last things we do are to light candles and place them around the room—on the fireplace mantle, on top of the bookshelves and on the end tables. Dana pauses to admire our work.

"This should set up a cozy little discussion."

"So how long do you think this is going to go?" I ask.

"I told people three hours. That will give folks time to arrive and settle in."

Three hours. Oh God. I start looking around Dana's living room for things I can count, just in case I need to distract myself. The doorbell rings and I look at the clock. It's still too soon for the others to be arriving.

"That's probably Dr. Brenda. I asked her to come a little early," Dana says as she goes to answer the door.

Great, I think, now it'll just be me, Dana, and another psychologist. When she opens the door in walks a striking looking woman and she and Dana hug like they're best friends. To my surprise it's the woman

I saw on the PBS station. She's taller than she looked on television, and she's casually dressed but very professional. Dr. Brenda looks over Dana's shoulder, sees me and walks over with an extended hand.

"You must be Carla," she says, shaking my hand with both of hers.

She knows my name. I wonder what Dana has told her about me. I hope she didn't tell her about my moods—or about me wanting to die.

"I see someone's been talking about me," I say, nudging Dana.

"Dana told me what a wonderful friend you are, and that you would be here to help her set up."

"Yes," said Dana. "I told her that you are my oldest and dearest friend."

Dana gives me a little wink—letting me know she didn't say anything else about me. Dr. Brenda looks into the living room, gives Dana a stack of forms for the participants—including me—to fill out, and goes into the living room to prepare. She moves about the room, setting up two flip charts Dana and I brought from her car, re-arranging pillows, and not paying any attention to Dana or me.

The doorbell starts ringing and Dana goes back and forth letting people in, thanking each one for coming. To keep myself busy I carry dishes of food out to the living room and place them on the TV trays, giving a small hello. I'm grateful for the job Dr. Brenda gave me, I'm to give each person a paper and pen, and ask them to please fill out the confidentiality form. It's a good distraction from feeling like I need to make small talk. The room is filling up with Black people of every skin color. There's one woman who I'd swear was white if I saw her on the street. Another woman has her hair pulled into a ponytail like the one Mrs. Jenkins wore during the home visit and when she came to the school. Both times she seemed tired and this lady seems tired too.

Where did Dana find these people? They don't look like her friends from the University, which I thought they would be. They look like regular working people. There are four men and five women including me, and then Dana and Dr. Brenda. It's almost seven thirty, the circle of chairs is full, everyone is looking down at their plates when I see Dana nod to Dr. Brenda that it's time to get started.

"Good evening, my name is Brenda, most people call me Dr. Brenda. I am a psychologist, and Dana, your hostess, asked me to facilitate tonight's focus group so she can be a participant along with all of you. Dana is doing research on the emotions and feelings of African Americans born between 1946 and 1964, a time when you might know our country experienced a tremendous birth rate. The information you share tonight will be kept confidential and if used you will not be identified. Dana, before we start is there anything you would like to add?"

"Thank you for coming and for signing the release forms which allows us tape the group tonight. All of us are black baby boomers, I would like to say something in my upcoming book about the feelings and emotions of those of us born during that time."

Dana nods again towards Dr. Brenda. I guess she's finished with what she wanted to say. I have to admit it surprises me that she kept it so short and sweet.

"Okay. Let's get started," says Dr. Brenda, "Let me remind you again what is said here is to be kept confidential, I also want to ask that one person at a time speaks, and that you respect all people's opinions. Can we all agree to that?"

Heads nod indicating yes and people quickly go back to looking at their plates.

"Let's begin with introductions. Please tell us your name, where you grew up and something about yourself today. I'll start first. You know my name is Brenda. I was born in the great city of New Orleans, but have lived most of my life in San Francisco. I've always been interested in how to bring more love into our lives and have written books on relationships and making good choices. I am fortunate that I am able to speak about this all over the country."

The next person to speak is Charles, a stocky man in a sweater straight out of Bill Cosby's closet who appears to be in his late fifties, he says he's from Georgia. He begins by sharing very personal details about his life. His parents divorced early, his father living three blocks away from him with a new family. He shares what it felt like being the oldest son.

I'm surprised when the others follow suit and share intimate details about their lives. One woman's husband died last year; another is going through a divorce, the man who appears to be the youngest of the group has four children. We're strangers to each other and yet everyone is saying things I'm sure Mama would say is their personal business. When it's my turn, I feel caught in the wave of telling folks about my life.

"My name is Carla. I have three older brothers. I'm the youngest child and the only girl. One of my brothers has a learning disability that inspired me to become a special education teacher. A year ago my mother moved from our family home on Chester Street to senior housing in Brentwood. I grew up in West Oakland and I remember when it was full of thriving Black neighborhoods and businesses. I still feel sad when I think how we've lost that. Our family was there when the Black Panther movement was just beginning."

"I lived a few blocks from you on Wood," says the only other woman born in Oakland, "I was a member of the Party. When I was sixteen I worked in the health clinic and helped with the breakfast program. How about you?"

She nods in my direction as if signifying our common history.

"I was pretty young then, maybe ten," I reply.

"Oh, you probably came to the breakfast program," she says, confident that I must have been involved somehow with the Panthers."

"I know it can be hard, but let's try not to cross-talk and just listen to what others have to say," says Dr. Brenda.

We just smile at each other and I don't say yes or no. I'm not ready to tell this group how I spent those years going to the park and a private school. When it's Dana's turn to speak, I'm more aware of what she doesn't tell the group about her personal life than what she actually shares. She finishes introducing herself and gives Dr. Brenda another signal. My dear friend is still trying to run things.

By now it's full on nightfall and the candles glow softly around the room. Dana gets up to dim the lights, letting just enough light stay to see what Dr. Brenda is writing. It feels like I'm in a tribal meeting, with village folks gathered to talk about important business.

"Dana, as a lead into the next question I'm going to ask you to tell us about your research on the history of slavery and the emotional inheritance we live with today."

Dana smiles when Dr. Brenda says this. By the way she has been sitting on the edge of her seat, I knew she couldn't wait to say something.

"Enslavement took many things away from our ancestors—their freedom, their human rights, their families," Dana says, "Our people lived in a state of terror and suppressed fear and anger. Their survival was dependent upon hiding their emotions. We are here today because they successfully learned how to do that. I believe this is our emotional inheritance, and as a people in order to truly be free we must recover the ability to have, and to feel, all of our emotions."

"Tell it, sister," says James, the youngest looking member in the group.

I notice he chose to sit in Dana's oversized talking chair and that he's leaning back into the giant pillow. At first his eyelids were so low I thought he was sleeping, but his comment clearly lets everyone know he's been listening. I've heard Dana say these things before, and truthfully, sometimes I don't want to hear her talk about those times. Though tonight, I have to admit what she's saying feels like it's about more than just the baby boomer book. The others nod their heads in agreement, and I notice that the white-looking woman is crying. Dr. Brenda hands her a tissue and turns back to the rest of the group.

"Thank you, Dana, for that wonderful lead-in to our next question."

Dana is smiling as if she just received a gold star from the teacher. I decide not to make fun of her though, and just smile. Dr. Brenda flips to a clean sheet of paper and uses a marker to write: what is your emotional inheritance? She reads the question out loud and then looks around the room.

"Who would like to start?"

We all look at each other like my students do sometimes when no one wants to be the first to speak.

"I'll go," says James. "I'm forty-six. I'm a baby boomer, born just on the tail end in 1964. And you know, I don't express shit. Excuse me."

He looks apologetically at the women and continues, "I go to work, come home to my wife and family, and just try to stay out of the way."

Dr. Brenda asks him to say more about how he feels about all of that.

"Like shit, excuse me, again. I feel like I'm not supposed to have anything to say about anything. Not at work, and not at home."

"Is there anything else you would like to add?" says Dr. Brenda.

"Nope. That's how I feel." And he leans back into the pillow.

Charles from Georgia raises his hand and starts speaking without waiting to be acknowledged.

"When I was coming of age I was one of those men you saw in magazine pictures wearing a large sign around their neck that said "I am a Man." I wasn't famous or anything like Dr. King, but I was there. We were angry. Jobs were kept from us, back then everybody was worried about how we was going to take care of our families."

"How did you feel about that?" Dana asks.

Dr. Brenda puts a finger to her mouth to remind Dana not to ask questions.

"Like it wasn't fair—I was a man too," he says. "Like James, I stayed out of the way but I found ways to keep myself busy. I learned carpentry, something I still do today."

I decide to just listen for a while. I guess the other women feel the same way as me because none of them are raising their hands to speak. Julius, who has been sitting on the edge of his seat, obviously wants to say something now. His answers during the introduction had been brief. I've noticed that he's extra polite, always saying ma'm, or sir, when spoken to.

"I was in the service, joined the army at eighteen."

His hair is short, neatly cut with a line, giving him a Denzel Washington look. "Back in Arkansas there were no decent jobs for a Black man," he continues, "so like my brothers and uncles, when I got old enough I joined up. The service gave a Black man something to hold onto, I knew I could count on a check and I liked the respect of the uniform. There was a lot I had to swallow to keep that check coming though, like white enlisted men saying things about us, or getting the worst tour of duty and assignments, but I learned to take it for me and my family."

Julius makes me think of Clarence. I wonder if the service has been hard on my brother, if he has had to swallow things as Julius is describing. He's never mentioned it, but there's a lot Clarence doesn't talk about. When Julius finishes speaking, my attention is drawn to Vincent who is sitting next to him. Vincent is reserved, not at all like Julius with his military manners, and he shows no sign of Charles or James' workingman's bravado. He seems almost aristocratic. In the introductions he said he grew up in Louisiana. His light skin makes me think he might be biracial, but you never know—both his parents could be black. His arm is bent at the elbow and his hand is slightly raised. Dr. Brenda calls on him to speak next.

"Well, my experience feels very different," Vincent says slowly, adjusting himself in his chair to cross his legs. "I was born to a Creole woman who was of a class of black women raised to find white men to sponsor their way of life. Many of you here in California might not know about this, but that was an accepted way of life for some in New Orleans. The movie *Feasts of all Saints* tells this story. I am a product of that history, in modern times my mother lived that life. In the past, the sons of these white men were sent to France, to become cultured men. They returned to a station in life different then the black men who came from the field. I was not sent to France, but I wore the clothes of a gentleman and went to schools that were only for the sons and daughters of these men. I was raised to be cultured."

"I could tell you had fancy ways about yourself," says Charles.

Dr. Brenda tells him to allow Vincent to finish speaking.

"It's okay," says Vincent. "It's true. When I was a boy I was raised to be fanciful, as Charles says. I was always told not to act like the boys whose grandparents came from the slave quarters."

"I knew it," Charles says, then he catches his tongue before he says anything else and nods an apology to Dr. Brenda.

Until now, the discussion has been going at a fast pace, though its' been mostly the men raising their hand to speak. But now the entire group is silent. Vincent has paused, and no one, not even Charles or James tries to fill the quiet space. I for one, don't know this story, haven't seen the movie. Like the others I just look at Vincent and wait. His hands are folded in his lap, his legs are still crossed, and his eyes lowered away from our stares, reminding me of when Rasheed looks away.

Dr. Brenda waits patiently, and we all follow her lead and wait patiently as well. I keep looking around Dana's living room for something to count, and my eyes land on the coasters. Vincent has uncrossed his legs, but he still holds his hands tightly in his lap.

"Is there anything else you would like to say?" Dr. Brenda asks.

Her voice is low, not at all demanding, it's as if she already knows there is something else. The others stir in their chairs looking at each other. James shrugs his shoulders at Julius and then shakes his head. Bobbie and Angela have stopped eating and Gloria, well, I don't know what she's doing—she left for the bathroom.

"Vincent," Dr. Brenda gently calls his name again. "Is there something else you would like to say, something important that you want us all to know?"

Whenever he has taken a pause between speaking, I've noticed how his lips have tightened. This time when his mouth opens, nothing comes out. His lips move up and down, until finally he's able to put sound to their movement.

"I want people to know," he says, struggling to get the words out, "I want you to know I rejected that way of life. I may have been taught I was to be different, even to think of myself as better, but inside everyday I was rejecting it."

The muscles in his throat are strained outward, and his mouth, is quivering as he speaks.

"It was demeaning to my mother for my father not to acknowledge her, to see him in town with the other family that was acceptable for him to be seen with in public. I watched him just ignore her. My father took care of her and my sister, but ... but, when I got older I wanted no part of what he offered."

He's crying. Vincent's words have stimulated an outpouring of emotion. Dana's living room has turned into a flurry of action. People are holding each other, talking fast. Bobbie and Angela put their plates down and are now talking to each other. The very light skinned woman walks over to Vincent and holds him, they're both crying together. Dana and Dr. Brenda move from person to person, consoling, rubbing backs, holding faces gently and whispering, *you'll be okay, I know, I know,*" and other soothing words to each person they speak to. I'm sitting, not talking, not crying and not sure what I feel. But I know there's ten people, four men, six women, six people crying, five standing, eight chairs, one couch, five pillows on the floor, three candles on the mantle, three more on the kitchen counter, four windows, two lamps...

By the time the last person leaves Dana's home, it's almost 11:00. It was Vincent. I saw Dr. Brenda speak with him privately in the hallway and hand him her card. When she closes the door she lets out a huge

sigh that Dana and I can hear from the kitchen. We look at each other
and then quietly start putting things back in order.

"That wasn't like any focus group I've ever led or sat in," Dana finally
says to Dr. Brenda once the living room has been put back in order.

They're sitting at the small square kitchen table that's really made to
fit two people comfortably, but they make room for me to join them.
Dana looks at me and I return her glance with a frown and shake my
head.

"Leave it to you to have me in something over the top," I say.

"I know you found it interesting. You shouldn't play poker—you'll
give your hand away."

"No, I should be more careful with what I let you get me involved in."

"I saw you staring at your plate, but your eyes told me you were
listening."

"Yeah, how could I not? But really is this what you wanted to happen?"

"I know Car, it didn't go as I thought it would, now I'm not sure
how to use it in the book. How do I write about all that?" Dana looks
worried.

"Maybe you don't put it in there. At least you tried," I say, her
worried look makes me want to help her feel better. I know she has
the book agent pushing her to finish soon.

"Maybe," Dana sighs, "but something really important happened
here."

At the same time our heads turn toward Dr. Brenda. While we've
been talking, she's been quietly sipping on her tea and watching us go
back and forth in our familiar way. Her grin now says she's amused.

"You two are definitely like sisters, reminds me of when my sisters
and I try to figure out who is to blame for something," She says.

Dana and I look at each other and start smiling too. When Dr
Brenda grabs my hand from across the table, I flash back to when she
touched the TV interviewer's hand who didn't get what she said about

slavery and Black women's health. I'm relieved when she tells me she's proud of me for not leaving the room.

"Thank you for noticing," I say. I don't tell her I took inventory of pictures, windows, furniture, everything down to the coasters in Dana's living room.

"I have to admit the things you said sounded different tonight," I tell Dana.

Dr. Brenda breathes in the light steam coming from her tea, and takes a sip.

"Yes, her opening on emotional inheritance did cause quite a stir of emotions."

"It surprised me too," Dana says, "I expected people to just name what they felt they inherited, but jeez louise, the stories came out like a flood gate opened."

I look at Dr. Brenda, who takes another slow sip of tea. I wonder what she has to say about all this—Dana, unlike herself, certainly appears to be stumped.

"Dana, it didn't turn out to be the focus group that you envisioned."

See, that's proof again I think, Dana had me in something over the top. I look to see what she has to say to this, but Dr. Brenda continues.

"And yes, something very important happened. I think your focus group turned into a healing circle. The food, the safe ambiance in your home, helped people to feel comfortable. All of that created a space where healing was able to happen. That's why I stopped writing on the flip chart. Think about it."

"I see what you mean," Dana's voice drifts faintly in the air and ended with a sigh.

Dr. Brenda smiles at Dana and this time it's her hand that she pats.

"Emotions come from human agitations and they want expression. For instance, let's look at Vincent. He wasn't in denial. He's probably found few places, if any, to tell that story the way he needed to."

"But Dr...."

"My friends just call me, Brenda."

"Brenda," I say, "he looked like a young boy when he finally started talking, which seemed to take forever."

Brenda gets up to fix herself another tea and asks Dana and I if we would like a refreshed cup also. She seems so calm with all this. I wonder if she's a breather like David.

"I noticed that too, he looked so young," Dana says. "When he spoke I saw someone who looked like Carla's fifteen year old nephew."

"Vincent is a good example of what happens when trauma occurs while we are still children. It can get stuck in our bodies. You can only imagine what his situation was like growing up. He knew the story in his mind, but his emotions had something to say too," Brenda says.

"But how did you know he wanted to say more?" I ask.

"His eyes and his body posture were trying hard to hold it in. That locked stare at the floor was a signal this was going on. When he uncrossed his legs I knew that he was ready and just needed gentle encouragement to speak his truth."

She and Dana continue to discuss every part of the focus group; why the women didn't talk much, why James said what he said, why the fair skinned woman didn't speak until she got up to hold on to Vincent. To me, they're like a special edition magazine on tape. Much of it sounds like psychobabble language I'm used to hearing Dana speak, only some of which I understand but now they're talking about neuroscience, nerve endings and things about re-wiring our brains.

I listen to them go back and forth and realize I'm getting sleepy. When Dana looks my way, I give her an obvious yawn, but she shrugs her shoulder and ignores my signal. They keep talking while all I do is sip tea. I think not to interrupt anymore—I can see how important this talkfest is for the both of them.

A little past midnight, Brenda says she ready to go home. Dana and I walk her to the door, and this time I'm the one who gives the first hug. While hugging Dana goodnight, Brenda nonchalantly says,

"You might want to do a focus group with just women. They will have a lot to say too."

"I'll think about it for sure," Dana says, "and thank you so much for coming."

A year ago, I never could have imagined that I'd be sitting and listening to these kinds of stories—from Mama's story to the things I heard in this group. I look at Dana, by her slumped shoulders, and the way she's leaning against the door it's obvious she's tired. It's like I am seeing her for the first time. She's a long way from her studded jeans and big fro, but like never before I see her soul cares about what's going to happen to us.

"I'm proud of you," I tell her. "Sometimes you're a mess as all get out, but tonight I saw, I mean really saw, what you want for all of us. I think you're trying to make a different kind of pot liquor."

Dana with downcast eyes looks visibly humbled, almost surprised to hear me say this. For a moment I feel colored girls guilt, because maybe I haven't told her how proud of her I am—how much she means to me. I'm making a mental note to fix that.

She hugs me and sways me back and forth like little girls hug, then steps back to do her little twisty dance. "Wow! I *am* something," she says with a laugh. "Thank you, Car."

CHAPTER TWENTY

It's hard for me to see. Cold mist hovers over the ground like smoky air from too many chimney fires burning at the same time. Off in the distance, I see a clearing the size of my bedroom. I look around and realize I'm in an old growth forest where the trunks of the trees are thick, and piles of pinecones lay on the ground beneath them. What looks like shadowy puppet heads hang suspended in the air, but as I walk closer light from the low-hanging moon reveals a ring of people sitting on the ground. They're so close to each other it makes me think they're trying to keep warm. I realize how cold I am, too. My bare feet are wet with dew, and my body is shivering. Why are they staring at a bundle in the middle of the circle?

"Sit, child," a woman says, as she grabs my hand and pulls me down to sit with the others.

She places her arm around my shoulders, and like the others I lean in close to her to shield myself from the frosty air. I count twelve people in the circle, all of whose eyes cast downward—they seem to be waiting for something. My eyes follow their gaze, and I now see that the bundle is a small body covered in heavy burlap bags. The head is turned sideways, resting on a makeshift pillow. A tiny face with fine features, small jaw and lips lets me know it's a female's body.

"Why is she on the ground like that?" I ask. I also wonder why no one has made a fire to keep them protected from the cold.

"Don't worry, she'll wake up, she always does. We just have to wait," says the woman who's taken me in.

I don't understand what's going on here.

"You following the North Star?" asks the man seated on the other side of me. "I don't remember you heading out with us."

Before I can answer him, a young boy, who can't be more than ten hurries into the circle, breathing hard as if he has been running through the woods.

"Mama, I heard something. You think its paddy rollers?" His shout is whispered and full of alarm.

"Quiet now," another says quickly.

We all freeze, still as statues. Not a breath can be heard. We listen, straining to hear beyond the forest. Through the trees the clang of wagon wheels travels to where we sit and we listen as the noise gets further and further away. We wait a while longer, then everyone lets out a sigh. Then there is just silence and the cold misty air.

The woman with her arm around me places her other hand low on my stomach. She presses down lightly.

"I see you done swallowed something you afraid to let out."

Her words make me squirm, but I don't try to pull away.

"I feel bad that I wanted to leave this life and that it took me so long to get here," I say.

"We been watching you," she says looking around the circle. "But don't you fret, some things will make you want to do that."

"I'm not sure I did my part, and now it's all so crazy," I say. "Will it ever be undone?"

"That one there, lying on the ground?" Her finger points at the bundle. "She know how to fix it. Just couldn't get more to believe, but you? You here. Now you can do different."

She starts rubbing my belly. Her fingers prod and push around the fibroids that crowd my uterus and my eyes grow big as I watch rays of red light dart out. I feel pulled upwards, but she holds me down to the ground, not letting me fly away. Strands of fire stream out and in time the glow disappears.

"Now there, that wasn't so hard was it?" the woman tells me.

I lean into her side and allow myself to receive the comfort of her arms around my shoulders. While we wait for the sleeping bundle to wake up I count the faces in the circle again and again, as many times as I need to so I can stay with the calm feeling that has washed over me. I almost lose my breath when I see a face that looks familiar. Is that Daddy? No? Yes—that is him! Before I can move, without any help, and not a sign of illness like when he laid in the living room, he stands up and crosses the circle. Strong calloused hands that I remember from girlhood reach out and lift me off the ground. We hold on to each other tightly. I can feel my body swaying, happy to be held by my father again.

"My baby girl, she's a beautiful woman," he says, just grinning and looking at me. Then seriousness takes over his face. "I know it ain't been easy baby. I'm sorry I had to go. Remember how I used to make you change what you was reading in the paper?"

"Yes, sir," I say.

"Well, life is like that, too. You can do something different. Maybe it hurts cause something done happened to you, but it can change."

"But, Daddy, I don't know how to change it."

His head rears back a little and he laughs softly, the others in the circle join him with their own whispered laughs.

"You'll learn baby—you'll learn. And remember I'm okay, you hear?"

"Daddy, I miss you so much," I say through tears.

"I'm always with you." He looks around the circle. "They are always with you."

He kisses my forehead and his body starts fading away until I can no longer see or feel his touch.

"Goodbye Daddy."

The sound of my own voice awakens me, I look at the blanket over the curtain that keeps the morning light out, and at the high ceiling, and I know I'm in my bedroom—and in my bed. Oh God, it was only a dream, but it felt so real.

The phone keeps ringing and ringing. *Dana, pick up.*

"Hello," her voice reeks with I-am-not-yet-awake.

"What are you doing?" I ask.

"I thought I was sleeping."

"I need to talk to you. I had this amazing it-felt-so-real dream," I say.

"Give me a few seconds to get up," she says. I hear her tell David that it's me and that she will be right back.

While waiting for Dana to return to the phone I get out of bed to sit on the couch in the living room. Dana's seconds turn into minutes and I wonder what she could be doing.

"I'm here," she finally says.

"What took you so long?"

"I went to the bathroom. Is that okay?"

"Yes. I'm sorry." I let my legs curl up on the couch, place a pillow behind my back and take a deep breath. My chest rises upward and then on the out breath I let out a deep sigh.

"Good one, I heard it through the phone. So tell me about this dream," she says.

I try to see myself back in the forest and close my eyes before I speak.

"It was so cold, the air seemed smoky and my feet were wet. A group of black people had formed a circle on the ground—now it makes me think of the circle we sat in during the focus group. In the dream they were all watching a tiny woman under these scratchy looking burlap bags, she was in the middle, another woman pulled on my arm and made me sit down with them." I hear my voice drift off as I try to remember what else was in the dream.

"Are you still here?" Dana's voice breaks the trance I'd fallen into thinking about what this dream means.

"Oh, I'm sorry. I'm thinking Harriet Tubman was in my dream. That she was the bundle sleeping in the middle."

"Why do you say that?"

"Well, remember when we were at the labyrinth and you asked me about my North Star? In the dream a man asked if I was following the North Star too, as if that's what they were doing. He also said he didn't remember me starting out with them."

"Really? What was the person on the ground doing?"

"She was sleeping. Just like Harriet Tubman suddenly fell asleep and they waited for her to wake up. I remember being cold, and going frozen because we thought slave catchers were coming."

Freezing? In this moment, I think how I've gone frozen, how Mama froze in her life. Oh, my God. Is this where it started? Hiding in a forest, reacting to something so big that all you can do is freeze? Stopped—cut off from what you want for your life?

"It's your dream and the meaning will have what you make of it," Dana says, oblivious that this realization caused me to check out for a moment. "But the sleeping woman, slave catchers, North Star—to me it sounds like Harriet was indeed there." Her tone sounded amazed that I could have dreamt all this.

"I know. That's what I believe too. I keep thinking about the woman who pulled me down to the ground. She said it looked like I swallowed something and when she placed her hand on my belly all this fire came out . . . Dana, I've never had a dream like this in my life."

"So what do you think it means?"

After her question, there's a pause of silence between us. What does it mean? I shift my position on the couch, my legs drop back onto the floor, and I sit upright while I take a moment to think about it.

"I've been wondering myself," I eventually say, "it's going to take a while to figure it all out. But you know Dana, when we lived on Chester I was always ashamed Mama took us away from what was happening in the streets. I know my brothers felt bad about that too."

"I can see how hard that must have been, but I think she was only trying to keep you safe. Many people died or were badly hurt during those times," she says.

"I know. She did what she thought was best. I think my dream is telling me no matter how we come, with whatever baggage from what we did or didn't do, we just got to get there. I know I want to stay in my life, because I can change it. Do something different, that's what the woman, and my father told me. Oh God, Dana. I told you Daddy was in it, right?"

"No," she says. "How'd you leave that part out?"

"I don't know but it was so real. I actually felt him holding me, and he kissed my forehead like he always did and then he just faded away. I was sad when he left again. But you know the best part about him being in the dream?"

"Was what?"

"We had our good-bye. I don't care if it was only a dream—it felt real."

I almost start crying. Even after all these years it's been something that still weighed on my heart.

"The hardest thing to accept is that before he died, I didn't have the chance to say my goodbye. And the dream gave me that chance back to me."

I tell Dana when I heard my voice say goodbye to him that's when I woke up from a dream I know will change my life.

"So what do you think about all this?" I ask.

"Well, to be honest," Dana says, her voice sounded like she is pondering, "I think more than ever, you need to follow your North Star—find Rasheed—and soon."

Hearing her say Rasheed's name brings a sad wave of reality to my stomach.

"Oh God Dana, I've been looking for Mrs. Jenkins' phone number all week and can't find it anywhere. I can't ask the secretaries, or even Mrs. Brown, who will get nosy and ask why I want the home number of an expelled student. They'd probably tell Ed that I'm up to something. I'm so mad at myself for being so careless."

"It's alright, don't be so hard on yourself," she says. "Let's think about it. There has to be a way."

"But I don't know where he is. He was expelled near the end of the school year. I don't know if he's at another school or what? Maybe he's just sitting at home angry about it all. I need to know what's happened to him. I looked through my files so hard that I didn't even hear someone walk into my classroom."

I think about when Miriam came in and saw me crouched over file drawers and tossing papers around. I feel bad because I snapped at her when she started asking questions about what was wrong.

"Yesterday, all I could think about was how he covers his mouth when he probably wants to cry out. I need to say something to him Dana, at least a good-bye, like I needed to say to my father. The way things are I feel hopeless about it."

"Well you know Jesse says *keep hope alive*. Here's what I think you should do. Just go by there. Do it today. You know where Mrs. Jenkins lives, right?"

"Go unannounced?"

"Yes, that's what I'm saying."

"I don't know about that. I haven't seen her since she came to that IEP meeting and that's when she told me to stay out of it."

"Look Car, the worst she can do is not let you in. But at least you will have tried. It's early and I'm getting back into bed," she says, and I hear her give David a smack of a kiss. "Eat some breakfast and go. I think it will be okay. Call me when you get back."

I tell Dana goodbye and stay seated on the couch to ponder what she just said. If I don't try it will be one more thing undone that I know will haunt me. If I'm going to do this I should eat a good breakfast. I go to the refrigerator and pull out peaches and frozen berries for a smoothie and two eggs to boil. With some toast and sweet milk tea I should be good to go. It may not be a big breakfast like Mama would make, but it's enough. I decide to wash the dishes and straighten up while I wait.

Everything is done. I even made the bed, wiped down the bathroom mirror and the sink and put out fresh towels. Now, what do I do while I wait? I plan to go to Mrs. Jenkins's around noon. I'm anxious and since I'm dressed and ready I want to leave now, but I know she's a working-woman and probably needs the morning to recuperate from her week.

Sitting in the living room, I notice how everything is so quiet. There's no Bose stereo or record player shouting crying songs at me. I guess the neighbors decided to sleep in, there aren't any sounds coming through the walls from their apartment. It's just still. I hope Rasheed will be home. Right now, I can't think about the possibility he'll act mad when he sees me; but I promise myself to be patient if he does.

My cell phone gives a little ping. It's a text message from Dana. *U can do this, David says breathe.* I send back a smiley face and a heart sign and realize it's finally time. One last look in the mirror tells me my brown pants, peach-colored blouse and orange scarf around my neck say I'm professional, but casual enough for a Saturday. I decide to take the stairs to the parking lot to get to my car.

Except for going to Charlene's, I don't come this way very often and it's been awhile since I've gone to the West Oakland station to catch a train to San Francisco. This time as I drive I pay more attention to the changes in the neighborhood. I guess they finally got Mr. Jimmy to sell his land to create a private parking lot across from the BART station. I wonder when that happened. His low, flat roof house had been there for decades. Young Black men are congregated in the parking lot of the check-cashing store, and when I turn on Chester there's another group gathered on the corner. They all wear the un-fathered son's street uniform. It saddens me that they seem worn down already. I hope they haven't given up.

I decide to drive by our old house on the way to Mrs. Jenkins. The gate is closed and on the porch sits a young girl. I think about how I waited for visitors to come not knowing our house had been shunned by the women in the neighborhood. Poor Mama—that must have been so hurtful to her, now I can see how back then, it would have been hard to explain to me why. I take the next left to get to Peralta. I'm looking for 6521, Number 7. There it is. Children are playing on the grass in front of the building, I wonder if any of them are Rasheed's brother or sister. I take a moment to sit in the car making sure I'm calm and centered, clear in my understanding of what I would like to see happen when I talk to Mrs. Jenkins, and hopefully, when I see Rasheed. I still don't know if he will be here, but if not, at least I will have started something that might allow me to help him continue his education. I think he's a really bright boy and deserves that chance.

When I knock, quickly a small boy answers the door, he's maybe six years old and he looks like a mini-me version of Rasheed.

"Hello, my name is Ms. Sinclair. Is your grandmother home?"

"Yes," he says, wide-eyed. "You Dub's teacher, huh?"

"Yes, I am. How do you know that?"

"Cause," his eyes turn downward, "he told me how pretty you was and that you like to wear orange." His compliment brings a smile to my face and eases some of my tension.

"May I speak to your grandmother?"

He opens the door all the way, revealing Mrs. Jenkins sitting on her couch watching television. Her eyes appear surprised and she waves her hand enthusiastically for me to come in. I take a deep breath, and step into her neat and orderly living room. When I attempt to shake her hand she gets up from the couch, and instead of a handshake she pulls me in and surrounds me with soft comforting arms.

"I just knew you wouldn't let my boy go like that. Thank you for coming."

"How did you know I'd be checking on him, Mrs. Jenkins?" I ask, relieved, and grateful she's welcomed me into her home.

"I saw in that meeting you was trying to speak up for my grandson, but them others had their minds set about him. And he tells me all the time how you gave him special attention, and that tide pool you made, well he just went on and on about that. Even tried to make one outside on the patio over there."

I had no idea, but then again, I guess I did. His eyes always told me he was present, watching, thinking about what was going on.

"Is he here? May I speak with him?"

"Sure you can talk to him. I sent him to the store for some baking powder. He should be right back. I'm making his cake. Funny you came today—it's his birthday. I know he will be real glad to see you."

God, my heart's fluttering, and I feel nervous again.

"I'm watching Judge Judy. That woman is something else. You want to watch with me?" She makes a space on the couch for me to sit beside her.

"Yes, that would be nice. My mother used to watch her a lot." I don't say anything about why Mama stopped.

"Your hair's different. Looks like you cut it some. It looks real nice on you."

"I did, thank you."

I'm wondering if she wants to make conversation while we wait, but I think I'll just sit and not interrupt her TV watching. I look in the direction of the television, but my eyes are on the pictures behind it on the wall. When I was last here, I don't remember paying much attention to them as we talked. Pictures in gold frames are gathered in groupings of four, and there are single portraits of each of the children. I'm sure the largest one is of her daughter.

Judge Judy is almost over and Rasheed hasn't returned home yet.

"He'll be here," she says, as if reading my mind and then pats my hand. "You know boys, going to the store is a chance to wander around. Go in there and get you some water. It'll help you relax."

Her kitchen is a two hip galley and there are no dishes in the sink. The counters are clear, not cluttered with old food or boxes of opened packages like mine used to be. While leaning against the counter and drinking my glass of water I hear the front door open. An adolescent voice brings excitement and delight into Mrs. Jenkins' home.

"Hi Grandma. I got baking powder and my favorite icing—chocolate. When you gonna make the cake? What time everybody gonna get here? Is my play uncle still coming? He said he would."

It's Rasheed. I've never heard him speak before and as he questions his grandmother I smile at how high pitched and excited his voice sounds. Even with all his seriousness his voice says he's still just a little boy. He's bubbling over, too thrilled about his birthday party to let his grandmother get a word in edgewise. I turn to leave the kitchen, but when a chill creeps into my stomach I hesitate. *You're okay*, I tell myself. Two deep breaths later I step back into the living room. Right away Rasheed sees me.

"Ms. Sinclair, you're here for my birthday!"

I'm happy to hear continued excitement in his voice, and immediately I see what he's been hiding for so long—except to those he knows care about him.

Rasheed has two double rows of teeth in his mouth, on the top and the bottom, giving him an appearance that would make most people stare. Oh, God—now I get why the nickname Dub. He walks in my direction with his head looking down at the floor. I reach out to pull him towards me, surprised that he doesn't resist. He puts his arms around my waist and we hold on to each other.

311

His embrace tells me I didn't lose him. When I step back to look him in the face, very gently I lift the bottom of his chin and trace his jaw line with my fingers. Over his shoulder I see his grandmother watching, her palms are pressed together in front of her mouth, as if she's in silent prayer. I think I see her eyes filling with pools of watery tears waiting to fall. Rasheed's eyes and mine start to tear up just like his grandmother. Lightly, I place my hands on both sides of his face and speak directly into his eyes.

"We can fix this Rasheed, we can change it. We're going to change a lot of things."

ABOUT THE AUTHOR

Debut novelist, Colette Winlock is a native Californian and lives in Oakland, California where she fondly says, "Lake Merritt is like having a front yard surrounded by water, geese, and zillions of people walking by everyday."

Colette has a M.A. in cultural anthropology and social transformation and is always looking for the truth of the matter in why cultures, traditions or human ways have come to exist.

In 1996, Colette was inducted into Alameda County's Women's Hall of Fame for her community activism. She is also in the Sport's Hall of Fame at CSU, Hayward (East Bay). As a former track and field athlete, Colette approaches writing with the discipline learned from countless hours of practice and concentration.

She currently directs a non-profit agency that promotes health and wellness through the expression of art and various holistic health practices. Colette conducts trainings and workshops on a variety of mental health related topics.

30 years of activism and community service provides Colette the opportunity to write stories with ordinary and extraordinary life experiences. She is currently working on her second novel.

ACKNOWLEDGMENTS

Writing a first novel I imagine is like becoming pregnant and waiting . . .

In this process I learned many variations of what done can mean—there were false labors—finishing came in phases, sometimes long periods of time went by and even I began to wonder if I would truly ever be done. The birth of my novel has so many people to thank. Without question, it took a village.

First, to all my family, thank you for your support and well wishes over the past several years as I wrote. I wish Louis and Loretta had lived long enough to read *Undoing Crazy*. To my brother Dr. Steve Winlock, and my sisters Lori Harris and Lisa Latimer, thank you for reading the first really rough drafts. Even still, you gave me encouragement. Thank you Sam, Jacqueline, Tristan, Lil' Anthony, Marcella, Samantha, Dee Dee, Mimi, and Lil' Lisa for believing I would finish. A very special thank you, again, to Lori, and her husband Marvin Harris, who knew what to do whenever I said, "I'm with Carla."

Melanie Tervalon, I will remember our walks around Lake Merritt when I proclaimed I wanted to be a writer and you patiently listened—thank you.

A particular, and special thank you to a bff, Michelle Brewer-Haygood, who meticulously read all my manuscripts and provided on point edits.

Dr. Brenda Wade, while I wrote, your words of transformation and healing were invaluable.

Rachel Bryant, from the beginning to the end you helped hold the vision, thank you for travelling this journey with me.

Demetra Fountaine, many expressions of gratitude for gathering up the community to buy me a new laptop when mine began to fail. Richelle Donigan delivering it on her motorcycle was priceless.

Tarita Gans-Thomas, your humor and wise insight during the early drafts helped to keep me going.

To my early readers, your feedback was so valuable. Felicia Ward, Ruth King, Patricia Rambo, Candice Francis, Patricia Jackson, Cynthia Merchant-Tam, Nicole Griffin, Marcella Pendergrass, Kymberly Upton, Anita Carse, Adella, Pam Dunn, Tisha Kenny, Anne Bacon, Mara Forsythe-Crane, Dr. Fabienne McPhail-Naples and Dr. Marye Thomas—thank you for your consistent encouragement.

James 'Mtundu' Armstrong, Dr. Taj Johns, Gina Breedlove, Dr. Penny 'Penro' Rosenwasser, Sandra 'Makeda' Mayfield-Hooper, Linda Dails, Asara Tsehai, Pamela King, Dr. Marye Jayne Sims and her mama Dr. Ella Sims, Annie Man, Bill Vink and Bob Matthews, thank you for reading drafts or listening to my process and always asking how my book was coming along.

Dr. Bola Cofield, your midwifery over the phone, helped me to enjoy the finishing phase.

To my Facebook family—all your likes and comments kept me inspired to get it done. ✪

Blessings to the angels who showed up along the way—Valerie Haynes Perry, a prolific and accomplished writer who gave time to mentor a newbie, assisted with editing and all things writerly; Lesa Hammond and Valerie thank you for our vision of forming the Oaktown Writers Collective.

Elaine Beale, a skilled author and teacher, from you I learned a great deal about writing fiction, and then I fell in love with it.

Monica Harris's developmental edits definitely made the story tighter.

Douglas Stewart and Grace Harwood your generous attention to my cover in the early days opened up possibilities.

Jeanette Madden, artist extraordinaire, your art brings life to the cover.

Kim Mason, you were incredibly generous, kind and patient as you created the design for the book cover. Lenn Keller, my sister Lori and I enjoyed the photo shoot that turned out to be a whole lot of fun.

Noa Mohlabane, thank you for being there during that final push.

And Luz Guerra, my writer coach and brillant copyeditor, I give a general's salute and say, "Gracias por todo." Yes, we finished the race.